Icing on the Cake

D0951336

Laura Castoro

Icing on the Cake

MIRA®

If you purchased this book without a cover you should be aware
that this book is stolen property. It was reported as "unsold and
destroyed" to the publisher, and neither the author nor the
publisher has received any payment for this "stripped book."

MIRA®

ISBN-13: 978-0-7783-2413-3
ISBN-10:   0-7783-2413-3

ICING ON THE CAKE

Copyright © 2007 by Laura Castoro.

All rights reserved. Except for use in any review, the reproduction or
utilization of this work in whole or in part in any form by any electronic,
mechanical or other means, now known or hereafter invented, including
xerography, photocopying and recording, or in any information storage or
retrieval system, is forbidden without the written permission of the publisher,
MIRA Books, 225 Duncan Mill Road, Don Mills, Ontario, Canada M3B 3K9.

All characters in this book have no existence outside the imagination of the
author and have no relation whatsoever to anyone bearing the same name
or names. They are not even distantly inspired by any individual known or
unknown to the author, and all incidents are pure invention.

MIRA and the Star Colophon are trademarks used under license and registered
in Australia, New Zealand, Philippines, United States Patent and Trademark
Office and in other countries.

www.MIRABooks.com

Printed in U.S.A.

First Printing: January 2007
10 9 8 7 6 5 4 3 2 1

For Drake Anthony, the newest member
of the Castoro clan.

ACKNOWLEDGMENTS

A big thanks to Scott McGehee, owner of
Boulevard Bread Company in Little Rock, Arkansas.
And a special thanks to his night crew, who let me in
on the secret life of bread making. After watching their
intensive efforts, I'll never complain about the
cost of a loaf of artisan bread again!

_T_he Pritikin diet almost killed me. Then along came Atkins, followed by the Stillman, Scarsdale, Hollywood, ketogenic and Zone diets. The South Beach was almost my coup de grâce. I've fought the good fight with all. I'm a baker.

Bread is the staff of life. Who could resist the warm yeasty fragrance of something loving in the oven? Plenty, to tell by sales at the No-Bagel Emporium during the no-carb years. After years of denying themselves steaks and chops, butter and cheese, the diet nation was ready to indulge in fat, as long as no flour was involved. But the mass hysteria couldn't last. The craze has fizzled. It's just a matter of time before bread is king again.

Yet New Jersey is not Manhattan. New ideas, even bad-diet fads, take a while to catch on and twice as long to fade out.

The morning rush, make that amble, has slowed as a well-toned woman in a workout camisole and low-rise pants gazes longingly at my bread racks. Then she sucks in her lower lip. She said she just came in for bottled water but I sense a weakness.

Shameless panderer that I am, I lure undecided customers with generous samples. Yesterday it was palm-size ciabatta slices spread with violet-flower honey. Today it's raspberry-almond butter spread upon chocolate sourdough.

"We were meant for bread," I whisper over my countertop like a desperate lover. "Try it."

She shakes her head, clutching her Nina Bucci workout bag to her chest. "I really shouldn't."

"Just a taste." I push the tray an inch closer to her. "If you're going to sin, do it for the best of reasons."

"I suppose one nibble can't hurt." She looks quickly left and right in my all-but-empty store, then reaches out and snatches up the smallest cube and pops it in her mouth.

I know what to expect, the sudden widening of her eyes, the slight catch of her breath, and then that little moan of animal satisfaction. I nod and smile. "I'll just pop a loaf in a bag for you. Pay now and pick it up on the way back from working out."

Before she can think better of her seduction I turn to bag a loaf, only a little ashamed of myself. I've become a pimp, and my madam is *un petit pain.*

Let me explain. I'm a bread addict. My grandparents owned the Bagel Emporium in Upper Montclair, New Jersey, for fifty years. They bought it from a Jewish couple from Hoboken, who were some of the first to emigrate to the new state of Israel in 1949. Five years ago Grandpa Horace decided they were too old to carry on and left the business to me, their only grand-child, and moved to Phoenix. It was a case of perfect timing. My career in advertising with my now ex, Ted, had begun to bore me to tears. I didn't have to think twice. I'm a Jersey girl, albeit one with a degree from a Swiss finishing school. Practicality is bred into my genes. The way I see it something that engages the five senses, makes arm-toning exercises an option and produces one of life's oldest culinary delights is a win-win situation.

Okay, Ted hated the idea. He said that in leaving advertising for an industry requiring physical labor I was "Opting out of an upper-middle-class career for a trade with all the cachet of cosmetology."

I consider his attitude bias. He has gluten sensitivity, which makes him swell with gas. Not a deadly reaction, just a very uncomfortable one. The sight of a floury kitchen counter is enough to send him reeling backward.

"Thanks." My customer smiles shyly at me as she pockets her change. "I hope Rodrigo doesn't smell chocolate bread on my breath."

"My pleasure." I offer her a Pez from my Snoopy dispenser. "This will keep it our little secret."

Ted's opinion aside, I was born to make bread. I compensate by making the best bread in the tri-state area. I have plaques on the wall that attest to the fact.

We're an artisan bakery, which is small enough so that each worker knows the whole process of making bread, and two or three of us can make enough batches to supply the daily requirements of the store.

From the beginning, we flourished.

The location was ideal, situated on the first floor of a three-story building whose second floor is home to *Five-0,* a lifestyle magazine for the woman of a certain age. The third floor houses Rodrigo's Body Salon, which caters to suburbanites with cellulite issues. Between them and street traffic, the Bagel Emporium had a readymade clientele of boomer women who no longer thought two lettuce leaves make a lunch, and health acolytes who reasoned they had earned a little sumthin' after burning two cinnamon buns' worth of calories. Burn two, eat one. It was a calculation they could live with, and I knew I could live on.

Within weeks of ownership, I invested in two used industrial mixers and a brand-new stone deck oven, and branched out from bagels to my personal passion: leaven bread. We make the basics like baguettes, ciabatta, pagnotta, whole wheat, rye and sourdough. But I love to experiment. Custom orders for chocolate-cherry pumpernickel and piñon-nut queso blanco con mango whole wheat garnered so many requests they quickly became store staples along with gourmet delights like bittersweet chocolate croissants, bourbon pecan cinnamon rolls and focaccia pizzas. Friends call my creations the haute couture of bread-making. Business was so good after the first year that I dropped bagels altogether, a decision appreciated by the deli down the block. Regulars nicknamed us the *No-Bagel Emporium,* and it stuck. Then disaster struck. Noodles, pasta and bread became the pariahs of modern life.

The bakery is definitely on the road to recovery but the bills accrued while it was on life support sucked up all my discretionary savings. The bread is better than ever, but once lost, one's clientele is difficult to lure back. We're a broken habit.

I glance around my store. Like me, it's neat but showing its age. Once I wore Albert Nippon and Ferragamos. Now I dress from the Gap sale rack. The No-Bagel Emporium needs a makeover to attract new attention. But there's already a lien on the bakery. Guess we'll both have to make do for now.

I check the front windows for the passing of a perspective customer. The *bump bump* vibrations of the body-pump class sound track that filters into my shop means my customer base is focused for the moment on burning calories, not consuming them.

To console my disappointment that there is no line around the block waiting to get in there's always the case for a cinnamon roll. One bite is all it takes to produce a smile. Its syrupy, crunchy texture cannot be bested anywhere in the tri-state area. I know because we won a taste test four years ago.

Just as I'm adjusting my mouth for the first bite, the door opens and in comes the skinniest eight-year-old I've ever seen. "Hey, Dupree."

"Hey, Miz T. You got a job for me today?"

I look around until I spy a broom. "Want to sweep the front?"

He nods but sticks out his lip. "When am I gonna get a real job?"

"Sweeping is a real job." Dupree is an entrepreneur. His parents could buy my store but Dupree likes to earn his own money, which he doesn't waste on things like sweet rolls. So I have to think up excuses to fatten him up a bit.

"Before you start I have something else I need you to do for me." I put my cinnamon roll on a napkin and push it toward him. "I think Shemar is slipping. Tell me if you think this cinnamon roll is up to his usual standard."

Serious as any adult, Dupree takes it, eyeballs it and then takes a big bite.

"You need some milk, to get the full flavor experience." I pull a half-pint carton out of my case and offer it to him with a straw.

"It's good." He cranks his head to one side. "Only, needs a little more cin'mon."

"I'll tell Shemar. Finish it, anyway, because you know I don't like wastefulness. I'll give you a dollar as my consultant, and your choice of a loaf when you're done sweeping." Wish I could pay him but I don't want child services coming after me for violating child labor laws.

Coffee cup in hand, I scoop up the mail and head for a booth. An ominous-looking envelope from my flour distributor sits on top.

I love the tone of dunning letters.

"We are sure you have overlooked... If not rectified in thirty days we will be forced... If the remit has been mailed please ignore..."

They manage to make you feel delinquent, a failure and possibly a good egg all in the same paragraph. Oh, and very afraid for your credit record.

I scan quickly through the advertisements and catalogs, until an industry magazine with the cover line *AWAKE from the No-Carb Nightmare* catches my eye.

I mumble as I read it until Celia taps me on the shoulder. "You okay, Liz?"

"Listen to this. The cover article says the low-carb craze

peaked last year. Yet on the very next page there's a piece about making low-carb bread. Instead of backing us up, the industry is still trying to cover every angle."

Celia smiles, which emphasizes the Kewpie doll contours of her face. "Those articles are written months in advance. Everyone knows bread is back."

I nod. "You're right. Got to think positively. Business will pick up after people sample our wares at the Fine Arts and Crafts Show. That's only a month away."

"So is the wedding." My blank look must give away the need for a prompt because Celia adds, "My friend Jenna's wedding?"

"Oh, yeah." How could I forget the topic of every other conversation with Celia since the invitation arrived two weeks ago?

Celia pats her twice-pregnant tummy. "Can you tell I'm working out with Rodrigo twice a week?"

"Absolutely."

Celia Martin is a former Wall Street analyst who quit three years ago because she had fertility issues to resolve. They resolved as two sets of twins born sixteen months apart. Yet even the most dedicated mommy needs a little time off. Luckily, Celia's husband has one of those boring-sounding careers in insurance financing that earns obscene amounts of money. Thanks to him, and her two live-in nannies, she can slum two mornings a week for me, ordering and pairing cheeses with our specialty breads. Twice a month, she goes into the city to get her hair done, and pick up our custom orders from Murray's Cheese Shop in Greenwich Village.

Working for the No-Bagel Emporium isn't usually an ego issue for Celia. But when a girlfriend from her "firmest" years is a partner in some disgustingly attractive IPO stock-optioned company, it's hard to say "cheese specialist" in the same *top that* fashion. According to Celia, Jenna was one of those friends who would steal your boyfriend and then still manage to keep your friendship by making you feel she's done you a service by freeing you up to find "someone worthy of you." Now, that's just Machiavellian. No wonder the upcoming wedding has Celia feeling the need to measure up to the world she left behind. She has, by my count, bought and taken back five outfits.

"Why don't we knock off early?" Celia waggles her perfectly arched brows at me. "Shemar can take care of the lunch crowd. Let's go get manicures and pedicures. My treat."

I don't hesitate on the issue of if she can afford it. But I'm in debt up to my no-longer-waxed eyebrows.

I duck my head. "You go. I really need to stay and help out."

"It's not a pity bribe," she says, reading my mind. "Think of it as girlfriend therapy. You're doing it *not* to embarrass me."

And just like that, we're out the door, after a quick reminder to Shemar, my baker and right hand. "Don't forget to bag up the leftovers for pickup by the soup kitchens."

One thing a bakery like ours simply can't do is compete with itself by selling day-old bread. It's quite frightening the number of customers who can't tell the difference.

"What do you mean, let's get tanned, too?"

Celia offers me a glib smile as she maneuvers her SUV into a parking space before a strip mall tanning salon in West Orange.

"The entire time I was trying to decide between dresses the

salesgirls kept saying any of the dresses would look hot if I had a tan."

"You have to be able to tan to tan, Celia. You don't tan."

Her Irish porcelain skin turns strawberry. "Spray tanning doesn't activate a body's melanin, just changes the outmost layer of skin, so even I can tan. If I start now, I will be able to squeeze in several sessions before the wedding. Let's try it. With your olive skin tone, you'd turn JLo honey-gold."

"Not me. I don't do chemical things to my body unless under a doctor's orders."

Celia gives me her mommy's-disappointed-in-baby glance. "Liz, life is about the decisions we make to live passionately or passively. Where's your passion?"

Okay, I know what this is about. Celia is like Noah, and thinks the world should be paired up. "I'm seeing someone, remember?"

"You are, to put it in your own words, nondating Harrison Buckley."

She's right. That relationship could be said to be living passively. Really should do something about that. When I have time.

I glance down at my feet and smile. We've had our toes and nails done. Celia got tips and a French manicure and pedicure. I work in dough and prefer natural short nails. However, my toes are the color of watermelon slices. The glue-on "seeds" were optional. If that's not living dangerously I don't know what is.

"*A-hem!*"

"What?"

"Tan? Now?" Celia points to a banner in the window of the tanning salon.

Change your outside to love your inside.

"I hope no one paid money for that slogan."

One minute later Celia and I are standing in the reception area of the South Beach Day Spa and Tanning Salon. Nearby a row of girls who look young enough to be cutting class flip through teen magazines and chat. Behind the wall of glass bricks flanking the reception area, colorful shapes move through a fogged kaleidoscope.

"Did you say Mrs. *Tal*-bot?" The receptionist's eyes couldn't be wider.

I nod.

She cuts her eyes to a young woman standing nearby, who is also openly staring at me, then says, *"O-kaaaay."* She pushes a button and announces, "There are a *Mrs.* Talbot and a Mrs. Duffy here for spray tanning appointments."

I wonder only briefly what that was about. Too nervous to sit I survey the menu of services on the wall that includes manicures, pedicures, facials and wraps. And, of course, tanning options.

I'm just wondering what sort of "options" there are to tanning when Celia says, "Oh, that's what I want." She points to a menu item: *Double Hot-Action Dark Tanning.*

"You're a beginner, Celia. Think Gwyneth Paltrow and Julianne Moore."

But she's not listening. She's picks up a flyer and reads. "Hot Action, also known as Tropical Heat, Skin Stimulation and Tingle, uses a combination of ingredients to increase the microcirculation of the skin, which increases blood flow. The hot-action lotion uses tan-extending walnut oil to produce an instant, intense glow."

"Intense glow? That doesn't even sound normal, let alone safe."

She flashes me a grin. "We're not here for safe. We're here for that outside to match our adventurous insides."

"You obviously haven't seen the unadventurous inside of my wallet."

"My treat!"

Before I can form another way to say N-O, a young woman, this one in a shrink-to-fit tropical-blue smock that barely covers the tops of her bronzed thighs says to me, "I'm your hostess, Lili. Follow me, please."

She pauses in a hallway of doors and says to Celia, "Did you bring a swimsuit?"

Celia nods and produces one from the depths of a purse the size of Pennsylvania. Since the twins were born, all her purses are the size of Pennsylvania.

"You may change out of your day clothing in here into a robe and shower cap. In the shower stalls you'll find exfoliating cleanser to use to help prepare your skin. Dry yourself really well before you put on your suit and goggles."

When she turns to me a big fat grin stretches my face. "I can't tan because I didn't bring a swimsuit. Or goggles."

"We provide goggles. You have the option of going into the spray booth in the nude."

"Not in this lifetime."

She gives me a quick up and down. Her expression says she agrees that my shelf life for public nudity has expired. "We have disposable paper suits available, for a small fee."

"She'll take it." Celia dares me to contradict her.

In spite of my anxiety about the paint job to come, I'm enjoying the idea of more pampering. Ask any woman of any age from any walk of life: self-affirmation can be most easily accomplished by a pampered hour consumed by such things as toenail length and shades of polish.

Five minutes later Celia and I are standing in a mint-green dressing room area, having exfoliated from chin to heels, putting on our suits. The locker room is a room away, and the cubbies provided for dressing don't have curtains for privacy. I guess the thinking is if you're vain/proud enough to tan it, you'd want to show off what you're working with.

"What do you think?" Celia's swimsuit bra top is a good fit. The low-waist boxer briefs make the most of her ample hips but hold in only part of her tummy. She puts a hand on the pooched-out leftovers. "Baby-making fat. I'm thinking lipo next year, after I lose another ten pounds. Good idea?"

"Maybe." At the moment I have worse problems.

Who decided a halter top made from what seems to be quilted paper towels could contain a real woman? One breast keeps sliding out of its triangle section while the weight of the other tests the elastic bandeau meant to stop it from slipping out underneath. The panties? It barely covers the lawful essentials. My cheeks are on their own.

Our hostess sticks her head in the door. "Okay, first one ready?"

Before I can answer, Celia's out the door. As I fiddle with the strings that claim to adjust hip exposure, the door swings back open and two young women enter.

One glance over my shoulder reveals a pair of deeply tanned

but un-sun-kissed babes in micro bikinis, the kind you only see in ads for Australian beaches or Brazilian wax jobs. They are also wearing shower caps and heels.

One holds out a slender arm to the other. "Does this look like a Brazilian tan to you?"

Her whole body is the color of maple furniture; who can tell? But I turn quickly away. They weren't speaking to me.

I hear her companion reply, "You look a bit toasty around the edges."

The first one sighs. "They say it will take several hours for the full effect. Still, I expected, well, you know. More."

The way she says this, I visualize beluga on toast triangles, chilled Dom, an ocean view and live violins.

I sidestep back into one of the dressing cubicles, hoping they will just ignore me. Now, not only do I feel sallow-complexioned and under-exfoliated, even my pedicure screams *amateur*. I'm a self-made woman in this spa-day world.

"Oh, look, a newbie," says one of them in a stage whisper. The reason that must be so crystal clear is because my pale June-moon posterior is turned to her.

Moving closer to me, she says, "Hi there. You will want to go slow the first time in a tanning bed. You're really untan."

"Thanks," I mumble without turning around. "But I'm getting a spray job."

"Should you tell her?" murmurs the other one. "About the, you know, uneven affects spray tans can have on aging skin. How it streaks in sagging areas?"

"No, that wouldn't be kind." Muffled giggles accompany this as they drift into cubicles to change out of their suits. "But I've seen what inconsistent coverage can do. The poor woman looked like she had a disease."

I suspect I'm being baited, even if they are whispering, but the partition blocks the nasty look I toss in their direction.

After a moment of silence one says, "Have you bought your wardrobe for Santa Fe?"

"Not everything. It's so hard to shop now that I'm between sizes. I saw these really cute capris at Bloomies." Big sigh. "But they were a size four, and positively bagged in the crotch. To make up for my bad mood, I bought two pairs of Michael Kors sandals, a gold-leather flat and wedgies with turquoise stones up the front."

"Oh m'god! I saw those. They cost a fortune."

"That's right. But I earn it." There's a muffled exchange and more giggles. "Teddy just loves my new abs."

"Ten days at a spa in New Mexico. You're so fricking lucky, Brandi!"

My head jerks up. *Teddy? Brandi!* "Oh…my…God!"

I step backward out of my cubicle just as she does, and find myself looking dazedly at a face and body that accelerates my heart. It's….it's…*her!*

Her gaze widens, as if I'm the one who needs help because I'm gaping at her standing there in the nude. "You know, I'm sure I've seen you somewhere before."

That's when I remember I'm wearing a shower cap and goggles. I hurriedly snatch off both, which is a mistake. My breasts heave and then drop, breaking the paper halter strings, so that they flop out over the top.

I reach back and grab for modesty's sake one of the paper

towelettes they gave us to dry off with. As I do, I hear a *rip*. The crotch of my bikini bottom pops, leaving me with two narrow triangles flapping free, fore and aft.

"Well, well. Liz." Brandi's lips twitch as her gaze flicks up and down my torso with mortifying interest in my wayward flesh. "It's always…interesting to see you."

"I—er, yeah," I manage but she's on the move.

"Got to run," she says as she sashays her tiny bronze butt toward the lockers.

"Who was that?" I hear her buddy ask as they disappear around the corner. I miss the reply. But I don't really need to hear it.

I strip off the remains of my wrecked suit with shaking hands. *Of all the bad-luck, unnecessary things to happen!*

I'm back in my own bra and panties when Celia reappears, which adds a second shock to the day. She looks like something that should be served up with clarified butter and lemon wedges.

"Holy cow! Celia, are you okay?"

"She's fine. She's just had a reaction to the tanning booster," Lili says calmly.

Celia doesn't look calm. She's vibrating as if she's got one of her new fingernail tips caught in an electric socket. "The hot-action cream said it gave maximum tanning results in the shortest possible time. I—I wanted to look—look."

I turn to our hostess. "I thought she was going to be painted bronze. Cherry-red is not a tanning color."

"It's temporary," Lili assures us with the perfect composure of a salon hostess accustomed to dealing with victims of a disastrous tanning job. "It will wear off."

"She can't go out in public like this," I protest. "She looks like a frankfurter."

"In twenty-four hours, she will look normal again."

"Tanless?" Celia questions in alarm.

"No, just not so—"

"Boiled?" I suggest.

Lili purses her lips. "She's not burned. Our hot-action creams simulate the same kind of heat you get from deep-heat muscle creams. Mrs. Duffy just has what we call an overt reaction. The overstimulation of blood vessels will wear off."

I turn to Celia. "Get in the shower and wash that stuff off."

"No!" both Celia and our hostess protest.

"She'll lose the benefits of the spray-on tanning," Lili explains.

"And now, because of my reaction, it will be two weeks before I can come back!" Celia's wail touches my heart. But my brain is busy reliving humiliations of my own.

She has just reappeared, wearing a blouse knotted high under her breasts and low-rider cuffed cropped jeans that expose a long lean bronze torso with a multicolor tattooed garland centered two inches below her navel.

Lili rushes up to her to gush, "Was everything satisfactory, Mrs. Talbot?"

She shrugs. "I'm not sure. I'll let you know."

"Of course, Mrs. Talbot. If there's anything I can do for you, just let me know."

I straighten my spine as *she* passes. I'm in my best underwire now. It's safe to thrust.

The corners of her mouth lift only in the corners. "I recommend next time you bring your own suit. They have designs that can work miracles with those little problem areas. Bye now."

If I wasn't holding in my stomach I would say something really vile.

Instead, I let *her* walk out the door, unchallenged.

Finally, Celia senses something is wrong. It must be the stricken look on my face. "Who was that?"

"Brandi with a ™ over the *i* Talbot. The husband-snatching chickie-babe who stole my husband!"

Chapter 2

" 'Night, Miz T."

"Good night, DeVon. Desharee." I step aside as two-thirds of the night crew troops out the front door of No-Bagel Emporium. DeVon wears camouflage and Desharee's in skintight jeans and a cropped tee. Neither smiles but I don't expect it. Generation Z projects a permanent bad mood. I can no longer afford trained staff so we recruit for on-the-job educating. DeVon and Desharee are two of my high school work-study-program students.

Bakers are a breed unto themselves. There are rivalries and rituals among my crew that I don't need or try to understand. Even so, I can't keep back a big sigh when spying the ricotta tub on the counter that acts as our "fine" box. The crew is young so we fine a quarter per cuss word to keep things polite. My grandfather didn't believe in cussing. Must be the only male to grow to manhood in New Jersey and not cuss. So we've kept the tradition alive in his honor. Today there's a five dollar bill sticking out of the ricotta tub.

"You don't need to know about the Lincoln, Miz T."

Shemar has poked his head out from the back. "We were breaking it down for the new guy last night. It's all good." He makes that sideways-fist-to-the-chest move.

But I'm unconvinced. The night shift is the heart of a bakery, when the mixing and proofing and shaping and baking are done. The *proof* of success is in the product.

I lift out one of the loaves of sourdough stacked in racks for the morning rush and inspect it. It's lightly brown, the crust texture thick and craggy. One stroke of a bread knife and the still-warm yeast aroma of fresh bread rises into my nostrils. Got to be in the top three of my favorite smells. I'm an olfactory person. The right smell can send me straight into ecstasy. Whatever occurred last night, Shemar got the job done.

"Would I lie to you, Miz T?"

I look up over my shoulder with a sheepish grin to see Shemar carrying a rack of pastries. "So what was the problem?"

"The fool didn't feed Ma before he left last night."

I blanch. "Is she okay?"

"True that. After I was done, he won't ever forget again."

Even so, I rush into the back and over to a large plastic tub that contains nothing less than our secret formula for bread-making. Lifting the lid, I lean in and inhale, reassured by its vague brewery aroma.

Every artisan bakery has its own Ma, or bread starter for the uninitiated. The fermentation processes caused by microbes that occur naturally in the environment give each bakery's Ma and the bread made from it its unique flavor and proofing properties. The rivalry among bakers over their batches of Ma is legendary.

I learned not to say Ma contains "bacteria" after a class of first graders on a field trip to a bakery stampeded out shouting, "The bread's got a disease!"

With a gloved hand I lift a glob of Ma to test its resilience. Like any living thing Ma must be fed or it will die. We put in fresh flour and stir it several times a day. Our Ma is five years old, and counting.

"You want a chocolate croissant?"

My empty stomach growls in expectation of a backslide in my resolve to lose a few. I *loooove* Shemar's chocolate croissants but, "No, thanks."

He crosses his arms high on his chest and leans back on a slant, giving me a smirk. "Watching your shape?"

I roll my eyes but smile. "How's Shorty doing?"

Shemar pats our oldest mixer. "Shaking her rump like she's in a 50 Cent video. Sounds like the gears are chewing on themselves. You are going to order a new mixer, right?"

"Soon."

Last night I tried to find a younger less-used mixer for sale online. But unless eBay is giving them away, I'm several thousand dollars short of a deal. Plus we need new tables and chairs, a better line of credit, and a new— Sigh.

"What can I do you for, Miz T?"

"Not a thing. I'm just going out front to mainline coffee until time to open."

"So then, I'm going roll on out of here. See ya!"

Shemar heads the night crew and is the only formally trained baker and pastry chef I have. With his cornrows and FUBU styling, he looks more like a hip-hop star than a baker. Desharee once compared him to D'Angelo. He is all laid-back sultry male. He's also a dedicated baker with a work ethic of which Trump would approve. Shemar could earn a higher wage in a larger operation but he tells me he's happy here.

The fact that the staff relates to Shemar makes my life easier. The fact he can get my deliveries to arrive on time makes him invaluable. This is New Jersey, and it seems every transaction has a back end. Sometimes he comes to work suspiciously mellow but I give him great leeway, and he gives give me bread fit for Trump Towers.

As I straighten up a stack of long slim baguettes as part of my morning inventory of breads, I'm reminded how he saved me from falling flat on my face when I went to take part in a Career Day program at a local high school last spring.

When it was my turn for a pitch I could tell by the rise of voices talking over me that I was going to lose out to the more sexy jobs like video store attendant, where slipping a free DVD to a pretty girl looked like a better opportunity for teen mating rituals.

Fortunately, Shemar interrupted my little speech and said, "Let me hit this, Miz T."

He plucked a long baguette from our display and stepped forward, a calm and smooth presence. Then suddenly he went into hip-hop mode. "*Yo, yo,* I'ma break it down for you. The boss lady, Miz T, she got a job situation with real po-*ten*-tial. You feeling me?" Without raising his voice he brought silence to the room.

He held up the baguette. "Making good bread with a hard crust and tender center is like making love. You gotta have the touch, aw-*ite*." As he spoke he ran a hand suggestively down its long length. The way he fondled that bread had me glancing nervously at a nearby knot of teachers.

Girls giggled and made *yum yum* sounds while the guys punched one another and grinned.

"You a baker, you can rest easy in your crib all day, get your party on in the evening, and still be steady stackin' ends at night. But you got to have the will to learn the skills."

Afterward, the faculty adviser told me the school frowns on using sex to advance one's career opportunities. But we had made an impression.

The next afternoon two young men and a young woman in a work-study program showed up at my bakery door. Over the next few days, a dozen more potential employees slouched through my door. Word on the street was we were conducting some sort of kinky sex class. A few stayed when they found out we really did make bread.

Satisfied that we are ready to open, I return to the front where I spy Mrs. Morshheimer tapping on my window, as usual, in hopes that I'll open early. I smile but shake my head, and point to my watch. I have ten minutes and I need another cup of coffee.

I reach for a copy of *Shape* that a customer left behind yesterday. As soon as my eyes fall on the bikini-clad cover model I regret my choice. There was a copy of *Newsweek* nearby, but it's too late.

Nothing can long block my mind from replaying the *gotcha* moment of *her* and me in the altogether naked nude.

Well, there was that string about my waist from the ripped paper panties. There now, and I thought she'd seen it all.

Until four days ago, the babe who stole my life was little more than a dim *Baywatch* silhouette. All I'd ever seen of her were quick glimpses because Ted has had enough sense to keep us out of the same room. Now I know up close and personal a few of the dimensions that ruined my marriage. And, boy, does she have my number!

How will I ever erase the image of *her* from my envious, small-minded mind?

Was I ever that slim, that firm, that everything?

They must be implants. Ted always bragged that I was a good size.

Yeah, right. Ted probably paid for them.

Get a grip! Lots of women get implants, normal, nice, non-husband stealing women.

Even so, I hate her.

It wouldn't matter if she were ten years older instead of twelve years younger. I'd hate her if she were shorter or taller, fifty pounds overweight, or skinnier than Kate Moss at sixteen. The truth is, when your husband leaves you for another woman, you hate the woman. Period.

If that's not modern maturity, at least it's honest.

Sure, I'd glimpsed her a few times, most notably in shop-aholic ecstasy in Short Hills Mall in the months right after my divorce, and her marriage. Once I spotted her perusing bags at Anya Hindmarch, formerly my favorite handbag store that I can not now afford. Then there she was at the launch of Burberry

Brit Red at Bloomies. Personally, I thought she'd only be interested in fragrance named after Britney or JLO. Another time, while window shopping, I spied her selecting triangle thongs at Dolce & Gabbana. And at Jimmie Choos—well, you get the idea. Oh, and once I saw her buy a tie for Ted at Bernini's and knew he must have a big event coming up because I started him on that habit of a new Bernini tie for special occasions.

In fact, the more I saw of *her* living what had been *my* life, the angrier I became. That kind of emotion can motivate a person out of bed and through many a miserable day. I didn't realize how corrosive it was to my psyche until I scared myself straight.

It happened one dark night of the soul. I had just had my card refused for insufficient funds at a drive-thru ATM when I spied *her,* on foot, crossing the all but empty parking lot and...

Let's just say I realized I could end up with a number on my chest, cramped accommodations in unpleasant company, and one hell of a wardrobe crisis if I didn't go cold turkey on her.

I never told anyone about that night. As far as I know, she told no one about what I'd almost done. That is probably what kept me out of jail.

Looking back I can't believe I'm capable of that kind of rage. The kind that makes the blood pump so hard and fast your veins burn and cold sweat drops the size of bumblebees pop out. Right after that I had my first panic attack. The doctor murmured something about rage turned inward and the need to get a life.

So I stopped even thinking about *her.* I don't even mention *her.* Ever. For four years, it's a plan that was working. Why mess with it?

A flip of my wrist and the magazine lands in the trash bin.

Mrs. Morshheimer is still leaving nose prints on my front window. And I'm supposed to meet one half of my twin daughters for lunch in SoHo.

Just before ten-thirty, I make a quick tally. We're average for the week. That's recent weeks. I'd like to stay and hustle the lunch crowd. But I promised Sarah, and she said it's important.

Chapter 3

$\mathscr{T}$he trendy restaurant on Seventh Avenue is full of lunch hour patrons. Sarah and I are stuck in a back corner at a narrow natural wood bar, teetering on stools half the width of my rear. I'm sure I'm instantly recognizable as a member of the Bridge and Tunnel crowd, suburbanites who come into Manhattan for shopping or entertainment.

For instance, Manhattanites wave off baskets of fragrant rolls as if they were being asked to partake of boiled eel eyes. One woman's unlined face draws tight in the corners as she refuses a basket, but her nostrils quiver from a whiff of the oven browning she denies. The frantic voice in her head may be telling her how virtuous she is, how strong-willed, how disciplined. But it's costing her.

When our waitress approaches I nod vigorously and she

places the wire breadbasket draped in white between my daughter and me.

Even so, I'm already contemplating asking for carryout before our orders arrive. At least it would cut short this "kindly meant but really I don't have the time to argue with my eldest child" lunch. It turns out this is a health intervention of sorts.

Sarah is ten minutes older than her twin Riley, but sometimes she seems ten years older. The genetic code split right down the middle with my girls. A performance artist who uses her family as her canvas, Riley inherited the Blake family temperament, which I'm told is a quite helpful state of mind for an artist. My mother has it. Sarah and I, no. Riley, oh yeah! For the past four years most of her Sturm und Drang has been directed at her decamped father.

Sarah got all the practical, disciplined, standards coding. Everything, from her thermal reconditioned straight hair to her dove-gray suit with tasteful pin to her kitten heels, screams reserved and rational. She has managed to find a rationale for being friendly, if not friends, with Brandi while Riley's hatred for Brandi puts my dislike in perspective. Sometimes I think Sarah is trying to make up for her twin's lack of self-control. But we all have issues, right? This no-nonsense approach works well for her career as a paralegal. But her brand of practicality also stops her from achieving her full potential. After one smack-down with the New York bar, Sarah decided that her law degree didn't require that she practice law. I think that she just lost her nerve, but a mother doesn't say that to a grown child. However, at the moment, she's lecturing me as if I'm her child.

"You need a vacation, Mom." That's her punch line.

"Vacation? I'm working the night shift starting tonight because my new baker walked out after a fight with Shemar over the flour-to-water ratio for making ciabatta in August. I don't have time for a nap. Forget a vacation."

"That is exactly why you need one. When is the last time you took time off?"

I take a deep breath. Sarah and Riley both live and work in the city so I don't see my girls that often. I don't want to argue. No point in mentioning my spa day. The face Sarah made when she saw my watermelon toes was priceless. "I was in Phoenix two years ago."

"That was for Grandpa Fred's bypass surgery."

I reach for a plump roll, perfectly formed and weighty enough to be genuine yeast bread, and place it on my plate. "What about the weekend in Kauai three years ago?"

"Didn't you go there as part of the New Jersey independent bakers association to broker a supply deal for macadamia nuts?"

"For my Hawaiian bread." I nod, happy to be reminded of a past culinary victory. "The secret is the bananas. Not the—" Sarah's frown cuts short my recipe revelation. "Okay. I've got it. Not long ago I spent a few days in Savannah. And before you say it was business I want you to know I took a whole day to sightsee."

"Mom, that was four years ago and you were scoping out relocation sites in case you went into merger with that Savannah frozen-dough plant." Sarah reaches out to touch my arm. "I'm sorry if it's still a sore subject."

"Just because they backed out on the deal without even a discussion? Of course not."

Out of habit I break the roll open with a thumb through the

crust, expecting a moist but lightly risen center. Instead it's damply dense. Clearly, it baked at too high a temperature and without enough moisture.

Disappointed, I lay it aside. "Okay, so I don't do down time well. What's the issue?"

"Let's see. Health? Mental regeneration? Health? Refreshment of the soul? Health? A social life? Health?"

"Enough with the health. My doctor says I'm fine."

"Really? When was the last time you saw a doctor?"

I look up as a waiter puts my order before me, hoping to avoid the trap I dug myself by mentioning my doctor. I've canceled my yearly checkup three times in a row. With my small-business insurance, I need to be deathly ill to be covered.

"Look, sweetie. I do appreciate your concern but I'm doing fine."

"What's this you're eating, Mom?" Sarah picks up half of my sandwich and lifts a brow. "Is that pork?"

"It's an Italian roast pork panini with organic basil pesto. Organic, get it?"

She shudders delicately and puts it down. "At your age, pork should be a rare indulgence, not a midweek lunch."

I hunker down in my chair as she forks the first portion of her field greens salad. "I don't eat this sort of thing often. This just sounded good and—"

"—I'm tired and wanted to give myself a little pick-me-up," she finishes for me. "I know that speech, Mom. You've used it all my life. For chocolate. For ice cream." Sarah shakes her head. "You're in need of far too many pick-me-ups lately."

I gaze longingly at the lovely pork sandwich I was relishing, get instead a mental picture of myself in paper-towel bikini, and put it down. "Fine. No pork." I snap my fingers to gain the attention of the waitress nearby. "Bring me a field greens salad. No dressing." I turn back to Sarah. "Happy now?"

Sarah reaches to squeeze my hand. "You don't have to tell me. I know it's got to be hard, with Dad and Brandi announcing that they're trying to have a baby."

"Baby! Baby?"

Now it's Sarah's turn to look stricken. "I thought you knew. Oh, Mom, Brandi called me last week. She's always wanted a child.... Oh, damn!"

"No, it's fine." I reach for my pork sandwich, the indulgence of which has just been justified by Sarah's revelation. "What's the big deal, right?"

Sarah leans forward. "I'm so sorry, Mom. She said Dad would call you before they left for their vacation in New Mexico. I should have broached the news more gently."

I wonder if news of this sort has a gentle approach.

A sudden too-tight sensation of warmth flames up inside me. Fricking great! A hot-flash reminder that I'm rapidly leaving the baby-maker category she's snugly in the middle of.

As I reach for my water I notice Sarah chewing her lip. "How upset are you?"

She shrugs. "I'm grown. What's another family member, more or less?"

"And Riley?"

"Riley's being Riley."

Which means Riley is furious. So, on to the next bit of family news. "Dating anyone?"

"Sort of." Sarah frowns but says nothing as I pick up my sandwich again. "He's a commodities dealer for the state of Montana." Her shy smile says volumes that I'm not suppose to comment on. "At the moment he's in Great Falls for a grain growers meeting."

"Interesting. And Riley?"

Sarah rolls her eyes.

Unlike her sister, who vets men as if she were trying to buy a condo on the Upper East Side, Riley's man-radar tracks exclusively for Mr. Wrong. No matter their backgrounds, the men in Riley's life are inevitably the same: emotionally unavailable, self-centered and generally relationship-phobic. She says nice men are boring. I say relationships shouldn't have to end with dramatic statements like "Come near me again and I'll set your hair on fire!" That one was aimed at a Goth high school boyfriend with skin the color of an altar candle and black hair that looked like an untwisted wick.

I tell her there are other types of men out there. I hope she will eventually discover this the way she discovered that a pierced tongue wasn't worth the cost of repairing the shattered enamel of her teeth.

"What's wrong with Riley's new man?"

"He's an ex-con."

I inhale for a big *whaaaat?* But the exhale never comes. In fact, the involuntary inhale seems to have sucked in more than a breath. That bite of pork panini has gone down the tube, my breathing tube to be exact.

A bit of pandemonium ensues while I'm slapped on the back by my daughter and then the nearest male waiter subjects me to the very undignified Heimlich. Thankfully the sandwich dislodges after only one try, and I'm left gasping and red-faced but generally okay.

Wiping my streaming eyes, I take my seat and then manage to rasp out, "I guess you were right about pork being a killer."

Sarah nods, her smile only at half power, and reaches for her ringing phone.

"Hello?" Her expression goes strange, her face gray, in response to whatever she hears.

Instantly, I know it's not good. Without a word she jerks the phone from her ear and holds it out to me. "Oh, Mom!"

I take it, certain it's Riley in some sort of jam, again.

But it's her, Brandi with a ™ over the *i,* hysterical on the other end of a lousy-reception cell phone call.

"It's Ted— Oh, God! He like—fell!" That's all I hear before the connection is lost.

Ted's funeral was yesterday. I went. I owed him that much. And my girls needed me. Riley and Sarah each clutched an arm so tight the circulation all but stopped in my fingers. *She* was there, of course, the center of all the attention in a broad-brim hat and veil as *she* sobbed softly into a monogrammed handkerchief during the service. We were relegated to bystander status. This, when you think of it, is our fate since the divorce. We are part of the past life of a passed life.

We didn't really exchange words with *her.* Okay, I admit that I did find myself saying something extremely awkward like "Sorry for your loss, I mean *our* loss," as we left the funeral home chapel. I didn't wait for *her* reply.

It's tragic when someone you love dies young. It's less tragic when that someone is someone you once loved but generally got over before the ink was dry on the divorce papers. It is less than heartbreaking when that someone left you for another woman, a woman he had secretly been seeing for months and married the day after the divorce was final. And yet...

I had just started working for a PR firm in the city when I met Ted. He wanted to open his own advertising firm in northern New Jersey. Did I want to join him as a partner, business and otherwise? Maybe not the most romantic proposal in the world but it sounded stable, ordinary, something I could manage. Falling in love has always seemed overrated to me. All that Hollywood heavy-breathing exploding fireworks stuff is marketing make-believe. I should know. I first made my living in advertising.

At first we were a good team. Ted was a natural-born salesman. I was good with ideas he often took credit for. I was also good with getting things done. Ted could sell but he couldn't make accounts balance or manage a staff. Yet give him a good pitch and he would knock it out of the park at a fashionable lunch spot, at an even more expensive dinner, or on a prohibitively steep greens-fee golf course. The unglamorous job of running the office and drafting ideas was mine. Five years into it, we were a big success. After fifteen years we were a major force in northern New Jersey advertising. But I wasn't happy, in the marriage or the business. If I drifted into an affair of the heart, it was with bread. Being wrist-deep in dough makes me happier than anything in my life besides my girls. I can be creative and eat it, too. But Ted took the more conventional approach to adultery.

The wife seldom knows what prompts her husband to stray. The unfaithful male usually just makes life so miserable that it's the wife who finally files for divorce. Not so for me. I didn't know *she* existed until Ted left with the uncharacteristic pre-emptive strike of filing first. How ugly was that? There are corporate dissolutions with less toxic vapor trails than our divorce.

I'll never forget Ted telling a judge that it was I who'd really opted out of our marriage by leaving advertising, and causing him to lose business. "Liz lost her nerve, her drive, her ambition. She gave up."

What, was he nuts? At the time, General Mills was dangling a contract before No-Bagel Emporium for producing frozen artisan dough. That was my doing and he knew it. Ted was always about money and more money. He threatened to sue for his share of "my" bakery if I didn't give up my interest in "his" company. His attorney claimed my leaving had cost the company. Business had fallen off so precipitously after I left that Ted was still recovering. Add to that, I'd borrowed from Talbot Advertising to pay for my new oven and mixers, while Ted had had to hire both an idea person and an office manager to replace me.

I didn't have the time or interest to invest further in the kind of ownership fight that might scare off General Mills. I might have been good at advertising but I didn't love it like he did. I was about to make it big on my own, and I didn't want him along for the ride. Ted got the firm and I kept my thriving bakery.

Looking back, my choice seems like a lousy bargain. Or am I just bitter because the General Mills deal fell through?

So, how do I feel about Ted's death?

I never wished Ted dead. Even in my worst dark days when I thought revenge had its uses, I never wished for his demise. Bankruptcy maybe, until I realized that with Sarah and Riley in high school and college ahead, I needed all the financial help I could get. Then there was that wish that all his hair might fall out overnight. Juvenile. But I can honestly say I hadn't given Ted an ungenerous thought in years—okay, months.

I did notice with a certain satisfaction that he never looked all that healthy after we divorced. Happier, perhaps, but never healthier. He was heading for a fall. I just didn't know how literally he'd take one.

Ted was afraid of heights. Even a quick rise in an elevator gave him the willies. He would never have gone near a ledge in all the time I knew him. But for *her* he went on a mountain bike trail ride in New Mexico, made the mistake of peering over the rim into the arroyo below, lost his balance and took a half gainer over the edge.

Some might say Ted had it coming. I think, wow, you just never know.

Chapter 4

It's been a strange month. Ted's death threw me, for all the usual reasons, and then some. You gain a new respect for life when one is snatched away by careless happenstance.

For instance, I've been driving a careful five miles under the speed limit. My response to the blare of car horns and ugly looks from fellow drivers is simply to smile and wave, as they are evidence of my very vital life. I always stopped for squirrels crossing the road. Now I stop, get out and shepherd them to the other curb. Live and let live, right?

I've made a few other changes. Pork paninis are behind me. And I decided to take a few risks.

I went to the bank this morning, with thoughts of expanding my credit line for equipment replacement and refurbishing.

"Your income has increased in recent months," my account

manager began, which seemed to be encouraging. "How-ever..."

This is when I knew that what followed wasn't going to make me smile.

So my Monday morning has begun with a fizzle.

As I am entering the bakery, it's scant balm to my pride to see that racks of ciabatta and sourdough are emptier than usual at 10:30 a.m. You can't exactly use photos of bread racks as evidence of improved sales.

"So, how did it go?" Celia asks as I slide behind the counter.

My neck warms. "Just because I was a few days late with a couple of mortgage payments last year I'm a 'risk factor.' Try back in six months was my consolation prize."

"Oh." Emotion registers in Celia's fair skin as if she's a mood ring. This mood isn't a good sign.

I glance about to be certain we aren't ignoring a customer, then grab Celia by the arm and pull her back into the corner. "Okay. What is it?"

"A couple of things. But first, just so you know," Celia glances back toward the front then whispers, "we didn't get a flour delivery today. Our check bounced. Shemar called and did everything but promise them his firstborn. We're just going to have to find another way to pay the bill."

We didn't get a delivery? *Our* check bounced? I have the most loyal staff in the world. And so, of course, I swell with tears.

"There, there, Liz." Celia pats my back but doesn't offer a shoulder to cry on for she's in a floury apron and I'm wearing my only decent suit, a Dana Buchman, so the bank wouldn't think I'm as desperate as I am. "It's going to be all right."

"No, it won't."

"Yes, it will—"

"No, it won't."

"It will."

"Won't!" I sound like a hormonal fifteen-year-old.

"What's up with Miz T?" Shemar frowns as he notices us huddled in the corner. "You're not sweating the delivery?" He scowls at Celia. "Didn't you tell her?"

"I was trying to." Celia reaches out and pats my cheek.

"Tell me what?"

"I paid for it." Celia flushes a natural pink.

An employee paid my bill? I feel worm high.

"It's all good, Miz T." Desharee has joined us.

Celia nods. "There's even better news. When I went into the city this morning to pick up our cheese shipment at Murray's I decided that we should stock up on an a couple of extra items for the Fine Arts and Crafts Show this weekend."

She reaches into the cheese case and pulls out a piece that looks, with its rough moonlike surface and a bright orange interior, like a slice of cantaloupe. "This is two-year-old Mimolette! It's rare to get a piece this old."

Rare translates as expensive. "We can't afford this now, Celia."

"We can if our display snags us the attention we deserve." Celia beams like a Girl Scout who's earned a new merit badge.

"That funky cheese will catch attention. No doubt." Shemar waves off the strong smell with a hand.

Desharee scrunches up her face and backs off. "Looks like maggots been at it."

"Actually, cheese mites do make the rind craggy. But the cheese has a sweet, dense, caramelized taste that matches perfectly with a microbrewery dark lager or chocolate malt, and slices of our eight-grain country loaf." Celia is in expert mode. "I also picked up wedges of HochYbrig and Pont l'Eveque. No food scout will bypass us with these on the shelf."

"That's a long shot." I can't keep the sour grapes mood out of my tone.

"No, it isn't." Celia beams. "I heard talk at Murray's that food scouts will definitely be checking out vendors at the local fairs this weekend!"

Desharee turns to me. "What's a food scout?"

"Consultants that major food companies hire to evaluate new food products in the field." Desharee give me a "speak English" look. "It's like when professional sports teams send out scouts to check out a high school pitcher or college quarterback for possible recruitment."

Desharee's usually bad-mood expression brightens. "Straight up?"

Celia nods. "Haven't you heard? Liz almost had a deal with General Mills four years ago. She was going to be famous."

"Actually," I say dryly, "they were going to hire a celeb to front the line."

"Celebrity endorsements? I'm all over that!" Shemar flashes me a really sexy grin.

"Why not?" Celia says with an enthusiasm ungrounded by experience.

Another chance at the big time! My mind boggles with possibility. I know better. I really do. I've been burned. But there's something about a dream lost. It's the sexiest thought on the planet: what might have been.

While I'm daydreaming Celia gives Desharee a short history lesson in food franchising.

"This is how franchising starts. The modern potato chip originated in a restaurant in Saratoga Springs, New York. Cracker Jacks first showed up at the Columbian Exposition at Chicago. And the Hidden Valley Guest Ranch near Santa Barbara, California, originated Valley Ranch. Oh, and Dave started Wendy's."

"What about KFC?" Shemar folds his arms together. "That old dude in the lame white suit started that?"

"Yes. So you see it's completely possible for our little bakery to hit the big time." Celia is nothing if not a positive thinker.

"*Aw*-ite!" Shemar snatches up a ciabatta, slaps the flat side of the rounded loaf against one buttock and starts rotating a bump and grind like a hottie in a video. "We *def*-initely calling our new item the JLO Loaf."

I burst out with laughter. Then we all start boogying around, as if it's a done deal.

Okay, so maybe we're thinking too big. While the Fine Arts and Crafts at Anderson Park is a great fair, Naomi's rhubarb pie isn't likely to become the next Stouffer's frozen pie. Still, I've been approached by corporate before. So, why couldn't I...?

"Liz, there is something else."

Celia's suddenly somber face pricks my elation. "You got another of those registered letters from Dunlap, McDougal and Feinstein."

She reaches under the counter and pulls out a slick plastic envelope. "This time they sent it by private courier."

"Thanks." I take it gingerly, as if it might be contaminated.

This isn't the first letter I've received from Ted's attorneys since his demise. Sarah and Riley got them, too, and say it concerns the reading of Ted's will. I can't bring myself to open any of them. The firm handled Ted's side of the divorce. Probably I'm being pressured to sign some papers returning my share of Ted's IRAs when I'm fifty-nine and a half, or something equally depressing.

When Celia and Shemar and Desharee have moved discreetly away, possibly with thoughts that I might open it, I toss the package aside. Sarah and Riley are attending the reading of their dad's will today. They can tell me what I need to know.

A while later the notes of "She Works Hard for the Money," playing on my cell phone interrupt me mid-preparation of a special order for heart-shaped scones. The readout says Sarah. "Hi, sweetie."

"Mom, where are you?"

"Where would you expect me to be at this time of day?"

"At the reading of Dad's will."

"I told you there's no need for me to be there."

"Dad's attorney thinks there is. He's refusing to read the will until you arrive."

This I need like another hole in my head. "I'm really kind of busy. Tell him I said to go ahead without me."

There's a pause, then Riley's voice comes on line. "Mom, get over here now!"

"Jeez! Okay. I'm coming."

I give three seconds' thought to changing out of my baker's white back into the Dana Buchman I carefully hung out of harm's way, but why bother? I am what I am. If this is so bloody important, what does it matter what I look like?

Chapter 5

"I'm glad you could join us, Mrs. Talbot."

The attorney of record, Lionel Dunlap, and I face each other across the conference table in the law offices of Dunlap, McDougal and Feinstein. He doesn't glance at his watch but he doesn't have to. Sarah has already told me that I've held up the proceedings by a billable top-attorney hour. Wonder who's paying?

Maybe I should have rethought my optional Dana Buchman. Every other person present seems to have realized the sartorial significance of the moment.

On my right, Sarah, prim and serious as her tweed business suit and tortoiseshell glasses, clutches my hand. At my left elbow sits Riley in a man's pin-striped seersucker suit sans shirt. The flexible dancer's leg folded against her chest puts considerable strain on the one button holding closed the jacket. A colorful batik fabric snugly wraps her head. I hope my urban Amazon aka vegan counter-culture purist hasn't shaved her head, again.

To one side and a little behind, *she* sits between two men-in-black-Halston attorneys. So far, we've avoided making eye contact. That's because *she's* wearing, yup, a mafiarina-style mourning veil. Yet her widow-black Carrie Bradshaw-goes-Goth micro sheath exposes enough leg to distract even me. If possible, *she's* even tanner, with deep red undertones. Swinging from the toes of her crossed leg is a Moschino black-heeled sandal with a crystal-encrusted suede-flower ornament. The pair would pay my flour bill.

"Shall we begin?" Lionel is an old-school lawyerly type, in an impeccable custom-made suit, terribly expensive and understated. Doubtless he would never wear anything as vulgar as a designer label. "For the record the date is Monday, September 12. The last will and testimony of Edward Duncan Talbot…"

I'm still at a loss as to why my attendance is such a big deal. Surely, Ted left everything to *her* and our girls. If he did leave me anything, it's probably something completely useless like a case of eight-track cartridges. Hmm. Collectors' items could be sold on eBay for cash. If that's why *she* brought in the former law review, to stop me from owning the Bee Gees and K.C. and Sunshine Boys, *she* can have them.

My attention swings back to old Lionel just as he reads aloud, "…I devise and bequeath to Elizabeth Jeanne Talbot all goods and possessions…"

My first thought is, of course he left everything to his wife. *Elizabeth Jeanne Talbot?* "Me?"

"Oh, Mom!" whispers Sarah.

"Holy crap!" echoes Riley.

"What!" she gasps, and jumps out of her chair like a goldfish jerked out of her bowl.

"This is, of course, a mistake," begins one of *her* attorneys as the other snags his client by the elbow to draw her back into her chair, "one, unfortunately, not uncommon in instances of divorce and remarriage."

"Teddy would never do that to me. He made another will." *She* points at Lionel. "Tell them."

Lionel nods slowly. "While it is true, Mrs. Talbot—"

"For the record, *I'm* Mrs. Talbot, too." I may be in shock but I've watched enough episodes of *Judge Judy* to know that if you don't protest these little items at the time, they can come back to bite you in the ass. "The Elizabeth Jeanne Talbot referred to in the will, that's me."

I can't see the expression behind *her* veil but I can hear it in *her* voice. "But you're not Teddy's wife, I am!"

Sarah grips my arm. "Mom, what does this mean?"

I lean toward her to murmur, "Who the heck knows?"

Lionel waits to see if there will be another volley before saying, "As I was saying, while it is true this office apprised Mr. Talbot repeatedly of his need to alter his will after his second marriage he never in fact signed the new document."

"What does that mean?" We all hear *her* whisper to her attorneys. After the more subdued whispers of counsel *she* wails, "But how could Teddy do that to me?"

I can answer her question, though I wouldn't dream of it.

"Dad didn't like the idea of wills," Sarah offers.

"What exactly do you mean, Miss Talbot?" *Her* attorney looks like a tiger that has scented prey. "Do you have knowledge that your father was coerced into signing this will?"

"What's that supposed to mean?" Riley snarls. A tigress in her own right.

Reluctantly I decide to weigh in on the topic.

"I'm surprised but not shocked that Ted didn't make a new will. This will is the result of the one and only time I could drag him to an attorney to make one. We'd just been in an accident. We escaped with a few cuts and bruises, but a totaled vehicle. It brought home to us the fact that the girls were just eight years old and would require legal guardianship if something happened to us."

"There! That's proof that Teddy would want his family, his new family, taken care of," *she* says to no one in particular.

Not looking *her* way I say, "Ted viewed having a will as tantamount to signing a death sentence." I've read that this is not an uncommon reaction even among smart, upwardly mobile men. "Mr. Dunlap can confirm that Ted paced like a caged bear the entire time."

Lionel nods his head. "He was a very impatient man." Of course, Lionel did present us with enough estate-planning and trust options to rival the choices on a Starbucks menu.

But I'm happy to take his side and give him a big smile. "As I remember it, Ted cut the conversation off by saying, 'Just give us the stripped-down, vanilla, no frills version. I die, Liz gets it all. She drops dead, it's mine. We both die—Jesus H. Christ! Liz's mother, Sally, gets guardianship of our girls. Okay?'"

Again, Lionel nods.

One attorney for *her* says, "Mr. Talbot may not have crossed all the t's and dotted all the i's, but certainly his intent was clear in his decision to have a new will drawn up."

"Mr. Talbot might be forgiven for thinking that the courts would understand when he named his wife he meant whichever wife held the title at the moment," says the other.

"Which-*ever?*" Riley snarls. "You make my father sound like a serial bigamist."

I lay a soothing hand on her forearm, then again engage old Lionel's gaze and smile. "There is no mention of a 'wife.' I am named in the will as sole beneficiary."

Lionel smiles back. For a member of the firm who dug my financial hellhole during the divorce, he seems almost amused by this turn of events. "It is not the usual wording for a will. I pointed that out to both of you at the time. Naming a beneficiary without a designation of the relationship can prove legally difficult should one's situation in life alter at a later date. However, as I have said, this is a legitimate will in accordance with New Jersey law."

Her mouthpiece says, "New Jersey law provides for a widowed spouse in ways that cannot be circumvented by any will."

Lionel's expression sobers. "Quite right. Mrs. Brandi Talbot is entitled to a significant share of the deceased's estate. Providing there are no other documents to supersede it, such as a prenuptial agreement."

She gasps. "Teddy would never have asked me to sign anything like that."

"You mean my mother will have to share?" Riley demands,

as if it's *her* and not me who has come into this dizzying windfall of unexpected possibility.

"In a word, yes. Possibly as much as a fifty-fifty share."

"Share?" *She* tosses back her veil. Her face is flushed, her eyes tight, and her mouth thinned by anger. "You were Teddy's attorney. Do something!"

Lionel says dryly, "Without evidence of the possibility of tampering, duress or diminished capacity on the part of the signer, a lawfully executed will should stand up in court, aside from the aforementioned widow's portion."

While watching *her* squirm has been fun, the last thing I need around my neck is another millstone business. "What if I refuse the bequest?"

Lionel leans back and steeples his fingers. "If I may, Mrs. Talbot, I would strongly caution you to consider every possible ramification for your long-term future. The Talbot estate is estimated to be worth in excess of fourteen million dollars."

Now it's my turn to gasp. "Fourteen *mill*-ion?"

Lionel picks up a bound folder. "This is a recently complied list of assets of Mr. Talbot's estate."

When I don't reach for it Sarah whispers, "Know thy enemy, Mom."

This feels like an invasion of privacy to which this Mrs. Talbot is no longer privileged. Scan it only for the essentials, I tell myself.

Okay, Talbot Advertising is estimated to be worth thirteen million. I knew Ted was doing well after the bobble in profit caused by my leaving the firm. But, this well? *Jeez!*

For one wild moment I envision myself rolling in a king-size bed full of crisp green dollar bills, feeling as flush as Demi Moore in *Indecent Proposal*.

The next, I feel the sting of a hundred paper cuts from those bills. This can't possibly be real. No court is going to give me Ted's company. The buzzing in my head is not, I realize, caused by evaporating euphoria but the next line of words swimming before my eyes.

"Well hell!" Ted had a second retirement fund the size of which my lawyer suspected but could never discover. *Worth one point three million.* Mental note to me: never hire cheap when it comes to divorce.

"A time-share in Vail?" I look up at my girls. "Did you know about this?"

They look off in different directions.

"That's in my name," *she* answers smugly, then leans in and whispers to one of her attorneys.

He nods then addresses Lionel. "The Vail property is in Mrs. Talbot's name as sole proprietor." He slips some paperwork onto Lionel's desk. "In addition, you have before you paperwork to prove she is the sole owner of her house and its contents, two cars and a string of tanning salons."

"What tanning salons?" I glance at *her* hard-body bronzed thighs with new understanding. That day with Celia at the tanning salon. Oh, no. That was *her* tanning salon!

She smirks. "Teddy said he wanted to invest his portion of the divorce settlement in something people could actually benefit from. So I suggested tanning salons."

My vision blurs. So, Ted took his portion of the divorce and invested it for *her?*

"The hell he did!" I toss the papers as if they'd suddenly burst into flame. "He—I...the bastard! What kind of—of—?"

"Mom, you're stuttering," Sarah points out unhelpfully.

"Don't let this weird you out, Mom," Riley adds in solidarity.

I swing my head toward Riley but I can't focus on her face. My eyeballs are jumping as if I have a tic in both at the same time. "I'm fine. Perfectly fine."

When I've subsided into my chair Lionel says, "Mrs. Brandi Talbot claims the aforementioned items seem to be in order. Therefore, the estate mentioned in the will would seem to include only Talbot Advertising and Mr. Talbot's retirement fund. His insurance has been left in trust to his daughters."

"How much?" I ask this after a second's hesitation because I know my girls are reluctant to.

"The insurance in is the amount of one million dollars to be held in trust until Ms. Sarah and Ms. Riley Talbot reach the age of twenty-five."

"Holy shit!" Riley says this in an unusually subdued voice.

"I would suggest," Lionel says, "that both Mrs. Elizabeth Talbot and Mrs. Brandi Talbot seek counsel, who will look for a solution that will keep this out of the courts."

"You're advising arbitration?" Sarah is taking notes. My daughters have assumed the sisterhood alternative to *her* suited sharks.

"It would behoove both parties to consider it." Lionel is one cool customer. "A protracted legal battle will tie up assets on all sides for the foreseeable future. An equitable agreement reached before the will is filed for probate would greatly simplify matters."

"Like hell!" *She* folds her arms under her rib cage, drawing attention to what money can buy. "My attorneys say I should fight this."

The other man in black, who until now has been mostly silent, speaks. "There's every possibility that there will be a second claimant against Mr. Talbot's will."

The hair on my head snaps to attention. Oh, that's right! *She* and Ted…

My gaze tracks down her front to where her dress wraps like cellophane about her torso. It's been two months since… could it be?

Unflappable Lionel says, "You have informed these offices of Mrs. Brandi Talbot's potential for procreation." Who, but an attorney, talks like this? "The real question is—"

"Are you pregnant?" Riley, who has been hunkered down in her chair like a military combatant, springs to her feet and approaches *her*. "Well, are you?"

She dips her head. "Possibly. It's still too soon to know." *She* lifts eyes swimming in tears. "It's what your father wanted. We were talking about it the day—"

It's a good performance. I am maybe the only one in the room who doesn't believe for a second *she's* pregnant. There are tests accurate to within days of conception. Yet I wouldn't put it past *her* to do something sneaky underhanded drastic.

But that's not the reason I suddenly feel threatened. I don't want anything to do with any of this. I don't need—who am I kidding? Who doesn't need half of thirteen million? I need any piece of it I can get. No! What I need is to get out of here and think. Think? What's there to think about? I won't know until I get a chance to do it.

I rocket to my feet, little puffs of flour escaping the folds of my baker's duds. "If you will excuse me I need to find the ladies'."

"Me, too. Me, too," my girls echo, popping up from their chairs.

"I'm going to sue. I can sue, right?" *she* asks as I head out the door.

Sweet as they are, I don't need daughterly advice just now. I bypass the ladies' and step into the elevator. Events of this magnitude require consult with a higher power.

As the door closes I hear my daughters, caught short on the other side of the closing door, chorus, "Mom? Where are you going?"

"To Olympus."

Chapter 6

"*Liz*, darling! Isn't this a nice surprise?" Sally busses both my cheeks. "But whatever are you doing here?"

She means how dare you, darling, show up at my apartment on the Upper East Side, and not telephone first. But, *kiss, kiss,* of course, I love you.

"I need to talk, Sally. Can I come in for a minute?"

She gives me a Carol Channing smile. "For you, darling, I have all the time in the world." This means, she's alone. "Come in, come in."

Sally Blake reminds most people of Jackie O. At five-foot-nine-and-one-half inches with thick dark hair and a willowy figure, she has the same square face, at once formidable and vulnerable. The same strong brows, as if the artist became too generous with his charcoal. A wide, pretty mouth proclaims her ultrafeminine and yet positively patrician. That's where the similarities to Jackie O end. Sally is as driven as Ethel Merman, with the same larger-than-life persona.

Oh, Sally is my mother.

From the crib I was taught to call her Sally because in 1958, *nice* girls didn't have babies out of wedlock. Certainly a potential Rockette didn't.

"Taking dance classes in the city," I was much later told was the official explanation when Sally went to a maiden aunt in Baltimore to have me. Meanwhile my grandmother, a taxi dancer during the Depression, announced that she and Grandpa Horace had decided to adopt. Sally dubbed me Liz Taylor Blake, in the hope that a famous name would inspire me to become famous. My grandmother, who saw the drawbacks to such a moniker, made sure I was legally named Elizabeth Jeanne Blake.

Three years later "big sister" Sally was high-kicking in the most famous chorus line in the world, the Radio City Rockettes, while I was learning to tell when a bagel was done.

I don't come to Sally for maternal comfort. I come for worldly advice. She's the ultraglamorous older sister who swoops in occasionally with dazzling tales of her globetrotting adventures yet willingly listens to my "what I did at the bakery today" type life stories.

She leads me through the maze of boxes and furnishings into a room with a panoramic view of Central Park. She moves when the mood strikes, sometimes as often as every year. Sally says a smart woman doesn't hang about Radio City Music Hall in a leotard and heels without finding ways to network. When the time came to segue from the stage into a different glamour profession, she had backers lined up. Today she owns a boutique Manhattan real estate agency. Successful, are you kidding?

When she pauses before a grouping of beige suede sofa units that could sleep three, her wide-legged stance opens the side slit in her Oscar de la Renta tweed pencil skirt. Who can blame her for showing off? Looking more than a decade younger than her sixty-three years, Sally can still high-kick a hat off a man's head.

"What do you think of my new pied-à-terre?"

I give the room's view a drop jaw gaze. What can I say? "It's spectacular."

"I'm undecided. Tony likes it."

Tony Khare is Sally's lover. They met five years ago when she sold him his first Manhattan condo. An Oxford-educated Indo-Englishman, Tony made scads of money long before it was news that American industry was outsourcing to places like New Delhi and Bombay. Tony is darkly gorgeous with that witty yet ineffable English reserve that's a perfect foil for Sally's old-fashioned glamour. The fact that he is twelve years her junior bothers neither of them.

"Look at you," she says just as I'm thinking, *let's not*. We may have the same thick dark hair but mine tends to frizz, and I am shorter with a not-so-willowy frame. You don't try to emulate a mother like Sally Blake. You only envy and adore.

"You look wonderful, as always. What are you doing?"

"Pilates." Sally runs a palm across her drum tight midriff. "You should try it. Customers would flock to the antioxidant properties of your spinach and tomato focaccia if they thought it gave your skin a refreshed glow."

"It wouldn't be true."

"Darling. Success is about selling the sizzle, not the steak."

For about three seconds I actually think about this approach, which just goes to show how desperate I am for new customers.

"I'll just ring for sherry. No, something more festive. " When her Brazilian housekeeper appears, Sally announces, "Gimlets, Ines!"

She waves me into a herringbone-stenciled leather side chair. "Tell me all about your life. Is it thrilling?"

"Let's see. I'm still parenting two grown daughters. I own a business trying to claw its way back into public consciousness. Oh, and I rent and have a business mortgage I can barely meet."

"So then, sell and relocate."

Sally always says sell the bakery. It's the only thing she and Ted agreed about, ever. But relocate? That's new. "Where would I go?"

"Miami?"

"Too hot."

"Tampa."

"Ditto. You know I blotch in tropical heat zones."

"There's no humidity in Tucson, or Santa Fe. Or Denver?"

"Altitude makes my head feel like the lid's on too tight."

Sally sighs and subsides onto her sofa. "I did try to help. Remember that, when you and the cat are moldering away."

"Can we discuss something else?"

"Certainly. What did Ted the Bastard leave you?" Though Sally has followed the family tradition of no cussing, since the divorce she always refers to Ted as if 'the Bastard' is part of his legal name.

I fiddle with the metal tip of the drawstring to my pants. "Why would you expect him to leave me anything?"

"The bastard stole you blind. If you'd have let me hire a real divorce attorney…" Sally's expression completes her thought. She's swimming in money and would gladly share an end of her pool with me, if I hadn't inherited her stubborn determination to live on my own terms. Even if it kills me. "Why wouldn't he leave you something if he cashed out first?"

"He had a new wife maybe?" I throw up my hands. "Oh, I don't know why I'm being coy. It's still so un-*fricking*-believable! Ted forgot to update his will. The one he had leaves everything to me."

Sally's brows peak in interest. "How much?"

I take a deep breath and say the words quickly. "Fourteen million."

"Darling!" Sally claps in delight. "You're set."

"Not quite. The will leaves Talbot Advertising to me plus one million and change in insurance to the girls. So, *she's* suing."

Not even Botox injections can keep faint frown lines from forming on Sally's face. "He left nothing to the slut?"

"Technically no. There were things already in her name, like the house, some cars, a few tanning salons—"

"A few what?"

"Don't ask. But the will itself leaves her nothing."

"How absolutely delicious!" Sally's smile is wicked. "Yes, yes, Ines, put the drinks here." She pats the place in front of her for her maid, in a black-and-white uniform, to lay out refreshments. She blows Ines a kiss then gives a little finger wave of dismissal.

She passes a gimlet to me then clinks her glass to mine. "To you, darling! Take the money and run!"

I can't drink to that. I can't even explain what I'm feeling. So I start with the least logical emotion. "I don't need charity from a man who walked out on our marriage."

"What charity? This is vindication. Ted saw the error of his way in leaving you and Mr. Can't Admit I'm Wrong used his departure to make it up to you."

"Sally, this was an accident, like a clerical error. He screwed *her* by mistake."

"You bet his screwing *her* was a mistake! And now *she's* going to pay for it. It's karma, dearest."

Sally believes in karma, kismet, ouija boards and pretty much anything else that will give a girl a psychic edge. "Ted created bad karma by cheating on you. So then forgetting to rewrite his will was the unpleasant ripening of the karma he created."

"How about being sued by my ex-husband's widow? This sounds like an improvement in *my* karma?"

Sally makes a moue. "Darling, I never criticize. Yet I've never understood how you thought marrying Ted young validated your need for independence. It should have been a starter marriage. If such things had been in fashion in my day, it would have saved so much fuss and bother."

"What bother? You said you never wanted to marry my father."

She shrugs. "If I'd known we were only practicing being married, I might have for your sake, knowing the relationship wouldn't outlive the sex. Of course, the sex was spectacular. But who knew at fifteen how rare that would turn out to be?"

"Too much information, Sally."

She gives me a strange look. "I've never understood how I reared a prude."

"Overcompensation."

"So then, dearest, listen to the voice of wanton reason." Sally drains her glass. "Take what Ted's will gives you. If not for yourself, then do it for every wife who's ever been dumped by her husband for the other woman."

"So it's as if I won the payback lottery?"

"But that's perfect!" Sally sits forward. "I know just how to capitalize on this! I'll call my friend in booking at *Good Morning America*. She's always looking for human interest stories from the American heartland."

"I'm only in New Jersey. Besides——"

"Oh, and I might be able to pull a favor and get you a small mention, as my little sister, in *Vanity Fair*. Well, maybe not, since you're not celebrity status with anyone but me." She blows me a kiss.

"Can we table this discussion for now?"

"Certainly." Sally tosses a throw pillow, which probably cost more than my phone bill, onto the floor and curls her legs up on the sofa. "So, what else is new in your life? Is there a wonderful man in it?"

The only topic that interests Sally as much as money is men. I hesitate only a second. "Harrison is fine."

"Oh, dear. Not the car salesman?"

"He owns two Lexus dealerships. That's a little different."

She shrugs. "Is he at least entertaining in bed?"

"It isn't that kind of relationship." I avoid her eye while trying not to think of my one-time sex act with Harrison. Micro-expressions are Sally's specialty.

"If he doesn't set your hair on fire, Liz, what's the point?"

"You're right. I'm going to stop seeing him, when I have time to explain."

"Darling, no! Never, ever explain. That will only cause an argument, which will make you feel bad. Remember karma. Cut him cleanly from your life. No calls, no notes, no regret. Why do you have such difficulty with men? You never learned it from me."

That's an understatement. "Do you know what my earliest memory of you is?"

Sally lifts a hand of protest. "Don't tell me if it's the reason you're in therapy."

"I've never been in therapy."

"Really? Good for you. Tell me."

"Grandma and I were waiting for you in a cab outside Radio City Music Hall. You came out still in full makeup, wearing a skimpy Santa suit with spangled tights and silver shoes. Following you was this good-looking man in a cashmere topcoat." Sally taught me to recognize quality materials when other girls were learning their shapes and colors. "He was shouting, 'Why? Why?' You simply closed the door and told the driver to take off."

Sally blinks. "I don't recall."

"Why should you? It must have happened many times. But I remember because no man has ever looked at me with the yearning I saw on that man's face as we pulled away from the curb."

"My, aren't we feeling sorry for ourselves today. At your age I was fielding three suitors at a time." Sally leans forward, as if to impart a secret. "The only reason you're not living the life you want is because you don't demand it. What have I always said?"

"There will always be the next great opportunity, the next great adventure, and the next great man." And this is why I come to Sally. She sees no roadblocks. Why should she? Life and love have always been willing to batter down her door.

We chat a little longer, wherein she gives me legal pointers about contesting a lawsuit and offers the services of her own attorney, which I promise to think about. Then she announces that she has an appointment and, really, I must come again when she has time to plan and we'll do tea at the St. Regis.

Once on the sidewalk I am reminded that, while Sally is high on life and it on her, I live on the ground level where a sudden chilly rain can blow in and soak a person who didn't think to bring an umbrella.

As I stand under the apartment awning shivering while I wait for the doorman to flag down a taxi, I wonder what sort of cosmic jokester thought it would be fun to dangle solvency before me with only one stipulation: that I deal with *her*.

Maybe it is the karma I deserve.

I should have been happy in my twenties and thirties being a striving career woman who worries about calories, checks her bank account obsessively because she can't pass up purchasing that "have to have" wardrobe item, and fields her share of disappointments in love and life.

But I am Sally's child, and whenever she swept into my

middle-class upbringing, contrary to what she says, she had expectations.

Being destined to be *somebody* is a burden, especially if it's someone else's version of your life. A plan like that needs the raw material of some kind of talent. When I grew up, Madonna had not yet made an art of doing nothing well, spectacularly.

When I was sixteen Sally coaxed her gentleman friend of the moment into footing the bill for me to attend a Swiss finishing school, Surval Mont-Fleuri on Lake Geneva. For eighteen months I lived with seventy-five nice but lonely girls from six continents who only had in common their parents/guardians desire that they become the *ne plus ultra* of international hostesses. The course load was surprisingly heavy: forty-two hours a week of French and German, International Etiquette, Protocol, Savoir-Vivre, PR, Floral Art and Table Decoration, Enology, etc. My electives were cooking and pastry classes. And I fell in love, with baking, again.

When I graduated, and to show off my education, Sally arranged for me to prepare a seven-course meal for my benefactor and his select friends. At the end of the very successful evening, Sally said, "Just think what she'll be able to accomplish after a term at the Sorbonne."

But I'd had enough of formal education and said that if another sojourn in Europe was required I'd just as soon it was at Le Cordon Bleu in Paris.

My patron said he hadn't spent twenty thousand—a considerable sum in those days—on somebody else's little sister just so she could become a pastry chef.

Sally, bless her, came right back at him and said that was

because he was too bourgeois to appreciate truly excellent cuisine. And, by the way, the "pasty chef" had inventoried his wine cellar and said it was execrable.

There was a howling fight. Shortly thereafter, Sally left for Paris. I stayed home and went to Rutgers. Then married, because Ted asked me.

Looking back, I can admit marrying Ted was a quick fix of stability. Women do that, knowing all the while that they are making a mistake, like choosing an inexpensive fun fur over a full-length mink because it looks so "right now" when waiting to have the money for the real thing that would have kept them warmer and remained timelessly chic.

What if by marrying Ted my karma is permanently skewed? That would be so sad.

As I enter the miracle of a rainy-day cab, my heart begins to pound in my ears. And I'm holding my breath. Panic attack?

"Oh, no," I moan, and stretch out flat on the back seat of the taxi.

"Lady, you okay?" I hear the driver ask nervously.

"Okay." *Breathe,* I command myself, *just breathe.*

The last time this happened I was a year past the divorce and trying to cope with being completely on my own. I went to see my doctor. He said that stress can have that affect on an other-wise healthy person.

"Can't you just give me a pill?" I asked.

"I could, but it won't help what you're suffering from."

"What's that?"

He smiled kindly. "In layman's terms, lack of a personal life. You're a healthy woman with needs. Go out and get a life."

Feeling the smothering sensation subside, I sit up.

The cabbie spares me a glance. "You need me to swing by an emergency room?"

"No, no thanks."

What I need is a few spectacular moments in my life. Sally's right. From now on, forget the steak. I'll take the sizzle!

Once inside Penn Station, I remember to turn on my cell. Sally detests interruption by modern conveniences. I scroll through to see Sarah and Riley have each called three times, Celia twice, oh, and Harrison once.

Oh, joy! His message reminds me of what I'd forgotten. We have a date for dinner tonight.

I've been avoiding him since we mistakenly tumbled into bed together.

So then, this is the perfect opportunity to break things off. A chance to change my karma!

Chapter 7

"I understand that you need your space, Liz. Still, I hoped after our last time together, we'd reached a new level of understanding." Harrison tries to take my hand, which I avoid by reaching for my glass of Shiraz. "I'd hoped you'd let me be the one you come to when you need someone to turn to."

"That's nice, Harrison." Oh, brother! What's a woman supposed to do with a man whose idea of romance is reciting lyrics from an eighties Carpenters' song?

Deprived of my hand he leans in to capture my gaze with his. The effect of this soulful glance makes him look slightly cross-eyed. "How about we drive down to Cape May for the weekend?"

There it is! It's the reason I'm as tense as he is nervous. He means when are we going to have sex again?

The answer is never. Not ever.

If it had been great sex I doubt I'd remember he tooted between thrusts.

Why hadn't I listened to my gut, which told me never bed a man as an "oh well, what the hell" response. I have only myself to blame.

"This is the weekend of the Fine Arts and Crafts Show. I have a booth to manage." I look around in hopes of spying a waiter.

Thankfully our waiter was waiting for a cue and comes over to take our orders.

I don't usually eat red meat but we're at Luigi's Trattoria, Harrison's favorite restaurant. Frankly, it's so-so. The marinara sauce is too tomato-y and lacks a "fresh" herb flavor. The pastas have a thick, cling-to-the-teeth gummy texture that is not what's meant by al dente. So I order the porterhouse, medium rare. There's only so much a cook can do to a steak.

Sarah says I'm too critical. Riley says I have an "elitist foodie bias against the proletarian need for basic food consumption." I remind her that basic consumption includes chemically enhanced beef and chicken, and potatoes deep-fried in trans-fatty oils.

When the waiter's done Harrison scrapes back his chair and rises. "Excuse me. I need to water the petunia."

I smile but think *jeez.*

Sally's right. "Car dealer" has a certain slippery-snake-oil-salesman image. But Harrison's not just another guy on the lot with the pompadour and picket-fence smile. He's "The Negotiator," the owner of a pair of northern New Jersey Lexus dealerships.

I was still working with Ted at Talbot Advertising when we came up with that slogan. Come to think of it, I came up with it. It's been one of Talbot Advertising's most successful slogans. It lifted Harrison out of the field of in-your-face car ads and gave him a profile with his targeted audience. I should have left the relationship at that.

A few months ago when I went in to get my car serviced, he came out to talk to me. It was easy enough to slip into the conversation that he divorced a year after I did and that neither of us was seeing anyone. When the bill came it was marked paid.

Now, I'm not one to knock free service but I was uncomfortable with the implication. I told him so when I handed him a check written for the full amount.

He said I was the first woman to turn down the offer. He went on to say that his high-profile business sometimes interferes with his love life. He was looking for someone who didn't want anything from him.

I told him his explanation of the "bill paid" test could be seen as bragging, paranoia or just plain manipulative. Anyway, I didn't like being tested without my consent.

There was an awkward pause before he asked if I'd consider accompanying him to a Rotary Club dinner the following evening.

I said yes.

There is something appalling about being single after a long marriage. It's like rising from your seat at the end of Act III, only to realize there's another play starting that you hadn't anticipated. The first three acts had such symmetry: career, marriage and children. To find that the next act of your life has

put you back in the prologue of a whole other play is discon-
certing and frightening. I felt the need to push on to the opening
of a new Act I. That explains my seeing Harrison Buckley.

Oh, we've had a pleasant time. I call him to escort me to a
Friends of the Library fund-raiser and he calls for things like the
Better Business Bureau or Kiwanis functions. But there's no
spark.

At twenty I was clueless. At forty-six my libido's stronger.
Not so surprising then that in a weak moment, a couple of days
after Ted's demise, Harrison found me rather distraught and one
thing led to another in a way that never should have been.

Until that night whenever we had the rare one-on-one dinner,
we ended up talking about our respective businesses over dessert.

Yes! That's when I'll break the news to him, over dessert.
I'll say that this was never meant to be a romance. We agreed
we were just friends. We both deserve a chance at more.

Yeah. That sounds good, nonjudgmental and positive.

Hungry and edgy, I stare balefully at a basket of rolls, bulk
manufactured like the kind sold in grocery stores. Even the
breadsticks come in individual cellophane sleeves.

"Here we are." I glance up to see Harrison's back. Our meals
arrive right after him.

"Now, that looks good." He eyes my steak in a way I don't
want him eyeing me.

I slide my knife into the meat and peel back a bloodred
center—no, the interior looks like it's fresh from the cow.

"Is something the matter?" the waiter inquires with dutiful
concern. After I explain that the cook didn't do enough with
this steak, he whisks away my plate.

"Here you are." Harrison holds out to me a forkful of fettuccini con pancetta.

I smile and shake my head, wishing I didn't have to wait for dessert. Sally would have sent him on his way months ago, thinking that he was just about the luckiest fella on the planet to have even known her.

I'm going to botch this. I can just feel it.

Harrison has stopped eating to stare at me not eating.

"I've been racking my brain, Liz, trying to decide on the right approach. A man can't just pitch a deal if the offer isn't right. You know what I mean?"

He's talking business before the dessert? His dealership must be in trouble.

He puts down his fork and spoon for twirling and wipes his mouth very carefully, drawing my attention to the fact that there is a thin sheen of sweat on his upper lip.

What's going on?

He pats his left breast pocket and begins to smile, only it's a "lips peeled back from dry teeth" kind of sheepish grin. "So, Liz, I've put together a package I think you're going to like. You don't have to make a decision now. Take it home, think it over. Terms are still negotiable."

Oh, Lord! He's trying to sell me a new car.

He stands up, the scrape of his chair enough to alert our waiter. "So here goes."

As he goes down on one knee, I have time to notice bits of minutiae. For instance, the red-and-green tweed carpet is actually a houndstooth pattern. He's wearing brown corduroy trousers in August. There's a splash of tomato sauce an inch long on his yellow silk tie. He's missed shaving a small patch of whiskers on the underside of his right jaw. A sweat stain wicks down the collar of his shirt. And why is he on a knee? Did he drop a contact?

Murmurs alert me to the fact that I'm not the only one staring. Harrison's actions have drawn the eye of patrons who wouldn't have glanced up if a waiter had tripped with a full tray.

There's something primal about a man going down on one knee in public. It's a rare moment of masculine vulnerability on public display. Like a Hail Mary Pass, it's fraught with the possibility of sweet triumph, or humiliation and miscalculation likely to end in crushing defeat.

Holy crap! It can't be—

A ring! He's thrust it before me, nestled in dark green velvet in a box sprung open on what must be two and a half, maybe three carats.

"—Not a deal-breaker. Terms are negotiable. But you're a sweet deal I won't let get…"

"No, no! Put that away!" I whisper as I reach out and snap the lid shut.

I must be looking at him as if he's offered me the finger instead of a ring because he flushes a deep red as he jerks the box back and shoves it into his pocket.

The whiplash of patrons looking away sends shockwaves of silent sympathy toward the poor bastard who couldn't close the deal.

"Oh, Harrison, I'm so sorry." I reach for his hand, which is clammy. "I didn't mean to react that way. It's just, you took me by surprise."

He doesn't even look at me. He fumbles with his fork as sweat runs in rivulets from his brow. "Obviously, it wasn't a pleasant surprise."

"I apologize. I do. But a ring? It was the la—least—something I didn't expect. We've known each other such a short time."

He looks up and if possible I feel even worse as the red-faced humiliation I've caused stares back at me. "Fifteen months, Liz. Nearly a year and a half of our lives has gone into this relationship."

"So much?" Good grief! Time flies when you're *not* having fun.

"But this wasn't that kind of a real relationship, Harrison. I had no idea you thought it was."

He glares at me. "We're sleeping together."

"Did. Once. It was a mistake." He flinches like a dog struck on the nose with a rolled newspaper.

Dear God! What happened to my no fault/no foul speech?

"I mean, we agreed, we were just keeping each other occupied. Casually. This was never a romance and…and we both deserve a chance at more."

He pauses with a forkful of pasta near his mouth. "You're seeing someone else?"

"No. I wouldn't…" Well, maybe I would, if there was someone else. "I'm not seeing anyone else, but we should. That's the point. You should, and I should. Okay?"

Instead of answering he just stuffs his mouth with pasta, and I guess I should be grateful.

We ride home in a silence only mortal enemies could appreciate after I insisted on paying for a steak I couldn't eat.

I go in, pour myself a well-aged Scotch, knock it back like it was cheap bourbon, and then go to bed, facedown in my dress.

About 2:00 a.m. I awaken unable to breathe. My dress has twisted so tightly around my waist it feels like a tourniquet.

I rise, dress for bed and return to a slumber where, in my dreams, farts instead of words issue from Harrison's mouth.

"Liz! Have I got something to show you!"

It's rare that Celia arrives early enough to open. Obviously something else has brought her in today because she goes right over to the TV-VCR perched above the counter and pops in a tape. Occasionally we watch a movie after hours as we clean up.

"I'm not always out of the shower in time to catch the local weather report so I tape and replay it while I dress. I'm so glad I did this morning." Celia picks up the remote and points. "Now watch."

For a few seconds the jerky movements of fast-forward animate the screen and then under the direction of Celia's thumb, it pauses and starts again in Play mode. There is our local weather guy chatting with the co-anchors of the show.

"For all of you who've ever wondered about the hype at North Jersey Lexus, I've got a scoop. Yes, an eyewitness account of my very own. It seems not even the famed Negotiator can close every deal, even if it's diamond-clad. Stay tuned—"

"Oh…my…God!" I turn in horror to Celia.

"So it's true?" Celia's Betty Boop face goes all wide-eyed with surprise. "Harrison proposed to you?"

"Er, sort of. But how did they hear about that?" I look back at the screen. "And why is it on TV?"

Celia shushes me, fast-forwards the tape through the commercials, hits Play again.

"Harrison 'The Negotiator' Buckley is well known to Jerseyites as the man who will not take 'No deal' for an answer. Well, old Harrison, car dealer par excellence, was certainly off his game last night. While dining at a local establishment…"

I turn away, feeling woozy. Who knew the local weather guy was at the restaurant last night, or that he'd make my proposal—no, refusal—the topic of his water cooler spot on the morning news?

"—So go by and give Harrison a break. 'Cause some little lady broke his heart."

"Your old man proposed?" Shemar has come out from the back. "And you shut him down in public. *Ouch!* Now, that's cold."

"He wasn't my old man. And I don't want to talk about it."

"I'm only saying, Miz T, you could be driving the hoopty of your choice off his lot, chilling and thrilling at this very moment."

I turn to Celia. "Isn't there a law against invasion of privacy?"

"John calls it a reasonable expectation of privacy." Celia's husband has twice qualified for *Jeopardy* and is waiting for the call. "He says Harrison proposed in a public place. He could have no reasonable expectation of privacy."

"What about me? I was totally blindsided. Don't I have a right to privacy?"

"Least that chump weatherman didn't catch the 411 on you, Miz T," Shemar offers as consolation.

I clutch at this realization. I wasn't named. No one will know it was me. So, maybe no real harm was done, except to Harrison. Poor Harrison! He's going to be in all alone in the spotlight of shame.

That fantasy lasts as long as it takes for the door to open.

"Who's Miss Picky this morning?" Mrs. Morshheimer actually simpers as she comes up to me. "I thought he was just right for you." She pats my arm. "At a certain point in life a girl can be too particular. Security and companionship are better in the long run."

She leans in really close to whisper. "The s-e-x never lasts." She looks up at me with a little shake of her head.

Great. Just great!

Chapter 8

Who marries on a Friday? This is a mercy wedding. At least my attendance is.

With the Fine Arts and Crafts Show opening tomorrow I should be at the bakery taking care of a hundred last-minute details. But I promised Celia. And this is Jenna Harris's wedding.

Jenna Harris is, by Celia's account, a whippet-size baby-blonde, the ethereal kind found only in Manhattan. Celia is "baby's mum" blond, meaning she's often too busy to keep the roots touched up. If Botticelli drew her she'd be one of the Three Graces of ample hip and stomach curves. But a bigger psychological barrier is that Celia and John eloped while Jenna's wedding is rumored to be *the* wedding of the season—even if it is being held in New Jersey. I say there's something fishy in that, but what do I know?

"You look lovely," I assure her for the fourth time. She's wearing a champagne silk dupioni sheath. "I can tell you've lost weight."

"And you. Sexy, sexy!" Celia seems as delighted as if she were speaking of herself.

What I've lost is my appetite. Hiring a lawyer I can't afford to fight for my share of Ted's will has me chewing my nails to the quick. Reason aside, I don't really want any part of Ted's estate. But I just can't stand the idea of handing everything over to *her!* How juvenile is that?

"I like your hair lifted back off your face," Celia continues. "Has anyone ever told you you look a bit like Jackie O?"

"No." Embarrassed, I turn away. Sally looks like Jackie O. I look, well, like not Jackie.

If I'm looking at all sexy it's the shoes. Periodically, Sally cleans out her closet and sends me pairs of last season's got-to-have shoes. Shoe size is the only size we share. Lucky me! The right pair of shoes can make even a simple black sheath look couture. Tonight I'm wearing Jimmy Choo sandals with curvy red patent leather hole-punched straps. Sex on a stem!

The black tie wedding is being held in one of the swanky hotels in the area. A block-long white Hummer limo blocks the curved entrance while double-parked guests wait for valets. I park myself. In my pennies-count world, I can't afford to show off.

When we finally break free of the crush entering the prenuptial cocktail area of the reception hall, Celia has parallel frown lines between her brows. Already set high, her envy meter is rising.

The theme of the wedding is "Under the Sea." The tones are champagne and mother-of-pearl pink with traces of silver. From tabletops spilling over with shells and pearls to a ceiling artfully draped to resemble ocean currents, the room is a stage set of seascape luxe. Granted, it's not as gaudy/tacky as it will sound when I describe it to Riley and Sarah, but my job tonight is to be biased on Celia's behalf. And Celia's turning an envious shade of green. Of course, it could be that she's holding her stomach in too tight.

"Would you look at all this?" I hope I sound faintly disapproving. "Who but a cruise ship still does conch shell ice sculptures?"

"Jenna took the Michael C. Fina wedding workshop course." Celia sounds positively subdued. "She must have made an A."

"And he made a bundle. Anyone can buy inspiration. She bought too much."

Celia gives me a funny look. "Don't you like it?"

I look around with a sigh of *so what*. "Honestly? It's as if Tiffany did *The Little Mermaid* in platinum and pearls."

A bubble of laughter escapes Celia and she steers me over to a diorama of the bridal place setting. The elaborately scrolled and painted pieces of Butterfly Garden bone china by Versa are presented as works of art. "John had a cow when I told him how much a setting costs. Oh, but it is gorgeous."

"Plates that decorative make it hard to tell when you have finished eating. And notice the size and weight of her silver. Elderly relatives will never be able to lift those forks to their mouths."

Celia giggles again. "I had no idea you could be so catty."

A waiter with tray approaches. "Have a Blue Bird or Abyssina martini."

Celia grabs the pretty blue drink with narrow strips of orange peel curling over the rim. After a sip she smiles. "Yum!"

"Gin, Monin Orgeat and blue Curaçao," the waiter offers in explanation.

I wrinkle my nose. "Nothing called a martini should be blue."

"You might prefer the Abyssinia," the waiter says. "It's cognac, crème de cacao and grapefruit juice."

"Have a lot of requests for that sort of thing?"

He shrugs. "It's the bride's selection."

Celia looks at me. "I can't wait to see what the appetizer plaza has to offer."

I nod. If Celia's ready to move on from sucked-in abs to self-indulgent grazing, my job, for the moment, is done.

I opt for the nearest bar station where I order a real martini. My limit is one before the wedding. Nothing gets me tight faster than a good martini. That tingling at the tip of my nose signals *stop* before all sense of decorum is lost.

There's a side galley for those with the preceremony munchies. At one stop hapi-coated sushi chefs make bite-size delicacies. After a tasting, we depart for tables laden with mini crab cakes, tiny beef Wellingtons and bite-size ham biscuits with béchamel sauce. My personal favorite is the lobster ceviche served in a silver conch shell. Heaven!

Finally Celia glances at her watch. "When are we going be seated?"

That question is being murmured in variation all around us when the doors are thrown open on a room with rows of velvet chairs and a wedding canopy at the far end. The throng rushes through to vie for the best seats.

As I would follow, Celia catches me by the elbow. "I wonder what that's about."

I follow the jerk of her head and spot a bridesmaid in a platinum silk chamois fishtail gown. She's waving to get our attention as she swims toward us.

She doesn't even introduce herself, just whispers, "Which of you is Celia Hart?"

"I am, was Celia Hart," Celia answers. "Now Celia Martin."

"Thank God!" She grabs Celia by the arm. "Jenna's locked herself in the dressing room and says she won't talk to anyone but you. Hurry!"

Celia must be doing marathon girlfriend counseling. It's been half an hour since the groom's mother announced that the wedding is off. After that, the hotel bar seemed a better location to wait than standing around at a celebration gone fractious. As I slipped out I overheard a guest refer to the bride as a "schizoid drama queen." No doubt from the groom's side of the aisle.

I'm gratified that my strapless black sheath with illusion yoke has earned me a few glances of approval. Possibly it's the Jimmie Choos. But I'm not interested in fending off upscale barflies. With a soda and lime in hand I chat up the bartender, Mitch, though he isn't above asking snoopy questions about the wedding. I've tried to divert him by talking about my favorite topic, bread, but he keeps coming back to the wedding.

"What'd you wager they spent on that shindig?"

"What do you think of the idea of pomegranate seed bread?" I respond. "I can't decide, does it sound like breakfast bread, dessert bread or a cheese-and-wine bread? I suppose it depends on how sweet it is, and whether or not there's a glaze."

"The kitchen staff has a pool going. My bet is three hundred thou."

Talk about a one-track mind.

"Excuse me," the man to my right says. "Are you here for a wedding?"

He sat down a few minutes ago, leaving a stool between us. I don't glance at him but I suppose there's no reason to be rude. He could be another stranded wedding guest. "Yes, the wedding that wasn't."

"Really? Tough break. So who called it off?"

I look over with every intention of telling him to mind his own business. But whatever I was about to say takes flight as I'm left just looking.

He's dressed in sport coat and open collar, definitely not a wedding guest. The rest of his assets click off in my mind: high forehead, cropped dark hair, bold nose and jaw set off by deep copper skin that no bottle, spray, oil or butter produced. Yet it's not his mature urbane looks that shut down my annoyance. It's his city-block smile. It's a smile of recognition, the kind you get from a long-ago friend who's eager for you to place him.

But I don't know him. Trust me, I would remember. The expectant look in his dark eyes only reminds me that I'm a single woman in a nice dress with time on her hands. So, *um,* what did he ask me?

"I'm here as moral support for a friend of a friend of the bride."

That smile widens a notch. "What kind of support does a friend of a friend of the bride give?"

The female response is a finicky business. One gorgeous male can leave a woman cold while the next average guy can have her crossing her legs and running a hand suggestively through her hair. I'm doing both before I realize it.

Not that I'd call him average. Actually, he's a really big guy. Like professional-athlete big. And he's talking to me. So why not keep the conversation going? The subject was? Oh yes, friendship.

"Oh, the usual. 'You're so lucky to be married to a great guy, and have two sets of twins, and a job with flexible hours. Look how long it took your boyfriend-stealing girlfriend to find a man to marry, even if he is a zillionaire.' As it turns out, she's had a change of heart about the zillionaire."

He nods, then says, "Excuse me," and pulls out his cell phone. "Hey. Yeah, I'm waiting in the bar."

I turn away, surprisingly disappointed. Of course he's waiting for someone. She's probably running late, to ratchet up his anticipation.

Mitch catches my eye, and I know he knows what I'm thinking. "I'm ready for that martini now."

"Try a perfect martini." He's talking to me again.

"What's your definition of perfect?" I say coolly.

He smiles and, yep, the eyes have it, deep-set and long-lashed. Girlfriend better hurry up. This is not a man who should be left waiting. "Four parts good gin, one part Chambery dry and one part Noilly Prat sweet, shaken with ice."

"Sounds interesting. But aren't you waiting for someone?"

He shakes his head. "Not anymore."

"You recover quickly."

"It wasn't a date. It was business."

"Sure it was."

He shoots me a knowing grin. "About that martini?"

"I'm paying," I say quickly. Hope it won't cost more than the twenty I stuck in my evening bag.

"Wait until you taste it." The deep grooves around his mouth become dimple trenches. "So, what do you do?"

"I'm a baker. I bake bread."

I watch closely for signs of a shift in his interest. Much as I hate to admit it, that "blue collar" comment from Ted has proved true for some.

"Why bread?"

"You know how some people crave chocolate? And others live for the next good vintage? Bread does it for me. A good loaf can satisfy all the senses." I stop, chagrined. "I know. I'm talking about a food most people use as bookends for meat and cheese."

"Not at all." He leans an arm on the bar and says, "Tell me more."

"Okay, but remember, you asked." Suddenly I want to sound fascinating, entertaining and sexy as hell.

"First off there's the form of the classic loaf to seduce the eye. Some are round and firm, others long and lightly ridged." I make the appropriate hand gestures. Shemar has rubbed off on me!

"The crust is paramount. Personally, a rich medium brown really does it for me." He smiles and I smile, and feel my pulse kick up a notch.

"What else?"

"There's how a loaf feels when you slip a knife through it, or tear it open. A good brioche or roll will open like a flower when you pull it part. A well-proofed loaf will fall open in firm slices before a blade."

He props his jaw on his fist. "Go on."

"The aroma of bread still warm from the oven." I close my eyes briefly in remembered delight. "It's one of my all-time favorite smells."

"Three senses down, you've got two to go."

"Okay, I love the tantalizing taste as a slice of bread reveals its nature as sourdough or poolish-based. Oh, and the crunch it makes when you take a bite."

He looks amused. "I never thought of something as simple as bread delivering an orgasmic experience."

What the heck? I lean close and touch his arm. "There are those who suspect that it was a pomegranate not an apple Eve plucked from the Garden of Eden. Imagine the possibilities of the pomegranate-seed loaf I'm working on."

As he chuckles, I look over at the drink set before me and frown. "There's fruit in my martini."

"You're a passionate and adventurous woman. Consider the possibilities of the cherry."

He snags the cherry in my glass by the stem and jerks it out. "Observe the color—red. The texture—smooth. The shape—round." He pops the cherry between his nice lips and rolls it around with the slow-motion deliberation, and then he chews as if he's relishing every bite. "The texture is crisp, the taste sweet yet with a touch of... *je nais c'est quoi.*"

When he's done I point and say, "You left the lemon rind."

He reaches out with two fingers, as if to dredge my drink,

but I move it out of his reach. "Okay, you win. I'll taste it." I close my eyes and take a sip.

"Well?"

"It's all right." *It's great!* Of course, his demonstration with the cherry has me thinking more about what kissing him would taste like. A second more considering sip brings out the blend of flavors. "Very smooth."

"To the perfect evening!" We clink glasses.

Might as well get the preliminaries over with. "Married or divorced?"

"Divorced." He shakes his head. "That sounded bitter. I'm not. Make that not anymore."

"You don't have to explain. I've been there."

"Was yours acrimonious?"

I pick up my glass. "What's your definition of acrimonious?"

"Did it include defamation of character or destruction of property?" His tone is light. "Were weapons involved?"

I contemplate the slightly oiled surface of my martini with a small smile. "What's your definition of weapons?"

His change of expression cracks me up. "Just kidding. So, what do you do?"

"Does it matter?"

"Actually, I couldn't care less." I finish off my perfect martini in two large swallows.

"Want to try another combination?" He points at my glass. "Or do you prefer more of the same?"

I meet his gaze and it's like looking over the edge of a high cliff. Is this the next great man? If so, "More of the same please."

"My pleasure and my treat."

After that we chat about nothing in particular. He's so easy to talk with. He tells a long story about his visit to a gin distillery. I listen only enough to make the occasional "Really?" or "You're kidding" interjections. I'd rather admire the way his ears lie against his skull. And imagine how much fun it would be to follow with a finger the wave of his hairline from the temple to where it swoops up over an ear and then slips razor-edge perfect down the column of his neck. Something about the smooth, hairless slope of his nape makes me weak-kneed.

When I reach out and touch his wrist to emphasize a point, he flips his hand over and captures my fingertips and gives them a quick squeeze. Our gazes meet and hold just long enough.

"Have you considered broadening your business?" he asks after the third set of drinks arrives. I've been regaling him with tales of the No-Bagel Emporium.

"Only every other day."

"What's stopping you?"

"Lack of capital. Lack of investors. Lack of distribution mechanism."

"Ever think about doing a deal with a corporation for distribution?"

I make a face. "Tried that."

"What happened?"

"Low-carb mania."

I rest my chin on my hand, only inches from where his rests, and am delighted by how daring so simple an act seems. The slight tingling in the tip of my nose signals that we're kissably close. Or, I've reached my martini limit.

He twists on his stool to fully face me. The result is my knees become nestled between his spread legs and I find it a little harder to keep my expression bland. "Is your product any good?"

"I'd match my bread against any bakery in the tri-state area."

He laughs and it's the most seductive thing. I feel this out-of-character-but-urgent desire to put my arms about his neck, and French-kiss him until we melt into a puddle on the floor.

A little perplexed by the force of my emotions, I look away from him. The truth is if I could have wild anonymous monkey sex with this man right this minute, I'd go for it.

I look up guiltily. "Did I just say something?"

He shakes his head. "But I'd give a dollar to hear what you're thinking."

Our gazes meet and I watch his pupils expand with the force of the desire in my expression. He's going to say something, do something, I just know it.

Instead he picks up my glass and waggles it at the bartender. "I'm going to buy you one more, and then we're going to say good night."

I glance toward the door. Has the girlfriend arrived, after all? I don't see anyone in particular, but then things have taken on a warm fuzzy glow. When I turn back he's staring at me, and it hits me. I want this guy. "Why break up a nice evening?" I hope I don't sound as giddy as I feel.

He takes his time before he says, "Because, what we're both thinking isn't going to be satisfied by an evening on a bar stool."

"So maybe we need a change of location." The words are out, and it feels liberating.

He reaches up and balances three fingers on the summit of my right cheekbone.

When the right person touches you he doesn't have to make contact with a traditional erogenous zone, your whole body simply becomes one. My cheek feels teased, titillated, and then abandoned unfulfilled as his fingers slide down and around before falling away. He smiles. "Why don't we find out?"

I didn't notice him pulling out a plastic hotel key but suddenly he's pressing it discreetly into my palm. "Eight twenty-eight."

Oh, my God! He's serious. I was just flirting. Not that I wasn't entertaining fantasies. But offers like this don't come to women like me from men like him. Or do they?

As he turns to signal for the tab, I spy Celia beyond his shoulder span, waving at me from the bar entrance.

The power of locomotion is still mine. I make it across the bar to Celia before I feel the full wallop of the alcohol I've consumed.

"I've been looking everywhere for you," Celia says in concern.

"I met this really great guy." I sound like a teenager at her first dance.

Celia grins. "So, who is he and what does he do?"

"I don't know who he is, but I do know he wants to do *me*." I find that remark hilarious and have to hold on to Celia's arm when the giggles seem to weaken my knees.

Celia tries to look stern but catches my giggles. "You're completely soused."

"I know. Just tell me this. Is he as gorgeous as I think he is?" I point in the direction of the bar.

Celia does a discreet "girlfriend checking out the other friend's guy." "Who am I looking for?"

I follow her gaze. *He's left!* Oh yeah, he's being discreet.

"Never mind." I fish out my car keys and hand them to her. "You take the car. I have a few details here to wrap up."

Celia looks doubtful. "What about the crafts fair tomorrow?"

I lean in and whisper, "If you were single and had gone years without feeling like a sexual being, and a great man invited you to spend some time, would you pass him up?"

She smiles. "Call me in the morning. But don't forget, no glove, no love."

Chapter 9

It takes forever to get an elevator. The hotel is filled with guests who seem to have nothing better to occupy the evening than riding from floor to floor.

What's worse, the wait is dimming my hedonistic high. Reason is whispering that I'm the mother who says to her daughters, don't pick up strange men in bars, don't do it on a first date, and *never* go to hotel rooms with strange men.

Yet here I am, contemplating all three.

What am I doing? I got carried away by possibility and gin. I'm sure—er, I don't even know his name. Shouldn't the next great man have a name?

Maybe not. I'm not looking for a future that requires the reality of name, career placement and credit score. I'm after a bit of sizzle. He is funny and smart. He is attractive. And that smile! Any way you slice it, he qualifies as the next great man.

My left knee, which has a tendency to shake when I'm really stage-fright nervous, is about to collapse under my weight.

This is what happens when you break out of a martini-blinkered lustful moment long enough to reconnect with reality.

When the elevator finally does stop, an overcapacity crowd, many still in evening dress, emerges. Left behind, wedged in a corner, is a young couple going at it like it's their personal private sex capsule. She's wearing a fishtail bridesmaid gown and he's in shirtsleeves. The jacket and cummerbund of his tux are at their feet. Well, his feet. Her legs are wrapped around his hips. Those standing with me quickly back off. But I've waited long enough. Before I completely lose my nerve, I step in and turn to face the closing door.

As the elevator rises, the muffled sounds of passion-on-the-hoof just behind me increase. Public sex seems unsanitary, not to mention illegal. What about the camera over my head? There, I'm too mature for hookups. I think about things like sanitation, privacy and the law.

No, I'm a mature modern woman who knows what she wants and how to get it.

Or I'm a middle-aged about-to-be slut. Bridget Jones's mom.

When the elevator doors part on the eighth floor, I spy him standing in the hallway in his shirtsleeves. When he sees me he looks relieved.

"Don't let me interrupt," I say, and leave behind the couple who've graduated to moans.

He reaches for my hand and gives it a hard squeeze. "I thought you might have changed your mind."

"I did. Several times."

He smiles. That little squeeze of my fingertips is awfully sexy. Thanks to my Jimmie Choos, I sashay down the hall.

When we stop before a door marked 828, he pats his pockets looking for a key. Finally, he turns to me with a sheepish look on his face. "I think I locked us out."

"Allow me." I whip out his key, the green light flashes, and we're in.

He walks over and picks up his jacket, fishes another key out of the inside pocket, and holds it up like a boy with a special rock.

I look around and say, "Nice room."

"Thanks. I decorated it myself." We both laugh, a little embarrassed by the unease of what up to now has been pure attraction.

It is actually a suite. Somewhere out of sight is a bedroom that will require a deliberate decision to move into. So, what now?

I need to lay some ground rules. "I think it's best if we don't exchange any information like names or phone numbers. What happens or doesn't happen here tonight is strictly between us. No strings. Okay?"

He hesitates. Maybe I should be hesitating, too. Then he shrugs. "Whatever the lady wants. I haven't eaten. Have you?"

"Not enough for what I've been drinking."

"I'll order some hors d'œuvres."

"Good idea." This is a good time to excuse myself to go to the bathroom to freshen up.

When I come back he's still standing. He's obviously waiting to say something. "There's something I'd better tell you."

I take a deep breath as my mind fast-tracks possible complication scenarios. "You are still married."

"Divorced, remember?"

The phone call he didn't explain. "Engaged?"

"There's no special woman in my life."

Okaaaay! He's cute, looks like he works out. "You're gay. No, after the way you kiss I guess that would be bi."

"Not even! I think you should know what I do for a living."

The funniest thing occurs to me. "You're an upscale drug dealer wanted by the police. No, don't tell me, you moonlight as a contract killer."

He stares at me. "You watch a lot of TV, huh?"

"Read. Stephanie Plum's a favorite character." His expression makes me chuckle. "So, listen, if what you want to tell me isn't life threatening or in some way casts doubt on our ability to be together legally or medically, can we skip the confessions?"

He looks a little doubtful now. "Is there something I should know about you?"

"I don't always floss daily. I answer the Myers Briggs the way I want to be, not how I am. And…it's been a while." I refuse to allow Harrison to count. "So, I'm not perfectly sure what happens next. Do we just strip and jump each other? Or, what is the latest conversational prelude to seduction?"

He laughs and motions me toward the sofa. "We just go with the moment, okay? For however long and however far seems right."

That seems fair. I sit down and set aside my purse, which I've been clutching like an emergency parachute. "Ah, about safety precautions?"

He nods. "I stopped in the store in the lobby."

Jeez! I don't know his name yet I'm asking him about condoms? I'm starting to sweat, which is not attractive.

He sits beside me, not so close as to be smothering but close enough to stay interested. "So, where were we?"

I lean in, as if I'm going to kiss him, but at the last second I turn my head so that we are cheek to cheek. First impressions are very important. The way a man smells, as much as his appearance and manners, tells me a lot about him. It's a clue to personality, a personal litmus test.

Okay, maybe I'm weird. But everyone has some instant measure of others. Clothing labels, sports shoe choice, musical preferences, choice of car, or hair color or bra size: these are more realistic barometers of personality? I don't think so. Something a man chooses to splash, spray or slap on his skin, now that's a personal choice.

"Um, you smell good." He does, clean but male, with a touch of something too faint to place. No aftershave. That's unusual.

He bends his head and lightly sniffs my neck. "You smell delicious, too. I don't recognize that perfume."

"Good." I pride myself on my perfume choices. I don't want to smell my scent in a room full of other women.

He lifts a hand and cups my face. "You're as soft and warm as you look. That's four senses down. You want to go for five?"

"Aren't you jumping ahead?"

"I've been looking and listening to you for hours. Taste is all there is left."

"Okay—oh!" He nips my earlobe and then backs up until our faces are in perfect alignment for a kiss.

My lips part slightly in anticipation of his. But we do not meet. When I grab his neck to close the distance he stiffens. Oh, no! In spite of the martinis, do I still have sushi breath?

"Something's wrong?" I venture.

"No, just testing." He breathes in slowly, as if he's sniffing out a new scent. "There's a practice in tantric sex where desire is heightened merely by the exchange of breaths. It's called an exchange of essence."

Uh-oh. He's into advanced sexual high jinks. My bridal-shower copy of the *Kama Sutra* is still in near pristine condition. Ted thought it was "cheesy."

"So you've—um, studied Eastern sexual technique?"

"Not exactly." He's so close I can only tell he is smiling because his eyes have crinkled in the corners. "Someone left a copy of *Five-O* in the seat pocket on my flight. The cover blurb was about tantric sex so I picked it up."

I decide right then and there to renew my subscription. The tension of not kissing is almost unbearable. "What else did the article say?"

"I'll tell you later. First let's break the rules."

He kisses me.

We're in no hurry. We just melt back into the cushions and kiss and kiss and kiss until there's a knock at the door. "Room service."

He lifts his head and says, "Leave it by the door."

And then we resume the kind of kissing that leads to exactly where we both want to go. Little by little, we lose contact first with the floor, and then with articles of clothing.

Very quickly sensation takes over, and cataloging seems like a waste of divided mind. He's touching that, rubbing the other and, oh, licking right there! Pretty soon I'm using my tongue to flirt with his lightly hairy male nipples. A little later I find his belt buckle and then open his zipper. What unfolds behind the cotton of his briefs is both urgent and prolonged.

The sex is...

I'd like to say we were urbane and sophisticated. That all sorts of prolonged foreplay took us to the brink again and again, that we measured up to some Olympic-style ideal of performance. But the truth is, once we were out of bra and panties and briefs, it took us about five minutes to get to, Oh! Oh, yes! Oh, oh, oh! Yes, yes, *yeeees!*

Or words to that effect.

When my world stops spinning and the color behind my eyeballs is back to black I say, "What happened to tantric?"

"Huh?" He's sprawled beside me on his bed, one heavy hairy thigh still tucked between my spread legs. "Oh, right." He turns his head my way and smiles the best after-sex smile ever. "I didn't want to scare you off."

"I'm lying here like a perfectly happy seal on the beach of your sheets and you're worried about that?"

"I did promise you a good time." He brushes the hair out of my eyes. No wonder he was a blur. "You still want to try it?"

"Nothing too strenuous. Yoga classes totally intimidate me."

He shifts his shoulders against the pillows. "You don't have to."

No pressure there. I can just pass up the opportunity for more sex with a man who knows what he's doing. For what, the hope that this offer will come again? And that that issue of *Five-O* is still for sale. And that I can find a guy I like enough to undress for who's willing to take a sexual performance hint from a women's magazine. What are the chances of that?

It's so much simpler to just say, "Yes, please."

He sits up. "We'll try something simple, called the breath of love. I hope I can remember how."

"Well, let's look at the magazine."

He actually blushes. "I left it on the plane."

"So, what do you remember?"

"First we sit cross-legged before each other." He obviously has no embarrassment in doing this, and I already know he has nothing to be ashamed of. He's a really big guy, broad and solid. While he may have a bit of a tummy it doesn't obscure his pride and joy.

When I've scrambled up into a sitting position facing him, and start to cross my legs I realize that a bit too much is going to be on display for a woman who needs a drape at the ob-gyn. I wrap the sheet over my hips. "What next?"

"No, that's not right." He scoots up to me. "I sit cross-legged. You straddle my waist then wrap your legs around my back."

The picture I'm getting prompts me to say, "I thought you said no sex was involved."

"We don't actually come together."

My mouth quirks up. "Perhaps 'unite' would be a less loaded phrase?"

"Right." He laughs. "Okay, now I remember. The position is called the *yab-yum*. You've probably seen pictures of erotic Hindu statues."

I eye him speculatively. "We won't be trying the one where the female hangs by her heels about the guy's neck while being penetrated, right?"

"Nawgh! I have a bad back. Besides I'd need a couple of feet to make it interesting."

I catch his eye. "You're plenty interesting just as you are."

After we unbend from laughter, we try this thing.

It's pretty embarrassing. His penis seems not to have gotten the news that the second act is not yet under way. It keeps wagging around as I try to straddle his waist. And no way will I be able to wrap my legs about anything. My nymphet-agile days are behind me. I end up with my knees under his armpits as he embraces me.

"Now what?" We are nose to nose, nipple to nipple. It's like being on the subway in rush hour, only sexier.

"Now, hold out your arms, bend them at the elbows, fore-fingers and thumbs together. And we breathe...through our sex organs." His voice already sounds labored.

As I breathe in—through my nostrils—I feel the thump of his penis down low, and wonder if he's accomplishing what I cannot.

"The point of the tantric experience is generosity," he says after a few seconds. "Being in the present for the other person."

"If you become any more present than you were a few minutes ago I'll need CPR."

His burst of laughter rocks my world, literally. I almost fall off his lap. When I've regained my balance I try again for the "centered" moment.

We breathe—very slowly—for several seconds but all I feel is that I'm about to get a toe cramp.

"Now, imagine," he says very softly, "a bowl between us that is filling with our energy."

His warm breath fans my face, and I think I will sneeze. Bowl of energy! This is so silly. I can't believe I actually agreed to this. We're at least two decades too old to go with this flow.

I'm concentrating so hard at not laughing at us that I don't even realize my eyes are shut until he says, "Look at me."

The second our gazes meet I feel as if he's touching my womb, from the inside. I tumble in through his eyes to meet in a place I've never shared with anyone before. Desire expands, as if I've taken a deep breath below. It's dizzying…and exhilarating, desire fills me up tip to top.

He's saying something about sharing energy

I feel…like he's set me on fire!

When he leans toward me we meet with our lips touching only at the edges.

We hover, for what seems like an hour, slowly breathing in and out. Finally I am only sensation…insubstantial…ephemeral…unbound by physicality.

Except for his very real and rock-hard penis, which is boring a hole in my inner thigh.

The kiss, when it becomes impossible not to kiss, gives me such an orgasm that I forget my position, throwing my arms about him as I shudder hard all over.

When the shaking stops he takes my sweaty face in his hands and rubs his thumbs across my mouth. "So, how are you doing?"

I want to say something sophisticated and worldly. What comes out is a fairly unenlightened "Wow!"

"Yeah." He's grinning into my eyes.

Within seconds, we've returned to the common practice of the westernized conventional sexual union we know best, and blow all to hell the basic tantric tenet that men should withhold ejaculation and prolong erection for energy containment.

There's something shockingly freeing about living in the moment.

I don't remember the order of anything after that. The thing I do remember is him cuddling in behind me as if we were a longtime couple after I said I needed a break. It feels so good I figure he must have liked being married. Whoever gave him up or threw him out never really understood what she had.

The bedside clock reads 5:23 a.m. when I roll over. In the time it takes to remember where and with whom I am I also remember that my tired but sated body was supposed to be at the bakery twenty-three minutes ago.

My bed partner doesn't even grunt as I practically step on him in a rush to get to the bathroom.

Showered and brushed, thanks to one of those throwaway-toothbrush amenities this hotel offers, I'm mostly presentable in fifteen minutes, for a woman in last night's cocktail dress and F-me red heels. I'm rooting around on hands and knees for one of those shoes when he snaps on the bedside light.

"What are you doing?" He looks unsteady and his hair is standing up in little tufts all over his head. He looks adorable. And I'm a little more embarrassed than I expected to be.

"Hi. I've got to go. Sorry."

"Oh." He rubs his eyes with both hands just like a kid. "Okay, so I'll call you."

I lever upright, my search for shoes abandoned. "No, you can't call me. We had a deal, remember? No strings."

He reaches over and picks up my shoe, which for some reason is sitting on the nightstand, and squints at the clock. "Do you know it's only 5:48?"

"I'm an early riser."

"So stay and have breakfast with me."

"Can't. I have to be somewhere. Give me my shoe."

"A woman of mystery and style." After an admiring glance, he hands over my shoe. "So, okay, you have to go. Come back tonight and we'll have dinner. Or see a movie, do whatever you like."

"No!" I bend down by the bed, trying to locate my other shoe. "This was just what it was. Nothing more."

"What was it?"

"A good time."

"That's all?"

"A very, very good time. But that's it. You don't owe me anything. I don't owe you."

"What if I'd like more?"

"Get over it." I locate my other super sexy Choo nestled, where else, between his Kenneth Cole loafers. "The truth is I don't do this sort of thing—ever."

"Really?" He sounds as if he suspected that from the beginning. Surely I wouldn't have done what I did last night if I wasn't hoping to see him again. "So this is going to be just a one-night stand?"

"Yes." I scramble to my feet and slip on shoes that feel much too high for a woman dealing with the low of a morning-after affair.

"But you just said you don't do one-night stands." He's now sitting on the side of the bed looking at me with those dark eyes I was skinny-dipping in a few hours before.

I want to touch him but we both know where that will lead.

"Let's be mature about this. We had an awfully good time. You're…" I stop and smile. "You're really something."

"Thank you."

"No. Really. A great guy. Funny and smart and generous and sexy as hell! But this—" I wave a hand around "—is not really my style. So let's not do or say anything that would spoil our perfect evening."

A half smile appears on his face. "You don't believe in per-fection."

I bend down a give him a quick kiss. "You've made a liar out of me."

Chapter 10

As I circle Anderson Park, searching for that parking space that won't materialize, the still-warm aroma of cornish splits arises from the backseat. I should be concerned about our potential for sales during the weekend, feeling guilty about not being ready for the early-morning crowd of hungry vendors, anxious about how well we'll do with a split staff and direct competition on either side and across the grassy aisle of the food vendors' row. Instead, I'm humming Aretha's *Natural Woman*.

It's like when you hit the jackpot in Atlantic City. You can only really count yourself a winner if you take the cash and immediately walk away.

And I made a great exit.

Of course, I got no farther than the lobby before I remembered that I had no way home. A quick call to Celia spelled relief. She was at the bakery where I should have been. She didn't ask a single question, just kept giving me funny sideways glances as she drove me home then headed for the crafts fair.

Ten minutes after arriving at my house, I was changed into jeans, T-shirt and baseball cap, and headed for the bakery where Shemar and company were loading the van with goodies for the day. As a cover for my red eyes and unruly hair, I made noises about a restless night. No one said a word but I swear they could tell something was up. Desharee kept giving me side glances and saying "um-hm" under her breath.

"Finally!" I spy a florist van backing out of a space a third of the way down the row ahead.

There's a car facing me at the far end of the row but it's momentarily blocked by the flow of visitors walking in that direction. Was it there first? Who cares? I'm closer, and swerve into the vacated spot with the breakneck speed of a pro rally driver.

A minute later, as I'm bent over in the backseat struggling to fill my arms with bread baskets I hear the annoyed tone of a man say, "Excuse me. You took my spot."

"Sorry. It's first come, first get." Without even a backward look, which might draw me into a confrontation I have no time or desire for, I reach back a hand with a peace offering. "Have a biscuit, on the house."

He hesitates and then takes it.

As he turns away I catch a faint whiff of a new and completely compelling fragrance, and the scent of something more familiar. The hair stands up on the back of my neck!

I straighten up and bang my head so hard on the door frame

that I see stars. By the time I've recovered enough to back out and turn around, he's gone.

"Who was that?" Celia asks as she rushes up to help me before I drop something.

"I didn't get a good look." Even so. My scenes are still in orgasmic overload. Could it be? "Did you smell him?"

Celia's eyes widen. "I certainly *saw* him. What? Does he have BO?"

"No." I close my eyes to concentrate. "He smells like talcum power and confectioner's sugar sprinkled over tart plums."

"That's a Gerber junior foods smell," says the mother of double twins.

"There was a distinct male smell too, like a hint of Hawaiian sea salt." And I'd swear that I've very recently and very intimately been involved with it.

As I fall into step with her Celia gives me a funny look. "Didn't you notice anything else beside the fact that he smells like dessert?"

I try to keep my expression bland as we enter the vendors' aisle. "For instance?"

"For instance, he looks like the Rock."

"The who?"

She does the eyebrow thing. "The ex-wrestler, now actor? Okay, this guy's a bit older, but he looks like he could be the Rock's dad."

Now that she mentions it…

Celia places my wares on the booth's tabletop and winks. "I'll be right back. I'm going to find out who he is."

Uh-oh! I can't have him waltzing up to my booth unprepared. "Wait, Celia, I need you with me. We have a lot of work to do."

But she's already on her way. "Here comes Shemar and Desharee. I'll be back in five."

I take a deep breath. Okay, even if he is who I think he is, and he didn't recognize my clothed rear end, maybe seeing him again wouldn't be so bad. Maybe.

Am I ready to have my wild night revealed?

A silly, giddy possibility sideswipes me, and leaves a grin that makes Shemar do a double-take. Perhaps he traced me here! Perhaps he couldn't take no for an answer because I'm the most sexy provocative woman he's ever encountered. He's here, seeking—

No, scratch that. He wasn't so infatuated that he recognized me when he spoke to my rear. This, when you consider how we spent the night, might not seem all that unfamiliar a territory. So, why is he here?

Celia returns five minutes later with a big grin and the answer. "TRD is corporate!"

"Who's TRD?"

Celia leans in close. "The Rock's dad. He's a food consultant for Nabisco in the environmental-health food division, stressing organic products."

"Oh, brother!" I know why she's grinning. She has no idea why I suddenly want to duck and cover.

"Is something wrong?" Celia's staring at me.

"I—uh, stole his parking space." *And, I'm pretty sure I had sex with him last night.*

Celia considers thoughtfully. "We could give him a gift basket as an apology when he comes by."

I shake my head. "Scouts like to make their own approaches. I hope he didn't think I was out to impress him," I add under my breath.

"Impress him? You didn't even really see him."

The things I've seen and know about the Nabisco scout couldn't be published in a corporate report. I need to think.

"Left something in the car. I'll be right back." I put on my shades, pull my baseball cap low and duck out the back of the booth. It's a short hike from there to the edge of the fairgrounds and into a shady grove where I pause to regroup.

Okay, there's no need to panic. People have relationships every day. So why, the one time I step out of line, do I find myself having screwed the man who could make my professional life better? Will he think I slept with him for a favorable report? He knew who, or rather what, I am. I told him all about my bakery while still at the bar. He could have told me then who he was.

Hmm. He did try to tell me who he was. I was the one who said no names, no phone numbers. Once he knows the truth, will he think I was being deliberately coy?

"Holy crap!" I remember bad-mouthing corporate types. He must think I'm an idiot.

So maybe I should just seek him out and tell him the truth. Will he understand if I say, "Excuse me, but I didn't know who you were when I screwed you. Now that I do, can we talk business?"

What are the odds?

I look up and there he is! Coming in my general direction away from the food booths is the best thing to happen to me in years. He's wearing cords and a suede sport coat, and a smile as broad and sexy as the Rock's. There's no longer any doubt. Last night I seduced the Nabisco rep!

He hasn't recognized me yet. He's talking to someone. Not just anyone, but a guy with the letters West Orange Bakery printed on his shirtfront. Who are they?

Reflex is a funny thing. My cerebrum is thinking, *step out and meet him like the grown-up you are.* But the cerebellum, with cowardly reptilian antecedents, wants me to duck behind a tree.

While I'm loitering in my mind I tell myself that whatever happened between us last night was private. He is a businessman. He's here in an official capacity. So, why shouldn't I…?

"Mrs. Elizabeth Talbot?"

I do an about-face to find a young woman in shorts and tee smiling at me. "Yes, I'm Liz Talbot."

She holds out an envelope. "I have something for you."

"Thank you."

In the space it takes to open the envelope my emotions shift from erotic to enraged. It's a court summons issued by *her* attorney.

"I'm being sued?" I look up but the summons server is moving quickly away.

Fan-*damn*-fastic!

I glance back over my shoulder but my mystery lover is walking away at an angle that won't bring him within range. I should go after him. Or, just maybe he did notice me and decided he didn't want his cover blown, either.

Fuming, I make my way back to my booth where Celia announces that there have been no further sightings of the Rock's dad, or "TRD," as she decides to refer to him so no one else knows who we're talking about.

By noon it's clear that the Nabisco rep bypassed our display. I try to look as sad as my crew, but something in me is defiant.

So what, if No-Bagel Emporium missed out on a chance to produce Nabisco's next hot product because I boinked their rep? I've got bigger problems. There's a summons tucked in my jeans pocket.

I should have known Ted's will was going to cost me. The question is how much?

Chapter 11

"I'm not here."

I yell this over my shoulder in answer to Desharee's summons to the phone. At the door of the No-Bagel Emporium, I do a quick right-left, looking for potential process servers lying in wait for me. Coast is clear. I'm outta here!

As I slide behind the wheel of my car, a young man on a bike approaches at Lance Armstrong speed. He brakes suddenly as I slam shut my door, his skinny tires sending up a puff of dust. I jab the key in the ignition and twist. As the engine roars to life, he holds up something and waves. It's long, white and slim. I gesture him out of my way with one hand while throwing the car into Drive with the other, and accelerate with enough force that the tires squeal.

"Special messenger delivery!" he shouts as I tear past him.

"Amateur!" I cackle in glee as he shrinks in my rearview. Who does he think he's dealing with? I've been subpoenaed so often in the past week that I've developed skills, can spot a server at twenty paces.

This is *her* doing, well, her attorneys'. Since the breakdown of the arbitration sessions last week they are like the Hounds of the Baskervilles, and I'm their prey.

First there was the court appearance three weeks ago in which I was labeled sole defendant in a civil suit titled *Talbot v. Talbot*. It took the judge only minutes to decide we were taking up valuable court time. The law nominally gives us a fifty-fifty share of Ted's estate, and says that we must go to arbitration to settle the details.

Arbitration means you have to come to an agreement. So said the retired judge who served as mediator. Due to the volatile nature of the grievance, we, the opposing parties in the lawsuit, were told to address one another only through our respective attorneys. The first session did bring us into agreement that the new and ex Mrs. Talbots have rights to Ted's estate. How much and what kind would be determined at the second session. So far, so good.

At the next session, last Monday, I directed my attorney, against his advice, to contest even *her* share of Ted's estate, to concede that Ted's spousal share of what he had accrued during his second marriage, i.e., the new house, tanning salons, time share, etc., should go to *her*. At this point I thought I should have been crowned Ms. Congeniality of Arbitration. The crux of the matter: Talbot Advertising and cash on hand, was reserved for round three.

We might even have worked that out if the mediator hadn't

unilaterally decided that the ownership issue of Talbot Advertising could only be resolved if one party bought out the interests of the other. He called it the "nonnegotiable option."

Being the magnanimous munificent sweetheart that I am, I had my attorney convey that I had no interest in owning Talbot Advertising, and that *she* should buy me out, as in I preferred to take the money and run.

To which, without benefit of attorney, *she* glared at me and said, "The agency belongs to me, by right of marriage in front of God and everybody. If anybody's paying anybody anything, it will be you!"

To which I replied, "When pigs fly."

To which *she* answered, "Jealous bitch!"

To which I replied, "Gold-digging, husband-stealing heifer!" or words to that effect.

To wit, arbitration went downhill faster than Picabo Street.

She got in what she thought would be the last jab with "We'll see what the courts have to say about who owns what after I'm pregnant with Ted's child!"

Pregnant. *Future tense.*

Her attorney tried to cover for her but even the exasperated arbitrator perked up at this up-to-then unmentioned topic of hidden assets.

Turns out *she's* not pregnant, but that could change. *She* has fertility issues. With in vitro as an option, Ted had made use of a sperm bank just before his demise.

My attorney then informs the room that since that was not named as part of the heretofore mentioned assets, in fact was deliberately omitted, I retain joint custody of the deceased's—

uh—deposit. *She* can't make a withdrawal without my permission, and until we've settled ownership of all the estate issues the possibility of a pregnancy is moot.

So, you might say I have the situation by the balls, except—*yeesh!* Who needs this?

The last comment from the harassed arbitrator was "You have no choice but to bury the hatchet because the two of you are most certainly in business together."

Given a chance we'd bury the hatchet all right, in each other's backs.

I scan my rearview twice for any glimpse of the stealth cyclist. And just to make sure I'm not being followed by either that Entenmann's truck behind me or the Volvo on my right, I go three miles out of my way.

Okay, maybe I'm overreacting. With millions more or less mine—whatever her threats, my attorney assured me we will eventually have to share the wealth—I should be happier. What I am is harassed. But, the way arbitration is going, I'll be collecting social security before I see a penny of this inheritance. Her attorneys have filed injunctions against the estate, the will, even the arbitration agreement, which effectively ties up the money. By suing the will, even Sarah and Riley can't touch their allotted portion. If that's not enough, *she's* suing everyone even remotely connected with the estate, including Ted's attorneys "for failing to adequately protect his assets."

In a weak moment I told my attorney I just want out of this mess. His answer was that I'd have to sue the estate *not* to receive my share. Now you know there's something wrong with a law like that!

But life is about making choices. So, I'm moving on. Literally. I never liked the condo I bought after the divorce. I need green space, however small, and for all the walls to be my own. So I decided to sell. Proof that this was a good idea? I had a buyer after only three days. They are practically newlyweds with a child on the way, and wanted immediate custody. It all happened so fast I've had to find temporary dwelling space until I have time, and the money, to hunt for the new perfect place. Meanwhile, I'll have some cash on hand to invest in my business.

"Maybe you should wait until you've fixed up the place a bit before you invite your daughters over," Celia offered by way of advice when she helped me move in last week.

"This place needs—damn!—everything" was Shemar's comment.

They have a point. As I pull into the long drive that leads to the back of the lot I can't help but have a twinge of misgiving. I was in a hurry when I took this six-month lease. Last renovated when Johnson was in office, the "historic apartment redo tucked away on a bucolic lane" was a bargain for a reason. It's small, really small, unreconstructed-carriage-house-apartment tiny. The redo part meant it needs new paint, new fixtures, new—damn!—everything.

But, hey, this is temporary, until I can find the perfect place for me. The thought of solvency has me feeling so at one with the world that I couldn't harm a fly, or even the wasp that's found its way into my new home.

A few moments later, as I'm trying to put into action this holistic approach to my new life, I hear my name called out in theatrical tones.

"Liz?"

"Sally?"

Sally's standing in my entry, dressed in slim-legged pants and a white turtleneck. No surprise that she's gained entrance since the doors and every window in the apartment are wide open. The surprise is she's here at all. She never crosses into New Jersey unless it's absolutely, unavoidably necessary.

"What on earth are you doing here?" we demand of each other at the same time.

I relent first. "I'm trying to shoo out a wasp."

As said wasp whizzes past my head, I make a swooping motion with a kitchen towel to herd it toward the nearest opening. When the wasp alights on a nearby ledge, Sally strolls over, picks up a magazine and swats the resting insect. So much for live and let live.

"What are you doing here?" I repeat. Sally's been on a Hawaiian cruise with Tony. They were scheduled to dawdle in L.A. afterward.

"I was bored and took an earlier flight. Why didn't you tell me you've moved?"

"No time." I don't need to ask how she found me. Real estate agents have ways we mere mortals cannot fathom. I've often thought *CSI* or *Cold Case* could benefit from the resources of a Realtor when tracking down a culprit.

"I suppose it's too much to hope this is simply storage space." She tips up her huge tortoiseshell sunglasses and looks about. Her expression says it all. "What were you thinking?"

"Low rent." I suck in my stomach to squeeze past a chair.

Her gaze has shifted beyond me. "Oh—dear—God!"

She propels herself toward the rear of the apartment. Has

she spied the return of the co-op eager pair of mice I've been playing catch-and-release with for the past week?

In the tiny space between stove and sink she stops and pirouettes. "You have no kitchen! There's not two feet of counter space. No place to put your mixers and kneading board and—" She opens and peers into a cabinet meant for glasses and plates. "Is that your microwave?"

I reach up to push close the pantry door she's opened. "This is temporary, okay?"

Desperate to divert her attention from the closet-size bedroom she is homing in on I grab a plate of warm buns and thrust it at her. "Try an Aberdeen butter roll. I'm in the process of modernizing the recipe."

Sally takes a roll, eyes it like a Forty-seventh Street diamond merchant looking for flaws, then takes a tentative bite. She chews a bit. "It's really quite good."

Satisfied I've sidetracked her, I turn back to the living room space with basket in hand.

Sally more carefully picks her way past boxes and piles to perch uneasily on the edge of a chair then throws back her head in a gesture of supreme distress I doubt Jackie O ever used. "Has it occurred to you that I make my living in real estate and that you simply had to ask for my help?"

"I'm trying to maintain my independence." I smile at her. "Besides, I took your last advice. I now own half of Talbot Advertising. And I found the next great man."

"Darling, you're blushing." Her expression brightens. "Tell me all about him." Obviously money comes in second to Sally's interest in my love life.

"There's not much to tell. We met in a bar, chatted for a while, and then went up to his hotel room where I got to know him in the Biblical sense. After that, we moved on to tantric sex."

"And?"

"I found myself doing things I'd never even heard of before." A prickly heat feeling envelops me just thinking about him. In fact, I can no longer imagine a single good reason why I shouldn't have tattooed my phone number on his rear after the evening we had. But then, I always was slow on recognizing the obvious. With a sigh I admit, "He certainly qualified as the next great man."

"We'll see about that." Sally pulls out her Blackberry. "What's his name?" When I don't respond, her brows lift. "You do know his name?"

"We met in a bar and decided not to exchange the details of our lives." I'm not about to tell her Celia and I dubbed him the Rock's dad. "It was just a wild, anonymous…" I *am* blushing! "Can I tell you something? I didn't know sex could be like that."

"Oh, dear." Sally snaps her BlackBerry closed.

"What's wrong? I thought you'd be delighted. I did something daring, totally out of character. I even amazed myself."

"Exactly. You are usually so practical, so deliberate, so…"

"Predictable? Reliable? Boring?"

"Blake women are never boring," Sally responds.

"This one has been. But I'm changing all that. The karma thing, remember? From now on, who knows what I'll do next?"

She flips open her BlackBerry again. "Are you free this afternoon?"

"Why?"

"I'm calling my analyst. It's Saturday and short notice, but he will see you as a favor to me, this once. It's so much simpler if one deals with these little annoyances of personality as they crop up. It's clear you have boundary issues. You were married a long time. It's only natural that you would make mistakes with men because you're no longer secure about yourself as a woman."

Okay, I should have learned by now that I'm never going to wow Sally. "I don't need a shrink."

"Of course not, darling! You simply need an adjustment. Analysis is the best thing that ever happened to me. I've made tremendous strides with Dr. Vidor. Tremendous!"

I've known Sally all my life and the only thing that ever changes about her is her nail polish color. "No shrink."

Sally snaps her BlackBerry closed a second time. "How shall I put this? This person you met might be a fabulous lay but, darling, if you found that out before you knew his name, why should he hang about to prove himself a truly great man? A great man is one who is willing to earn the title. That requires effort on his part, great restaurants, thoughtful notes, sumptuous bouquets—"

"Fabulous jewelry?" The story behind the five-carat canary-yellow diamond ring gracing her right hand is legendary.

Sally smiles indulgently. "Darling, your foray into impulsivity is the flipside of your life-long reticence. Both are proof of your sense of a lack of control of your life."

"So then, it's just as well I'll never see him again." When Sally begins talking like this, it's time to change the subject. "How's Tony?"

Sally produces a smile as wide as the Cheshire Cat's. "Perfect. So perfect, I've decided to leave him."

"What?" I should have guessed she didn't just show up at my place out of curiosity about my new digs. "What did he do?"

"Nothing. *Hmm,* my analyst says she's booked." Sally looks at her watch, a sure sign she's about to bolt. "I just detoured through to tell you my news." She types a short text message. "This will have to wait until Monday. Now I really must scoot. My driver is waiting."

"Wait, you can't leave me hanging. You and Tony have been together four...?"

"Five years."

"That's grounds for common law marriage in some states."

"Exactly." Her bright smile flattens out as she finally looks directly at me. "Yet marriage has not once occurred to him."

I try to remember when Sally last mentioned marriage. Can't. She doesn't believe in it. Oh, right, there was what she once referred to as a "lost weekend" when I was about fourteen. It began with a weekend in Vegas with an Argentine cattle baron and ended in divorce in the Bahamas three weeks later. So, what's up? It must be something traumatic.

"Oh, Sally, you're not...?" I can't say it. The thought of her nobility of strength in trying to spare Tony the agony of her last days pushes the panic button in every cell in my body. "Oh, Sally, you're dying!"

"Don't be ridiculous." She sniffs. "When have I ever been ill?"

I sit back and cross my arms, willing my heart to slow to normal. "So then, what's changed? Didn't you tell Tony that if he ever even mentioned marriage you would never speak to him again?"

She waves this away. "It's what I've told every man I've ever been involved with."

"Then how do you know it hasn't crossed Tony's mind, but he's been reluctant to mention it?"

"I know men. If marriage is on a man's mind he knows only one way to think about it." She holds out an elegant but bare left hand. "What do you see?"

She's serious! I suppose even the most dedicated singleton can have a change of heart. Then it hits me. "You're in love!"

"You needn't sound so incredulous."

"I'm not. Wait. Yes, I am." I'm grinning so hard I can barely form words. "You've left Tony because you want to marry him? What am I missing?"

"I've left Tony before it occurs to him to leave me. He's hired a new personal assistant." Sally adjusts her shades to bandeau position. "A female. English."

"Oh. You suspect it's...um, an arrangement?"

She glares at me as if I'd suggested she's put on a few pounds. "Tony would never be so clichéd."

"Okay. So?"

"Oh, for heaven's sake! Look around you." Sally shoots to her feet. "Who is getting married these days? Secretaries, assistants, babysitters, caterers, flight attendants, researchers and fact-checkers! They've even got a name—nanny wives."

"What's that got to do with Tony?"

She makes an impatient sound. "I read about the phenomena on the flight to Honolulu! It's humiliating to admit but I'd been so involved with those condos at the Park Imperial that I completely missed the point of his hiring her. The article made it painfully clear what Tony's up to. It said after years of powerful men seeking equal companions with brains *and* sex appeal, they've gone completely retro. Rich and influential men are once again marrying women who are trained to tend to and care for them."

"You're throwing away the best thing in life because of what you read in an in-flight magazine?"

She gives me a pitying look. "Ted dropped you for a nanny. *She* adored him, isn't that what he told you? Picked up his dirty socks without complaint!"

"I could have lived a long time without that reminder. But Tony adores you."

"For now." Sally folds her arms resolutely across her chest. "But he's not getting any younger. The day will soon arrive when he's feeling a bit wobbly and needy. Will he look my way for security? No, that little English chippy who's making his flight plans and reminding him to wear his Burberry and forever hovering about will seem a more reasonable choice. And, frankly, he'd be right."

"Why?"

"Because I'm no domestic goddess, and never intend to be."

Sally drops her shades back into place like a jet pilot snapping closed his visor. But I catch a glimpse of the pain in the tiniest tremble of her chin. It makes my own world quiver. Sally's the strongest woman I know. But she's also my mother.

"Want me to drop a hint? I could ask him to meet me at Van Cleef & Arpels."

Instead of a reply, she gives my place another once-over. "When I get back to my office I'll see what I can do about finding you a sensible place to live."

* * *

Sarah calls early on Sunday morning to commiserate over Sally's breakup. Seems Sally left the girls text messages about her new single status. "Riley and I agree someone should do something."

"It's not really our business," I reply. This applies to most family landmine subjects. When dealing with Sally it's more like a commandment, thou shalt not meddle!

"But Aunt Sally and Tony are perfect together." Sally doesn't want to be called "Mother." Imagine what she thinks of "Grandma."

"They will work it out." Or not.

"I hate men!"

Naturally, my motherly ears prick up. "Which men are we talking about now?"

"Mr. Montana Commodities for one. He's married."

"Oh, and he didn't bother to mention that before."

"He wasn't married before. Mom, he saw an old girlfriend while in Cheyenne, they hooked up and pulled a Britney!"

"A what?"

"They went to Vegas for the weekend and got married."

"You can do better, sweetie. Lots better. What about that junior partner at your law office?"

"An office relationship is just not practicable." Translated that means she's very interested but he hasn't given her the right signals yet.

Sarah reflects in a moment of silence. "At least I do better than Riley. Her new guy has piercings in places people in their right minds wouldn't."

I don't ask where or why Sarah knows this. "It's really not our business." But I'm worried. Riley retains a lot of anger about her father. I hope in releasing it, she doesn't do something she'll regret forever. Mothers worry.

"By the way, did Riley tell you she's got a new job? She's a horticulture technician."

"She's a leaf hopper, Mom. She drives a van from one office building to another where she spritzs and wipes down leaves."

"The flexible hours allow her to go to auditions." I end our conversation with "He's out there. You just have to let it happen."

On the other hand, I'm swearing off men. For the time being. Sally's right. Mind-blowing sex with a stranger in the night is not my style. Besides—

Aaahhhyyyyah.

You know you're past forty when a huge yawn can interrupt musings on the mind-blowing sex.

Later, with a large cup of coffee in hand while perusing the newspaper, I notice an ad I haven't seen before. It's for the West Orange Bakery. Two locations are listed below with "soon to open" superimposed over a third. In the lower right corner I spy a small "TA" logo. Damn!

It's not that I think that there's no room for another bakery within a twenty-mile radius of the No-Bagel Emporium. But when its slogan is "Best Bread in North Jersey" and Talbot Advertising is their PR firm I have to wonder whose idea that slogan was. And if they are so wonderful why haven't I heard about them?

There's a loose confederacy of bakers in the area who swap stories, traumas and triumphs a few times a year. Let's face it, who else can really appreciate what sweltering temperatures do to dough unless you, too, are dropping ice shavings into the mixer to keep the heat from killing the leavening process?

Then I remember. A guy with West Orange Bakery printed on his shirtfront was talking with my—the Nabisco consultant last time I saw him. What was he doing there? West Orange Bakery didn't even have a booth.

A pricking sensation of trouble sweeps through me. Just where did these guys come from, and how good is their bakery? I must have Shemar check them out.

Or I could call up Talbot Agency and ask for a gander at their file on the West Orange Bakery. I am, after all, a proprietary owner, so far. Even if the judge gave Lionel's firm the responsibility of overseeing it until the suits are settled, I'm entitled to walk in and check the files. With one phone call, I could find out how old company is, who owns it, and perhaps a general figure of what their earnings are. Know that enemy.

But no, that would be cheating, a conflict of interest, and just plain lowdown. The guilt creeping across me outweighs the premonition of trouble. I'll have Shemar check them out.

Chapter 12

There's a breed of customer a proprietor can spot at ten paces. They're going to complain. The meat's too fatty, the mustard's off taste, the bread's too hard or soft, or maybe the cheese is too "cheesy." Any mishap will be pinned on bad service. It's always some version of "How can you call yourself a business when you don't cater to your paying customers?"

"I'm sorry about your mishap." I smile just enough not to be rude to the furious woman on the other side of the counter. "But accidents do happen."

"What about my jacket?" The woman points to her plum suede top where a big glop of bright yellow mustard is bleeding into the leather. "You put too much mustard on my sandwich." Her eyes snap with challenge.

My expression freezes. "Sorry about that."

"Then you'll pay my cleaning bill?"

"Sorry, no."

Mouth agape, she swings around to the table where she's been having lunch with two other shoppers. "Did you hear that? She's refusing to pay for damage she caused." She whirls back to me. "Let me tell you something. This jacket cost more than you'll take in today. How can you call yourself a business when you don't cater to your paying customers? You can be certain I'll never step foot in here again. And I'm telling my friends!"

I nod, smile and say, "Good luck with that." I think, *Whadaya think, I'm a moron? Get outta here!*

Grandpa Horace taught me well. Don't let some poor schmuck who couldn't make up his mind about what he wanted back up the order line, or complain about the food.

"Whadaya mean you don't like it?" Grandpa Horace would boom. "Do I look like I stand here all day working just so you can come in here saying you don't like it? I don't need your kind in here. People come in to eat, not to complain. Get outta my place!"

I watch as Plum Suede and her friends leave without clearing their places. Typical.

The No-Bagel Emporium closes at 2:00 p.m. No one lingers past cleanup. Yet after I lock myself in today I spend a little extra time making the store spotless. One never knows when a dissatisfied customer like Plum Suede will turn vindictive and call the health department. Heck, even good news can go wrong. I once heard about that very popular restaurant in Short Hills whose interview for the local paper, complete with pictures, caught the eye of the local board of health official, who dispatched an inspector. So many violations were written up that place had to close for a month.

We can't afford to be done in by so much as gum on the underside of a table. Anyone who thinks people have stopped doing that should have been there for the scraping-down party we had this week. Jeez! Some people are pigs!

The phone interrupts my final check.

"Mrs. Talbot? This is Bill Nash from NJN TV. We met at the Fine Arts and Crafts Show last month?"

"Hi, Bill." When the NJN news crew stopped by the No-Bagel Emporium booth for a snack during the weekend Bill and I naturally fell into a discussion of what makes an artisan bakery "artisan." He seemed pretty impressed. Maybe he wants to place an order. "What can I do for you?"

"Sorry to bother you on a Saturday, but I've got a proposition I think you're going to like. We're thinking about doing a segment on artisan bakeries for *New Jersey Works.* Are you interested?"

Yes! But I try to make my tone thoughtfully interested. "Sounds intriguing, Bill. What's the angle?"

"After we talked I came across this article that says bread is on the eve of a renaissance. We want to look at it as an industry. What the artisan bakery is, why it's gaining in popularity, how it differs from commercial bakeries. Think you can speak to that?"

Boy, can I!

We chat for a few more minutes and he agrees to come in on Friday and observe the whole process of making bread. "By the time you've seen firsthand our production process with its own little dramas and suspense, I'm sure you'll agree we have a compelling story."

When I hang up I do the Snoopy Dance, from one end of the room to the other. More exposure is just what we need! Take that, West Orange Bakery. Take that, Nabisco! No-Bagel Emporium's going to be on TV!

Some girls go all gooey inside over Manolo Blahnik alligator sling backs or a Hermès Birkin. Others treat Century 21 as their temple/cathedral/Mecca. Whenever I'm deeply stressed, deliriously happy or just need solitude, I bake something.

At the moment I'm so happy I could fill a week's bread orders by myself. So why not channel all those good vibrations into an afternoon perfecting a new bread sensation to be debuted on film?

It's a bit startling to find what first comes to mind is an image of TRD, drenched in warm millefiori Italian honey with only a cherry clutched between his teeth for decoration. Suddenly sweaty desire is pumping out of me, and for once none of which is attributed to "that time of life." O-*kay*. Step back from the horny aspect of receiving good news.

The truth is, I've been wrestling with fantasies like this for weeks, so many that it makes me wonder if I'm remembering him—us correctly. Was TRD that wonderfully funny, confident and sexy? Was the sex that good? Or are the memories tinged by a middle-aged woman's four years of celibacy? What, am I nuts?

He was there, I was there, and I'm damn lucky to have been counted in the equation.

But I'm not going to turn out a heterosexual phantasmagoric loaf of bread. So, what's the next best thing?

Italy. I've been in Umbria in early fall. The cologne of al fresco meals invades my memory banks with orgasmic whiffs of olive oil, millefiori honey— *Uh-huh, stay on track!* Black truffles and Montepulciano grapes. And I think *bingo:* schiacciata con Umbria!

Within an hour I've produced two variations on our ciabatta dough. For savory *impasto,* Italian for dough, I added olive oil. For sweet *impasto* I added olive oil and honey. After proofing, I will roll them out until they resemble thick oval pizzas. While I wait for them to rise, I sip a fresh-brewed green chai tea and think up suitable toppings. This is the part where I get creative.

The savory dough would be divine basted with a paste of pâté with lemon peel, pressed fresh garlic and red Hawaiian sea salt. Or sprinkled with bitter black olives and a few well spaced anchovies, or perhaps slivered roasted almonds and rosemary. Drizzle with olive oil and honey and bake.

Black seedless grapes from a local farmer's market would be delicious covering the surface of a sweet schiacciata. I'd love to splurge on imported dried uva fragola grapes. And ripe black plums, several kinds of figs and, oh, luscious fall pears.

Next I raid the refrigerated cheese case looking for inspiration. What about shavings of *formaggio alle noci* with pears and grape sauce? Or crumbled Umbrian goat cheese, ribbons of pancetta, black olives and fresh green peas?

I pick up a wedge of *pecorino di fossa* whose tag says, *Brushed with olive oil and aged for months under layers of straw and juniper, walnut and bay leaves.* Sounds perfect for a sweet schiacciata layered with figs, chicory and chestnuts.

The knock at my door comes as a surprise but I'm so mellow

that I've rounded the counter before I remember my newfound caution. That's because it's been three days since the last summons delivery attempt. Oh, damn! I forgot to pull the shade and am in plain sight. But it's too late. Peering in my bakery window with an Estee Lauder-perfect face is *her*.

I think about just turning my back, but then, why should I? We were going to have to do this face-to-face eventually. Why not in my territory?

Even without the stiletto mules she's taller than I am and her baby-blond hair tumbles perfectly over her shoulders as she slides into the space of the door I open.

Extensions?

Of course, I don't know that's not her real hair.

But I now know wheat-blond ain't her real color!

I shut the door behind her, pull the shade and turn the lock before saying, "We're closed."

She doesn't exactly greet me, just pauses out of hand-shaking range and looks around. "Business isn't so good, huh?"

"We open at 6:00 a.m. By two we've put in our eight-hour day."

"Whatever." Maybe she's not smirking. Maybe it's just a personal tic. Or maybe she's remembering my humiliation day at the tanning salon. Now, that was a joke.

In true female fashion we eye each other.

I'm my usual floury sweaty-face self. No news there.

Is it just me, or is she a different shade of tan each time I see her? Today she's biscotti beige. Her former widow's black, such as it was, has been traded for Miami-neon capris, shrunken T-shirt, jeweled flip-flops and a coveted canvas tote bag embroidered with 11968, Southampton zip code, slung over her arm. How on earth did *she* get——no, I don't care. Nothing about her can make me miserable today.

She does a quick scan of the shop. "Who else is here?"

"Just me."

"Good." She gives me a speculative look. "There's something I have to do, and I'd just as soon there weren't any witnesses." As she says this she reaches deep into her canvas tote.

All of a sudden I'm aware that I've given entrance and cover to the only real enemy I ever had. Last time we were in the same room together, with a lot of witnesses, she was really pissed off. As in maybe trigger-happy Jersey girl PO'd?

I am her worst enemy. What if she's come to whack me?

Adrenaline supernovas through me. I can take her. I've got twenty, okay, twenty-five pounds on her. I've got desperation and survival instinct on my side. *She's* only got puny pique motivating her. And greed. And——

"I've got something here for you." She whips out not a snub nose .22 but—— Ah, *jeez*. Another summons?

Relief makes me nauseous. "What's that for? You're already suing me six ways from Sunday."

When I don't take the envelope she looks like she'd like to swat me with it. "Fine." She lobs it onto a nearby tabletop and then looks around. "Aren't you going to offer me a latte or something?"

"No." I've just had a bad scare, even if my imagination did provide the grist for it. I've still plenty of reason to want to see her take a long leap off a short Jersey shore pier.

She shrugs elaborately. "You try to be professional, but with some people——"

"How about you just say what you have to say, and then you can leave and I can get back to my life."

She visibly pulls herself together like you see lousy actresses do in daytime soaps: shoulders wing back, stomach sucks in, chin lifts, breasts, well, you get the picture. She gives me an annoyed look. "Okay, we don't like each other. But we have to be practical, right?"

"Not at all."

She gives me an annoyed glare. "This is strictly business. I need to ask you something but I don't want you to overreact. Okay?"

To tell the truth, I don't know how to answer that. Thanks to her efforts of the last couple of weeks I've run through just about every emotion I'm capable of: anger, despair, contempt, revulsion and fear. What's left?

"I want you to sign over the running of Talbot Advertising to me."

Chapter 13

*L*aughter!

In all the frustration of the last weeks I'd failed to see one scrap of humor in any of this. But now tragedy has turned to sitcom farce. Give *her* control of the company? Hilarious!

By the time I sober up she's eyeing me as if she's reconsidering what else might be in her designer bag. "You could just say no."

"Oh, no," I gasp, trying to conquer another wave of giggles. "You wanted to talk. Talk. And you can begin by telling me why such a crack-brain idea would ever enter your mind."

"Someone has to do something. It's obvious that you don't care about the future of Talbot Advertising."

Right. *She* wants to save the company from me. This should be good. "Have a chair and tell me all about it."

As she moves past me to sit down at a nearby table I catch a vaguely familiar whiff of peach and raspberry scents overtopped by a vinegary baby powder smell. It is her perfume or her bronzer, or both?

She sits and crosses her long bronze legs. "I want to sell my share of the Talbot Agency."

I cross my arms and remain standing. "Your injunction against the estate prevents either of us from selling, remember?"

She examines a paisley-decorated fingernail. Always the Jersey girl. "My attorneys say we should both sell our shares to a third party, and split the profits."

"Really?" Dollar signs start lining up in my mind's eye.

"There's just one teeny problem."

"Oh, yeah?" I knew there'd be a catch. And her perfume is beginning to bug me. I think I know that fragrance.

She glances up, her baby blues narrowed between barbed-wire mascara lashes. "Talbot's earnings have tanked."

"How much?"

"A lot." She reaches to pick up the papers she'd tossed on the table and holds them out. "It's in the quarterly report. Which you'd know, if you'd bothered to keep up, like I have, with Teddy's assets."

"Let me see that." I snatch the papers and scan them. "Twenty-five percent! In one quarter?" I smell a rat. "How is this possible?"

She eyes me speculatively. "You really don't know, do you? Teddy's two assistants left the firm for other companies as soon as they heard there was a legal dispute over ownership. Some junior munchkin is now in charge." Her glance suggests that this, too, is my fault. "Our best customers are leaving because they say the company can no longer provide for their needs."

How does she know this and I don't? Okay, so maybe I've been focused on the legal battle and not enough on Ted's company, but I didn't think I'd have to get involved. Guess that was wishful thinking.

I give the numbers another glance. They are dramatic in their depression. Revenue from the three top earners has dried up. "Seems like Talbot has a public relations problem."

Her eyes narrow. "What do you mean?"

"When a business is small, the reputation of the owner supplies the juice. Ted *was* Talbot Advertising. You need another Ted."

"As Teddy's wife, I have instant recognition with his clients." Who knew one could preen in a chair? "And I have a plan to recoup our losses. The agency needs a high profile ad person to attract attention. I plan to hire someone from the city."

"Don't count on it. Anyone with that kind of juice would rather wash dishes than give up a Manhattan business address. Besides, New Jerseyites can be pretty frosty to city ways. You need that local connection. And, you need someone who understands Talbot's niche in the business world, and can capitalize on its history. That's what the clients meant about supplying their needs."

It's her faintly amazed gaze that finally shuts me down. Damn! Start talking business, and I'm like Pavlov's *frickin'* dog. But the sight of a bad bottom line, even one with Ted's name attached, brings out my fighting instincts.

Annoyed with myself, I drop the papers back into her lap

and shrug, hoping to effect a so-what attitude. "But that's just my opinion. When you find the right person, come back and talk to me."

She gives me an impatient gesture. "I think you're trying to destroy Talbot Advertising. You don't want me to take control because I know how to run a business. My tanning salons are doing great business because, for instance, we offer incentives."

"Don't tell me. Free tans." I'm sorry but I can't stop my smirk.

"Yes," she replies in all seriousness. "We offer them to popular students so they will talk up my business. The wannabes line up for days after."

"That might be effective with the high school set but—"

"Oh, no. We start in middle school. High school is much too late to develop brand loyalty."

"I see." I decide not to think too hard about the fact that even getting a tan has become a minefield of faux pas for the training-bra set.

She smirks. "So what do you think?"

I could tell her exactly what I think. What I've thought from the first, that she's a shrewd and conniving cow, with a wide-eyed act only a besotted man like my ex couldn't see right through. Instead I take the marginally higher road, smugness.

I glance up with a smile. "With Ted's assistants out of the picture I can think of only one person who can fill the bill. Me."

She looks away. "They told me that would be your attitude."

I blink and refocus on her. "Who told you?"

She shrugs. "It wasn't my idea. It was Lionel's, but I didn't think you'd agree to it."

"Agree to what?" She's now on a first-name basis with Ted's attorney? This can't be good.

"Ted's law firm thinks that under the circumstances that you should be asked to take over the running of Talbot Advertising, temporarily. The judge agrees." She should never play poker. Her face gives away her every expression large and small.

The subject of this discussion has changed course so radically that I need a moment to catch up. "So Ted's law firm thinks Talbot Advertising needs a savior. And, aside from you, even the judge thinks I'm it. Is that correct?" I want her to say the words out loud, so we both know she said them.

She looks annoyed. "I told them I could do it. But, yes."

My laughter is a little choked this time, but still enough to raise her hackles.

She stands up and the fragrance wafting from her distracts me again. The faint though distinctly familiar notes of jasmine, mandarin and ylang-ylang emanating from her are so like—no. Surely it's just coincidence. Many perfumers develop similar scents. If I could just get a good whiff!

"I knew you wouldn't do it. But Lionel thought you'd see it as a challenge or something. Teddy always said you were a whiz at business."

"Ted *what!*"

Her expression turns pouty. "He said that no matter how difficult and unreasonable you could…well, whatever. When it came to business, you'd be the person he'd go to for advice."

"Ted said that?" Ted never once told me I was wonderful. Good at the tough stuff, a people person but never brilliant at business. I give her a big fat grin. "What else did Ted say?"

Her expression turns to ice. "He said what really fried his bacon was that you left the firm without thinking about what was best for him. Your desertion cost him plenty."

Her words don't touch my smug smile. "It was my company to leave."

"I'm not agreeing to this. I mean, you could say yes, and then run everything into the ground, leaving me with nothing."

"You think I'd destroy a multimillion dollar corporation just to spite you? You overestimate your irritation value." Though, admittedly, not by much.

"No, of course, you wouldn't do that." There something creepy about this woman. One instant she's all snotty witch. The next her lashes lower, her voice rises half an octave and becomes breathy, and she's the incarnate of "frailty thy name is Brandi." "I mean, why you would want to hurt me…now."

"As opposed to when you were deliberately stealing my husband?" Little lost lamb, my ass! How could she imagine I'd forget for an instant what we are? Can I have an *E*—an *N*—an *E*—an *M*? Etc.

"Sometimes I think I shouldn't have done that, breaking you guys up. But Teddy and I were so happy together that, well, I think it was destiny." She looks up through her Spider Woman lashes. "You know, meant to be. And you're happier now, too, right?"

"I'm fine." Except for the sudden desire to gag. The heat has kicked in, blowing warm air from a vent above her head directly at me. I know that perfume! That's *my* perfume! She's wearing Casmir by Chopard!

"So then, things worked out for the best." She fiddles with

her earring. "My therapist says sometimes people marry for the wrong reasons, thinking they are the right reasons. Like the way they think certain tasteless cereals are good for you because of the fiber factor? But marriage shouldn't be a box of prunes, good for you even if you don't like it. One should look for the source of the emotional blockage, eliminate it and push through to happiness."

I inhale slowly. She's just compared my failed marriage to a blocked bowel! And she's wearing my signature fragrance! No one I know wears my fragrance. That's the whole point of a personal fragrance.

Satisfied, I suppose, that she's made her point, she picks up her purse. "My attorneys say you would have to accept a salary in the position, to keep your working for the company separate from your supposed ownership share of the business. Because we don't yet know how that will turn out." Her expression says what she thinks of that. "They said that perhaps it would be easier if you think of your position as a consultant to Talbot Advertising, with a vested interest."

"The thinking being I won't sink the ship if I'm standing on the deck?" How can I sound so normal when, inside, I'm running around with my hands in the air? *She's* wearing my perfume! How is that possible? Why is it possible?

She glances speculatively at me. "I guess this means you're going to accept."

"Actually, no. I have no interest in running Talbot Advertising. I'm thinking of selling the bakery, which is a very hot commodity, and moving to Phoenix." Now where did that come from? It's just a gut reaction to doing anything that would benefit her.

"Oh. I understand." She looks completely thrilled that I'm turning her down. She gazes around the bakery, her gaze coming to rest on the single missing square of tile near the bar. "You must be, after all, close to retirement."

Oh, she's good. She insulted my business acumen and my age in the same sentence. "What is that perfume you're wearing?"

She lifts her wrist and sniffs. "Oh, this? It's called cashmere, like the expensive sweaters? Teddy gave it to me just before our vacation. I don't really like it but...Teddy...if you'll excuse me."

She turns and hurries to the door, fumbles with the key and lets herself out.

What the hell? Ted's last act of generosity was to give *her* the fragrance I've been wearing for ten years? I'm so many kinds of appalled, I can't even name them.

I rush over to turn the key in the door and then bolt it.

That's it! I wouldn't do a deal with her now if we were both tied to a...!

And yet, I can't get her revelation out of my head.

Ted told *her* I was a smart businesswoman! That's tantamount to saying I was better in bed. Well, sort of.

And yet...

I feel like I've just been manipulated ten ways from Sunday. How did she do that? One minute she says she wants to run the company. The next she's practically asking me to do it. Did she think I was dumb enough to fall for her bait-and-switch tactics—if only I knew what she really has in mind?

I pick up the quarterly report she left behind. Maybe I should have read this when it came. But I didn't want to be pulled back into Talbot's work life. I just wanted, hoped, dared to dream of making a few million without having to get my hands dirty.

Okay, so maybe that was a dumb wish. If I had something to prove, I bet I could turn the business. Which, I don't.

As I sit and reread the report more carefully it becomes apparent that many of the accounts listed here are familiar to me. Long-forgotten details of my old life nudge back into my consciousness. I know what to say to him. And as for them, well, they always did want to be hand held. I could, if I set my mind to it, recoup this loss and add to the bottom line in the very next quarter.

Which, I don't. But I bet I could.…

Before I realize I'm doing it, I've found a pencil, a pad, and have picked up my calculator to run some of the numbers on the spreadsheet before me. In no time I have outlined a tentative strategy to win back three of the accounts.

Yet I have to wonder if I'm not just blowing off steam. We make great bread. So if I'm this great businesswoman why isn't No-Bagel Emporium doing better?

Through the thick fog of my thoughts, I realize that the timer is going off in the kitchen, in fact, has been going off for—"Oh, crap!" My schiacciata con Umbria!

It's toast, or rather a molten black cheesy slag. One thing is certain. The creative impulse for making bread has left me for the day.

With my thoughts on long ago and never again, I dump both burnt and freshly risen dough in the trash, and replace the cheeses into the refrigerated case. Celia will have a cow when she sees the mess I've made of her tidy display, but I don't have the energy to make it right. I suddenly feel like a loser, an also-ran, a middle-aged, hips-of-a-mother-of-twins has-been.

Sunday is a slug day. I don't move from the bed but twice. Once to make coffee and collect my newspapers. And later to bring enough victuals to keep me fortified while I catch up on bills and work the *Times* puzzle. I'm asleep by 7:00 p.m.

It's cave dark when the phone awakens me.

"Miz T?" Shemar's voice is oddly pitched. I glance at the clock. It's a little after 10:30 p.m.

"What's wrong?"

"Ma died."

"Your mother? Oh, Shemar, I'm so sorry."

"Nawgh, *the* mother, Miz T. The sourdough starter."

I bolt upright. "Ma? I'll be right there."

I arrive at the bakery in pjs and flip-flops to see for myself that Shemar's news can't be improved upon with a viewing. The usual Saturday routine includes storing Ma in the walk-in re-frigerator where the low temperature will put it in stasis but not kill it. That way no one has to flour and stir it for a day. But between the joy of the impending TV interview and the pain-in-the-butt aftermath of dealing with *her* I forgot to put Ma in the fridge.

Left out in the warm store from Saturday afternoon until Sunday night, it has turned cadaver-gray and sludgy. Revival, if that is possible, will be more like a miracle of resurrection.

It's been like an ICU waiting room here while I've tried to coax Ma back to life, the heart of my bread business. I've postponed the *New Jersey Works* taping until I'm sure we have a product worth selling. Bill understands, saying he can wait a week or so, but don't expect his program director to stay hot on the subject for long.

We continued to make bread, all but the sourdough, with the piga and poolish, which are made fresh daily. But without a true mature sourdough Ma, we're just marking time.

By Wednesday the bubbling vat of Ma is still not the right color. Give it a week, other bakers advise. As it matures the flavor may develop. None offer to share their Ma with me. That's just not done. Mas have unique properties that make the breads made from them distinctive in taste and texture. It's every artisan baker's secret weapon.

Customers mean well when they say, "You know, I can't really tell the difference."

That only makes me feel worse. How would Caruso feel if told by his audience that while they like his singing, they're just as happy with the cantor at temple?

They say trouble comes in threes. I wish *they* had chosen a smaller number.

Yesterday, Shemar tripped playing b'ball and broke his arm. No rolling and shaping for six weeks. There goes the New Jersey Live shoot. I'm good, but Shemar is a wizard with pastries. We can't put our best PR foot forward without him.

I switch him to days while I yawned my way through the next three nights in a row of pastry-making.

Saturday morning I've just pulled out of the oven what appears to be a successful test loaf with our new-risen Ma when the phone rings.

My condo buyers have backed out. The Realtor says there has been reorganization at the husband's place of business, and he was downsized out the door.

I'm so upset for the couple, with a baby on the way, that it takes me a while to feel justifiably sorry for myself. Now I have a mortgage on a condo I'm *not* living in, plus rent!

That's it. I'm crying uncle—ah, Sally!

When I call I get Ines, the Brazilian housekeeper. She tells me, "Mr. Tony has move out. Mees Sally go to Swedish Spa. In Sweden. No phones. No fax. No e-mail. She don't talk to nobody."

I suppose I could try to send her a message by reindeer.

No. I'm forty-seven years old. I have to face facts. My inheritance is tied up in arbitration for only God knows how long. That doesn't mean I can't benefit from it in the meanwhile. Why, the bonus alone from turning Talbot around, which I would demand if I was going to take the job of savior, should pay off my immediate debts. And the best part is that *she* still wouldn't see a penny as long as we are in arbitration. Now, that's a plan I can live with.

I've assembled the troops: Shemar, Celia and Desharee. They have to know what's going to happen and why.

"I can't believe it!" Celia's voice rises in alarm. "The thought of you working for *her,* that's like going over to the Dark Side."

"I'm not working for *her.*" I look at the three glum faces before me. "I'll be working at a business in which I have half ownership. And believe me, as soon as the agency sells, I'll be right back here full-time."

Shemar shakes his head. "You don't have to do that, Miz T. I'll take a cut in pay. After all, I'm gimped up." He lifts his cast to remind me in case I'd forgotten.

"No. In fact, I plan to increase your salary because I want you to become the full-time manager of No-Bagel Emporium."

Shemar's face lights up. "True that?"

"Can you start in the morning? It will mean inventory and bookkeeping."

He nods.

"Celia will back you up."

"Of course, anything you need," Celia answers, looking like she's going to cry.

I turn to Desharee. "That means you step up to be lead baker. You and DeVon will have to train a third."

"No *problemo*." Desharee flashes a rare smile. "You can work for whomsoever you want, Miz T. Just don't let *her* get in your face."

Celia nods. "And, Liz, don't go drinking any corporate Kool-Aid."

They are all so loyal they make me want to cry.

$\mathcal{M}$y palms are sweating and my left knee is shaking like half a maraca, which makes my foot unsteady on the clutch. Nearly four years have passed since I last set foot in the building I glimpse through the trees as I exit Highway 287 in Metuchen. Ted paid too much for the space because he said it was an ideal location for an advertising firm, with companies like Bristol-Myers Squibb, Merrill Lynch & Company, Telcordia Technologies and Prudential Insurance within easy reach. He was right. Companies had just begun outsourcing their needs. Now outsourcing is a major practice of every business large and small.

Lionel Dunlap and I have worked out the terms of my new employment as special consultant to Talbot Advertising, which includes a legal document signed by *her* that will turn the sperm bank deposit into permanent withdrawal and discard.

So, here I am the new decision-maker at Talbot Advertising. Ted's junior associate, Edward Suskind, has been running things. He will now answer to me. That doesn't mean I have free rein. Joint ownership means I still have to deal with *her*.

Which reminds me, I've got to get a grip on that.

I lift my wrist to my nose and sniff. A new personal fragrance is in order. This is one of a bunch of samples from the mall snapped up when I went to forage the fall sales for a presentable business ensemble. Baker whites can take a girl only so far.

No, this fragrance isn't quite right. Tried L'Eau d'Issey last night, which was touted for its "sparkling water scent with highlights of lotus, cyclamen and freesia." Not enough fragrance. One can smell like water anytime. Celia suggested Fragile and Beautiful. Too light and young. I'm on a mission. I'll know it when I find it.

Just as I'm rummaging around in my bag for lip gloss my cell phone rings. It's Riley. "Hi, sweetie. How are you? " I check in the rearview to make sure the light I just went through is green.

"I am so okay, Mom!" The level of adrenaline in her morning voice is impressive, which makes me suspect she has not yet been to bed. "I've got a gig. In an off off off Broadway play."

"That's terrific. But just how far off is off off off Broadway? I mean will you still be in one of the Five Boroughs?"

She laughs uproariously, as if this was the funniest thing she's heard since Chris Rock was on HBO. "We'll be down on East Fourth Street. The play's called *Horizontal Fairytales.*"

Artists must have leeway in order to be creative, but something deep in the mother in me winces at this title. I try to find the least intrusive way to ask. "Are there costumes?"

"Of course. There are masks and wigs and body paint."

"Doesn't qualify."

"Don't go Moral Majority on me, Mom. You've been to plays where there's full frontal nudity. What about those actors?"

"It involved OPC."

"Come again?"

"Other people's children."

"This is my break, Mom, I can feel it. Just wait until you see it. We go into rehearsal next week and—*ooh,* hold on." I hear a low male voice murmur something in answer and just like that I know she's not alone, and probably not in a club. I hope it's not the hole-punched guy. "We premier in November, so there'll be plenty of time to cash in on the holiday tourists."

Wonderful. My daughter will be the talk of the Midwest.

"So Mom, have you heard from Sally?"

"She's incognito in Sweden. Why?"

"Just let me know me the moment she returns."

"Riley, if you're plotting something, then stop!"

"Someone's got to do something about her and Tony. Gotta go!"

No, actually, I think as I flip my phone closed. When it concerns Sally, someone shouldn't even think about interfering.

I hope it won't cost Riley too much to learn that lesson.

I was expecting many feelings to ambush me as I enter the agency front office. But not what assails me. A very agitated man in a gray pin-striped suit is thumping the top of the receptionist's console and shouting.

"I don't give a shit about that. Get Suskind out here! Now!"

The young woman looks duly impressed by the man's heat. But her reply is remarkably self-contained. "I would, Mr. Healy, but Mr. Suskind isn't in this morning."

"Where the fuck is he?"

"He's out of the office on business."

"Business, hell! I'm his business. Make that *was* his business. He's fired!"

I have no idea if the customer's right, a bully or just plain nuts. If he's a big customer he can be wrong, a bully and nuts, and we would still need to cater to him. Bottom line always trumps self-respect, Ted used to say. Another reason I didn't mind leaving advertising behind. Still, with the bottom line bottoming out, I've got to try something.

"Excuse me, may I help you?"

The man swings around so fast he almost oversteps. The belligerent expression reminds me of a bulldog with a bad combover. When did Trump hair get to be a fashion statement?

Almost at once his snarl widens into a wolfish grin as he gives me the up and down and up, to chest level. "Well, hello there."

I had wondered about the wisdom of wearing a demi-cup bra under a fine-gauge knit sweater but I was behind on my washing. And here it is showing advantage already. "I'm Liz Talbot. How may I help you?"

"Al Healy. Pleeztameecha."

His pinkie ring leaves its painful imprint on the underside of my little finger as he squashes my hand. He's still smiling and I suddenly understand the receptionist's rabbit-in-the-cross-hairs look.

"I'm sorry, but we've had to temporarily suspend certain services."

He frowns up like a fist. "Whadaya mean?"

Good question, since I have no idea why he's here. I glance at the receptionist, who only shrugs. Fine, I can spin-doctor with the best of them. "The late Mr. Talbot was our resident expert in many advertising matters. As he is deceased, we have had to defer some of our more technically advanced services."

His eyebrows do a deadweight lift. "You're kidding?"

"I regret any inconvenience our very personal sorrow may have caused you. We value customer loyalty, and wish you only the best in future." Much as it seems like sidling up to a snake, I slip my arm through his, and amazingly, he allows me to steer him toward the door. "If you leave me your card, I'd be more than happy to check into your account. Should it be that we cannot fill your business needs promptly, we'll contact another firm that can provide whatever you require."

He doesn't answer, most likely because he's too busy giving my chest sidelong glances.

At the door I try to detach. This isn't easy because he's clamped down with his elbow, pinning my arm to his side. "Your card?" I repeat sweetly.

"Oh, yeah, right." He digs in his left breast pocket. "Who are you, the widda?"

"No, I'm the ex. As of today I now run the firm."

He throws back his head and roars. "My kinda woman," he says, and slaps me on the bottom before heading out the door.

Okay, that was awful.

Ignoring the curious glances of the other two clients sitting in the reception area, I approach the young woman behind the desk. "Good morning. I'm Liz Talbot. Mr. Suskind isn't expecting me but I've just come by to introduce myself."

The young woman stands up and offers her hand. "Good morning, Mrs. Talbot. I'm Nancy Ferguson. Mr. Suskind should be returning shortly. We were told to expect you this week." She dimples and leans toward me. "Oh, and thanks for taking care of that other matter. How did you do that?"

"It's called the hustler's hustle."

Nancy's forehead wrinkles thoughtfully. "Can you teach me?"

"Sure." I wink. Then it hits me what I should have asked before. "Is Mr. Healy a big client?"

"No." She folds her arms primly. "He's waiting for an overdue back order of baseball caps for his son's Little League booster squad."

"Oh."

Edward Suskind turns out to be a perfectly nice young man with an open face, brown hair and a ready smile. Twenty-six, he tells me. I size him up as date material for Sarah, until I notice the picture of a two-year-old on his console. "Your son?"

He nods. "Sean. I call him Tiger."

"I don't want to make this awkward, Edward. I have no desire to micromanage you. Once we're up to speed on pending matters, and if you feel you are up to handling the firm's day to day, I should not need to be here full-time." One can dream, can't one?

He nods but looks thoughtful.

"I sense a *but*." If he's found a new position, too, I'm going to scream.

"I was just wondering, Mrs. Talbot, if you will require office space?"

"Call me Liz. We have an embarrassment of Mrs. Talbots at present. Is office space a problem?"

"Not exactly space." He looks a bit tense about the eyes.

"What is the problem?"

He pinkens. "Mrs. Tal—Brandi hasn't wanted anything touched in Mr. Talbot's office."

I stand up. "Show me the office."

Edward opens the door of the corner office that was Ted's pride and joy. Today it exudes all the ambience of a crypt. Black bunting flanks the desk and covers the mirrored wall he thought expanded the space. Every picture has been taken down and turned to the wall. The drapes are drawn and—I don't think it's too tacky of me to notice—the small American flag on a desktop stand has been lowered to half mast. Ted would be appalled.

I march over to the windows and draw the drapes, flooding the room in light. "All the black must come down." Sweeping up an armful of bunting, I pull it down. "This is a place of business not a mausoleum."

"Okay." Edward looks at me as if I've just performed magic.

Next I jerk the rope to bring the flag back to full mast. "Have a flattering sixteen-by-twenty picture of Ted framed, in black with double-gold-and-cream matting. Make it tasteful. Order a small brass plate for it with his full name and the words Founder of Talbot Advertising. No dates. We'll hang it in the reception area. No other tribute is necessary. No flags, no drapery. Not one flower bud. Understand?"

"Yes, Mrs. Talbot."

"Call me Liz. And get custodial services in here to shampoo the carpet and wipe down every surface, baseboards included. This is a business, and the business is alive and thriving. I'll take this office."

"What about the other Mrs. Talbot?"

He doesn't really deserve the look I give him. "We'll think of something." Broom closet maybe, or fire escape.

Just so the day won't be a total success, I run into Harrison at the grocery store. He's in the vegetable and fruit aisle, over by the casaba melons, wearing tennis whites. I'm still dressed to kill. Wonder if an ex-wife invented that phrase?

"Hello, Harrison."

He takes so long to respond a stranger would think he's trying to remember if he knows me. "Hello, Liz. How are you?"

"I've never been better. Hope things are going well for you."

"Sure." A funny sad smile flickers through his expression.

"I'm so sorry about, well, everything." No point in pretending that I don't know about his public humiliation on the morning TV news even if it is old news. "It should have been our private business."

He winces. "I bungled that possibility."

"No, you had class, and always will."

He doesn't say thank you and I don't say sorry again. I simply touch his wrist with a quick firm pressure and push my cart down the row.

Since our public breakup, I've tried not to be anywhere I thought Harrison might be, to save us both the embarrassment factor of trying to be polite with others watching.

I did think about sending him a letter of sympathy after the morning show hazing but then he might have called, and then I'd have had to be nice, and he might think I was being nice because I'd had a chance to think things over, and had had a change of heart, and if he did and said something about marriage again I'd have to say it all over—that's where my thinking got me.

A sign saying pomegranates are on sale sends a white-hot dart of desire through my body as I recall a conversation in a bar about pomegranates just before one thing led to another. One second I'm feeling up the day's fruit, the next I'm remembering a scene to melt glaciers in a very private world behind my closed lids. My stranger in the night is there with me, with that luscious smile and a maraschino cherry clutched between his teeth.

Funny I should keep cueing in on that particular fantasy. But who says daydreams have to make sense to anyone but the person having them? *Sigh.*

There must be a least a hint of my lascivious thoughts in my expression as I turn to my basket with a pomegranate in each hand. An elderly man with a box of instant potatoes, a family-size package of steaks and a bottle of Pepto-Bismol in his cart wiggles his eyebrows at me as he passes by. I wink back.

Chapter 15

It's Friday. I'm up, I'm dressed, and I'm driving into Talbot Advertising. In spite of my misgivings about how awful the experience of a return to daily panty hose and heels might be, I have tuned into my inner compass and found my mind-body-survival connection. It's as simple as learning to cleanse my basement psyche. This is an excellent opportunity to be rid of the fungus and cobwebs of past experience, and choose to find the small joys in the difficulties of my present life.

In other words I cracked open a few of the armloads of positive-think help books Celia brought me when she heard what I was about to do. And it's working. I have found a new calm. Absolutely.

Even if I dropped the glass carafe to my coffeemaker before I had both eyes open.

Even if I burned two fingers while trying to hold up the lever to release brewed coffee directly into my mug.

Even if the filter backed up after I couldn't fill my cup and overflowed streaming hot coffee onto the counter and floor, where it splashed my suede pumps.

Did I indulge in a quick drive thru pick-me-up that will do damage to my new health regime? I did not. There's coffee at work. Patience and my new inner compass preserved my mind-body survival connection

I rushed to the fridge, grabbed a spotted apple I'd brought home from the bakery, and hurried out the door.

The mess I made will be there when I get home.

And ruined shoes are, after all, just shoes. They're four-years-old with really pointy toes, practically out of fashion. I'm determined to go forth, caffeine-deprived and bleary-eyed. See, it's working. Really.

If only I don't meet another disgruntled customer before I've drained my first cup.

That's been my first order of business, calling departed customers, letting them know I'm now in charge, if temporarily. Listening to litanies of supposed business errors that really are all about "Attention-hos in need of ego fixes," as Shemar calls difficult customers, I've been tempted to say, *Whadaya think I am, a moron? Take your business and get outta here!*

But I don't because we are making progress. Two customers have agreed to at least come in and hear what I have to offer.

Nancy greets me with a touch too cheerful, "Oh, hello, Liz."

"Hi, Nancy." Experience tells me something's up. Yet the three clients seated nearby seem normal, no foaming at the mouth. *Don't look for trouble,* one of the books advises, *you reap what you expect from life.* Fine. "Is Edward in yet?"

"Oh, yes." Nancy gaze shifts sideways. "He's with Brandi."

"Really." There goes the dream of getting through the first week without seeing *her,* a subbasement experiment I'm ready to jettison. Yet positive-think has prepared me, or will once the caffeine flows.

I smile blandly at Nancy, who seems to expect some sort of dramatic response. "Good. We have a few things she needs to sign."

I turn toward the hallway to my office when something catches my eye.

"Where did *that* come from?" I whirl around and point to an enormous urn of flowers that hides the lower half of the wall beneath the newly installed picture of Ted.

"Brandi had them delivered." Nancy looks down quickly, opting out of whatever I may say or do next. We had an office agreement. No flowers or memorials.

I stare at the arrangement that can only be described as hideous. Half a dozen bird-of-paradise flowers dominate it, looking as if they'd peck to death whoever came near. There are bloodred leathery heart-shaped anthuriums from which protrude erect shiny yellow phallic spikes. Spiny pink torches of bromeliad, ramrod bamboo stalks and sprays of purple orchids all spring up from a black-and-gold mortuary urn. The effect is funereal, in a Fire Island festive sort of way.

Closing my eyes I think positively. *This is not important. This appalling lapse in taste will not become my problem.*

I turn to Nancy with a plastered smile on my face. "That is

so unfortunate a choice. I need coffee, the biggest mug I can find."

Nancy's brows shoot up in alarm. "Oh, *um,* Liz, there's a problem with the coffee."

"I don't care if it's wretched. Just need some caffeine. Tell you what, I'll get it myself."

But when I've hurried down the corridor to the mini lunchroom I can't believe my eyes. There's the microwave, the fridge, the hot plate. There is a new blender and some other sort of machinery on the counter. But there's no coffeepot or espresso machine.

I hurry back down the hall to Edward's office and stick my head through the open space. "Where are the coffee and espresso machines?"

"I took them out." She's there, in the flesh, wearing a suede micro mini and matching Claudia Ciuti knee high boots in fuchsia with a black turtleneck. "Caffeine's so bad for the complexion. And it yellows the teeth."

She uncrosses her nut-brown legs very slowly and rises from the chair she's been perched on the edge of. "Everybody knows caffeine revs the system and ruins one's nerves. In our business we should thrive for calm. Oh, and at your age, aren't you worried by the fact that caffeine decreases a woman's bone-mineral density?"

I could just kill her now and end my agitation. But no, one must seek to maintain a calm and positive outlook. Otherwise one is the mere pawn of circumstance.

I smile so broadly I feel muscles near my ears contract. "Caffeine drinkers are less likely to commit suicide than the general population. And they score higher on IQ tests. Caffeine can cure headaches. I need revving in the a.m. I want the coffeemaker back."

"No, really, this is so much better for you." She picks up from Edward's desk a clear plastic pitcher full of a pinky-orange concoction. "I made it myself. Fresh-squeezed carrot juice with a little beetroot. I like to add a touch of açai and a hint cupuaçu, which is very hard to get because of customs regulations. But I know this Brazilian hairdresser. His mother sends it to him in shampoo bottles. It's tasty, isn't it, Edward?"

"Not bad. Not bad at all." But Edward is a man with a death grip on his cup of vegetable goop. I bet he swallowed worms to impress fifth-grade girls.

She pours a cup and hands it to me. "I always follow up a cup with a wheat-grass shot for an all-natural energy boost."

A health tip, from a woman who spray-paints her body with chemicals containing traces of arsenic, lead and mercury.

"Try it." She nudges my hand. She sounds so eager. But, she knows Edward can't see the narrow-eyed I-dare-you daggers she's sending my way.

"No thanks." My new feeling of well-being is gone. Even the corpuscles in my veins are beginning to percolate with annoyance. "There are potential risks in the consumption of unpasteurized juices."

"That's why I dip my fruits and vegetables in chlorine bleach solution."

I take a breath, exhale and breathe in again. "This is a place of business. All places of business offer coffee. It's in the business handbook."

She looks at me with the clinical detachment of a counselor. "Caffeine is addicting."

"You bet it is." That comes out a little too snippy for even me to past off as nothing.

Smiling triumphantly, she starts toward me. "You need a cup of Yerba Mate. It will relieve your stress and boost your mental capacity."

As she tiptoes past me I turn and notice several other pitchers of stuff lined up on Edward's credenza.

She reaches for a mug and begins to pour. "I've ordered a juice bar to be installed next week. Until then Edward's being a dear and letting me keep a variety of my organic drinks in his office." Again she offers me an unknown brew. "Yerba Mate is an Amazonian tea that contains mateine, a chemical cousin of caffeine. But without the ugly side affects."

I don't want a fight. I don't want a lecture. I only want a lousy cup of coffee. "Where is the coffeemaker?"

"We dumped it." She wrinkles her nose. "It was old and really cruddy inside. Very unhealthy."

Probably true. I'm willing to work with her. I am. "And the espresso machine?"

"Gave it to the cleanup crew. And the coffee and the filters..."

That's when I know, she's doing this deliberately.

If Ted talked about me to *her,* he would have mentioned my caffeine habit. It's legendary. Like the time I refused to be wheeled into delivery with the girls until I'd had my morning cup. Thank goodness they had not yet told pregnant women to give up caffeine for nine months. I might have had to think twice about becoming pregnant. And she knows that.

I take a deliberate step toward her. "Have you ever seen a junkie in need of a fix?"

"I, *ah,* only in the movies." She's turned berry-pink, which means she's lying.

"Imagine what it's like, the need, the all-consuming craving that will make you do crazy stuff, dangerous insane things, in order to get to the next hit."

I take another step so that she's pinned between me and Edward's desk. "There isn't a Starbucks within one thousand feet of here. And I need coffee. Now. Here. Each and every day. End of discussion."

"If you say so, but..." Whatever comes into my expression makes her think twice about finishing that thought. "I suppose we could have both, coffee and a juice bar."

I don't give myself the opportunity of a reply. I make a beeline for the door, headed for the only place I know where I won't have to wait in line or be asked to pay for a refill.

"I can't believe you missed him!" Celia is practically dancing on toe point. She doesn't even seem surprised to see me at the No-Bagel Emporium though I'm not supposed to be here today.

"Missed who?"

"Him!" Celia makes a comical face, wiggling her eyebrows up and down as I brush past her. Finally she gives up and uses a forefinger to push up one brow. "TRD."

"The Rock's Dad?" I swing around, my drive for caffeine momentarily arrested. "He was here?"

"Ten minutes," answers Desharee, who is stacking bread in the baskets. "And looking good, too. Like you, Miz T. Anytime you tire of them Marc Jacobs shoes they got my name on them, for real."

I nod. Desharee shares my mother's shoe fetish, if not her deep pockets. I home in on the coffeepot behind the counter I've driven thirty minutes to reach. Coffee first, men second, shoes whenever. Wait. Men?

As casually as possible I fill my sixteen-ounce java mug. "So, did he say what he wanted?"

"You," they answer in unison.

"He bought some buttery rowies and two loaves of bread." Celia waggles her brows. "I think he was checking us out. He asked if we make pomegranate bread."

Pomegranate! I turn to hide my smile, and pour milk in my coffee. That's got to be secret code for *I know who you are.*

"You want to see him?" Desharee slips her ever-present cell phone from her pocket and offers it to me. "Flip it open."

Inside is a cell photo backlit by the glare of the store window of a man. I can't tell much about his features. I recognize his impressive big tallness, and the frisson of lust within me those particular dimensions inspire.

"How'd you get him to pose?" I ask.

"He didn't. I was making a phone call when he walked in. When I see a fine man, I snap him. He doesn't ever have to know about it."

"You go, girlfriend!" Celia cries.

I shake my head. "You two scare me."

"He left his card." Celia whips it out.

I take and look at it. It says Marcus T. James. There's a St. Paul, Minnesota, PO box and phone number. I look up at Celia.

"This doesn't mention Nabisco. Maybe your info on him was wrong. He could be anybody."

"He's somebody, all right." Celia giggles. "He's somebody you need to meet. He wants you to call him." Celia indicates the card I'm holding. "He wrote down a number on the back."

Sure enough, in bold strokes is a local exchange for what is probably the same hotel where he stayed last time. For two seconds I think about calling him. But, the man is being way too mysterious. I'll have to think about it. And I don't want an audience.

Nonchalantly I walk over to the wastebasket by the cash register and drop the card into it.

"Now, that's just cold, Miz T." Desharee shakes her head. "You seen him, you'd not be dropping his digits so quick. The man is fine, even if he is old."

"He's not old," Celia pipes in. "Not even old enough to be the Rock's dad. More like his big brother."

"That's what that TRD means? The Rock's dad?" Desharee cranks her head back on her neck. "You make that up, Miz C?"

Celia nods.

Desharee squints at her cell phone image. "Now you say it, does seem like he looks sorta like the Rock." She grins at me. "Now, you know Miz T needs to jump on that!" She and Celia break into giggles and high fives.

While my would-be yentas huddle together, I go in search of a broken scone to go with my coffee. "Don't touch that trash," I toss over my shoulder. I wouldn't put it past them to call and make an appointment for me.

"She ain't never getting no action with that attitude,"

Desharee says at a pitch only someone who keeps the volume on her iPod way too loud would call a whisper.

The real question is, how much more action, and what kind, do I want from Mr. Marcus T. James?

Marcus, that's a nice name. And he knows who I am. But if he was interested in doing business with me, he would have introduced himself right then and there in the hotel bar last month. Instead, he just let me babble on about bread and guzzle martinis, and then screw him.

I'm getting a buzz from the caffeine but it's not making me happy. It's mixed with a sort of urgent quasi longing churning in my middle. If this is desire, it's the morning-after kind, when you feel the need to squirm even if you were delirious the night before.

So, why is Marcus at my bakery door? Is it business? Big businesses like to keep even slim-slot options open. Tastes and trends turn on a dime. Yet, he didn't say a word to Celia about business. Why not?

Because, maybe he's here for strictly personal reasons. He could be thinking that, since he's back, he might as well start up a "friendly whenever he's in town drop-in for a screw" sort of relationship.

Or maybe he can't let me go. Maybe I just knocked his socks off.

And, yes, it's thrilling, he tracked me down!

Or do they call that stalking these days?

When I'm not at my best, I can play ping-pong with my emotions.

There's only one way to answer my questions.

I head toward the register to count the morning receipts. When I'm done, I causally fish Marcus's business card out of the wastebasket and slip it into my bag.

Okay, I'm fortified with coffee. The receipts look good. It's a half hour drive ahead in which to regroup and figure out how to deal with *her*.

"Hey, Miz T." Shemar meets me going out as he's coming in. "Did Celia tell you about the jamming freakizoid bread monsters we're creating for Halloween?"

I feel a thump of surprise. Halloween is usually a bust for us. Why try to compete with candies and apples and lollipops? But I did promise Shemar free rein. What could it hurt?

"No, but do whatever you want."

He holds up his hand for me to slap him five. "We be steady stackin' ends this Halloween, Miz T. For real."

As he passes I spin around. "Wait! What's that cologne you're wearing?"

He grins and nods. "You're feeling it?"

"Well, it's really intense."

"It's called Premium by Phat Farm. It's got aromas of hops, driftwood, tobacco flower and leather in it. And just for the pleasure of the ladies, they added pink peppercorn."

Now, that's different. "Do they make a fragrance for women?"

When I returned from my foray for coffee I find her sitting behind what was formerly Ted's desk in the office I now claim as mine. "Is this just a one-time visit? Or do we need to find an office for you?" I say this as civilly as any mortal could.

She hops up, all smiles. "Oh, no. Now that we're partners, I was thinking that we could share the main office. Redecorated. Each with her own desk, of course."

"No!" I swallow. Coffee means I can be pleasant. "What I meant was, you'll be spending so little time here, office space won't be necessary."

"Oh, but I will be here, lots." I follow her hand flourish across *my* desktop where paint, fabric and carpet samples are spread in colors of a rain forest. "I thought we should strive for a harmonious palette. Something that will provide a naturally soothing habitat."

"Businesses don't have habitats. Advertising is all about presentation. We need to be neutrally appealing, forward-looking without seeming so trendy we frighten off the more tradition-minded customers. Got it?"

"No." She picks up a piece of fabric and runs it through her fingers. "But I will."

It doesn't even require my anti-bimbo radar to read trouble into that statement. But if I ignore it, it might just vanish along with her. I take a step to round the desk. "Do you mind clearing out for now? I have work to do."

She looks past me toward the door. "Oh, thank goodness. You're finally here."

The who-is-here turns out to be her buddy from my tanning salon debacle. We recognize each other with a reflexive widening of the eyes. In tow is a slender young man with Niles Crane blond hair in a four-button European-tailored suit.

She's more than happy to make introductions. "Liz, this is my best friend Tami. Tami, you remember Liz, from the tanning salon?"

"I sure do." Tammy's smothered gurgle of laughter makes me want to grab one of those fabric samples and hold it up in front of me. I do a quick gaze-drop to be certain that my beginning-to-crepe thighs are not again on display. Some humiliations die hard.

"And this is Logan."

Logan offers me one of those bent-wrist, downward-angled handshakes that leave one feeling stirred but unshaken.

Turns out he's an interior designer. "He did all the rooms in my home," she enthuses. "Now he's agreed to do the agency."

For five minutes he chats in a quick, nervous tone about "a botanical color palette" with names like Bermuda palm, succulent gray, Key lime and intense teal.

After I explain in an edgy tone about our need for neutral appeal, he suggests selecting Asian-Pacific accessories. "African ebony carvings, hammered bronzes and palmetto baskets will rev up a sophisticated urban oasis vibe."

"We don't have this budgeted," I say in resistance to what sounds like a showroom display at ABC Carpet & Home.

"I've personally budgeted for it." She strokes a carpet piece called ginger beer. "This is my treat."

I hate tale bearers. From the age of three I've despised anyone who cries, "She hit me!" after a normal playground tussle.

But here I am, while she and Logan are "taking lunch," blabbing to Lionel Dunlap over the phone about my morning with her. "We simply don't have the financial resources to undertake an office-wide renovation."

"As a matter of fact, Mrs.—Brandi came by the see me about

this very matter. She offered to use her personal funds to subsidize the redecorating project. Frankly, Liz, I don't see the problem."

"What about liability? Control of the workplace? Disruption of business? Removal of caffeine products? Arbitrary choice of color palette?" I think I was gaining Lionel's sympathy until the last two complaints.

"Let me set your mind at ease. Brandi is well within her rights to remodel since at arbitration you agreed in principle that she is part-owner. And when it's at her expense, frankly, I'd think you'd be delighted not to have to share the cost."

That's when my little house of hostility cards folds into trite reality.

I'm flat pea-green jealous.

She has money free and clear from other sources to hire an interior designer who talks about carpet shades of cantaloupe and casaba, while my share of Ted's estate is so tied up I can barely scrape together a week of presentable clothing.

"It just seems a waste of money," I manage after a moment.

"I think we need to give Brandi time to grow as a businesswoman. She's most eager to learn from you."

"Really?" I feel a squirm coming on.

"She said she wants to learn all she can from an astute businesswoman such as you."

Why do I think that is a lie of the proportions only the *Titanic* could hold? She's up to something. And that can't be good for me.

Chapter 16

"Oh, am I late?"

Four heads lift as Brandi tips in through the doorway of our conference room.

I make an elaborate gesture of checking my watch though I know the time. We are holding a staff meeting on a Friday, which I assumed she'd miss. But here she is, wearing a tight-fitting black turtleneck, 7 For All Mankind Cropped Boycut jeans, a hip-slung studded leather belt, and boots with stiletto heels. Perched on her hair is a teal newsboy cap with beading. "You're late."

"I had an appointment for a custom spray tanning. Chita is the best in north Jersey. It takes weeks just to get an appointment. She offered me, as a professional courtesy, a free session but could only fit me in first thing this morning."

The fact that she looks rested and tawny on a rainy October morning after I spent a nearly sleepless night going over the company books doesn't improve my attitude. She's in her charm-and-disarm mode. I'm in search-and-destroy mode.

"You don't have to participate in staff meetings, but if you do, you need to be punctual. We haven't time for remedial reruns."

Edward, who popped up gentleman fashion when she stepped in, offers his chair.

She gives him the kind of smile you give someone who has personally saved baby seals from furriers' clubs. "Thanks."

Don't know why I sound so pissed off. Maybe it has to do with the fact I came in to find my desk missing. Logan had all my office furnishings moved into the hall so that the painters can set up scaffolding in preparation for the weekend paint job. I'm stuck working in the conference room.

The coffeepot is back, so I'd call the week a draw.

She looks around. "If this is a staff meeting, where is everybody?"

"This is the staff." Edward dodges my eye. "The rest were laid off—"

"Old business," I say.

"That's right. Talbot's revenue is in the toilet." Her voice has gone as cool as her expression is now icy.

But I'm not taking the bait. "Obviously, there won't be enough of us to do the work once I regain the accounts of our former clients." Even if this is proving more difficult than I hoped. So far, only one has returned my calls. "So, we've already agreed to rehire immediately. Edward will call Paul Burgess, our former computer graphic designer, and Suzi Sloan, who was Talbot's ad copyist."

"I remember Suzi." She smiles. "Fabulous hair."

"So then we were finished. Everybody has their assignments."

Brandi frowns. "I don't."

I force myself to smile in her general direction. "What are your business skills?"

"I own a tanning salon business." She fiddles with the clasp on her hobo bag. "Of course, my managers do most of the work. But I know how to calm unhappy customers."

"Providing help for a client after a bad tanning job isn't in quite the same league as dealing with one whose hundred-thousand-dollar campaign tanked."

"Oh, you can do that, then. I don't really like dealing with angry people, anyway. It ruins one's karma."

Everybody with the karma. *Jeez.* "Any other unique skills?"

"I do feng shui. I've taken classes. Why don't I bring the office into harmony?"

I want to say that the easiest way for her to accomplish that is to leave the premises.

"For instance, we should change Natalie's desk location. Out there in the middle of the room she's confronting every kind of energy coming through the door. It's too much and disruptive. She should have her back to a wall, so she's protected from hostility."

"Furniture mover. See Brandi." I write that down.

"You said my name!"

I look up. "What?"

"You never say my name." Brandi turns to Edward. "Have you ever heard Liz use my name?"

"I—uh." Edward looks like he's caught something in his zipper.

"Brandi, Brandi, Brandi! Can we move on now to your other areas of business acumen?"

"I'm good at client relations." Brandi smiles confidently. "People are always stopping me to ask where I got my tan."

"We don't need for our customers to be well groomed, only well heeled. Next?"

She turns to Edward. "I give good phone, everyone says so."

I have to stop myself from saying something really inappropriate. "We have Natalie. Next."

"How about I create ad campaigns? I like to watch commercials. I never miss the Super Bowl, mostly for the commercials, and I can always spot the winners. At the parties every year, friends take bets on how many I will get right." She turns to Edward. "Never bet against me."

I slam my pen down on the table. "You see, Edward. There was no reason for you to get a graduate degree at Syracuse or for me to finish Rutgers. Brandi can just go out and win us accounts, then dream up winning ad campaigns while watching TV."

She casts me a sidelong glance and half smile, as if PO'd has suddenly appeared on my forehead. That's when I know she was deliberately trying to get the best of me. "I have a degree from Wood Tobé-Coburn. In fashion."

I stare at her. "Do you even know what we do here? Our business is to create business for our clients. Simply stated but very hard to do. There are 47,000 advertising and public relations businesses in the United States. Less than half write copy and prepare artwork, graphics and other creative work. Then those ads must be placed on television, radio or the Internet or in periodicals, newspapers or other advertising media. We don't even have an experienced PR person at the moment. Most advertising firms specialize in a particular market niche. Talbot Advertising specializes in small and independent businesses in New Jersey. Oh, we occasionally get small jobs from the big guys, distributing circulars, handbills or free samples at a local sales convention. Right now Edward and I aren't enough brain power to generate all the ideas we need, like yesterday. So if you think you can do it better, be my guest. If not, please don't make what professionals do sound as easy as watching the Super Bowl."

"I, well, maybe I——" She rises from her chair, looking like she's going to cry. Am I the only one who thinks it's an act to make me seem unreasonable? "I suppose I'll check on how the decorating is coming along."

When she is gone Edward sends a thoughtful glance my way. "Maybe you could ease up a bit? Brandi is trying."

That's right. Let her well up and most men will do anything to dry those babe-blue eyes. "I think you should thank me for making it clear how hard we work."

He shrugs. "I thought her enthusiasm was sort of cute."

"Her cap's cute. She wants to learn the advertising business? She can start by learning to dress professionally."

I'm behaving badly, but I don't seem able to stop myself.

I look over at Edward, who is collecting his paperwork from the conference table. "Since you two have a rapport, why don't you take Brandi under your wing, show her the ropes, all that clichéd stuff, and see what she has besides enthusiasm."

Edward looks sideways. "I don't know."

"You just said you believe in her. She just might have gleaned some very clever ideas from TV advertising by the big boys."

Edward brightens. "She is able to talk to people. Clients always want to meet her."

"The male clients?" I don't need his blush to confirm it. "Tell you what. Let's give her a client to work with." I go through the motions of checking my folders because there's only one I'm looking for. "Ah, here's a good one."

Edward takes the folder and looks at it. "West Orange Bakery?"

"I can't very well work on it, conflict of interest and all that." And if she royally screws it up, so much the better!

Oh, but when I'm bad, I'm very bad.

The rest of the day passes in relative calm, if one doesn't count the raucous voices of the painters, and the oohs and aahs from Nancy and Brandi and Tami—heaven forbid this has become a daily stop on her shopping round—when Logan drops by with more samples. It's not that I don't care what my office is going to look like. It's that I can't trust myself to be involved. I cannot be reasonable with her in the room. She's like a rash I can't scratch, a pimple I can't squeeze, a—a reminder of a mistake I can't correct.

Instead of going out for lunch I'm calling Marcus T. James. Four days late.

I didn't want to seem overeager or pathetically bereft of a social life, both of which I am if I stop and think about it. Don't know what I'm going to say to him. Surely, hearing his voice will trigger some emotionally honest reaction. If he's still in town. If not, nothing lost. Right?

It is a hotel number. I ask for Marcus.

After five rings it's clear he's not in his room and I'm being transferred to an answering service.

"Hello. Uh, this is for Marcus. Hi, Marcus. This is Liz, the owner of No-Bagel Emporium. If you are who I think, um, anyway, I'll be at the bakery tonight, working. After seven. So, okay, bye. Oh, the number there is…"

There are 911 calls by three-years-olds that sound more mature.

So now I've put myself in my least favorite of all positions: waiting for a call back.

Of course, I don't have to wait. I have to go back to work.

No one darkens my doorstep until closing when Edward gives the open door of our boardroom a light rap.

"Spoke with the on-leave staff. They're coming back." He smiles the same smile as his toddler son. "Oh, and Brandi mentioned she's found a new prospect as a major client."

The hair on my arms lifts. "Who is that?"

"She didn't say. Someone she talked with during the lunch hour, I gather. She's bringing him into the agency as soon as he can schedule."

I'm amazed by how incensed this news makes me. I don't believe she wants to be like me. I think she's up to something. I just don't know what. How could she land a client when Edward and I are battling just to keep the ones we have? Can I believe her? I'll have to wait until next week.

I pick up my portfolio, unfurl my umbrella and head out to join the Friday evening traffic crawl home.

Marcus won't call. He was just casually curious about a woman who picks up strange men in bars. Maybe he thought he'd get a quick boink in while passing through.

I can understand how he'd have that impression of me. I have a few of him I'd not trade for fifty other feel-good memories.

I slide behind the wheel of my car and hit the windshield wipers to clear raindrops. Oh, God! Don't let that be all he thought of me.

I put my car in gear and head out into major rush hour traffic. So what if he doesn't call? Does that mean that just as I'm ready to admit that I want a relationship with a man whose buttocks I recognize and admire—I can't find one? Of course not! It just means I need to start looking. Where does a woman my age meet a man, anyway?

I met Marcus in a bar.

It could be that bar clientele has improved dramatically in recent years. Perhaps Marcus isn't as singular as I suppose. The few good men left may be drinking perfect martinis all alone in upscale bars all over northern New Jersey and wondering where some wonderful me is keeping herself.

Oh, right. I'm going to go out again, alone, dressed to the nines, and buy myself expensive drinks? I don't think so.

I'm just beginning to see daylight at the end of my financial tunnel. I'm not going to get run over by a train of emotional desperation.

Next thing you know I'd be in civil court, suing some deadbeat ex man friend for back rent and loans of a few thousand, while he tells the judge I'm a jealous pity boink who wanted him to have a few dollars for services rendered, until he left me.

I don't think so.

I'm a modern woman. I'm a role model for my girls. I will not go home and sulk. I will go and make bread.

And just maybe Marcus will call.

By 6:45 p.m. I'm back in my comfort zone, the No-Bagel Emporium, measuring and weighing flour, salt and Ma. Finally, Shemar and I agree, Ma is back to its normal-tasting self.

At precisely 6:57, I stop and reapply my lipstick, in case of a phone call. Thanks to Celia, who browses makeup counters the way other women stalk shoes, I have all the fall shade samples. Today I'm trying Bobbi Brown clove lip stain.

Women are weird. Smear a little pigmented wax on our lips, and we feel like we're ready to take on the world.

At 7:03 the sounds of someone rapping at the front door pull me from the tension-induced mantra: *He's not going to call. He's not going to call. He's not going to call.*

I suspect it might be a late delivery. Or, more likely, DeVon, who has forgotten his key again.

It's neither.

It's Marcus T. James.

He gives me a little salute through the glass when he sees me, and I feel the need to reapply my lip stain. Instead I hurry over to let him in.

Chapter 17

He looks good, in a cashmere sweater the color of blue spruce and gray slacks. He could be on a date. "Hi."

"Hi." I am in a T-shirt and jeans because it never occurred to me I might actually *see* him without prior notice.

I can see it in his eyes, the adjustment of disappointment. The sex-on-a-stem lady has vanished. In her place is a nice middle-aged woman with flour on her hands. I really should stop using scrunchies. My hair is a knot of dark curls at my crown.

"What are you doing here?"

He looks surprised. "You called."

"Usually a return call is all that is required."

"Can I come in?"

"Sure." I'm a little slow at comprehending that he's come all this way just to see me. "How did you get here from Somerset?"

"They've developed this system for travelers. It's called rent-a-car."

I feel a sudden blush. "What I mean is how did you know where to find me in the first place?"

He smiles that got-you smile and I feel that little flip-flop inside that started a night I intend never to forget. "You talked a lot about what you do for a living the night we met. No-Bagel Emporium is the kind of name that sticks in the mind."

My hand comes up to my forehead in a "duh!" moment of chagrin. "Some mystery woman."

"Let's say you were keeping it more real than you realized."

"So why didn't you say who you were?"

Instead of answering he looks past me. "What are you doing?"

"Making bread. It's my therapy."

"I thought bread was your aphrodisiac."

I turn away from that statement because I remember everything we said, pretty much word for word. And, where it got me. I'm also registering things like how really large he is, and as handsome as I remember, and his shoes are Italian, hand-sewn leather. I'm, well, frankly surprised I attracted him. But since I have, I say, "Come on back."

He follows me into the room with the proofing table.

"Sometimes, when I've had a tough day, I like to do the kneading by hand." I begin folding and pushing with the heels of my floury hands. "It lets off steam."

He watches for a few seconds and then says, "You might want to try kickboxing instead. The way you're going at that dough, you could be getting ready for a bout with Laila Ali."

"What would you know about it? Oh, that's right. You're a professional."

"I've got a few skills." He walks over to the sink, pushes up the sleeves of his sweater and begins washing his hands.

I stop. "You're right. I'm ruining perfectly good dough."

He comes back, slips on a pair of disposable gloves from the box that hangs by the sink, and nudges me aside with his hip. "Want to tell me why?"

Actually, talking about my problems with *her* is the last thing I want to do when the best thing to happen to me in years is standing hip to hip with me.

He knows how to handle dough, using a technique that takes time to master. Which reminds me how much I'd liked having those hands on my thighs. Oh, dear. I'm wandering down a path I surely won't take this night.

"I should begin by fessing up." He cocks a brow in my direction, and I think Celia's right! He's got the Rock's move down pat. "I stole your parking place at the Upper Montclair Fine Arts and Crafts Show back in September."

He frowns for a second and then it clears. "That was you?"

"With the buttery rowies, yes. And though I didn't actually see your face, I do remember something memorable about you."

"Really?" He stops kneading and half turns to me. "What would that be?"

"Your smell."

He looks like he'd like to check his armpits. "I smell?"

"Not bad." I shut my eyes to conjure the aroma. "It was a great smell, though not one I'd associate with a man. You smelled of talcum powder, confectioner's sugar and tart plums."

He grunts. "Must have been something I ate."

"Oh, no, it was much too strong for that. It was cologne, or something like it." My toes curl just thinking about it. "I'd recognize it anywhere."

His dark eyes widen with interest. "You responded like that to a smell and yet didn't turn around for a look?"

"I had my hands full. By the time I extracted myself from my car, all I saw was the back of your suede jacket."

His brows rise. "*Aaahkaaay.* Now I know what you're talking about. My daughter, Hayley, was trying to decide what perfume to wear to her summer school finals. I asked her what difference it would make to her grades. She squirted me in reply. It took weeks before the smell wore out of that jacket."

He has at least one child, and since he says he's single he must have at least partial custody.

"Hmm. I liked it. A lot."

"Yeah?" He leans a little closer. "What about the unadorned me?"

I lean in to almost kissing range but stop short. I inhale deeply then sigh in disappointment. "Too bad you don't have any more of that fragrance. I really *really* liked it."

"I'll call Hayley and get the name in the morning. Good enough?"

"Good enough."

He goes back to work on the dough, as if something important has been settled between us. When, in fact, nothing is settled. I don't know why he's here, if it's business or pleasure. And if it's the latter, why has he waited all this time to get in touch?

But I'm a woman and we tend to overthink these things. "What can I get you to drink?"

He smiles. "A latte would be great."

I prop open the door that divides the kitchen from the front of the store, so we can talk while I move behind the counter to make espresso. "Tell me what you do for a living."

"You know. I'm a consultant for Nabisco."

"How does a man who looks like he once played for the— Where do you live?"

"At the moment?" He looks as if the question might have more than one answer. "Minnesota."

"So how does someone who wanted to be a Viking end up in the bread business?"

"I'm surprised at you, pegging me as a cliché. Not every big guy plays sports."

I stop and look at him. "But you did."

He grins. "I did. No major league aspirations."

"I, um, don't suppose you ever did any wrestling?"

He gives me the eyebrow.

That's what I thought. "How'd you get into the bread business?"

"Long story."

I check my watch. He grins.

"I'm an army brat. Dad was attached to the United States Defense Attaché Office. We spent a lot of time overseas. I have a diploma from the American International School in Nairobi, Kenya."

"I thought you played football."

"I did. They call it rugby."

"I can see how that sparked your interest in food."

"You don't grow up in houses with full-time staffs, including blue ribbon chefs, and not become interested in the process. My first crush was our Italian cook, Magdalena." He smiles. "She knew the way to a young man's heart."

"Just how much did she teach you?"

He grins. "A gentleman never tells."

"And so you decided to follow your *impassionata* into cooking school?"

"After college and a stint in the service. Let me tell you, boot camp is easier than the first weeks at Le Cordon Bleu." He wags his head. "Give me a drill sergeant anytime."

"And now?"

"I own James Consulting Group." He turns the dough he's been kneading into a proofing tub, strips off his gloves and comes out front where I am.

"We provide high-quality consulting services for small to mid-size independent specialty food shops, restaurants and other food and beverage-related businesses in the organic foods market."

The espresso machine beeps to indicate the coffee is ready. "You sound like a commercial."

"Want the whole spiel?" He takes from me latte glass that I was about to fill and puts it on the counter. He reaches for the stainless pitcher I use to steam milk. "Our services include identification, evaluation and acquisition. In addition, we offer program development, marketing-concept development and evaluation, prototype, testing, market potential and joint ventures for new products."

He pauses to froth the milk because the whoosh of high-pressure steam would drown him out, anyway.

Fascinated I watch him pour steamed milk into two latte glasses, which is opposite of the way most lattes are made. As he draws espresso into a shot pot he says, "Our national client list includes Nabisco, numerous restaurants, microbreweries and a couple of high-profile upscale spas. Do you have—ah, here's one."

He extracts a spoon from our utensil pot and then carefully pours espresso from the shot pot over the back of the spoon into the milk. When he's done, he uses the spoon to arrange a layer of milk foam from the steaming cup on top. The color bands from bottom to top are cream, coffee, and cream. The effect is called a layered latte, which he hands to me.

"Where'd you learn that trick?"

He clears his throat, then says in tones that could get him commercial voice-over work, "Marcus Terrence James, president of James Consulting, received his undergraduate degree in business and finance from Howard University, Washington, D.C., and then received a grand diplôme from Le Cordon Bleu, Paris, France."

Oh, my! I'm in love. A man who knows food, and can prepare it to perfection!

When he's made a latte for himself he clicks his glass to mine and we each take a sip.

"Perfect!" No other word describes it.

He accepts the praise with a smile, then points to a chair and we both sit.

For a long moment we only sip our lattes and smile silently.

He seems to be having serious thoughts all of a sudden. I don't want to break his concentration so I happily sip and savor until he decides to speak again.

"Liz, we're not going to approach your bakery with a business venture."

"Oh." I didn't expect it, I didn't. But honestly, I did hope. This is a blow.

He sighs. "If I'd thought we were going to do business I wouldn't be here like this. This is personal." He smiles and leans toward me. "Very personal. I'm glad that business won't interfere."

"Oh." I'm still caught up in the fact my little world isn't good enough for his.

His smile veers back toward a serious edge. "You've got to come at me with something else besides a letter in the alphabet."

"So you didn't seduce me to improve your bargaining position?" I had to ask? I had to ask.

He lays a hand on my thigh far enough beyond my knee to convey his message. "I like the position we were just in just fine. But, no." A single brow lifts. "You didn't seduce me to improve your position?"

"I didn't know who you were until the next day at the crafts fair. My cheese specialist told me."

"So, see? Complications filed, concerns tabled."

We chat for a little while about life in the food industry. It really doesn't matter. It's obvious to both of us that being together is reason enough. We could be discussing Tibetan lamas for all I care.

Finally he takes my empty latte cup out of my hand and puts

it down. He then folds both hands over my waist and pulls me out of my chair and into his lap. "It's just you and me. Feeling lucky?"

"This will never work." Even if I am impressed by his ability to lift un-petite me into his lap at one go. "You live a thousand miles away."

He leans in and kisses my left cheek. "There are long-distance flights daily."

"But I don't, can't travel."

He drags his mouth across mine to kiss my right cheek. "So, I'll come to you."

"There's another problem." I just can't think of any because he's kissing me full on the mouth.

My hands find his shoulders and then slide around to his back. And just maybe I was overdoing it with the dough but I know how to knead a man's back to get him seriously excited. And then gradually, I move on to other even easier-to-arouse parts.

I can never *ever* tell anyone what we did next.

Chapter 18

$\mathcal{S}$ally's back.

That's the good news, and the bad.

Riley explains when I call her back after returning home from my personal boink-a-thon. Sally had called Riley, standard procedure lately when Sally wants me to know something but doesn't want to discuss it with me, because I might ask questions. Riley revels in these calls from Sally, and so does Sally. She dotes on the only one in the family to go into what she calls "the business," show business that is.

First, before I hear about Sally, Riley tells me she's been relieved of her day job. "Dealing with corporate management is so surreal. Rehearsals went on until after 4:00 a.m. I couldn't *fooking*—" she sounds like just John Lennon when she says this "—be expected to be on the job wiping leaves at a bank at six-thirty, could I?"

"You were fired?"

"They call it being put on the on-call list. Backup leaf hopper."

And here I was, worried that she might never come into her own. "What did Sally have to say?"

"She said I was right to walk out. One must have principles. And that it's part of life to suffer for one's art. She's putting a check in the mail to cover my rent. But here's the worrisome part. She has no plans. Can you imagine? Sally is at home on a Friday night."

Riley's right. Even when Sally's positively too tired to do another thing, that only means that she will be at her favorite spot at Café des Artistes, sipping Pernod with water, and holding court with passersby.

"We've got to cheer her up. Have a party. This weekend."

"I don't really have time to plan anything right now."

"This is an emergency, Mother. This is Sally."

The reason these words resonate along my spinal cord with deep dramatic impact may have less to do with the extremity of Sally's emotional state and more to do with Riley's practiced delivery after all those rehearsals. Whatever the cause, I'm agreeing to a meeting of the Talbot/Blake women in Manhattan tomorrow night.

But first I need at least half a night's dead-to-the-world sleep.

I wasn't this active as a young adult. Marcus brings out the wild woman in me.

He has beautiful control. And they say there's nothing good to say about men and sex and aging! That's why we tried so many positions, and I came like it's all new to me every which way.

First we did it right there in the dining area on the broad

expanse of a tabletop. Well, I was on the table. He was on his feet. Then he retreated to a chair and I came astride. Then we sort of decided without much conversation that the only surface that was really going to be satisfactory to this production was the stainless-steel preparation table in the back.

Which is why this could never be a serious relationship. Serious relationships bring out the adult in me, the serious woman who worries about financing and faucet drips and hourly wages. Relationships aren't built of the perfect martini, the expert layering of a latte, or sex that makes mind-blowing, body-slamming, earthquaking climaxes seem first-thought fresh.

Right. Tell it to the marines.

When Marcus was finally content, as in spent, I tried to regain strategic clothing so that we wouldn't shock the first baker, DeVon, who was due within the hour.

Swiping back curls from my overheated face, I made one last stab at reason. "This is it. Absolutely, positively the last time."

Marcus was pulling up his trousers over standard-issue briefs, which I find kinda sweet. "Whatever you say."

He didn't have to sound so agreeable about it. But then he put his hand on my bare breast and I thought about how final "positively the last time" sounds, and thought why not one for the road?

We didn't because DeVon likes to play his car stereo really loud, and I heard him coming before he was midway up the block. His bass makes the walls vibrate.

Instead, Marcus wrestled on his sweater while I grabbed disinfectant and lots of paper towels and started the process of eradicating all evidence of the board of health violation that had just been committed.

Marcus's final kiss shmushed my nose. "I have a helluva busy week or two coming up. But I'll call. We need to get a few things straight. Don't sit by the phone. I travel a lot. But I'll call."

I won't sit by the phone. But really, does he have to say as well as do all the right things?

There's something I don't know. There has to be. I just hope it's not so awful it will completely ruin this good feeling I intend to nurture until he does call.

Karma? Stay outta this!

Alone, Sarah and I wouldn't have a prayer of getting into this new fashionable spot on a Saturday night. But Lassie and Ma Kettle could get in if they were accompanied by Riley and Sally.

Tonight Sally is channeling postwar Lauren Bacall in a Ralph Lauren gray fitted jacket and long pencil skirt with a bit of fur wrapped about her long neck to ward off the chill of fall. She's let her hair grow out a bit and rolled it under, pageboy style. As always, she's showstopper regal.

Riley is channeling Euro trash waif with a vintage silk kimono over a fifties strapless evening gown, Indian hand ornament and Chinese embroidered silk boots. By comparison, Sarah is Wall Street and I'm—what else?—wearing my ubiquitous Dana Buchman suit. I will go shopping for luxury garments the minute we have two profitable months in a row at Talbot's.

As we enter the pastel-paneled walls of Juniper Suite, strangers look up from stylish wood cocktail tables set between sleek wooden seats that look like pastil chairs that have been told to stand up and stop slouching.

Sally is animated, greeting both the hostess and three patrons by name. Everyone we pass is certain she's somebody, they just can't place her.

Yet something is missing. Sally seems on, acting her role in life.

Soon we are snacking on venison lollipops and fried olives stuffed with fontina cheese, retro-dining and sipping the signature drinks: the Juniperotivo. It is concocted from Junipero gin, lime juice, pomegranate molasses and mint. Sarah opts for a hot Suite in C Major cocktail made with gin, lemon juice, strawberry hibiscus and rose syrup. They are both quite pretty and joyful on a cool October night, a touch of Tahiti in Midtown.

During it all Sally regales us with her latest spa tales. Of course, her personal trainer looked like Viggo Mortensen. The way she describes it even I, who doesn't like being covered neck to ankle in squishy concoctions, admit that a luxurious chocolate wrap, all fudgey and deep brown warmth, has appeal.

Sally says she has her limit, and green is it. She didn't like one bit the mint wrap because with it came the almost overwhelming urge for a Kentucky bourbon julep, which they didn't serve at the health spa.

Speaking of which, there is another thing. Sally doesn't drink, unless it's the occasional Pernod or champagne. Tonight she's swilling down Jumiperotivos as if they are bottles of Perrier.

"Younger men, darling——" she leans toward me to confide "——they are the only way to go after a woman reaches fifty."

"Something to look forward to," I say, and take another slug of pomegranate-flavored gin. I'm happy right here and right now with my mystery man Marcus. Of course, it could be *très gauche* to mention such happiness in this company.

Sarah announces that she's thinking about taking the bar again. She says legal aid is all very fine but now that she's seen law up close as a paralegal she's ready to join the rank of attorneys we all love to hate. And she's got a tutor for the bar. A junior partner, Lissette Kawn, offered to coach her.

However, as soon as we all make the appropriate encouraging noises, Sarah begins backpedaling, saying she will see how she feels when the time comes. Maybe she won't take the bar, after all.

Then it's Riley's turn. She holds forth on the not-so-pleasant aspects of full-body waxing, which is necessary for the heavy body makeup to adhere correctly.

"The guys are complaining about ingrown hairs in the funniest places. We girls laugh and say now they understand the cost of wearing a thong. For guys it's called the 'tackle box' wax!"

We giggle uproariously, because we've drunk too much by the time orders of boudin blanc with whipped potato and apple ketchup arrive. We are so determined to have a good time that after a while my face aches from holding an ebullient expression.

I don't even know why I thought of the word *ebullient*. I suppose it expresses my desire that all our lives be filled with the joy teetering on euphoria that I feel.

But something is missing. Maybe it's the lack of "bull" in our e-*bull*-ient.

Not that a man is a requisite for joy. But when you get three generations of talented, accomplished, healthy, good-looking women together and they can't produce a single "my guy" story, it does give one pause.

Not one word has been spoken about Tony. We are waiting for Sally to mention him. But she seems equally determined to avoid all mention.

I recognize the moment Riley decides to crack that ice. She leans forward, propping her chin on her hand, dark eyes flashing in a sparkly persimmon eye shadow that completely encircles her eyes from brows to top of her cheeks. Lash pearls dance on the tips of her fake lashes. Dew drops from a bottle by Givenchy, she informed us earlier. The new play sans garments has freed her to dabble in the art of makeup. When Riley takes something to heart, there are no half measures.

"So, about Uncle Tony."

I gasp softly. If there were a way more calculated to get a rise out of Sally, I don't know what it could possibly be. Riley's hit the sourest spot of that relationship. In order for Tony to be an "Uncle" there'd first have to be a M-A-R-R-I-A-G-E.

Sally lifts her brows in the faintest of inquiry then says, "Never heard of him."

This is the moment when lesser beings retreat. Riley blurts out, "But I love Tony. Aren't you being just the tiniest bit unfair to the rest of us?"

Oh, now she's done it, swatted the lioness in the nose.

Sally sits a little straighter, if such a thing is possible, and slowly turns her head in Riley's direction.

I'm a mother, and a daughter. I don't know which of them

to throw my body across to provide protection. Yes, I do. Riley's younger and scrappier and can peel the steel off a taxi at five paces. But Sally is... Sally. No contest. My kitten will be mauled.

"Isn't that Kevin Spacey?" I say a little too loudly for a New Yorker whose life is rife with celebrity sightings. Heads at the nearby tables swivel toward the main entrance. Only Sally is left staring at Riley, who seems suddenly younger than twenty three, and quite fragile.

And then the only thing that could possibly be worse happens. I spy Tony at the entrance, looking gloriously finished in the Salvatore J. Cesarani suit and turtleneck Sally gave him last Christmas. And there's a woman on his arm. Not just any woman, a much *much* younger woman.

Holding Tony's arm is a six-foot-tall Eurasian with lovely almond eyes and a ribbon of blue-black hair piled high, wearing a storm-cloud-colored sweater and wrap skirt, and ankle strap Dolce & Gabbana heels. I recognize them because I saw them in the latest issue of *Five-O*.

I whip my head around to see Sally's mouth quiver, just the barest shiver of vulnerability, the kind Mount Helen's must give off when molten-hot magma surges beneath. An eruption or implosion is eminent.

This is awful. I want to cower and hide my eyes, to protect my optic nerves from the searing image of Sally's moment of humiliation.

Sally rises slowly to her feet to meet them. There's no doubt that Tony has seen her, and vice versa. And yet there's no greeting. No exchange of words. The room grows strangely quiet in Tony and his companion's wake. They don't know who or what or why, but Manhattanites know gossip-worthy drama unfolding when they see it.

"Mom, do something." Sarah punctuates her whisper by reaching to grip my arm.

We're like commuters who've noticed a man in the subway standing much too close to the edge contemplating the rails. We don't know whether to cry out or keep still. Only Riley stares upward, her face alight with the magic of live theater.

Sally touches a shoulder of the girl's sweater, rubs it lightly between her fingers. "Sonia Rykiel. Very nice. If you're very smart, as well as very pretty, you might even one day be able to afford her. But, of course, even a mountain goat may wear cashmere."

And then she whispers something to the startled girl in Russian—I didn't know Sally spoke Russian or how she knew the girl knew Russian.

Whatever Sally says causes the younger woman to blanch and then flame up pink. The words that suddenly spew from her are quite obviously vulgar, if unintelligible.

Sally has the remedy. She reaches down, picks up a hibiscus-laden vase and flips the contents up into the girl's face.

"The only way to calm a hysteric," she says in a conversational tone to the table next to us. "Quite déclassé." She turns and walks past Tony toward the exit.

The first to recover? Riley, naturally.

Riley stands up, hopping mad. "You said you'd be here ages ago, Uncle Tony! And what's she doing here?"

Tony smiles. "Do calm yourself, dear girl. We've achieved enough of a spectacle for one evening." He turns to his companion and offers her his pocket handkerchief. "You were superb, my child. Superb."

She actually blushes but looks in doubt. "You said I could have this dress but look what she's done to it!" The thick Russian accent all but obscures her meaning yet her accompanying gestures paint the picture.

"Not a worry, love. It will clean. Send me the bill."

Am I the only one left still gape-jaw by the last minutes?

I rise and give first Riley and then Tony considering looks. "I would like to understand just what's been going on here."

Tony smiles, the brilliance of it quite blinding against his rich Indian coloring. "Riley, little lamb that she is, wanted to effect reconciliation."

I turn a heated look on my child. "You thought up this scenario?"

On this rare occasion, Riley looks absolutely subdued. "I invited Uncle Tony. I didn't know he'd bring a date." I believe her because Riley never lies, even if it costs her dearly. She calls it the privilege-of-being-alive tax.

I turn back to Tony. "That was cruel."

"Frankly, my dear, you don't know what you're talking about. The shock has done Sally a world of good. Didn't you notice? She walked out in a magnificent huff." He sounds like the proud parent of a new babe. "It's just what she was wanting, a good gobsmack to get her juices flowing again. She will be plotting revenge all the way back to her apartment. "

I study his face, all proud lines and sensual curve. "You do know what this is really about?"

He looks at me as if he is dealing with a dimwit. "I trust you will stay out of it." His gaze flicks over to Riley. "Sally needs no further help from amateurs."

When he has escorted his damp companion up the curving stairway to the more exclusive Swizzle Lounge, Riley gushes, "That was *fooking* brilliant! I've got to find myself an Indo-European lover. They are *sooo* classy."

"Mom, you don't think he's actually...?" Sarah has that worried-about-proprieties expression.

"What I think is that Tony's right, we're amateurs. And that it's time for me to go home."

I look around for a waiter to ask for the bill, remembering belatedly that it will be high, and Sally's not here to cushion the expense as we all expected.

"It's taken care of," the waiter tells us with a genuine smile that must mean the tip was more than adequate.

I glance up the stairway toward the Swizzle Room. The old darling!

Chapter 19

The office has been abuzz with speculation for three days about who Brandi is bringing in as her first big client. Today is the day.

Why am I the only one to suspect this won't go well? In fact, the urge to leave the building is so strong that I'm formulating an excuse to get the hell out of Dodge when I come up short.

Harrison!

He's standing in the foyer of Talbot Advertising talking with Nancy. I overhear him say, "I'm here to see Mrs. Talbot," just before he looks up and notices me at the opening of the hallway that leads to the firm's private offices.

"Hello, Harrison."

"Liz, what are you doing here?"

"Working." He looks puzzled, and caught in a quandary at the same time. *Jeez*. How long are we going to have these awkward moments? "Weren't you just asking for me?"

"Oh, hello, Harrison." The familiar voice coming from behind me is smooth and creamy, yet grates like sandpaper on my nerves. "I'm ready for you."

Brandi slips past me, leaving a wake under the influence of Echo perfume. Already scratched that one off my list. I notice she's wearing a tailored navy jacket and skinny pants and four-inch-heeled sandals. Today she's Jamaica bronze.

"So glad you could make it." She offers Harrison a two-handed clasp of greeting. As she turns about to face me she brings him along, making them a pair and me, well, confused. "You two know each other?"

Harrison looks as if he'd like to burrow under the carpet, which wouldn't be a disaster since we're having it taken up next week. "I didn't know you worked here, Liz."

I want to believe him though his lack of knowledge surprises me. I thought everyone had heard about the *Talbot v. Talbot* match in progress. Of course, since his was one of the first accounts to desert after Ted's mishap it might not have occurred to him to inquire, or maybe… My stare swerves to her.

"You do know each other!" She looks so totally surprised I know it's an act. My face prickles with chagrin. She knows about us.

The arm she slips through his is sporting a silver-and-red-string bendel. Some call it Jewish chic. I happen to know she married Ted in a Congregational service. "I dropped by Harrison's dealership last Thursday to get my SC430 serviced." Her lashes drift low. "It's so difficult to have to think of all these things now that I'm alone."

I've already had the joy of learning that Ted bought each wife the same make car at the same dealership. Of course, my 2002 GS300 sedan is no competition for her 2006 sports coupe with the teeny rear seat most useful "as a padded place for your purse or some impulse purchases from Tiffany's," or so goes one commercial. For a man who left his wife for her "inadequacies," Ted certainly didn't let that get in the way of duplicating the details of my life from perfume to auto. Or maybe he was just too lazy to make a change.

But she is chattering on.

"Harrison just happened to be on the floor of the dealership when I came in, and personally offered to see to my needs. Isn't that just so amazing a thing for the owner to do?" She looks at Harrison and makes a wrinkle-nose cutesy face. "He was perfectly delightful company, even drove me home."

Harrison's ears turn boiled-shrimp pink. He knows I know he never personally drives anyone home. He has an assistant grease monkey on standby to do that.

Brandi pats his arm, the one she's linked to. "And what do you think? While I waited he told me all about how awful his life has been since that woman embarrassed him in public."

Harrison winces, so do I, but she just keeps talking. "I mean what sort of woman would turn down a proposal from a man as handsome and sweet and romantic as Harrison?"

Just possibly she doesn't know I'm the cow who jilted the Negotiator. Just possibly he was gentleman enough not to mention that fact. Just possibly I'm not the only one who wishes she'd vanish, and take him with her.

And then I see his face. He said something. The bastard!

For an instant I'm paralyzed. My throat won't work. And though self-protection is urging me to get the hell out of here, my motor skills are stuck in neutral.

But then I've been around long enough not to let even utter humiliation hold sway for long. "I'm sure Harrison would never speak badly of a woman he once hoped to marry." My tone says "let's move this excruciating moment along."

"Well, he wouldn't confide in just anyone." Her tone suggests she had to pry it out of him. "But I can tell by the attention he lavishes on me, his customer, that he must invest a lot of time and care in all his relationships."

"Now, Brandi," Harrison begins, only to be distracted by her patting his arm.

"*Now,* Harrison. I think it's so completely shining armor of you to shield her even now." She turns her babe blues on me. "I mean, who didn't see the news the morning after that woman broke his heart? In public, too."

"I, for one, don't watch sleaze TV." Take that.

Her smile only deepens. "Then you don't know that Harrison bought her an oval diamond engagement ring that was three point eighty-two carats?"

Harrison cocks his chin at an angle that seems to say, *see what you missed?*

I answer with a *big deal* roll of the eyes. Diamonds do not a relationship make. Maybe he's not in on her plan, but clearly she is working up to something nasty that has my name on it.

"So, to make it up to him, and so he won't think all women are so callous, I told Harrison that if he brought his account back to us we'd do a deep discount rate on a new campaign to replace his tarnished 'Negotiator' image."

I stare at her in utter shock. Then emotion floods me. No, *hell* no! Over my dead body! Over his dead body! No, over *her* dead body! But none of these homicidal thoughts escape me, except perhaps as an expression of *what the fook?*

"Maybe this isn't such a good idea." Harrison's voice trails off. Now he's getting the picture.

"Oh, but I promised, and a promise is a promise." She gnaws just half of her lower lip, so the pouty effect is not overshadowed by teeth buffed daily by Opalescence Whitening Toothpaste. I know because she keeps it on the shelf in the employees powder room.

They both stare at me. Okay, let's see what I've got. "Our other clients might object. It might be considered price fixing, or worse. I'd have to get the approval of Ted's attorney." Yes, let's bring Lionel into the conversation. So far, he's the only male I know impervious to her charm.

She turns to him. "If the attorneys don't think it's a good idea then I vow to make up the difference out of my personal account. A woman should stand by her word."

He looks askance. "Oh, no, I couldn't allow that."

You bet your sweet assets he won't! If he thinks I've been a cow about things, he ain't seen nothing yet.

"Harrison is aware of how it would look if he took advantage of Ted's widow." Every ugly suggestive pejorative innuendo I can muster goes into those words. "He's a wealthy man. He can afford our prices. And he knows we'll do him proud." Who said that? *Sheet,* and I was doing so well.

Something flickers in Harrison's eyes, could it be relief? "I really wasn't planning to accept Brandi's offer of a discount. Ted was a good friend. He did a really bang-up job for Luigi's Trattoria near my dealership. That ad was the reason I started going there."

This just goes to show that you can sell anything to the public some of the time.

That's when it strikes me that maybe I do owe Harrison something for the embarrassment I, however unintentionally, caused him. Luring back a campaign for the top luxury car dealer in northern New Jersey would be no small achievement. And we need the work.

I could just spit she thought of it. But the bottom line triumphs.

I smile at him. "Why don't you come into the conference room and let's discuss your needs."

He does a little adjustment of his belt buckle with a hand. "That will be fine."

As he leans down to hear what she's whispering in his ear I notice that he's suspiciously tan where his sport shirt collar gaps away from his neck. This is new, and I should know. I've seen a lot more of him, and thought at the time it was all a little pasty. Did she talk him into a hose-down tan? *Eeeyew!* I shake my head to jog that thought loose.

She giggles and points down the opposite hallway. When he's gone she looks at me. "He needs to water the tulip. Isn't that sweet?"

Just sweetie pie yucky doodle! I don't dare look at her or I might not be able to resist the urge to put both hands around her neck. "I'll be in the conference room."

She calls after me, "You might want to be extra nice. Did you know Harrison gives free lube jobs?"

This isn't as difficult as it would have seemed. Harrison is a decent guy, if a little bit of a predator with attractive women who come into his dealership. Within minutes, Edward, Harrison and I are ready to map out a general strategy. Brandi's playing hostess, offering juice drinks fresh squeezed by her own hands and organic snacks.

I begin with the obvious. "In the past, Harrison, you've played up your deal-making skills. Why not turn the tables and play up the cars? The new campaign needs to be something sustainable yet flexible so that it can change in details over time yet retain its identity."

"Like the bull's-eye that represents Target," Edward offers in explanation.

"Oh, I know that one. Not that I ever shop there," Brandi is quick to say.

"That's called a signifier, a target represents Target," I say to Harrison.

She perks up. "Like Brandi with a ™ over the *i?*"

My opinion of that is best left unsaid. "The kind of campaign I'm thinking of has a theme but with different features highlighted from time to time."

"Kind of a flavor-of-the-week approach." Edward likes sexual suggestions in campaigns. "We could get women with great sexy voices to do the voice-overs."

"And women with sex appeal who drive a Lexus for the TV spots," Brandi suggests with a sly smile.

There's a bit of male-grinning and Brandi-twittering as I try to think of a way to remove myself from the moment. Boys and their toys!

I tap the picture from a Lexus brochure Harrison brought along. "What makes a top-end car buyer pull out his or her credit info? Better yet, what takes any car out of the adequate-to-drive category into a dream ride?"

"The luxury details," Brandi says quickly.

"Engine power," Edward answers.

"The name association," Harrison offers. "And a break on the bottom line."

I shake my head. "Too prosaic. It's something more ethereal, the feeling one hopes to capture in sliding behind the wheel."

I get three puzzled looks. Not good when two of the three are earning a paycheck for this sort of thing.

"How about we call it passion for the sophisticated driver?" I jot that thought down. "Or maybe sophistication for the passionate driver."

"I like that." Harrison looks pleased. "My dealerships are among the first nationwide to get the new limited edition of the GS300. That's because our volume is so high."

No wonder he could afford what had to be at least a ten thousand dollar diamond. "What's so important about the car?" I ask.

"It's the car of the year. The equipment level is so comprehensive that there is no 'options' list. But wait." Harrison suddenly shakes his head. "That won't work. The edition is already fully sold and it hasn't even been shipped."

"No, that's why it could work." I sit up with renewed interest.

"The 'dream car of the passionate driver' is the point of this campaign. But we mustn't actually say this. It must be subtle."

Edward nods. "Like *zoom zoom?*"

"Oh, I love that little boy." It takes so little to make Brandi gush.

I drift off in thought. "What compels the passionate driver to a purchase? Its exclusivity, its luxury… It's the must-have car. What were you saying before, Harrison?" I scramble through my notes until a big smile breaks over my face.

"This is it, our campaign slogan!" I grab a black marker from the pile we lay out for meetings, move to our easel pad. "It's what the passionate driver feels when he sees the right car. There's no doubt. No substitute. There is—" I flip over to a clean sheet and print in bold letters. "No Option!"

"Excellent!" Edward leans forward with a nodding head.

I grin. "We open the campaign with a display of the limited edition of the GS300. Eye candy for all the poor suckers who can only press their noses to the glass at Montclair Lexus, and dream. This is what you *can't* have."

Harrison grins. "Our customers with the back orders will love it."

Edward grins. "Layout ideas are unreeling in my head."

"Take them and run."

Feeling pretty pleased, I turn to Harrison. "We'll follow that ad up quickly with information about cars that are available. But we need to be careful. What's so good about second best? What will the other guy settle for?"

"The standard GS300 has an all-wheel-drive system featuring a planetary gear set and a wet, multidisk clutch to couple the primary drive wheels, at the rear, to the front."

"That's not exactly what I'm talking about."

"We want to hear about all the sexy bits," Brandi offers with a quite suggestive laugh. She reaches out a hand that stays on his arm.

Not wanting to lose Harrison's attention, I point to the words I've written. "What's available for that car that's on the no-options list in the limited edition?"

"Well, there's a comprehensive air bag system available, plus bags dedicated to knee preservation for the driver and front passenger. Also a new optional 'precollision system' that uses adaptive cruise-control radar to evaluate closing speeds and decide whether collision is imminent, in which case it cinches seat belts and pre-initializes the brake system for quicker response."

"What about the interior?" Brandi pats his arm. "I just love luxury interiors. They really should make mink seat covers."

Harrison's gaze shifts to her. "We have wood trim in golden bird's-eye maple, black bird's-eye maple or red walnut, depending on interior leather color." He rubs his chin while trying to think of sexy bits, other than the one by his side. No doubt because *she* pats his arm each time he names an option.

"When the keyless entry is activated, door handles as well as puddle lamps under the side mirrors light up."

"Love that." *Pat*.

"There's a push-button start ignition, no key required."

"Very cool." *Pat*.

"Oh, the Mark Levinson Premium Surround Sound Audio System has fourteen speakers."

"Sweet!" she chirps. *Pat, pat!*

Given this kind of encouragement what man wouldn't go for the gold? Harrison's voice rises in tone and intensity.

"There's a voice-activated Lexus DVD Navigation System with auditory and visual cues. Tiny lens at the rear of the vehicle transmits a wide-angle color image to your NAV screen so you can see behind you better than in a rearview mirror."

"How cool is that?" Brandi shifts to the forearm squeeze, crimping his jacket sleeve. "I may have to trade up."

Harrison is flushed-up happy. "With Bluetooth technology you can find a location even if you don't have an address. It enables the NAV system to search by importing the location's phone number directly from your compatible cell phone."

"Stalkers don't usually buy Lexuses, I suppose." Okay, my comment wasn't worth the effort but I had to say something. Harrison is getting glassy-eyed from all the touching and patting.

"How about rain-sensing variable intermittent windshield wipers with mist control, headlamp washers...?"

"Okay, Harrison!" I put up my hands. If she touches him one more time I may have to roll up my notes and swat *her* on the nose. "We get the picture and more important, your customers and potential customers will. That's enough for today. Edward and I have plenty to work with. Give us time to go with the ideas and get back to you in, say, a week."

"This is so exciting!" Brandi practically levitates from her chair. "Harrison, you're a natural at PR. You practically wrote your own campaign."

Harrison beams like a champ after a TKO. "Guess I'm better at this than I thought. 'No Option.' I like it."

"You should. You thought it up," she assures him. "Didn't he, Liz?"

Now, wait a minute. I'm supposed to let Harrison think that my ideas were his? That sounds like one of Ted's tactics. He'd consider that damn clever PR strategy. Even if it diminished my contribution.

Boy! You think you understand your life and then the mirror falls off the wall, giving you a whole other view. I am good, no, really good at what I'm doing. And that made Ted a teeny bit jealous.

"You were a great help, Harrison." I offer him a sincere smile. "If you'll excuse me, I'm going to go and put your money to good use with my time and my expertise. Brandi will be in touch to talk with you about contracts in a few days."

Brandi gives me a sudden fierce look as I head out the door.

Let her struggle through the legalese of the contract I'm going to spend the night preparing instead of sleeping. With luck, she'll pat him into signing it sight unseen.

I'm not jealous. Instead, as I slide into my new cream leather office chair, delivered this morning, I'm comparing her total hotness performance to my actions the first time I met Marcus.

Did I seem that obvious, that eager to make physical contact? Did I fiddle with my earring; repeatedly gloss my hair back with a slow sweep of my hand? Or cross and uncross my legs until the friction of nylon on nylon could have set off sparks? Yes, I probably did. The truth is, when a woman is deeply attracted to a man her actions go on automatic pilot.

And I'm deeply attracted to Marcus, even if he did bypass No-Bagel Emporium. Come to think of it, he never gave me a satisfactory explanation as to why.

We sort of got sidetracked.

I can't imagine what his report must have been when he returned from the field in September.

Nice woman, decent bread. But she's not focused, impulsive. Don't think we can risk our organic bread future on a woman who knocks back martinis while trying to seduce the business rep.

$\mathcal{S}$ince bringing back North Jersey Lexus as an account, Brandi's been feeling her Wheaties. Make that her wheat germ funny-smelling blue-green algae smoothie pick-me-ups she peddles to the staff for high energy performance. I won't touch the stuff.

But she is so gung-ho that she even talked Harrison into allowing her to pose for the premier "No Options" print ad.

She's hijacked the staff meeting with the news. The print shoot is scheduled for next Tuesday, in order to take advantage of an auto insert in the weekend newspapers.

"Using a real person says so much about the attainability of one's dreams." Brandi pauses to give us a Paris Hilton pose. "Everyone knows a celebrity gets paid to say she or he likes something, even if it's not true. But a real person, well, that's from the heart."

"It's an interesting concept." I'm feeling unusually diplomatic toward her. "But launching a modeling career so soon after your bereavement might not be well received by the public."

"Teddy would want me to stay busy." She says this with the kind of passion that sweeps lesser emotions before it. "Getting directly involved with the agency makes me feel like I'm still connected to him."

Amazingly Edward, Paul and even Suzi nod in agreement. But they all drink her funky Kool-Aid.

I'm sure the fact that the budget for the first "No Option" shoot includes a stylist, makeup and hair personnel, plus a wardrobe allowance, has nothing to do with her decision. She is wearing rhinestone-pocket pink jeans, rhinestone flip-flops and carrying a pink Crystal Suede Shopper on a November morning.

"What about conflict of interest?" I turn to Edward, expecting he will have to admit to that objection.

"I don't see any," says the traitor. "It'll be great PR for Talbot Advertising. Shows our commitment to the customer is not confined to ideas. We're so certain of our work that we're not afraid to put a personal stamp on the campaign. It's brilliant!"

"Fabulous!" Suzi echoes.

"Sweet!" declares Paul.

Whatever.

When I swallow my pride, ignore the irksome factor of her presence, try to be objective, I can almost tolerate the idea of Brandi being useful. But mostly I wish she'd go back to her tanning salons and leave the agency to me.

But she won't, and so we keep fielding "Brandi's finds." She doesn't understand our need to screen prospective clients. She tells any and all she meets to drop in for a demonstration of what we can do for their school, business, team, club, et cetera. As if dreaming up a PR campaign is what we routinely do before we are hired by the client.

By the end of the week I'm not sure that saving this company is worth it.

Worst interview of the week? The Monleigh-Exeter girls lacrosse team. My clients were a pair of juniors from the local prep school who didn't understand why we wouldn't print posters of their lacrosse team posed provocatively in Fergie of the Black-eyed Peas nano-mini skirts. What was wrong with looking like an ad for an R-rated jailbait skin flick? Our attorney could tell them. It is spelled l-i-a-b-i-l-i-t-y.

The girls were equally underwhelmed by my suggestions, and freely expressed their opinion of our alternate ideas for a poster.

"It sucks."

"Sucky."

"Now that's jacked up."

"Sucks, major!"

This from juvenile Cameron Diaz and Lucy Liu look-alikes.

"I'll get my brother to do the posters," "Cameron" finally said to "Lucy." "He's got a Canon 20D digital camera and access to a major Colortrac 5480e scanner on his campus. He'll make hot posters, for free!"

Their parents will be so proud.

At least when Shemar checks in it's to say things are going well at the bakery. He's decided to go ahead with his plans for Halloween.

He tells me he and Desharee have been practicing with batches of sourdough. They've worked up an assortment of bats, spiders, cats, ghosts, snakes and piranhas with saw-edge teeth. "Some jamming freakizoid dough monsters. We'll be steady stackin' this Halloween, Miz T. For real."

Why not? What could it hurt?

TGIF! In fact, after a quick check of my mail, I'm heading out to Liberty Outlet Mall in Flemington. I've been paid! I'm going shopping for clothes, real grown-up clothing with upscale labels and this season's styling.

I thought of asking Sally if she'd like to supervise my first real foray into clothing in four years. Before I could decide, Riley called with the latest bulletin from the Manhattan high-rise set. It seems when Tony dropped by to see Sally the day after our evening at Juniper Suite there was a row of proportions that prompted her co-op board to call an emergency session. Sally is now on probation, not good advertising for her real estate business.

So I'm going solo. Leaving my office with a swing in my step and joy in my heart!

"Oh, wait, Liz," Nancy says as she sees me headed toward the door.

I put a finger to my lips. "No, Nancy. You don't really see me. I'm already gone." I move rapidly toward the exit.

"Stop!" Nancy glances down, running her finger over the day's appointment book. "You have a ten-thirty and then an eleven-forty-five with new clients."

I pivot smoothly on one heel and opposite toe the way Sally

taught me at age four. "I didn't make any appointments for today."

"Brandi did, but she won't be in."

"Then reschedule them for her for Monday."

"She called and said she had a personal emergency. And she won't be back until at least midweek."

"I hope it's not family." She could have one. I just never thought of her as actually connected to anyone but other women's husbands.

"Actually, she said it was more of a tanning crisis."

I retrace my steps to her desk. "Did you say tanning crisis?"

Nancy nods. "She said she needs authenticity in her work so she's gone to Miami for a long weekend to 'catch a few rays' before filming the TV ad." Nancy leans forward and lowers her voice. "I suspect there's more to it because she was very evasive when Edward asked her where she was staying, in case we needed to check with her about Tuesday."

"Really?" I know we are both thinking the same thing: there must be a man involved.

"She told him to call her cell, but only in an emergency, if we really need her."

She could move to Miami permanently, the agency needs her so much.

"Better reschedule all her appointments for the next week, then."

Nancy looks doubtful. "Mr. Rybezynski has already called to confirm. He sounded stoked about the meeting."

"Then Edward can handle him." I see her reach for the office phone. "Don't bother, I'll tell him."

Edward is not happy about my decision. He's pushing papers around on his desk and not meeting my gaze. "I can't keep fielding these cold calls from Brandi's acquaintances. It's embarrassing."

"I agree. But I'm the boss, and I elect you to pinch hit today. I have plans."

"You were right. She doesn't have a professional bone in her body." He shoves a hand through his well-behaved hair and leaves crooked rows of exasperation. "She makes us sound as if we're a home-party business and she's selling plastic kitchenware. 'Oh yes, you must drop by. We have so many new and lovely items for sale. Buy several and get a bonus.'" His mimicry of her is dead-on.

I chuckle but he's not smiling. "We've got to do something about her, Liz."

"Take your complaints to her. She likes you."

He pinkens. "That's kind of an issue, too."

"Your wife?"

He nods. "Deirdre can't stand her. Not since she saw the sketches for the new Lexus ad I brought home."

I smirk. "I saw it."

The idea of your husband working in close proximity with a known home wrecker who's about to lounge provocatively on the hood of a limited edition GS300 in the little red patent leather skirt that barely covers the essentials is bound to raise any wife's blood pressure. Perhaps I should cut Edward some slack.

"Just for today, I'll take the ten o'clock. You get the eleven-forty-five. When she comes back you tell her that she is not allowed to make business appointments without checking with you first."

Edward says nothing but looks really pained. Being the boss has its privileges.

It's twenty-five minutes past ten and I'm out the door. Don't know what happened to Mr. Rybezynski and don't care. I'm so anxious to shop till I drop that I practically slam into the man in a quilted down vest who's coming in as I go out.

"Sorry." He's curt almost to the point of anger as he brushes past me.

"And a sweet good morning to you, too," I say, and shift my purse strap back up onto my shoulder. He doesn't even grunt.

His hostility makes me pause and glance back through the glass door to watch as he marches up to Nancy's desk. One can never be too careful these days. Crazies come in all sorts of packages.

He says something loud enough for me to hear the impatient tone through the glass. Nancy shakes her head. He slaps both hands on her desk, obviously making a demand. She's shrugs, expression apologetic, and points to the clock on the wall. He thumps her desk. She stands up. He's gesticulating. She looks past him, sees me staring at them through the glass, and—uh-oh—points at me. Damn. That must be Rybezynski.

He whips around and sees me.

I push the door open and reenter, determined to be pleasant but firm. He's late. I'm busy. Make another appointment with Brandi.

"Yes, may I help you?" Now that I get a look at him, crossing over to me, he's not as rough as his tone of voice first suggested. A thick shock of dark hair rises up from a very pointed widow's peak in a face that, while not handsome, isn't unpleasant.

"I'm Sam Rybezynski." He doesn't offer me his hand, which means he's royally pissed. There are deep furrows in his brow. "I have an appointment with Mrs. Talbot. But you're not her."

"Hello, Mr. Rybezynski. You're late." I say this in the coolest possible tone and I don't offer my hand, either. "And you're mistaken. I am Mrs. Talbot. Mrs. Liz Talbot."

He looks sheepish. "I beg your pardon. I'm here to see Brandi Talbot."

"Unfortunately, she's out for the week."

His face loses any hint of congeniality. "What do you mean, out for the week? I called this morning to verify my appointment. Nobody said anything about Brandi being out. She—" he points at Nancy "—assured me my appointment would be kept."

"And I would have seen to it personally had you been on time." Actually he is sort of attractive—dark hair, hazel eyes, deep-chested—if one discounts his bear-with-a-sore-paw attitude. "But as you have just seen I'm on my way to another appointment."

"Lunch?" He smears enough sarcasm on the word to raise the hair on my nape.

"As is happens, Mr. Rybezynski, I have another business to run." Obviously news of my shopping spree isn't going to impress him. "And I'm late."

"Whoa, wait!" He takes a step after me as I turn toward the door. "You can't do this to me. I had to rearrange a lot of things to get here. And I drove over an hour in traffic."

"I'm not impressed. You are more than thirty minutes late. My time is valuable, too."

He folds his arms across his chest. The sleeves of his shirt are a little short and ride up to reveal well-developed forearms lightly sprinkled with dark hair. But those hands! Is that grease under his nails?

He notices my staring, unfolds his arms and puts his hands behind his back. "I hadda change a flat on 78."

"You have a cell phone?"

He reddens a bit. "Sure."

"You might have called."

"I didn't have the number." But he doesn't sound completely convincing. "Look, I'm sorry I'm late. I changed the tire myself and thought I'd make up the time but I took a wrong turn. This is not my stomping ground."

"Really?" Didn't call because he didn't want to admit he got lost. At least that explains the grotty hands. "Where did you drive in from?"

"Basking Ridge. I own a small French restaurant there. Brandi and a friend came in for dinner one night last week and spoke with our maître d'. She convinced him that this was the best advertising agency for independent restaurants in northern New Jersey. So here I am." He folds his arms across his chest once more. "Knock my socks off."

That's when I catch a faint whiff of—him. He's a nice cross between fresh basil, lemongrass and, yes, grease. He is not only the owner, he's the chef, or spends enough time in his kitchen to qualify as the genuine article.

"Very well, Mr. Rybezynski, since you came all this way." I

put my purse down and take off my coat and sit on one of the unoccupied chairs in our empty waiting area. "You have fifteen minutes. Tell me what you think we can do for you."

"Uh-uh." He shakes his head and glances at a wristwatch face the size of Cleveland, but he can carry it. "My time is expensive and you gotta give me more than fifteen minutes."

"I really do have another appointment. Can you come back at, say, two o'clock?"

He shakes his head. "I've got to meet a pickup at Newark airport at two. You wouldn't believe what customs can do to truffles if you're not there to watch. So, I tell you what I'm going to do."

He reaches in his breast pocket and pulls out a card and pen, and scribbles something on the back. "You want my business, you come to see me Sunday night at seven, and we'll discuss it then." He holds out the card.

I don't take it. "I have plans Sunday evening."

"I do half million dollars gross a quarter, and I'd like to expand. I'm prepared to throw some decent business your way if you impress me. You want the job or not?"

I pluck the card from his hand. "Seven, did you say?"

He grins, and it's a nice smile. One would think he was civilized. "We're a classy place." He gives me the briefest of once-overs. "Wear something nice."

I check out the card he's handed me, with a smudged oil thumbprint, and then allow my skepticism to show as I give him the once-over, from his L.L. Bean storm chaser boots to his down vest. "Arnaud's?"

He grins. "Would you drop a wad at a French restaurant named Sam's?"

Chapter 21

$\mathcal{I}$have been waiting for an excuse to wear the lovely chrome-yellow suede pumps with the rounded toes Sally sent me. Now I have one. Dinner at Arnaud's.

Even so, I wouldn't want Mr. Rybezynski to think I was trying to impress him. So the shoes are paired with a brand-new black cashmere sweater and my tried-and-true gray flannel slacks. For warmth I add the grey pashmina opera stole Sally gave me last Christmas. Those chrome-yellow suede pumps from Kate Spade make it all seem fresh.

Not sure I should have agreed to drive so far for an evening meeting on my own I have enlisted Celia's aid.

When I locate the restaurant, I'm a little dismayed. The lights are on inside the French-blue awning storefront that has a simple tasteful sign reading Arnaud's hanging out front. But there's not a single patron inside.

Someone notices me peering in and comes to unlock the door.

"You came. Come on in." It's Sam. And he's in a tux and looks, wow!

Once inside I look about. "Where's your usual clientele?"

"It's Sunday." He's smiling a little too hard. Is it nerves, or a barracuda grin? "We're closed on Sunday."

"Most restaurants close on Monday." I watch as he relocks the door then say, "You said this was a business meeting."

"It is. Sort of. I didn't want us to have any interruptions."

"People know where I am, and with whom."

He nods. "I know you are a smart lady. Don't worry. This isn't anything shady."

He comes up to me with both hands outstretched. "I closed the place in your honor. You can't represent us if you don't know what we serve and how we serve it. So I've arranged for you to sample our menu without distraction. Afterward, you can work up a presentation to show me."

"I'm not sure this is the best idea." I back up a couple of steps, noting the keys are still in the lock. "We should have the full creative staff here for something like that."

"You want a chaperon?" He looks up over his shoulder. "Derek, Jake, Sasha. Come out front. Now!"

The imperative tone of voice brings three people dressed in chefs' uniforms hurrying out from the kitchen.

Sam scowls. "Where's Dimitri?"

"Just here, Mr. Rybezynski."

A small narrow man dressed as the maître d' comes forward from the direction of the bar. "At your service, Mrs. Talbot." There's a slight accent in his speech I can't readily place. "May I show madam to her table?"

My cell rings. It's Celia. "You okay?"

"I'm fine, thanks. I'll call you later."

I glance at Sam, who winks at me. "Satisfied you're safe with me?"

"Yes, thank you."

I'm ushered to a table set for a special occasion. There are silver roses, white tapers, and the crispest, whitest linens I've seen in a long time.

Once I'm seated with the customary flourish of the napkin settled in my lap, Sam pulls up his chair as if he's about to sit in on a hot poker game. "I should apologize for my manners yesterday."

"Yes, you should." He looks a bit annoyed that I'm not melted into acquiescence by the trouble he's gone to.

He looks at me as if sizing up the opposition. "You're kind of tough, aren't you?"

"Did you really expect I'd just smile and say, 'Oh no, that's okay, you didn't really insult me'?"

"Maybe. So, if I was to tell you that you don't need to be tough no more tonight, would you listen?"

I shrug. "One should always listen to good advice."

He wags a finger at me. "You and me. I don't know what it is but it's something. You gotta stick around until I figure it out, okay?"

"I'd be more likely to follow that advice if I were, say, sipping a glass of wine."

He flicks a finger at the waiter hovering. "What do you want? It's on the house. Whiskey? Champagne?"

"How about we start slow? A glass of Shiraz."

He grins and nods at the waiter. Then he leans forward and folds his arms on the tabletop. "I like that. Start slow. Then you got options, eh?"

I smile.

"You're going to get the chef's sampling, a little of our best cuisine." He pauses. "You okay with that?"

"Sounds wonderful."

"Okay." He rubs his hands together, then signals to his head waiter. "Dimitri, get on it. Serve it just like I wrote it."

He looks back at me. "You wanna pace yourself. We're going to start you with scallop mousseline with dill sauce, cresson and chicory salad, then shrimps in a cognac sauce and a pâté of baby vegetables with a fresh tomato relish. Dimitri will take care of the wine selection. You okay with that?"

"Absolutely." I'm glad I wore trousers with a little room in the waistband.

The wine is served, opened and tasted by Sam. When we are served he lifts his glass. "To a genuine classy lady. And there're not as many of them as they'd like to make out. I know."

We clink glasses and I take a sip.

And just like that, I'm having a very nice time.

Maybe this is just for my benefit as half owner of Talbot Advertising. But then, I should be courting his business, not the other way around. So this is his apology. I must admit, I'd never had nicer. And I'm not slow. He's interested in me, which is flattering. There's something of the lust of life in him, and it's attractive.

Even so, Sam isn't exactly what I'd call choice partner material. He begins by telling me he's been married, "Three, four times, if you count making the same mistake twice. But Anna is the mother of my boys. Still, a man's gotta have his head up his ass—excuse my French—to wanna deal with that kinda irritation twice. Know what I'm saying?"

"I'll keep that in mind."

"What about you? I didn't know about the, you know, two Mrs. Talbots."

"You're forgiven. I'm the first and ex. Brandi's the second. We inherited joint ownership of the ad agency at Ted's death."

"You lie! He left it to the pair of you? And you accepted that? He musta been some kinda man."

"No, the usual bastard sort."

"Guilt made him do it, huh? I get some of that myself. Still, that'd make a movie. So what, you left him? Or did Brandi wiggle her nice little ass at him first?"

"You're losing the ground you gained with me, just so you know."

"Nawgh! Some women use their heads, some their asses. There are men who prefer one over the other, but enough to go around. Natural selection, right?" He shrugs. "But what do I know about women? I got half a dozen who can't hear my name without calling me everything but a child of God."

"I can't possibly understand why."

He laughs as though I've said the funniest thing he's heard in a month. "I like you. You don't back down, and you aren't out to impress."

That could be a backhanded compliment but I'm in much too

good a mood to care. I know I look as good as I can. And that ain't no small potatoes, as Sam would put it.

The food. Let me just say that it's this surprising: I've never had better food in my life. This is genuine French cuisine with all its butter and cream and sauce, and panache.

It's been forever since I sampled everything a professional kitchen has to offer. Ted didn't like dining at a restaurant's kitchen table where you watch the food being prepared and sample orders. He said he felt like he was eating with the help. Sigh.

After five samples of the first course, I can't believe there's more to come. I want to stop right here, polish off these plates and—

"Hello? Yes, Celia, I'm fine. Really fine. You don't need to— Okay. If you want." I hang up and smile.

Sam nods. "You got people looking out for you. That's good. A beautiful woman alone, anything could happen, and sometimes does. You tell her I said good for her."

Okay, I have to point out the obvious. "You're not French."

He laughs and all but slaps his knee. "Me, I'm Italian and Polish. Grew up in the Bronx."

What a surprise. "So then, what brought you to this?"

"The merchant marines. After finishing high school I wanted to travel and see the world. Only I wasn't so hot to carry a gun while I was doing it. So I graduated from Kings Point first, then I saw the world. But most of the time, I was at sea. And let me tell you that can be all kinds of boring. One time we had a Cordon Bleu chef on board to break up the monotony. He took a shine to me because I liked to drop by the galley and ask lots of questions. One thing led to another and pretty soon when I was off duty I was cooking with him. I had practically a whole year of courses. I coulda gone for a diploma but what would that look like, a seaman in a chef's hat? So, when I left the service, I vowed to hire the best chef of cuisine I could find and open a real French restaurant. It took a while to get going, what with the wives, and all. A wife doesn't want to live frugal while her husband wines and dines them that's got. Know what I mean? So, there are you. No wives but one hell of a kitchen staff."

I nod in sympathy as the next set of courses begins arriving. Foodies understand that there are simply too few pleasures in life to rival a truly excellently prepared meal using the best ingredients.

Soon, we're busy swapping recipes and stories of good meals as we sample our way through many dishes and several wines. The evening passes quickly. By the time I'm cleansing my palate with a champagne sorbet, I've begun to think Sam's rough edges are just a front to keep anyone from thinking he's hiding his Bronx roots.

"So what do you think?"

I roll my eyes and kiss my fingertips à la Maurice Chevalier. "Where do I begin? The salmon quenelles were excellent. The Tasmanian sea trout with grapefruit and ginger, wow! The duck with green olives, really remarkable. The lamb with cumin crust, divine. The crabs in ginger, I would order every time. The sugar snap peas with champagne dressing, who knew? The quail and star anise, unprecedented. The roasted asparagus with black truffles, and fricassée de champignons des bois, quite delicious. Ah, *la piece de résistance,* the tarte tatin?" I kiss my fingertips again. *"C'est tres bon!"*

"What do you mean?"

As if he doesn't understand. "The caramelized apple torte was perfection."

He scowls. "No. That's not right. Something's wrong. You're holding back and that don't do me no favors. I put two hundred and ten dollars' worth of food before you, not counting the wine. You should be shattered." He searches my face. "You aren't shattered."

"Nothing's wrong exactly." I look for the proper way to say it and then, what, he can't take it? "It's more like a few details are not up to the level of the rest of the service." I pick up a leftover roll. "It's this. You use frozen dough."

He grins. "Just for the bread basket. How do you know?"

"It's my business to know. I'm a baker. I own the No-Bagel Emporium."

"So, and what, you make the bread in your spare time?"

"You bet I do. The best in northern New Jersey."

He rears back in his chair and claps his hands. "A kindred spirit. I knew there was something about you. You and me, we got food on the brain and in the blood. We're gonna have a really good time, you and me."

He leans forward so that his chair smacks the floor hard enough to crack the rails. "Only tell me this. That best-in-northern-New Jersey thing you said. I've seen that slogan some-where. That your place?"

"No." But the fact that Sam knows about the West Orange Bakery rankles.

"So, what? You make better bread?"

"Any day of the week."

"What restaurants do you supply?"

"None in this area."

"So, you think I should buy from you?"

"I didn't say that. That would be another conversation for another day. Tonight, I'm here representing Talbot Advertising. I don't this want to be a conflict of interest."

"'Cause you got ethics."

"Something like that."

He smiles. "I like you."

I pick up my wine. "It's mutual. Now, shall we talk business?"

He picks up his wineglass and clinks it against mine. "If you insist. But I'd rather feed you dark chocolate mousse. 'Cause, you know, you got my business."

By the time I'm ready to leave, and Celia is calling for the sixth time, Sam simply takes the phone out of my hand.

"Hi, Celia. Sam here. She's fine. More than fine. You got one great gal for a friend. She's feeling a little happy with wine so I'm gonna drive her home. Of course, to her house. What do you think?"

He scowls at the unseen Celia. "You don't need to say that, you know. Why do you think I'm talking to you? That's better. Okay, I'm gonna drive her car, my head waiter's gonna follow us, and I'll ride back with him."

He rolls his eyes in exasperation. "You do what you gotta do. We can meet tonight or tomorrow at the No-Bagel Emporium when I come to make my restaurant order. On second thought. You call those bakers tonight. Tell them I need three dozen baguettes for in the morning. You heard me. And the three dozen, it's a standing order, Tuesday through Sunday." He winks at me.

"You're right, I'm a good guy. Now, you go back to bed, Celia. Your boss is in good hands. Yes, safe hands."

He hands me back the phone. "She's a regular barracuda, that one."

I'm in an excellent mood when I wake up the next morning. Stellar mood, actually.

Sam asked me out. We're going to a Devils game Saturday night. He has box seats and he said he can't give the tickets away. Would I like to join him?

I probably should have said no. But he seems the kind of client who likes to show off, and I learned from Ted that if you thwart that kind of client too often you won't have him long. So I told him I'd have some preliminary plans for us to go over at that time, just to keep business on the table.

Marcus hasn't called. He told me it could be a while. I'm a big girl. I'm not holding my breath. But I wish he would call, soon.

There are three messages on my answering service I neglected to listen to the night before.

Call number one is from Riley. She wants me to come into the city tonight to watch her in the first of her show's previews, and then bunk in at her place.

I'm torn. The last time I bunked in at her place, which she nominally shares with two other girls, there were nine of us. Two boyfriends, plus some out-of-town friends of friends. Frankly, I'm too old to sleep on a blanket spread upon a suspicious floor only to wake up to the sight of unknown bare male buttocks lit by a fridge as some guy searches for a hit to satisfy his middle-of-the-night munchies habit.

Before I can move to the next message, Riley calls to tell me that Sally agreed to come to the rehearsal.

"You did warn her about the nudity?"

"That's what decided her, Mom."

Of course. So why doesn't the promise of lithe nude males move me to equal exertion? They will be cavorting with my equally unclothed daughter, that's why.

"You have Sally for preview night. How about I wait for opening night?" By then Sally will have filled me in, in great detail, on the parts where I need to avert my motherly gaze.

Surprisingly, Riley thinks this is a good idea. "Sarah says she'll wait for our opening, too."

Message number two is from Sarah. *"Hi, Mom. Call me."*

I dial.

"Where were you last night?" is her opening gambit. She's going to make a wonderful parent.

"Sorry, I had a business dinner last night."

"With a man?" See what I mean?

"Yes. I didn't tell Riley because she will tell Sally and, well, you know how Sally will respond. It wasn't a date."

"Who is he?"

"A restaurant owner and potential client."

"He must be single if you're worried about Sally's response. That's great, really great, Mom." Sarah sounds like me when the subject of a call is her date, positive but reserved. "Why not bring him to Riley's opening?"

"I'm trying to win his business for the agency. I'm certainly not going to invite him to ogle one of my daughters starkers."

"I suppose you're right. Suppose I shouldn't have invited Ed."

"Who's Ed?"

"Someone from work."

"The junior partner someone?"

"Maybe." Sarah's reluctant to say more but I can tell she's happy about what she's not saying. "So how are things at Talbot's going?"

I have deliberately not talked with my daughters about my life with *her*. But Riley did catch me midweek and I let slip a few things. "Have you talked to Riley?"

"Riley's not fit to speak to. When I said good luck last night, she nearly came after me through the phone. I forgot about the good-luck vs. break-a-leg tradition."

"She's just nervous."

"She's a mess. She and this guy named Sakdu, who sounds like a really horrible person, were not speaking to each other, at the top of their lungs. He was yelling in some foreign language. She kept interrupting me to tell him to stick it. When I said something about him being a jerk, she said he was wonderful and stay out of her life. Really, how could you have produced such different daughters, not to mention at the same time?"

"Just lucky, I guess. Love you. See you soon."

So there's a Sakdu in Riley's life who cares enough to yell. That could be a good sign. Usually Riley has to supply all the emotional life for both parties.

And Sarah is seeing Ed, whoever that is. More good news.

And I've got new business on two fronts, thanks to Sam, plus a personal life that's looking up. Could the day get any better?

Message number three is from Marcus.

"Liz, sorry I haven't called, and the timing could be better. We need to talk about something that's come up. I'll be in your area next weekend. We'll talk then." There's a pause. *"This didn't have to happen if just once we could sit and talk. Just talk."* He chuckles. *"What the hell am I saying? I'm on the road. I'll call you."*

I listen to the message twice more before I save it. He sounds like a man with a fairly high level of sexual frustration. Poor baby.

Chapter 22

It occurs to me that it's been two weeks since I set foot inside the No-Bagel Emporium. Before that, I hadn't missed more than a day or two at a time. How could events at Talbot's have so completely embroiled me that I'd forget to drop by the most important thing in my life?

That question gives me the same uneasy sensation I had when I was eight years old and found my goldfish floating belly up in the bowl because I neglected to feed it for a week.

No, no reason to panic. Business is up. Shemar called on Saturday with the week's tally. Halloween weekend alone pushed us up by fifteen percent for the quarter so far. He's doing a great job.

Still, something could be going wrong that only the owner

would recognize. Businesses are like fine old cars, they have to be monitored, constantly tweaked and babied along.

At the last second I take an exit into a jug-handle turn that has the man behind me shouting abuse as he passes.

How could I have left Shemar with so much responsibility? He's a great second in command but he's always counted on me to be the leader and make the big decisions. My support and guidance is the least I can offer in return for his loyalty.

A quick call to Nancy at the agency is all it takes to free me up until noon. Who knows what problems the bakery is having, or how long it may take to sort it out? Poor Shemar. Why didn't he call for help?

My usual spot on the side of the bakery is available. The aging brick facade of No-Bagel Emporium reminds me that soon enough money will be in the bank to start renovating. That should cause business to pick up. Yet once I turn the corner I scarcely recognize my bakery sidewalk. A dozen baby strollers are chained to the protective metal fences around the trees along the curb.

We've never been big on the preschool mommies' circuit, catering more to the business and gym world. But as I peer through the front glass into the interior, it's plain to see that this morning the nine o'clock crowd at No-Bagel Emporium is predominately stroller mommies. And we're just about packed. Maybe someone's having a birthday breakfast. That would be a novel event.

In my eagerness to get inside I almost stumble over the new sandwich board outside the entrance. My gaze latches onto the essentials. It advertises new hours. The No-Bagel Emporium is now open Monday through Thursday from three to five, exclusively for the after-school set. Pastries, drinks and slices of focaccia are half price. Students must have a student ID to get in. Hmm, that will never work.

I brace myself and push open the door. It sounds like a daycare inside, a happy daycare. While mommies gather at the tables drinking lattes and chai teas, kiddies munch on what look like soft pretzels or zoom around in a cordoned off area full of soft toys, gigantic foam puzzles pieces and plastic building blocks. Definitely, this is new.

It's easy to walk up to the cash register and surprise Celia, who is counting change. "Is this a private party?"

Celia squeals in delight and rounds the counter to give me a big long-lost-friend hug. I guess it has been a while.

"No party." Celia sounds breathless with joy. "This has been the usual morning crowd for the past week. Every since our Halloween ghoul breads were a hit, we've been featuring a different bread animal every weekday for the kiddies. It's packing in the mommies whose kids are too young for fast-food play places. What do you think?"

I'm not sure yet. "Whose idea was this? Yours?"

"Not me. Shemar. That young man is really talented. He's making lots of changes."

"I see." Good changes. Happy changes. Why am I not feeling the thrill?

Just then Shemar comes out of the back in a T-shirt emblazoned with a bagel stamped with a red No symbol over it. The word *emporium* is written in fancy script beneath. "Miz T! How's the advertising business?"

"Not as much fun as this."

A big proud grin stretches his face. "Yeah. What do you think?"

"Looks like you're on to something. But aren't our pastry doughs a little rich for two-year-old tummies?" Okay, I'm looking for flaws.

"Got it covered. Rodrigo gave me some health specs on nutrition for the shorties. Desharee's sister is a social worker who's specialty is childhood diabetics. We had her check out the nutrition issues, too. Now we're baking with my own special creation for the ankle-biters. It's a low-salt, low-sugar whole wheat pretzel dough. We work it into everything from snakes to spiders to kites to butterflies. The older ones can get fruit-juice icing, raisin-cream cheese dip or granola sprinkles."

"Tell her the rest." Celia beams at Shemar as if he were her own star pupil. "Shemar suggested to Rodrigo that he begin an 8:30 a.m. exercise class for moms with toddlers. We created a punch-card system. Moms get a discount here when they attend the classes."

"One hand washes the other," Shemar says with a grin. "Like a mutual-benefit thing. Aw-ite?"

"I'm impressed." I am. But I'm also feeling something not altogether positive or nice roiling though me and try to squelch it. "What about the new hours?"

Shemar looks sideways and strokes his chin whiskers with thumb and forefinger. "It's like this. I was looking to clear our shelves at the end of the day. Desharee happens to mention DeVon's been doing business in day-old pastries on the corner near the high school. So I checked it out, and the girl's Gospel."

"He's been selling our pastry instead of taking it to the soup kitchen, and pocketing the money?" There! See, that's what happens when the boss takes her eye off the ball.

"Not to worry, Miz T. DeVon and me had that discussion. I told him to find another way to make some bank, and then I cut him a fiver to drop flyers by school cafeterias in the area. From three to five we cater strictly to junior and senior high. You got to be twelve to get in and no more than seventeen, with ID. DeVon does the carding at the door. We don't allow no drugs, no madness, no cussing. The bucket made us a Hamilton the first day. Since then, we keep out those known to mix it up, know what I'm saying?"

As he says that, a younger child in a stroller screams in dismay. A second later a little boy of about three streaks past holding a bird-shaped pretzel over his head.

Quick as he is casual, Shemar scoops up the little thief by his underarms and lifts him shoulder high. "We don't roll that way up in here. You feeling me?"

The little boy starts kicking so Shemar hauls him in until they are nose to nose. "We…don't…roll…that…way…up…in… here." He says each word distinctly in his deepest voice. "You…feeling…me?"

The child has gone limp. The only part to move is his nodding head.

Shemar puts him down gently and turns him toward his mother, who is coming our way. He gives the child a little push. "Give back what you took, then ask your mama for something if you want it."

The little boy races past his mother's outspread arms to hand the pretzel back to the child he took it from. Then he turns to his mother. "I want a bird pretzel like Charlie's!"

Shemar nods. "Another satisfied customer."

Celia and I exchange impressed glances.

Shemar turns back to me. "What was I saying? Oh, yeah. We're busting business so bad, I have to make extra pastries just to have leftovers for the afternoon."

This explains why business is up fifteen percent the first two weeks of the month. Who am I to quibble about the costs of extra utilities and wages? However…

"Those shirts must cost something." It took me a moment to notice that beneath her cheese apron, Celia, too, is wearing one.

"It's a marketing tool, Miz T." Shemar smiles. "Desharee's got a boo that works at a T-shirt printer stall in the mall. We pitched in for the cost of the shirts from a discount place. Desharee did the design." He grins and rubs his shirtfront. "The girl's got skills. Her boo took care of the printing costs of the first batch. We sell them for ten dollars. Ka-*ching!* Let me get you one while Celia makes you a latte. On the house."

I'm being treated as a guest, if an honored guest, in my own shop.

I follow Shemar and Celia behind the counter, where she gets called away to make another sale. "You never mentioned these sorts of innovations to me before."

Shemar stops and looks thoughtful while a hand goes automatically to check the tightness of one of his perfectly neat cornrows. "I guess it's like the man says, you don't know what you can do till you got to. It came to me, how was I going make a success of being a manager? So I checked out some of those business magazines you read. Now I understand why you do things like shifting the business, changing the merchandise with the season, making customers comfortable. I'm just riding on the tracks you laid down, Miz T."

"That's amazing! I'm proud of you."

He bobs his head to some internal music. "It's all good."

The truth is Shemar's done more for business in a couple of weeks than I've been able to do in months.

Latte and T-shirt in hand, I follow Shemar to the back to talk about supplies and deliveries and staff. It's not quite the same as before. I have questions and he's got the answers. His initiative makes me proud. Yet it feels strange, too, as if I've lost control of something that has defined me for nearly six years. The No-Bagel Emporium is doing better without me.

What sounds like something or someone rummaging in the garbage cans awakens me. A glance at the clock tells me it's 4:13 a.m. There's a sudden racket like someone dropped a garage can lid and then a muffled curse. I mutter and roll over. Must be trash day. Then I remember. Thursday is trash day!

I sit up, wide awake now. There are more sounds. Someone's out there in the dark, near my bedroom window.

Before moving in I had only one real hesitation about taking this carriage house apartment. Location. It's located at the back of a deep lot and not easily seen from the street. Which means a burglar or thief—aren't they the same thing?—could hide in the bushes without being noticed.

That thought propels me out of bed. I don't believe in firearms but I'm not afraid to wield an andiron, which is conveniently acting as a bedroom doorstop since I'm sans fireplace at the moment.

But just as I'm dialing 911 for the first time in my life there's a loud knock on the front door.

"Who is it?" I cry.

"Mom? It's Riley!"

"Hello, this is emergency services. Can I help you?"

"No," I say into the receiver. "Sorry, a mistake," and hang up.

I flip on a light and throw open the door. It *is* Riley, and she looks awful. She's been crying and her skin feels wet and sticky—

"Riley, you're bleeding!"

I drop the andiron and pull her in out of the cold. "Where are you hurt?" I try to feel around but she's bulked up by backpack and an enormous poncho of nubby texture that smells suspiciously like a wet horse. "What's happened? Were you hit by a car?"

"No, Mom. I—I'm all right." She pushes me angrily away and tries to catch her breath. "No, no I'm not!" Surprisingly she erupts in a fountain of tears.

I fumble for the phone and punch redial.

"What are you doing?" she asked between sobs.

"Calling an ambulance. You're bleeding!"

"Hello, this is emergency services. Can I help you?"

Riley looks at her hands. "Mom, this is stage paint."

"Hello?"

"Sorry, wrong number." I punch the off bottom and pray they don't send the cops to check me out as a nuisance caller.

I flip on another light. It quickly becomes obvious that she's telling me the truth. In proper light the "blood" is revealed as smeared paint in colors of gold, orange and red. There are large flakes of glitter and a couple of feathers in her short frizzy hair, which is now dyed robin's-egg blue. Costuming, I assume.

She looks around. "Mom, where are you living? I practically killed myself trying to find the door."

"And you nearly gave me a heart attack. Why didn't you call to say you were coming out?" Her lip begins to tremble ominously. "Never mind. Get out of those damp things and sit down. I'll make coffee."

"Hot water for me," Riley says between teeth that have begun to chatter.

In rapid succession Riley divests herself of her belongings. Off comes the poncho to expose a torn T-shirt over sleeveless leotard and leggings. I watch all this happen in silence while she hiccups and gulps, curses and stomps, tosses and throws these bits of her life around. To know Riley is to appreciate the finer points of her moods. She's using all the four-letter words, and some combinations I never heard before. This is serious.

When she runs out of steam I say in my calmest voice, "What's this all about?"

She pauses and looks at me, every fiber of her being stiffening until she could be picked up and used as a javelin.

"You've got to do something about your mother. Sally stole the man I love!"

Chapter 23

This family's beginning to resemble a Chekhov play. Or maybe a Pedro Almodóvar farce where husband-stealers date ex-wives' former lovers, and grandmothers steal granddaughters' boyfriends. Actually, I don't think he's done that one yet.

I'm a caffeine-first, talk-second person. Coffee brews for me while Riley empties some vile-looking herbs retrieved from a pocket of her backpack into boiling water to make tea.

When we each hold a mug of the poison of our choice, we settle on the sofa, face-to-face. "What happened?"

"Sally, that's what!" That's all it takes for Riley's composure to crack. She pops up, cussing and kicking a nearby unopened box.

"Stop!" I reach out and grab her arm to pull her back onto the sofa. "If you break anything you will owe me. So start over, from the beginning. Exactly what happened?"

Riley shoots me a look. "Sally came to the pre-preview re-hearsal. And she—"

"Stop." Thinking quickly I decide that diversion tactics are in order. "Why a pre-preview?"

"The director thought that in order for us to perfect our roles, the cast needed to get comfortable performing before a live audience."

"So, really, it was an *un*dress rehearsal."

She gives me a look that makes me sorry for the injection of levity. "Each performer was allowed to invite four guests we trust so that the environment would be real yet safe for artistic expression." She pauses in reflection. "Our director is really into organic relationships. He says there's a natural embarrassment for all nude mammals. Did you know even a dog or cat will slink around or hide in shame after they have been shaved? Sheep, less so, because they become accus-tomed through domestication to being sheared. But it's a scientific fact—"

"Riley, it's 5:00 a.m. Your mother's a bit vague. Can we stick to the main subject?"

The hurt returns to her expression. "I invited Sally because not only is she a relative but she's a fellow thespian. But then she shows up dressed all in black, turtleneck, skinny capris, ballet slippers and a tam. Like a beatnik."

I sigh. "She embarrassed you." Been there, done that, over it.

"Oh, no. She charmed everyone. I mean, a Rockette!" Riley's eyes shine in admiration that for the moment outweighs treach-ery. "She even high-kicked the hat off a guy wearing a Stetson. Who wouldn't grovel?"

Been upstaged, too. It's a natural hazard when Sally's present, like falling rocks in Yosemite. "So, when did the trouble begin?"

Riley sits cross-legged on the sofa, then hunches over her tea, like Buddha with bad posture. "Somewhere near the end of the first act."

I don't know how to ask this. "Was it something she saw on stage?"

Riley's mouth twists into a knot. "I don't think she saw a thing, not one moment of my big scene. She was too busy making eyes at him. Touching him, even. At one point her hand was on his—"

I gasp.

"—knee. Are you okay?"

"Fine." Dirty minds are their owners' responsibility. "Back up. I thought this guy was an actor. Who is he?"

"His name is Sakdu Jaru-Ampornpan."

Ah, yes, Sarah mentioned him. "Is he Thai?"

"How did you guess?" Riley seems inordinately pleased I can contribute.

"I learned a few things about names from our former neighbor who is half Thai. You should remember Andrea Frabregas-Prem. She gives wonderful parties."

"And has all the crazy Brooklyn relatives who come in the summer?"

I nod and laugh. "They were a bit exuberant. So, where did you meet Sakdu?"

A dreamy look comes over my daughter's face. I've never seen anything quite like it before. On another girl's face, I'd say it was infatuation. Riley says she doesn't believe in love. Bondage to chemical enhancement, I believe she calls it.

"He was at the casting call I went to before *Horizontal Fairy-tales*. His family is backing an experimental Bollywood-style Thai musical bound for Broadway next spring. The family has money but Sakdu is its artistic soul."

"Nice work if you can get it," I murmur.

"We began talking while I was waiting to try out. Sakdu is so cerebral. It was like I was talking to myself."

"That must have been fun."

She gives me another look. "You know how I am when I don't get a part. But this time it didn't even matter because he asked me to stay after. He said later it was because I thought to borrow a genuine Thai costume and Srivijaya-style headdress for my audition." Riley totally immerses herself in parts, like Daniel Day Lewis. And, yes, it can be just as scary for friends and family.

"So then we went to this incredible place near Gramercy Park for a raw-foods dinner." She wrinkles her nose, which means she didn't really enjoy the food but she's much too avant-garde to admit it.

"We talked and talked. He's traveled the world. Really traveled it, not just stopped in all the right places so he could say he's been there. He believes that it's imperative for a person to change his or her reality constantly. That it is no longer enough to be just a New Yorker or just Thai or Ghanaian. Such identities weigh down the mind and encapsulate the soul."

"And he is beautiful."

Riley offers me a goofy smile. He must be something!

So, then it's easy for me to understand what attracted Sally, no matter the age difference. But that doesn't explain her actions. "So how did he meet Sally?"

Riley's softness vanishes before the more familiar antagonism. "I introduced them. And then Sally spoke to him in Thai. I didn't know she spoke Thai."

I shrug. Who knows with Sally?

"And they started conversing in French and German, and he was completely taken with her. And I had to go get ready for the first act. Of course, she made him sit next to her." Riley's expression grows tight. "I sort of kept an eye on things from behind a curtain in the wings. She kept making comments during the play that he would laugh at, and it ruined everything."

"That doesn't sound like Sally." She might be self-absorbed but my mother has faultless manners and as a performer she knows the burden of an inattentive audience. She would never deliberately hurt anyone less than a mortal enemy.

"I couldn't believe it, either. My own grandmother. Feeling up my boyfriend!"

We both lapse into subdued silence to let that thought settle.

Riley sniffles. "And then, while we were still taking our bows, she blows me this kiss from the audience and leaves, with him!"

"She must not have realized how interested you are in him."

"So?" Riley sniffs again. "She should stick to men her own age."

"I don't think they make a male model comparable to Sally." Except, perhaps, Tony.

"What am I going to do? How can I face anyone?"

Before I can make a suggestion she jumps up, splashing tea all over herself, but she doesn't seem to notice. "I know what I'll do. I date someone older, disgustingly older and wealthy and—"

"Like Hugh Hefner?"

"Who?"

Oh, dear. My references are too old. "The Donald? Between marriages, he dates women almost young enough to be his granddaughters."

"*So* not interested!" She thinks for a second. "What about someone *much* younger?"

"You're twenty-three. I can probably arrange a play date with Celia's son, Trey. He's three."

She sighs so deeply I think she won't have air for speaking, but she does. "What am I going to do?"

"Do you really want my opinion?" I've learned to ask.

She subsides back onto the sofa. "What?"

"This has nothing to do with your guy and everything to do with Tony."

It takes her a second to process this. "You're saying Sally's just pissed, and out to prove something after Tony brought that teenager to the Juniper Suite?"

I nod. We've since learned that the girl with Tony that night is the new hot stuff seventeen-year-old Eurasian model namedYasu.

"Maybe she thinks he'll hear about tonight's escapade from you. After all, you did help him engineer the Juniper Suite meeting."

"*Sheet!*" But then her expression brightens. "Sally did wink at me just before they walked out. You think it was a sign? Like, don't worry, this is all for show?"

I devotedly hope so.

She looks doubtful again. "I really like him, Mom."

"You really like every guy, Riley. For instance, what happened to the one with the, *um,* unusual piercings?

"Who? Oh." She blushes. "I made that up. Sarah's always on my case about the men I date. So I made up this really disgusting scenario to gross her out and get her off my back."

"The boyfriend you described was a figment of your imagination?" I sound awfully giddy glad.

"No, he's in the play."

"Oh."

"We have a scene together, if that's what's bothering you."

"That, among other things. So, what now? If you were to see Sakdu again, do you think you'd still be interested?"

"God, yes! You just have to meet him. He's…" She heaves her shoulders and moves in to lean her head against mine just like she used to do when she was a toddler.

"I know I always claim to be against exclusive relationships. But that's because I never met anyone like him. He's…different. And even if the circumstances stink, and I'd like to claw his eyes out for what he's doing, being so stupid as to be with, well, I still want him."

I nod my head against hers. "I'm feeling your pain." Marcus hasn't called.

There's a long pause before Riley says in a quiet little girl voice, "So you don't think Sally's at this very minute screwing Sakdu's brains out?"

I look at the ceiling. "Let's suppose *not.*"

Before she leaves at noon I ply Riley with her favorites, fresh scones I made while she slept, heaped with strawberry jam and clotted cream. Then I tell her everything will work out for the best. I absolutely believe it. And, yes, I will be at her opening night on Friday.

After a few hours' sleep on my bed, Riley has the presence of mind to think about something else besides herself. She turns on the TV to catch the "biased government-whipped infomercial news" and sees, instead, the new slide commercial for Harrison's Lexus dealership.

"Ugh! It's *her!* Feeling up that car!" Riley whips her head around to look at me. "How'd this happen?"

"Long story."

"But that's disgusting. Brandi's pawing that car as if she was told to give it the forty-dollar special."

"I believe titillation is the point."

Riley clicks the TV off. "How do you do it, Mom? Working side by side with my mortal enemy would curdle my guts."

"It has its moments."

I take a deep breath, knowing this is a rare moment to talk to her about her dad. "Sometimes the most you can do for someone you love is forgive them. Sometimes the worst you can do to someone you detest is be nice. Loved your dad, hated what he did, but I'm over it. And if I can make her life miserable by being in it for a little while, well then I've done a service to jilted wives everywhere."

Riley grins at me. "When I grow up I want to be just like you. But not for a while."

This is the very first time Riley has ever alluded to marriage without recoiling in horror. This Sakdu must be some kinda fellow. We hug and wave at the train station and I wish her well for Friday.

Things as a mother I didn't say: *Sakdu is smart, handsome and seemingly a man with a plan: not your usual type. He has money, which means he is not bound by the usual necessities of job and stability to live. Ditto. Marriage is commitment: Sakdu believes in changing his reality often.*

I can't bring myself to warn a daughter, whose previous string of boyfriends I have actively disapproved of, that this paragon might actually be a world-hopping, grandmother-*fooking* hedonist. She's seen the warning signs with her own eyes.

As for Sally? Sally I can scold, as soon as she returns any of my six phone calls.

When Sally does call, she sounds as if she just stepped out of the shower, freshly ready for an evening of elegant decadence.

"Darling, what did you think? I'd absconded with the boy?"

"Sally?" I can barely lift my head to check the time. It's 1:00 a.m.

"He offered to see me home. I twisted my ankle getting out of a taxi at that wretched warehouse-district location. Why do young people think good theater can only take place amid squalor and danger? After he saw me home, I sent Sakdu right back to Riley."

"Not so right back." I recall Riley saying she waited in the dark outside for an hour after the theater closed for his return. Only then did she hop the train for New Jersey and her mother. "Strange, you never mentioned a sprained ankle when you were high-kicking that Stetson off that man's head."

"Yes, well, a trouper never lets on about personal tragedy."

Unless her confessor looks like Sakdu! "So, what did you do with him?" I deliberately didn't say "to him."

"I offered him tea, as he insisted upon looking through my Rockette album."

"Did he just happen to trip over it on the foyer?"

"I might have encouraged him to tarry for an hour, or two. But it was for the very best of causes."

"So that, if rumors of a young lover reach Tony's ear, he'll be able to verify it, and the time frame, with the doorman?"

"How very clever you are! I'm quite proud of how well you've turned out."

At the moment I'm more worried about how my daughter is turning out. "You served Riley a terrible blow. She believes she could be in love with Sakdu."

"Then that only goes to show how poorly love serves a woman. Look what it got her? Bother and heartache and loneliness."

The drama in Sally's voice would play well in summer stock. That just makes me wonder if we aren't talking about her at this point.

"I believe in love, too, Sally. And you did everything to encourage that belief."

"I did nothing of the sort!"

"Who carted me to every Broadway musical from the time I could toddle? In every one, the girl always got the guy."

"I had no idea you thought that was *real* life. I was trying to ignite your acting talents so that you could avoid real life."

I smile. "Thank you for a most entertaining upbringing. Now, find a way to clear this matter up with Riley. I hear Sakdu is a very nice young man."

Her laughter is amazingly suggestive. "Yes. He's a very clever boy!"

"Mother!"

There's a gasp on the other end of the line. Maybe I've gone too far. I've used the "M" word.

"There's no call to be rude, Liz. I will make up with Riley in my own way, though you must admit she had a lesson coming."

So this *is* about what Riley and Tony did to her. Still, someone has to be the adult.

"There are some things a girl shouldn't have to fight her grandmother for. Like her boyfriend."

There's a long pause. Did Sally hang up on me?

"I suppose that would compare to snatching a cashmere top from a friend's arm at a Filenes's basement sale." This logic seems to have an impact on Sally that propriety never would.

"Never fear. I will think of some way to make amends. I always do."

Chapter 24

We do look smarter since the remodel.

Thankfully there was no tearing down of walls, or erection of any, that would have turned our transformation into months of misery. Just a bit of paint, paper and fabric went into brightening us up. I would have liked to suggest a soundproof partition cutting *her* off from my side of the office, but one can't have everything. And I'm not about to give her the space that by rights should be mine.

Equally gratifying, the decorator concurred that flowers beneath Ted's portrait were anathema to customer relationships. Why remind them of what the company has lost? They must do business with those present.

In the end, Lionel suggested that the redecoration come out of mutual funds, so there'd be no question of parity. If the faintly

Pacifica theme seems vaguely out of place on a November day,
I can deal.

I'm on my way to solvency again. We have brought in two more
returning clients since Harrison's "No Option" ads began running.
We've hired back more staff to cover it. In fact, all the company
seemed to need was the appearance of stability to stabilize it. That
means freedom from dependence on this job should soon be mine.
Best of all, Brandi has been absent a full week. We run smoother
without the disruption. By the first of the year, we should be
looking very attractive to a buyer. Once sold, my millions' share
will go in the bank, and I will go back to being the happy baker.

Across from the coatrack in the hall are little cubby spaces
that serve as in-house mail slots. Mine is so crammed with
items that it takes both hands to jerk them out. A flurry of en-
velopes takes flight, some sailing right down the hall toward
Edward's office door. I follow the scattered mail as if they were
breadcrumbs from Hansel and Gretel until I hear voices behind
the almost-closed door.

"—Don't think it's too soon."

"Really?"

I pause dead in my tracks. She's back! Eavesdroppers never
hear any good…all the same

"—Have your whole life ahead of you."

"You're so lucky, with your little son." Her voice drops and
I miss something.

I kick a flyer from Wal-Mart nearer the door and follow it.

"Of course, you do. So, say yes." Edward sounds more so-
licitous than I would have thought after our last conversation
about her.

"It wouldn't seem a conflict of interest?"

"Why would dinner with a client be a conflict of interest?"

Because she's thinking about more than a business relationship!

Guilt makes me look back over my shoulder to make certain I won't be caught snooping before moving closer to the door.

Maybe she's already begun a new affair. There was that suspicious trip to Miami. But with who? I know. Harrison!

It was bound to happen. Harrison's many trips to check over the details of the new campaign were so transparent as excuses to chat with her. So obvious. Like the flowers I spied on her desk the last day she was in. She said Harrison had sent them to the office as a thank-you because our initial "No Option" ad drew favorable response. Yet, she totally hogged them.

I snatch up the last piece of mail and walk quickly to my office, where I shut the door and lean a shoulder against it.

I take a quick emotional inventory. How do I feel about this revelation?

It's not my place to feel indignation that she is defacing her husband's memory with this whiplash recovery. My allegiance is long gone.

Poor Ted. The force of memory has lost its staying power. Soon he will be a footnote in her life. He would have had a better shot at a long memorial had he stuck it out with me. After all, he was the father of my children, and that's a larger imprint.

I don't care either way, but Sarah might be hurt and Riley might, well, they won't like knowing their dad's widow is dating within the first six months.

It takes me another thirty seconds of staring at our twin-desk setups, arranged back to back at my insistence, before my subconscious reflection kicks up a more uncomfortable fact.

This is the second time she has usurped a romantic attachment of mine. Can't she find her own men? One would think she's emotionally stalking me.

If anyone's actions are a little creepy in the matter, it's Harrison's. You'd think he'd not want to be seen in the company of the second Mrs. Ted Talbot so soon after being dumped by the first.

So, if the news that they are an item should become public, the gossip won't reflect well on her.

Just as I'm feeling hunky-dory about it all, Brandi appears at the door. "Oh, you're back."

"Oh, *you're* back," I echo. This time she's the shade of an oiled pecan with reddish undertones, though there are white patches around her eyes from sunglasses.

"How was Miami?" If that's where she really went.

"Oh…it was lovely." She looks around, running a finger down the length of the rainforest stick mounted by the doorway for aesthetics. "Miami. In fall. Not like here. Cool. Chilly, even. At night. Here, not Miami."

Is it me or does she sound more inane that usual? "Is something wrong?"

"No… that is." She comes in and closes the door behind her. "Can we talk?"

"I'm really busy." I wave a fistful of mail as proof.

Never one to take a hint, she comes and perches on the customer chair before my desk, anyway. "I thought you should know. I wasn't in Miami just for fun."

Out of sight, I grip a drawer pull. If she's about to share the news of her romantic romp with Harrison I just may be ill.

"I went to the Atlantic Bakers' Convention with the West Orange Bakery."

That revelation stings me in an unexpected way. I remember seeing a flyer about the convention back in May. At the time the only way I could afford to fly to Miami was if I sprouted wings. "Did you clear this with Edward?"

She gives a little nod. "He said it was absolutely fine. They invited me, as their advertiser person, to help them make a pitch to some Nabisco execs."

Every hair on my arms comes to attention. "Why is this the first I've heard of it?"

"You asked not to be involved in anything to do with the West Orange Bakery."

I manage a nod but it's hard. I was only hoping not to be blamed when she royally screwed up the account. But it sounds like they are thriving. They went to Miami! They talked to Nabisco!

"Liz?"

I open my eyes and force myself to release the drawer pull. There's a deep dent in my palm. "Okay. Go on."

"The owners of West Orange Bakery thought I'd be good PR for them."

"So you already said."

It's not fair! the juvenile side of me cries. Marcus didn't pull punches when he told me No-Bagel Emporium didn't measure up. Did I personally screw up No-Bagel's chances? Did Marcus choose West Orange over us? Or were we done in by a campaign designed by my ex and followed up on by his bimbo widow?

I have to ask. "So, did they get good feedback from Nabisco?"

"We won't know for a while. This was sort of an audition. But I'm feeling very positive." She does that shoulders-back-boob-forward arch that she calls stretching her back. "If we land this, I will be the first to bring in a national account to Talbot's. That should be worth millions, don't you think?"

Just shoot me now!

I grip cold metal and ask an obvious question. "What sort of presentation did you and Edward go with?"

She frowns, as if she doesn't know what to call what she did. "Oh, the usual. You know, PowerPoint. Product-line schedules. I gave out samples by the pool."

I try not to think of her in a teeny-weeny bikini giving samples of honey buns. It makes me seem like a very jealous, insecure individual. Oh, but it's a struggle to imagine her not using her over-the-top sex appeal to gain advantage in any venue. But then we have a unique history.

Marcus never said why we weren't chosen. And he certainly never said anything about who was. Is that why he's flying in this weekend, to tell me? Or congratulate the winner?

I take a deep breath. She can leave now. She's delivered the bomb and it struck my personal ground zero.

"There is one other thing you should know about." She's twisting the edge of her cropped scallop-edge sweater into a knot. Her gaze falls before mine. "I've met someone. A really nice guy. But, well, do you think it's too soon?"

Oh, *hell* no! I'm not doing Dear Abby with her. Especially since the "really nice guy" is Harrison.

I spread out my mail on the desk and pick up something at random. "Listen, I'm really busy. Your personal life no longer affects me one way or the other."

She looks across at me. There's something about her expression but I can't quite guess at. "I admire you, I do. The way you've just gone on alone, without anyone these last years. I could never do that, be alone the rest of my life."

"You mean the way you think I'm going to be." I force myself to look up at her and not come across my new desk after her. "It just so happens there is someone in my life. We've been seeing each other since September." Twice counts as an ongoing relationship, as opposed to a one-night stand. Sure it does. "Not that it's any of your business. Just as your business is none of mine."

"Do you mean that? No hard feelings?"

"Don't push it."

"Okay, fine."

She pops up from the edge of the chair. "I'm glad we had this little chat. Because it's best to get these things out in the open, be aboveboard."

"Right. What do you have to hide? It's not as if you're sneaking around with a married man." I see the arrow strike home and I can't say I'm sorry. What did she expect after that crack about me being home alone the rest of my sad little life?

"So then, since we work together and all, I thought I should probably deliver this myself." She smiles and lays a suspiciously thick envelope on my desk.

"What is it?" I glance down and recognize the law firm's return address. "Another summons?"

She shrugs. "We didn't complete arbitration. I thought it was time we moved along."

Too angry to speak, I pick up and tear open the envelope and gasp. "This is a writ to break the will!"

"I need clear and final title to Teddy's business." She tosses her hair. "We don't work well together."

"You've got that right." I feel steam rising behind my eyeballs.

She puts a hand on each hip. "You're constantly pointing out my mistakes and overriding my decisions. You like to embarrass me."

"And you still come in. What's changed?"

"I was talking with my attorneys and they say I don't have to keep to our arrangement. In fact, after they heard what I had to say about how things are going here, they think Teddy was wrong. You aren't that wonderful at business. I mean, who brought back Harrison's account? And what about Arnaud's? Now the West Orange Bakery made it to a look-see with the big corporations as my account." She perches her perk rear on the edge of my desk. "I've brought in the bulk of the new revenue. If not for me we'd still be in a hole."

It takes every ounce of maturity I have not to leap across the table and pull out every blond hair by its dark roots. She does a fan dance and gets clients all hot and bothered, then I have to follow up and do the hard work to make it happen. This is like dealing with Ted all over again, with boobs. Only this time I'm not going to lose.

I use a single finger to tip the writ off the edge of my desk.

"Go ahead and start papering my life again. It won't do you any good. I checked with my attorney, too." I was hoping to be able to ban her from the premises. "This fifty-fifty thing is airtight. Business is up and we're prospering because of my leadership. You spin a good story but you have no real leverage with which to try to oust me."

"Well, just maybe I do."

She slides off my desk to face me. It takes only a second for the animated, girlish, wide-eyed waif she seems to be to submerge behind the gleaming, steely-eyed gaze of a hacked-off Jersey girl. "You've tried to kill me."

"What?" And then it clicks. "You mean four years ago?"

She nods. "You tried to run me down with your car."

I smirk and relax back into my chair. "Did I? I'm pretty sure I just lost control of my wheel for a second."

"You swerved when I did. Three times! You did it on purpose."

"If I'd meant to kill you, you'd be pushing up daisies, or those god-awful arthuriums you're so fond of."

"Those are very expensive flowers."

"Those flowers are tragically phallic symbols of a male-dominated mindset."

Her eyes flash, just like they talk about in books. "You just hate men!"

"Wrong. I hate you!" The words are out and it feels good, really good.

She sniffs. "Teddy wanted me and you just can't get over that."

I breathe in through my nose so strongly my sinuses almost

collapse. "Let's be clear. I don't like you. I'll never like you. But this is the deal left to us by the man you claim loved you so much. Deal with it. Or buy me out."

"I'll never give you a penny!"

I stand up slowly. "Then, sister, we're still in business and we're going to stay in business together until we sell. If you try to change that I won't hire a team of lawyers to fight you." I lean forward from the hips. "I still have a driver's license!"

We stare at each other, both a little impressed and appalled by what's been aired.

I move first, picking up my purse, scooping up my mail and deliberately stepping on the writ as I leave the room.

In a blur of adrenaline-powered action, I march through the foyer and out into the bracing cool of a bright November afternoon. Every nerve ending is tingling. It feels so good I could cry.

For the first time in more than four years, I've told the truth, the whole truth, and nothing but.

And, as we all know, the truth will set you free!

Chapter 25

"*A*re you sure it was a good idea to get out of the cab on the corner?" Celia has a hammerlock on my arm.

"The driver said he's not allowed to drive through an alley unless it's an emergency."

"Looks like an emergency to me." Celia is walking so fast I'm practically at a trot. "Where are all the streetlights?"

On the street, and we're in an alley off Avenue C.

"Think of this as an adventure," I say, then wonder again about how smart I am to be in an alley thinking of adventure.

"Right." Though a former Wall Street analyst, Celia was born in Jersey and never really took part in the more colorful delights of city life, for instance experimental theater. The fact that she left two sets of twins at home for a night in the East Village says a lot about her desperation for recreational time.

I now know what Sally meant when she said that the best theater in New York these days is on the fringe. There are still a great many districts in the city where you might disappear for days. Some areas of Alphabet City still qualify. There used to be a saying about this community: Avenue A, you're Okay. Avenue B, you're Brave, Avenue C, you're Crazy. There's a reason *Rent* was set here.

The truth is I, too, wish it were brighter, and that there were a couple of policemen and—ah! That's better.

As we turn a dark corner we see that the entrance to the performance space is lit by a big portable searchlight that moves across the sky to attract attention. Near the light a long line of people huddle together next to the building for protection from an alarmingly strong wind on this November evening. I have on a coat, but with the way the wind blows up my skirt I might as well be naked below the waist. So much for my new Rebecca Taylor jacket and lace skirt, mother-of-the-star outfit. I need wool and denim on these mean streets.

"Wow! Look at the audience," Celia says. "You think someone knows something we don't?"

"I have no idea. Riley didn't say anything about any early reviews. This isn't the kind of event to draw much attention. Maybe they've papered the audience with free tickets."

"More likely they hired someone to be Producer of the Public."

"Do what?" I say as we press forward to the head of the crowd.

"Bring in people who have a special interest in the subject matter of the play, even if they aren't particularly interested in theater. John was telling me all about it. It's called casting the audience." Celia has to shout the last sentence because we are getting cat calls and less pleasant responses from those waiting in the line we are breaking.

We flash the special VIP passes Riley sent me and a doorman, who looks like a younger, taller, healthier version of Don King, gives me a single jerk of his head and lifts the velvet rope.

"Guess there's a job for every idea born," I say by way of finishing the conversation with Celia as we squeeze into the tiny lobby. "Although I would think a show featuring nudity would have a ready-made audience anytime anywhere."

"You really need to get beyond the nudity, Liz." Celia sounds suddenly so worldly. "This is a play, not burlesque."

"Chris Rock says if your daughter's on the pole, you have failed as a parent."

"Riley's an actress. She's bound to get a part with a wardrobe allowance next time."

"Tell me that when your Daphne and Chloe are old enough to decide to join the cast of a revival of *Hair*."

Of course, Celia is right. This is a production with a playwright and a producer and a director and professional actors who just happen to be acting without reasonably sized costumes. There, that sounds more like it. They are sartorially challenged. And my daughter's among them.

I take a deep breath. I can do this. I really can. And I won't cringe or crawl under my seat, no matter what.

We are ushered into a former town house space turned into a black box theater, thanks to stepped platforms that form bleacher seats for the audience. The risers are painted black.

The curtains that form walls in the open space are black. The floor has been painted black, crisscrossed by silver strips of tape to hold down the cables snaking across the opening. A few rows of folding chairs on either side are for the overflow.

"This could be fun," Celia says, and releases my arm.

It's not much warmer inside but there's no wind, and that's something.

"Mom! Over here!" Riley waves us toward the stage.

She's in a robe, covering what I know is not much of a costume. Got to get beyond that!

I give her a big but careful hug that won't smudge things. "You look great. You're going to be great. I'm so proud." And I mean every word. My kid, her life. I want for her what she wants for herself.

She hugs Celia and then looks back and makes a beckoning gesture. "I want you to meet someone."

Sakdu would be hard to miss, even if he wasn't wearing a tuxedo jacket over a white tank top, a tied-on batik sarong and barefoot. He's beautiful as only some few men can be described. That doesn't mean he's not very male. The hook-you-in glance from those glowing dark eyes is scorching. No wonder Riley was prostrate with grief over his disappearance.

Of course, that much heat would kill me these days.

"You must be Sakdu. I'm Riley's mother."

He takes the hand I offer. "You cannot be the mother of one so grown. I must think sister." As he says this he is lightly massaging my hand with both of his. No, it's not creepy. I don't know more than two men in the world who could get away with it. Tony comes to mind. That leaves Sakdu.

Celia blushes and practically drools as he charms her. When we've had a surfeit of his charisma and sophisticated banter, he looks at Riley as if to say, the rest of your family doesn't match up with Sally. But then, who does?

I kiss Riley again and wish her the traditional break a leg, and then we try to find the seats we've been assigned. Third row center, according to Riley. That means three bleacher steps up. Reason number two to wear pants. Oh, well.

We've just settled when Sarah comes in, looking a little forlorn.

"He couldn't make it," she says before we even get out hello. "Work."

"Bastard," Celia says under her breath as I hug Sarah. To Sarah she says, "Good, now we have you all to ourselves."

If Riley has always skated far out on the edge of thin ice, Sarah seems to have spent her life making tight little circles at the edge of the pond. With hair hidden under a black beret, she's dressed in a tweed cigarette coat, trousers and turtleneck. It would take Carnac the Magnificent to divine what she looks like under all those layers. Sally says Sarah's like me. But I don't know. I made some mistakes but I took some chances, too. Something needs to shake my eldest up at bit. But not tonight. Tonight is Riley's night.

We're beginning to warm up as the theater fills. A full house is good news for the cast. A full house is usually enthusiastic, and they are young so there is already a buzz of energy in the room, and body heat.

I'm just beginning to feel at ease when Celia gasps so dramatically conversation hushes in a ring around us. "Who invited *her?*"

Three rows of heads swing toward the entrance. It's Brandi.

She catwalks on impossible stilt heels to within ten feet of us before she spies me. Looking smug, she turns and wiggles a finger in the direction from which she's come. A man steps into the theater space and I feel all the air go out of me in an *oohff!* of surprise.

"Liz, look! Isn't that TRD?" Celia asks, as if I need the confirmation. "What's he doing here?"

Like someone who's been knocked breathless by a pancake fall onto cement, I stare as he approaches and pauses—this can't be happening—beside her.

Smiling at him she leans in to whisper something. Oh, my God! They know each other.

Marcus looks up and locks gazes with me. He looks stunned.

I feel something, too. I think it's the desire to retch. My stomach has taken a half gainer off my liver. When it lands I suspect I will not be pleased with the results.

Some masochistic instinct sends my gaze veering from him to her. That triggers a memory of her kitten purr of a voice confiding in me just the other day.

I've met someone.

Oh, please, not him. Tell me this isn't happening.

As they climb the bleachers toward us my mind loses track of what's important, and takes ostrich-like refuge in the nonessentials. Like the fact that she's wearing one of those shrunken jackets that fit tightly to the upper body and stops short of the waistline. That leaves plenty of toned torso available for a clingy top that just touches the top of her low-slung jeans. She should be blue with cold. Of course, she's got Marcus for body heat.

Something's come up. We need to talk. That's what he said in his phone message. Did he really mean someone?

They pause before us and she offers a big smile. "Hi, everyone!"

All I can do is stare just past them like someone suddenly gone blind. I should be so lucky to have been struck blind! The image of them together is now stuck in my mind.

"What are you doing here?" Celia asks in a tone that I wish I could muster.

"Sarah invited me." Brandi glances at Sarah, who turns a painful shade of red.

"I, er, told Brandi about Riley's debut." Sarah glances pleadingly at me. "She is family, after all."

Brandi is her family.

Sarah, the family Miss Manners, sees no reason for exclusion at a celebratory event, even if her mother and stepmother hate each other's guts? Remarkable.

"Ah, Liz." For once her voice is not pitched to irritate.

I can't even manage a civilized hello.

Of all the times, and in all these years, I've never hated her with such pure unadulterated feeling as at this moment.

When I'm myself again I will have to think about that.

"Cute top," someone in the audience calls out to Brandi.

"Thanks. It's Robert Rodriguez." Brandi looks back at me with smug assurance that for once she has the upper hand. "I want you to meet someone."

She tugs on Marcus's arm.

While Marcus still looks uncomfortable, he isn't nearly as agitated as I am. I'm making and releasing my fists. I suppose a catfight in the audience would upstage my daughter's official Manhattan stage debut.

I'll call you, he said. So what's he doing with another woman, even if he didn't expect me to be here? On so many levels my ego has taken a suicidal nosedive.

"Marcus James, I'd like you to meet a temporary consultant for Talbot Advertising, Liz Talbot."

"You're a consultant, Liz?" Marcus looks really confused as he offers me his hand.

"No. I own half shares in Talbot Advertising."

I'm cross-eyed furious with him but when his hand closes over mine I get a sudden body flush just as if he'd stuck it up my skirt instead. I try to let go quickly but he hangs on a fraction longer, enough for Brandi to notice.

"You two know each other?" She sounds really annoyed.

"The bread business is a small world," Marcus says smoothly, which allows me not to have to explain. But him, he's got a helluva lot to explain. "I know Liz as a baker. But apparently, I've missed a few things."

"It's complicated," I say. If he's waiting for clarification he can just go fish!

Brandi gives me a speculative glance, then turns to Marcus. "Liz came out of retirement to lend a hand, until we hire a real professional. And, anyway, this is my step-daughter, Sarah."

Marcus shakes Sarah's hand, but his gaze comes immediately back to me with a question.

Suddenly my voice, the snide snotty one, comes back. "Actually, Sarah's my daughter." I jerk my head in Brandi's direction. "She was the second Mrs. Talbot."

TRD's eyebrow hikes up as he says softly, "Damn."

"Yeah." Even in my situation there's a flutter of sympathy in my chest for him in his newly realized predicament. We've all sophisticated adults, yet there's something not quite politic about dating one ex after the other.

I get a soft push from behind to step aside.

"I'm Celia." Celia sticks out her hand to Marcus. "We've met before, too. At No-Bagel Emporium." She sounds like a fan who's in the presence of her idol.

"I remember," Marcus answers, and shakes her hand.

Celia giggles like a teenager. "You've met Liz's daughter, Sarah. Her twin, Riley, is one of the stars of the evening's performance."

"So I've been told." He gazes speculatively at me. "This is an unexpected pleasure."

"Then you're a party of one," I murmur.

Now that I'm breathing again, it's in tiny fiery puffs of fury. How dare he! How dare *she!* Wait! I think I singed my eyebrows.

"So, now you know everyone, Marcus." Brandi sounds a little unhappy.

"He doesn't know me!" We all turn toward the sound of that irresistible stage-pitched voice.

Sally!

Sally is wearing a body-fitting rouge-and-burgundy glossy leather coat with tan trim and golden button detail. Her hair is perfect, her face is perfect. She, as usual, is perfect.

"Great coat!" someone calls.

"Dolce & Gabanna," Sally answers. It seems impromptu fashion retailing is a part of Manhattan's social fabric. Then she spies Marcus and turns her full focus on him. "And you, darling man, are a friend of our Liz?"

Was she eavesdropping before I noticed her?

"That's right." Marcus's sexy grin finally appears as he takes Sally's hand in both of his. "And you are?"

"Sally's Liz's mo—" I can't see the expression Sally turns on Brandi but am in a position to see Brandi flush up to her hairline as she falters.

"Sally is family," I say quickly.

Sally wraps an arm possessively about Marcus's free arm. "And you're obviously a friend of the family. So then you absolutely must sit with me. I've seen this production before. But *you* I haven't seen before. Let's find a cozy dark corner. I want to know all about you. Every little teensy-weensy wicked thing!"

Marcus sends me an SOS glance but I just shrug and cross my arms. He's far from safe in Sally's clutches, but anything is better than having him spend the evening snuggled with *her* while I suffer alternate attacks of rage and mortification. This is one of those impossible-to-believe moments that only happen in real life. Why my life?

Caught up in Sally's irresistible tide, Marcus moves on, leaving her to either follow them or relinquish his arm. Why am I not surprised she hangs on?

"No wonder Riley lost Sakdu to her," Sarah says in awe. "Sally is like a female tornado."

Celia nods, then leans toward me to whisper, "You called him back after he came to the bakery, didn't you? And you never said a word! How could you hold out on me like that?"

"Ask me about it another time."

"Okay, but how did Brandi find out about TRD?"

"Bad karma."

I plop down in my seat, feeling the drain of adrenaline like an outgoing tide. I should be grateful Sally came along and did what I could not. But now Sally's got wind of Marcus. *Hmm.*

"I'm sorry, Mom. I had no idea you'd be so upset about Brandi being here." Sarah looks contrite. "I thought, with you two working together and you always saying that things were fine between you, that you wouldn't mind. But the look on your face when you saw her. I had no idea."

"Don't mind me, sweetie. What's family without its little dramas?"

Not that we need any more drama but, of course, why not?

Just as the lights flicker a final warning that the production is about to get under way, Tony enters. Not alone. That would be too easy. At least she's not underage. She's closer to my age. In tweeds. English? Oh, brother!

"My dear, Elizabeth! Sarah!" We do the Continental kissing thing while I wait, stiff-backed, for the first grenade to land.

But Tony doesn't even blink when he spots Sally. He simply straightens and says, "I say, isn't that Ted the bastard's slut sitting with Sally?"

I sigh. "Yes."

I follow his gaze to where Sally is deeply engrossed in conversation with Marcus while Brandi sits staring off into space. Marcus looks relaxed and happy, and an unfamiliar tug of emotion catches me by surprise. Unlike Sakdu, Marcus is the kind of man a mature woman could take seriously.

Okay, now I'm even unhappier. Brandi I can still run over. Sally, that's something else.

When I look back at Tony, I have the suspicion he's feeling what I'm feeling even though it doesn't show.

I put my hand on Tony's shoulder and lean in to whisper. "It's okay. That's Marcus, and he belongs to me. Sally's playing on my team tonight." I think. I hope.

Tony gives me a pleased look then leans in and whispers, "Still and all. Word to the wise. Don't leave him with her for very long."

I understand perfectly.

"So then, has the chap been warned that there's going to be full-noodle frontery?"

Sigh.

Just then somewhere a gong is struck. As it resonates through the dark cavernous space it rises in intensity until we are practically levitated off our chairs. And then we're plunged into blackness.

Horizontal Fairytales is just what I'd expected. Freud would be proud. Bettelheim might frown on the stretch for sex in every scene. Like the lesbian relationship between Snow White and the Wicked Queen. Who knew? Seven dwarves are gay kind of figures. The Three Little Pigs are sluts and the Wolf, well, the Wolf is a pimp with a bad attitude. Hansel and Gretel are happy if incestuous siblings who give new meaning to the phrase oral fixation. The Witch, natch, a child molester.

Not that I'm actually watching the enthusiastic but rather un-professional performances that closely. The music, sometimes lyrical, other times rap, occasionally sounds like someone stepped on a cat, and cannot be called compelling. After a while even the procession of sexual perversities in fairyland becomes monotonous.

My own sexual entanglement is taking up the larger portion of my mind.

Marcus is sitting a couple of rows back and a few seats over, across the makeshift aisle. It's all I can do to keep from glancing back over my shoulder every ten seconds. Of course, when my purse slides off my lap, or when I need to adjust my coat draped about my shoulders, when I yawn or lean over to whisper to Celia, if I happen to catch sight of him, well, that's okay.

It doesn't take me too long to figure out where and how Brandi met him. It must have been at the baker's convention in Miami. Does that mean the West Orange Bakery is Marcus's new client? I feel ill all over again.

Twisting around on the pretense of adjusting my jacket, I catch his eye and shoot him a hostile glance. He shrugs and smiles. I look away before *she* or Sally notice.

He did hint that he might go another way, professionally, that is. On the other hand, he might have warned me that he invited my rivals to Miami to do their thing. He never said a word!

So then that's probably where he met Brandi, showing off her wares.

And what about that call? *We need to talk.* Obviously, he was interested enough to call her before he got back to me.

As for him being here? Maybe he asked her out and she suggested the play so she could boast about her step-daughter being in a New York production.

This is not my idea of family entertainment.

When Riley first steps on stage, I barely register that she's nude but for a red ruff about her neck, a lot of artistically splashed body paint and glitter, and the three inches of cloth covering her yum-yum. She's Red Riding Hood and for some reason she slips in and out of the woods between every vignette. As she goes she gathers more feathers and glitter and paint, but never any more fabric.

Finally, before the end of Act I, it's Hood's story. Yeah, yeah, grandmother's basket of goodies—is that a dildo? Trip through woods, the Wolf appears. I spend no time in speculation on how his bushy tail is attached. He's got a shiny brass ring hanging from his thing! But a little later when Riley's triangle is ripped off by the Wolf in Grandmother's clothing—make that a frilly night cap—my gasp is submerged in Celia's. Then the lights go out, a scrimshaw screen descends and a shadow pantomime backlit by red lights takes place that would give Marcel Marceau pause. Eaten by the Wolf never meant that before!

It's staged, I remind myself. Think the Blue Man Group. Cirque du Soleil. This stuff is old hat. It's a perfectly legit theater experience. I'm a modern person. I'm a woman who meets a strange man for sex.

"Are you okay, Mom?" Sarah whispers.

I turn to Sarah. "Fine. Why?" I whisper back.

"You've got your eyes squeezed shut, and a death grip on my sleeve."

The lights go up, and my eyes open just as the curtain descends.

That was the longest twenty seconds of my life, so far.

There's no intermission, and the second act goes by so

smoothly that I'm not even fazed by the Ugly Duckling, in which nine naked young men leap in one direction as their equipment swings off in another. All this indiscriminate dangling of men's appendages does nothing for my libido. My funny bone, yeah! Tackle box waxing only magnifies the ding-dong factor. I'm pinching my lips so hard near the end that I fear I will need collagen injections to revive them. But I can't laugh. It wouldn't be right, adult, sophisticated.

When I think I'm about to burst from withheld giggles, I glance at Marcus, and see Brandi holding tight to his arm. All humor in the situation leaves me so fast I feel that little sick feeling again in the pit of my stomach. It only marginally helps that Sally is holding his other sleeve. Wonder whose grip he'll displace if he needs to scratch his nose?

Oh, this is awful. I'm feeling possessive about a man I don't really know.

I know some things. I know some essential things. We have things in common. Like bread, and cooking school. And sex. If there are better experiences than us together I don't need to now about them. Unless I lose him. Unlike Sally, I'm not cut out to keep turning up the next great man. Find me one, I'm done. It's the plowing through so-so that's discouraging.

And that's when it hits me. Brandi has a nasty track record. Ted. Harrison. Marcus?

Am I going to let her take another thing from me?

Oh, *hell* no!

When the curtain goes down there's a lot of clapping and whistling, cries of approval, and the general noise of people getting out of their seats.

Someone from behind me pats me on the back. "Great play! Your daughter's got a perfect set of assets for this kind of work."

"Er, thanks." Can I crawl under the seat until the theater empties?

I watch Sally, Marcus and Brandi ahead of me troop toward the lobby. Sally is laughing. Brandi looks superbly annoyed. Marcus looks back in my direction, but I look away too quickly to register his mood. He's seen my daughter naked. He must think my family comes from a long line of sluts. *Jeez!*

"Can I get you something, Mom?" Sarah questioned.

"The next act in my life." This one has lost its charm.

Chapter 26

There's nothing to equal the drama of a roomful of exuberant young actors after an opening night performance. Add to that half the audience, some of whom I'd swear weren't even at the theater, and there's a serious party going on. The cast party is being held at the director's loft apartment around the corner. The lighting consists of spots of brilliance shot through cavernous darkness. The music is experimental club, which means it's loud, with rhythms that pound internal organs and are not especially easy to dance to if you're over twenty-five.

For the rest of us there's booze, lots of it, and weed, lots of it. The air is smogged. One doesn't even have to take a hit, just breathe in. The aroma is expensive. I'm not a partaker, but in my youth my roommate at Surval Mont-Fleuri was a regular. She preferred high-grade Cambodian, flown in by Daddy's

LAURA CASTORO

courier. The smell of good weed is unmistakable. My head is buzzing within half an hour though I've only had one mojito. Ah, the bad old days.

I'm so happy and embarrassed, proud and ashamed! I've hugged and kissed Riley repeatedly to compensate for my own conflicted feelings. There are smears of glitter on my cheeks to show for it. Sakdu has hugged and kissed me a couple of times, too. On his breath is the expensive herbal experience he, no doubt, shared with the group at large. The weed doesn't exactly mellow his gaze, just veils it with an erotic tease.

I'm out of my element, and know it.

The heat is unbelievable. Rain forests are drier. The air is saturated by a heady cocktail of human breath, body BTUs and hormonal flow. In short order I've shed my coat, my jacket and even my silk blouse. Thank heavens for a camisole underneath. Some of the guests are wearing much less coverage.

Tony didn't join us. Sally did. With Brandi and Marcus in tow. Sakdu made a quick backward step when he spied her. Smart boy. At the moment she's taken the most comfortable seat in the house, with Marcus beside her, while playing center stage to a half-dozen starstruck ingenues.

Celia took a cab straight from the performance to Pennsylvania Station. She and half her kids have a Saturday morning mommy-and-me play date.

Sarah couldn't be convinced to stay long. She said she had a load of work in the morning. But as she was leaving I saw her being approached by one of the cast, the wolf of "Red." Not sure how I feel about that, having seen what I've seen. But he wouldn't let her pass and she seemed to be okay with that. That was ten minutes ago. Last seen, Sarah had shed her coat and turtleneck, and was flinging her body one way and her head the other to the music while the wolf swayed and watched. She's having fun. This is not a bad thing. I hope.

That's the terrible thing about being the mother of girls. You want them to find men, the right men. You want them to find love and passion, enough passion to make the business of marriage attractive but not so much that it obliterates common sense. At best, the wolf is a one-time deal. Fine. Sarah needs to jump-start her social life. But a mother doesn't want to know the details of these things. Unfortunately, I've seen too many of this guy's details already.

There are other things on my mind, for instance the way Brandi keeps eying Marcus as he listens to Sally. I suspect they wouldn't be here but for the fact Sally strong-armed, in the nicest way, Marcus up here.

Marcus doesn't look happy. He appears to be for the very first time since we met a man unsure of his next move. The Sally/ Brandi tag team might well do that to the Rock.

Just as I'm turning away to call it a night Marcus looks up across the room. For an instant our eyes meet and a sudden-heat feeling catches me by surprise. And here all I thought I felt at this point was cross-eyed anger.

Another second passes before he stands and makes a discreet move in my direction. But I lift a hand in a "don't" gesture. This is not the place for a discussion. If it took him that long to decide to say hello a second time, there are things going on in his head that aren't all "happy to see you." I feel the same. We will have to wait until another day.

Brandi takes this as her cue. She rushes over and takes Marcus by the hand, leans in close to say something, and then leads him into the dancing crowd on the dance floor.

I move to the other side of the makeshift dance floor yet linger at the edge, curious to see what happens next. What was once simple if chancy is now so complicated by relationships, business and personal, that I'm not sure what I really want from him. Well, maybe I do and it's a little uncomfortable to admit.

After a moment someone's hand slips down over my hip and cups my rear in an intimately interested way. As I turn around to tell whoever he is that I'm not the fruit of the week selection, I come eye to eye with the yards of curly red hair and navy-blue eyes of "Rapunzel."

"Hi," she says in a husky voice, and gives me another little squeeze.

"Hi." My voice is equally husky, but for a far different reason. "Sorry, but you're playing the wrong hand."

She removes hers. "The way you were staring at blondie I thought…"

Ah jeez! She thinks I'm eyeing Brandi. "She's dancing with my guy."

Rapunzel swivels her head toward the dance floor. "Want me to break that up?"

"Thanks. I'm on it."

"Too bad. I like classy." She shrugs and turns away. She's gorgeous. I think I'm flattered. A little freaked but flattered.

In quick order I finish a second and third drink, and consider that maybe a hit on a toke might not be totally out of the question, considering the circumstances. But then there's nothing more pathetic than a middle-age woman in a life crisis trying to be "cool."

What I should really do is go home. What I really want to do is breeze past Marcus to say call me in the morning. If I leave now, then I won't have to watch them leave together later.

My stomach contracts hard at that thought. Got to get out of here!

Sally saunters over to me as I'm collecting my blouse, jacket and coat...where's my coat?

"Darling! But this is a marvelous party!"

"Someone stole my coat!"

"Happens frequently at these functions."

I look up from the pile of ragged sweaters and distressed leather and torn denim outerwear. "But I just bought it for the winter season."

Sally seems suspiciously mellow. "Think of it as a donation that will improve the winter survival for some young starving soul."

What it is is another bill coming due without the benefit of the purchase.

Sally slips her arm through mine. "I'll make it up to you. But right now you need to go home. My home."

A few minutes later we are snug in the back of the town car Sally leases with a driver. She doesn't do cabs in the city. She says they are so unreliable, and too often smell.

At the moment I wouldn't know the difference. Now that the cold November night air has cleared away all else, I realize I'm drunk, and high. And I'm not enjoying either. There's a strange emotion curling through my stomach. I'm pretty sure it's a noxious combination of jealousy and fear.

Sally is well into the ritual of retouching her lipstick and powder, in case she might be spied by someone she knows between her curb and her door. "So, Marcus is your next great man. Good choice."

My shrug is noncommittal. "How did you guess?"

"The drool on your chins as you stared at each other before the performance." Sally takes a breath mint from her vintage Tiffany pillbox then offers me one. "You certainly weren't aware of my approach. I heard every word you three exchanged. Want to talk about it?"

"No." The power of her breath mint is too strong. Must be the "high" part of my intoxicated state coming into play. I roll down my window and toss it out. "So, who was drooling more?"

"No comment. However, it was remiss of you to allow the slut to know he exists."

"I didn't know she knew he existed until tonight."

"So I gathered. She was going on and on about their time on the beaches in Miami so I switched the conversation from English to French." Sally smiles. "The slut doesn't know French."

"What made you think Marcus did?"

"I was pointing out the fact of nudity in the notes in the handbill, so he would be prepared, and he pronounced *au natural* correctly."

I have to admire a woman who can steal a man from her adversary simply by changing languages. "So, what did you find out? How interested is he in her?"

Sally makes a moue. "Darling, it is not about what he wants. It's about what *you* want."

"I want him." There, I've said it.

"What are you willing to do to have him?"

"I certainly wasn't being myself when we met." I slump farther down the wide cushy seat. "He thought I was mysterious and carefree, a wild woman."

"Perhaps sleeping with him first wasn't a mistake, then. Sex with the right man is just the sort of thing to get a woman over a bad patch. As I recall you said he set your hair on fire."

"Hmm. He knows tantric sex."

Sally's laughter is throaty. "Clever boy! Lucky you."

I don't want to whine. It's not really my style but it comes out, anyway. "He's already had the best I have to offer. What do you do after you've done everything?"

"You do something else."

"Translation, please."

"Truth time, darling. After a while every partner's allure begins to fade. Women are better at fantasizing so we make up for the wear and tear on our men with creative reimagining of them. Men just let their eyes wander. A clever woman doesn't allow that."

She touches my cheek. "When you married I hoped it wouldn't last. But you do have staying power. I admire that. Detested Ted the bastard, but admired your ability to make it work."

"I didn't make it work."

"Darling, nations have crumbled quicker than your marriage."

I giggle, and giggle again. "I think I'm high on secondhand smoke."

"Sakdu had it flown in specially for the celebration."

The nose knows.

I sober as we turn onto Fifth Avenue. "I can't lose him, not to *her*."

"You may be a Talbot but you were born a Blake. If you want Marcus, the slut doesn't stand a chance." Sally's voice trails off as she finishes because we have arrived at her apartment building.

Tony is standing under the awning of her apartment building, legs apart and both hands braced on his furled umbrella. He looks like a man with all the time in the world on his hands. Maybe it's the tilt of his James Lock homburg.

I glance at Sally. Her expression is one part amused, one part field marshal. "I really should do something about the assistant," she pronounces with sibilant *s*'s in excess.

"Maybe I should get a hotel room." Not that I can afford it.

Sally reaches into her purse and pulls out her key and hands it over without even a glance in my direction. "Sleep well, darling."

I step out, Tony steps in, and the town car slips off into the night.

Chapter 27

Marcus called my cell at 6:00 a.m. *Thought I'd find you at the bakery. We need to talk. Call me.*

I was still facedown on thousand-thread-count cotton linens in Sally's guest bed.

He called at 10:00 a.m. *Must have been a long night. Are you angry? Call me.*

I was sitting before a plate prepared by Ines. It consisted of an egg-white omelet with truffles and feta, fresh-squeezed de-pulped orange juice, and a cup of coffee made from kopi luwak beans. I could have taken a pass on the meal but nothing keeps me from caffeine. Not even if it is made from beans passed through the digestive system of an Indonesian palm civet. The passage is said to improve the flavor of the beans.

I'm a foodie, but some things don't bear much thinking about.

Marcus called again just before noon. *I have to go out for a while. I'm in town for business and I have to fly out early in the morning. Call me. Please.*

I listen to all three messages and then put my cell back in my purse.

On the train ride home I try to make rational sense of things. If Marcus lived around the corner or say in Basking Ridge or even Philly, there'd be something to think about. But honestly, Minnesota is a prohibitive distance for a guy to live that I'd like to see regularly enough to say I have a relationship with. Even so...

Reason says it's my move. We met by mutual interest. Our second encounter came of Marcus's pursuit. So what if Brandi jumped in? He called me, three times. That proves it's my turn. And I have a lot of questions.

My cell phone plays "She Works Hard for the Money" as we pull into the Newark station.

"Sam here. You ready for tonight? Pick you up at five. I hate the traffic. We can eat at the game. Okay by you?"

Sam! The Devils game. Tonight. Can't check out on a client. "Hi, Sam. Yeah, sure. Sounds good."

"Dress comfy."

That takes care of that. What I need to say to Marcus can't be done by phone or a fifteen-minute conversation over coffee. So there's no point starting what we can't finish. I call his hotel, find him out and leave a brief message. *Got your messages. Sorry, but I have plans today. Call me next time you're in the area.* If there is a next time.

Our meal at the game turned out to be Sam's personal tailgate party complete with foie gras, duck comfit, white asparagus, an aged cabernet and bread that he thoughtfully picked up from No-Bagel Emporium. What is it Shemar likes to say about a good meal? Sam knows how to burn some groceries!

I tried to talk business but he wanted to talk about food and celebrity clients he knew, and those he thought the right campaign could help him reach. Fine, it was his dime.

I like Sam. He's funny and enthusiastic. I'm Jersey bred, even if my antecedents have been somewhat eroded by a Swiss boarding school education. I can appreciate his frank view of the world. Although, at one point, I thought we might get put out of the game. The man has a mouth on him. The ref took exception to his pungent comments on more than one occasion. So we leave a little early, to miss the traffic, Sam says.

By the time we're pulling up in front of my door, well, the path to my door, Sam has made me laugh so hard I think I've sprained something. Merchant marines have a lot of stories in their repertoire that a girl's not going to hear just anywhere.

I turn to him. "Thanks for a really great evening. It was just what I needed."

His brows go up. "That's it? How about a nightcap? Coffee? Water?"

I smile and slowly shake my head. "I had a really late evening last night. I need to turn in early."

"Fine by me." I meet a still friendly gaze but the subject has definitely changed. "You didn't get dessert yet."

"I have to watch my calories." I'm not completely surprised when he reaches for me. And I'm not uncurious about what it would be like to kiss him.

Can't explain it. Woman's intuition or just the weird

workings of my own peculiar mind. He kisses very nicely, but within seconds I know I'll never be interested in his goodies. I work both hands up between us and am surprised I have to shove really hard on his chest to break contact.

When my lips belong to me again, I say, "I'm going to give you the benefit of the doubt and assume you've been a few too many places in the world where no doesn't mean no."

He releases me immediately but then chucks me under the chin. "You liked it. Come on, admit it."

I angle my back to the door and reach for my bag, which has slid to the floor. When I've fished out my key, I get out of his truck. He's out and around to the other side before I get both feet on the ground.

"Look, I'm sorry. Okay? I got a little worked up at the game. I was being friendly. No harm meant."

His stock is dropping so fast I feel the urge to sidestep him. But do I want to blow a promising deal while Brandi's stock is soaring, and she's got the men in black looking for ways to make fresh misery for me? I need a friendly but firm way out.

I smile just a fraction "You're a nice guy, Sam. But you need my professional expertise a lot more than you need another woman in your life. I can grow your business, but it's a trade-off. No more friendly dinners for two."

He lifts both hands palms facing out. "Whatever you say. You're the boss."

"Then we agree to keep our relationship strictly businesslike from now on."

"You're tough." He laughs. "I can respect that. Now, I'm going to walk you to your door because my mother brought me up right. Then I'm going to go home and take a cold shower and beat my head against the shower door until I've knocked some sense into it."

Good as his word, he waits until I'm inside, shoots me a little salute, and then heads back up the path.

Ugh! I hate dating. I hated it at sixteen and twenty and now.

It takes me about five minutes of stumbling aimlessly about my apartment to realize that I'm not going to be able to wait until Marcus's next flyby to see him. Sam fanned a flame that wasn't meant for him. I'm no longer sure I should be holding a torch for Marcus, either. I need explanations and I need them tonight.

I check my watch. It's a little after ten. I dial Marcus's hotel.

"Hello?"

"Hello, Marcus."

"Liz! I'm glad you called."

"Are you busy?"

"I am sitting here watching the Devils lose on TV."

I take a deep breath. "We need to talk. I'll be over shortly."

My left knee is shaking as if it's palsied as I enter the hotel. Could be because my heels are high and I'm missing a winter coat. The flirty chiffon skirt and deep vee silk sweater I bought on my recent shopping spree aren't made for November weather. But a woman needs to look her best when she's confronting what could be her worst fears.

And just maybe I want to remind him that I'm an attractive woman he's attracted to.

Marcus answers the door almost before I finish knocking. "I

thought you'd changed your mind." He is shoeless, and his rumpled, half-buttoned shirt is hanging outside his trousers. He gives me the up and down. "Been out on a date?"

I smile. It took like forever to redo my hair and makeup. But I'm not here to answer questions. That's his task.

Yet, the moment I see him all I can think about is that when I leave here, it could be the very last time I'll ever see him. All the rationale in the world has not prepared me for my reaction to actually being alone with him again. Because what I'm thinking is that I don't want a fight, after all.

A phone call might have been safer.

He pushes the door closed and locks it before turning to me. "About last night."

"Yes?" Wish the word didn't sound so tentative, but it's hard to sound forceful when one is holding one's breath.

He meets my gaze. "It was business. Sort of. I'm not seeing Brandi socially."

I fold my arms across my chest. "Could have fooled me."

A smile flirts with his face. "What do you want to know?"

That's a good question. What do I want to know? "What I don't want to know is that anything happened between you and Brandi that would make me not want to see you again."

"I suppose I have that coming." He exhales. "My grand-mother always said believe only half of what you see, and none of what you hear."

You have to like a man who's not embarrassed to quote his grandmother. Okay, so maybe I believe him. It's *her* I don't trust.

Yet, I'm still angry. At him! "You could have told me that you'd chosen to represent West Orange Bakery."

"No decision had been made last time we spoke. Even if there had been, telling you would have been unethical."

"You might have at least warned me that your company was looking at other bakeries in the area."

"That would be tantamount to telling you." He looks past me. "You want to sit? This could take a while."

I look toward the sofa. The pillows are squashed, as if someone had been sitting in the same position for a long time. I walk over, very aware of his gaze following me, and perch on the edge of a nearby chair. Sofas offer way too much temptation to a woman not certain of her emotions. "So talk to me."

He sits on the sofa and stretches out his legs, completely at ease. "I'm a businessman with partners and clients. I have responsibilities to them. Premature rumors can wreck a deal."

"Yes, well." He's being reasonable and I want to pout. "I just can't believe you chose that white bread bakery over No-Bagel Emporium."

He glances up, his gaze rising no higher than my breasts. Okay, that's what the deep vee in the sweater is for. "Want to tell me why you're partners in an ad agency that's touting a rival bakery?"

"That happened before I got involved."

"Okay, then how about this. Brandi says she's the widow of the former owner. She never explained how you fit in with Talbot Advertising."

Just wait a minute. He's asking the questions? I'm the one who came here for explanations. But I suppose my reluctance to speak up at the beginning of our relationship contributed to the confusion now. I could tell him the story of a middle-aged ex-wife with a floundering business hooked by circumstance into partnering in business with her ex-husband's left-me-for-Barbie-type widow. But the truth sounds pitiful. Might as well cut to the chase.

"My husband forgot to change his will after the divorce. When he died his will left everything to me."

Marcus does the brow thing, which is kind of cute, except I should be too annoyed to notice.

"It gets better. Brandi is his widow. She sued the estate, and me. We went to arbitration, sort of. Now we each own half the ad agency."

He whistles softly. "You're in business with the woman who stole your husband?"

"Cute, huh?"

He stares at me. "My ex would dig me up, shoot me and bury me all over again if I did something like that."

I smile. "No, you only boink an unsuspecting prospective client and then do things behind her back that could cause that person to lose her bakery."

His lips twitch. "You call it boinking?"

"Don't change the subject. So how did you meet Brandi?"

"In Miami."

"Care to elaborate?"

He grins. "You're cute when you're mad. Okay. You know I'm a consultant. I don't just work for Nabisco. I put investors and small businesses in the food industry together for mutual benefit. There'd been some interest expressed by an investor so I extended an invitation to the West Orange Bakery to make some important contacts at the bakers' convention. Brandi came along as their PR person. Turns out their bread is not only inferior to yours, they have some other issues that made my investors nervous."

This makes me sit up. "What issues?"

"Issues." The way he says it lets me know I'm not going to get the full story.

"So if they didn't make the grade, what were you doing out with her last night?"

The eyebrow goes up. "Jealous?"

"Avoiding the question?"

He nods. "I came in to deliver our decision. When Brandi found out I was coming into town, she invited me to dinner. A business dinner. Then when I arrived she suggested we go to the theater instead. She said her step-daughter was starring on Broadway and it was opening night. How could I refuse?"

"That sounds like her brand of hype."

"By the way, your daughter's a lovely and very accomplished performer. Like her mother in many ways."

"Um." He can say that after he's seen both of us naked? Move on!

"So you told her the deal was off last night?"

"I told Brandi this morning." My eyes must narrow in response to that suggestive statement because he adds, "At brunch. With the West Orange Bakery representatives."

He could have called and invited me to dinner. Of course, I can't say that. "You might have let me know you were in town."

He sighs. "After last night I'm sure I look like a royal screwup. But I thought I would take care of business first and then, when it was over, we could just be about us. How was I to know you and she and Talbot Advertising were connected?"

I think I'm mollified. Except that, "You didn't even give No-Bagel Emporium a chance."

"Actually, I did." He looks away, and I know he's thinking of how to tell me the bad news. "You're not ready for a serious investor. You don't have the staff, the production schedule, the output, the focus or the broad reach into the community you say you serve."

"I have all the focus in the world."

He shifts closer to me and for the first time in our relationship the hard-nose prove-it businessman expression appears. "I came by your bakery to introduce myself. I left my card but you didn't return my call for four days. When you did, it wasn't about business." His smile makes me want to squirm.

"Do you know that I interviewed your head baker? Or that I came in more than once to count your morning bread stack? I did a survey of neighborhood restaurants and storefronts and delis to see if any of them carry your products. They don't. You have no marketing program, no expansion or retail prospects. You're overmortgaged and barely hanging on."

Jeez! He even knows my financial status. "Things are different now that I've inherited the ad agency. I'm solvent, or will be as soon as the estate is settled."

He nods and shrugs at the same time.

"Did you really speak with Shemar? He never mentioned it."

"He doesn't know who I am. Discretion is part of my business. I know how to take care of it."

"I see." Implication, I don't. I can't look at him any longer.

He touches my shoulder but I jerk away. "Liz, ask yourself a question. If baking is your passion, why are you messing with advertising?"

I glare at him. "You don't know anything about my life."

"And whose fault is that?" His sigh of exasperation lifts his shoulders. "I like your version of fun and games but there's something going on between us that isn't being best served by mystery. You want to tell me what is going on in your life?"

"It's complicated."

"Okay, say you've got your reasons, good reasons. But then why aren't you using this gift of advertising clout to promote No-Bagel Emporium instead of a rival?"

My mouth drops open. "I hadn't thought of it that way."

He shakes his head. "Then I think you don't know what you want."

I grow very still. At the moment all I want is his mouth on mine again. And a few other places besides.

But wait! He just called my life's work crap. And my managerial skills pathetic.

He's right. I've thought this myself lately. Shemar's doing a better job of community outreach than I ever did. Even Brandi with a ™ over the *i* is holding her own at the agency. But to hear Marcus say it out loud, that hurts.

"I'm a baker. I want to bake. And share that love of baking with the world."

He frowns with a thought that lasts a while. "If you want to improve your market share, you need to first raise your profile within your community. What if you started an offshoot business? Something like a direct-to-the-customer retail business?"

"Now, there's a specialty market. FedEx Bakery Products."

"I'm serious. A few years ago, Oprah's spot on hatbox cakes delivered nationwide by overnight delivery made them so popular that no one stopped to question the three-figure price tag. I thought a specialty bread market would be next. But no one has really followed up. Put a fresh baked loaf in a hand-painted decorative tin and you've got a high-end, noncontroversial corporate gift."

I stare at him in frank surprise. "I like your concept. I really do." I sigh and lean my chin on a hand. "But, really, how good could bread be that's been shipped across the country?"

"You're missing the point. It's about the presentation, and uniqueness of the product."

"My philosophy of baking is that you must meet the discerning customer's expectation or you won't get that customer again. That's why I use only quality ingredients, however costly."

He lays a hand on either side of my face. "You're a clever woman. So find a way to make your passion for bread work for you."

I don't feel like a clever woman. I feel like a black hole of need. A mature black hole, adorable on a good day, but awfully needy.

I place my hand into the still unbuttoned space of his shirt. "Just so you know. Last night wasn't a total loss for me. There was a woman at the cast party who was interested in me."

"I'm not surprised." He looks down to observe the path of my hand. "You're a very interesting woman."

By mutual instinct we rise to our feet while I concentrate on the feel of his skin. It's warm and smooth, a few strands of dark hair curl about my fingers as I lightly explore.

"I thought we were going to talk tonight," Marcus says after a few heartbeats.

I move in closer and tip my head back to look up into his eyes.

"Think again." I add my other hand to the first, undo all the buttons and then spread open his shirtfront and push it back off his shoulders. He's tanner, his skin richer and browner. Oh, yeah, he's been in Miami.

He sighs. "What are you doing?"

"I'm exploring my options. If you don't want to be involved just say so."

His breath catches as I brush his trouser placket with my knuckles. "I'll stick around."

His hands find my waist and move to my back, the touch turning personal as his fingers begin to brush my spine. "For the record, nothing happened."

"That defense covers a lot of territory."

"With Brandi."

I want in the worst way to know the specifics of that "nothing." Was there not anything more than hand-holding, arm squeezing? How about a kiss? She passed up an opportunity to kiss this man. Who's going to believe that?

Damn! Maturity exacts a toll on a person. Maturity requires that I give him a pass on this. And never mention it again.

"Fine. It's history."

He shakes his head. "I just wish I'd known about Talbot, about everything before now. You really are a mystery."

"Good." I think I'll hang on to what's left of my air of mystery for a little longer.

I lean in to kiss his chest but come up short. "That smell. That's it!"

"Narciso Rodriguez For Her." He grins. "Hayley let me borrow hers. I put a little on especially for you. Like it?"

"I like."

"Don't expect me to wear it in public. It's a bit girlie for my tastes."

I lift my head and kiss him, really putting everything I have into that kiss, lots of emotion, intensity and tongue. Yes, this is more like it. This is the right kiss from the right man.

Then I reach for his belt buckle.

He laughs against my mouth. "You must have found new reading material."

"No. Improvisation."

I find his zipper and drag it down.

He's smiling but there's something of a question in his eyes. "You're sure we shouldn't talk first?"

"Yes!"

"You sure you know what you're doing?"

"I've been here before."

"Yeah, but usually you offer me a martini or latte first. Something to get a fella in the mood."

I reach the end bottom of his zipper. "Are you feeling nervous?"

"I'm feeling a lot of things. You?"

I'm feeling everything! I slip my hands under his waistband and back over his hips. His trousers slide away and drop to his knees. As I kiss him again a full body heat flash engulfs me. I've never actually taken the lead in a seduction. It's quite heady. No wonder men get off on it.

"So, are you really that fond of my briefs? Because there's something more substantial inside you might want to get a grip on."

He takes my hand and puts it inside his waistband. I curl my fingers around him and we both sigh.

They say anything more than a mouthful is a waste. They lie!

Just before sunrise, as I'm heading toward the door, I look back toward the bed.

"And about last night…"

"I know," Marcus says, head shaking slowly. "This is the very last time."

I smile. "You wish!"

Chapter 28

"You have a personal letter." Nancy hands me a sealed express envelope. "It came by private courier so I didn't think I should put it in your office cubby."

"Thanks." I check out the return address.

"Good news, I hope." Nancy doesn't ask me who it's from but it's obvious she wants to.

Don't recognize the sender's business name, JTM Inc., or the address in Parsippany, New Jersey. Call me crazy but I have a feeling I'm not going to want to open it in front of an audience.

I notice a gorgeous bouquet on the credenza behind Nancy. "Nice flowers."

"Aren't they? They're from James Consulting."

I bite back my first thought. "For Brandi?"

"The card just says 'better luck elsewhere.'" Nancy leans forward. "I think it's a polite kiss-off."

"Hmm."

I head for my office, leaving the letter unopened. Something tells me I need to be completely alone before I open it. And I have to stay focused on the morning's goal.

Marcus said I wasn't focused. He said I didn't know how to make the best use of what I had. He said I was in the wrong profession. That makes three strikes against me. I need to prove to myself that he's wrong on at least two of those. I know I don't belong in advertising. No, scratch that. I belong, I just don't want to be here long term.

There's not a single thing I can point to yet as proof but it still feels like I haven't reached my full potential as a businessperson or woman. Both those things are about to change.

The No-Bagel Emporium needs a marketing plan, something that builds on what we've got, what Shemar's doing, and what we're capable of. Why not hire my own company to take on the job?

If only it were that simple. The company comes with strings attached to *her*. The last thing I need is for her to have access to my business. Think I'll ask Edward if it's possible to do business here, and keep her ignorant of it.

I stop by Edward's office but he has a note stuck up saying he has a morning appointment out of the agency. Okay, then I'll start on my own.

Brandi arrives just before noon. The vase of flowers is clutched to her black velvet YES jacket, which I recognize from the fall Bloomies catalog. But she doesn't look all that happy.

She puts the flowers down and fluffs them before speaking. "Did you have a good weekend?"

"Hmm." No point in trying to hold a conversation. She will only succeed in infuriating me, and I'm busy.

"I thought Riley was wonderful. Of course, I do wonder how she will cope with all the attention that kind of perform-ance will bring. But then, she's a professional."

"Umm-hmm." I pretend to be working at my laptop.

She picks up a fallen petal and rubs it between her fingers. "So, you know Marcus James?"

"Umm-hmm."

"I think maybe he's not all he seems." She eyes me from beneath her mascara-gunked false eyelashes. "What do you think?"

"Uh-umm-hmm."

"I'm not sure, either." She walks to the window, adjusts the shades so that a shaft of sunlight angles across my computer screen, the glare blanking out a third of it. I look up at her.

"Oh, my bad." She readjusts.

I go back to not working. Every instinct tells me she's come to talk about Marcus and that we're going to have to do that.

She wanders back to her desk but doesn't sit. "You know how I said I'd met someone? He's the one." She gives me a look.

Suddenly, I feel like a target at which she's aiming knives. Nat-urally I take the coward's way out and look away before I give away too much. "How interesting."

"So, since you know him, maybe you can help me. Ever since his company expressed interest in West Orange Bakery he's been sending me these sweet little e-mail notes. Not that I'd allow anything skeevy. I'm just out of mourning. But a woman can tell when a man's interested, right?"

"Hmm?" I don't look up because I know I'm going to hear nothing good. But since I gave Marcus a pass last night that doesn't mean I'm not human enough to want to hear some version of her and him. Perhaps she'll lie like a rug, but I have to know what her version of them is, even if it gags me.

"Things changed when we were down in Miami. That's when Marcus really came on to me."

"Hmm?" Out of her line of vision I do my clutch-the-drawer-pull thing.

"There was this extraordinary poolside party." She drops that line lightly, as if she were fly-fishing in my psyche. "Well, anyway, certain things were understood."

"Uh-huh." Since she's about as subtle as a Lil Kim video I'm sure she made certain things understood.

"But then he comes to town and offers to take me out and, well, nothing happens."

That pops my head up. "Really?" Now, this is an unexpected development.

She starts to come toward my desk but stops short. "What I mean is, he's so good-looking, and I hear he's very rich and single. He says a lot of the right things but when it comes to action he's a dud. Know what I think?" She glances back at the open door and then says in a whisper sure to carry down the quiet hallway. "I've been reading about men who are on the 'down low.' Living double lives. What do you think?"

I have to look away. "I don't think Marcus James is a closet homosexual."

"Well, something's definitely wrong there. He was positively odd Friday night." She looks really annoyed. "And then he dumps West Orange Bakery as an account on Saturday morning."

"Really? I'm sorry to hear that." *So not!* "Looks like you'll have to find another account if you still want to bring in a national sale."

Her expression is suddenly void of emotion. "So, Marcus knows you as a baker. He must have been interested in No-Bagel Emporium at one point."

"Something like that."

"Too bad you didn't even make the cut to go to Miami." Crocodiles would shed a tear before her. "So, like, even though you didn't do business together, you must have been thrown together. And he never came on to you?"

I don't dare make a sound. After a few seconds she smiles, so she must take that as a no. *Fake!*

At that moment Edward stops in the open doorway and raps on the jamb. "Hear you got a letter by courier."

Brandi's head whips from Edward to me. "What kind of letter?"

"Personal." What's with everybody nosing into my mail?

"If it's company business I have a right to see it." She looks down and spies the unopened envelope lying on my desk and snaps it up. "Is this it?"

"It has my name—"

She must have a lot of experience with opening packages. I can never get that paper zipper to cooperate. She rips right through it in one smooth motion.

I suck in an angry breath. "That's my mail!"

But she's already pulling out the contents. "It's just a white envelope without anybody's name on it."

"Really?" Now Edward is curious. "Open it."

"My mail...?"

"Oh, my!" Brandi's eyes are like mascara-fringed saucers. "It's a cashier's check for fifty thousand dollars."

"Wow." Edward looks over her shoulder and then up at me. "It's made out to you."

"That was my point." I stand and reach across the desk to snatch the check out of her fingers.

Brandi turns the envelope over and shakes it but nothing else drops out. "Who would be sending you a check for that much money?"

"The tooth fairy." I hold out my hand. "Do you mind?"

Edward takes the courier envelope from Brandi and passes it to me. "I'm sorry. I guess we got a little carried away."

"Yes." Brandi folds her arms across her chest. "Sorry."

I close my laptop and collect my purse. "If you two will excuse me. It's my lunch time."

But I don't head out the door. I go into the ladies' and lock it. My hands are shaking as I pull out and really look at the check. My heart lurches.

It's true! There's only one person I've discussed money with recently. Marcus.

Brandi gets flowers. I get a cashier's check for fifty thousand dollars.

Sounds fair.

I find my cell phone and dial.

"Darling! You caught me moments from my bath. How are you?"

"I'm coming into the city, Sally. I need to talk."

"Oh, dear. I'm scheduled for a flight to Milan this afternoon. Could we possibly chat now?"

Since bathtime is sacred to Sally I know she's making a sacrifice with even this suggestion. I double-check the lock and then go into the single stall. "I seduced Marcus the night after Riley's party."

"How delicious!"

"Not necessarily. A letter came by courier from him this morning. He's sent a check to help with financing for No-Bagel Emporium."

"That must have been some seduction!"

"That's the problem. He had just been telling me what a risky business proposition I was."

"I see. Then *you* propositioned him and he thought better of it. It has been known to happen."

"Then you agree? Sleeping with a potential investor is a breach of business ethics."

Sally is silent for a moment. She could be contemplating my moral dilemma, or she could be choosing bath oil. "You had a relationship before he offered you money. So he sweetened the deal. You haven't exactly joined the world's oldest profession."

"That's true. It really was sweet of him. He doesn't know that I'm, well, going to be a millionaire soon—when we settle the will. He only knows that No-Bagel Emporium has been in hock for the past two years."

"So then he's a gentleman gallantly helping out his lady. Darling, you really did find the next great man."

"Even so, I can't accept this check, not and continue to have a relationship with Marcus. It would be like having sex with the bank."

There's a sigh on the other end of the line. "Darling. If you both had as much fun as your dilemma suggests you did, Marcus isn't thinking that you prostituted yourself for a few measly dollars."

"I'm holding a cashier's check for fifty thousand."

"You don't come cheap."

"Sally!"

Sally chuckles. "I'll say one thing for him. He certainly makes you a more interesting person."

"You are supposed to be the voice of reason."

"Then listen to me, darling. The reasonable thing would be to take the money and enjoy the man for as long as they both last."

Not quite what I wanted to hear. It's time to change the subject. "How did things turn out with you and Tony the other night?"

"Don't talk to me about that—that man!"

I'm almost afraid to ask. "What happened?"

"He had the audacity to waltz into Café des Artistes last night with a five carat diamond."

"Arpels?"

"Harry Winston. As if our split was only about a piece of jewelry! As if I could be bought! I belong to no man, and no man belongs to me. We won't ever belong to each other."

"Thank you, Holly Golightly." I wait a heart beat. "So, it was an engagement ring?"

"How should I know? He ordered Krug's Clos du Mesnil and then set this little gift box before me without even a *'Ciao, bella.' Ciao,* by the way, originally translates as 'I am your slave.' But, of course, he wouldn't say that."

Jeez! "Anything else?"

"There was a wretched violin player. I'm certain Tony hired her right off the street. Juilliard, she said. Unlikely. And there were flowers. Scads of them. Peonies."

"Your favorites."

"Exactly! He was being obvious. And he knows I hate melodrama."

I end the call completely undecided as to which of us, Sally or I, is more confused about what constitutes a relationship with a man.

I look at the check once more and then fold and tuck it into my bra. It's not every day a girl gets to be up close and personal with this much money.

I almost get through my lunch salad when "She Works Hard for the Money" sounds on my cell.

"Don't have a cow, Mom, but I think you should know Sarah went AWOL over the weekend."

"What do you mean? She's missing?" The two mothers with preschoolers in the booth next to mine whip their heads toward me.

"It's okay, Mom. I found her."

"That's good news. Isn't it?"

"Here's the problem. Sarah spent Friday night at my place and then went to Saturday evening's performance with me. She said she wanted to show support but I knew she really went to see Jon again."

"The wolf with the...odd piercings?"

"You noticed. She said they were going for coffee after, but she never came back. And then Jon didn't show up for last night's performance."

"Oh, God!" The mothers of preschoolers send me "pipe down" glances.

"Turns out Sarah has been with Jon. That's a problem because he's a——"

"Sadistic killer!" The mothers begin gathering their children's belongings.

"——a real muff hound. I told her all she's going to get from him is a lot of good sex."

Oh. "Has he had his shots?"

"You're not taking this seriously."

"Yes, I am. I'm also trying to avert a heart attack. Go on."

"I tried to talk to her but she told me she's taken a few days off from work to be with him and I should butt out. That's not like Sarah."

"No." Sarah went in to work last winter with a hundred-and-two fever.

"My sister's an amateur where men are concerned. She has no experience with being sexually strung out. She wouldn't say exactly where she is but I think she's at Jon's place. Someone should find her and talk some sense into her."

"I'll call Sally. She has connections with the NYPD. Maybe they will send someone to Jon's place to check on her."

As I dial Sally I think, please, God, let this be a sitcom situation. A lark, with no major repercussions.

When I've filled Sally in she says calmly, "I know just how to handle this. Don't fret, darling."

I do fret, and worry and stew. Unlike the mothers of toddlers who are still gathering items, I'm out of the store and behind the wheel within seconds of speaking with Sally. I can't bring myself to go back to work. I go to No-Bagel Emporium to make schiacciata with grapes and olives while I wait for a call back.

It comes in less than two hours.

"Mom!"

"Sarah! Where are you? Are you all right?"

"I'm fine. No, I'm furious! I've never been so embarrassed in my whole life."

"What happened?"

"These two goons who say they are private security broke into Jon's friend's apartment. They had a note from Sally. They said they had orders. And then they hauled me out of bed—in my underwear!—and now they say they are taking me to Sally's apartment."

"You're in your underwear?"

"Well, no. They let me dress but they won't let me go home. They say they have to produce me for their client. They can't do that, can they?"

"You'll have to ask Sally." Who knew she'd call in black ops forces?

I hear a scuffle and then this really intimidating voice says, "Your daughter's A-OK, ma'am. No drugs, coercion or perversity was involved in her situation."

"Thank you. Sir." I decide not to ask how they know.

I hear Sarah say, "Give me that phone!" More scuffling. "Mom, Sally is so going to get a piece of my mind!"

"Are you okay? Really, okay?"

"I'm…" She giggles.

Big sigh. "Be careful. And promise you won't pull a Britney."

"It was just sex, Mom. Jon's not my type."

Bigger sigh.

It seems to me that lately the Talbot/Blake women are behaving very badly.

Chapter 29

"Celebrity Retrieval? I've never heard of them."

"All the best families use them, darling." Sally's voice sounds far away, as if she's already in Milan. She's at Kennedy International airport.

"They're a kind of private Blackwater. Everybody but everybody uses them. Occasionally a client will call me when a child they left in their rental slips off the family radar. It's so much quicker and less messy than dealing with the police. Sarah's fine so I sent her home. But what if she had been found in compromising circumstances? She might have been arrested and booked and we'd be posting bail."

"You're such a comfort." That never occurred to me. Okay, it wasn't my first thought.

As I've thought before, a real estate agent should be

included in any missing person's investigation. Sally's resources seem unlimited. However, I am appalled that a business has grown up around such a need. I'm hopelessly conventional about some things.

"When will you be back?" Could be days or months.

"Soon. Ta-ta!"

I check my watch. It's only three-thirty. Time flies when you're having fun.

Have moved my base of operations to my apartment for the week. That way I've been able to go into the bakery for the night shift and still get a few things done after dawn. At the moment I'm working on my laptop on my lap because I don't have room for even a kitchen table in this place. Definitely need to start looking for a little cottage with a small patch of garden. Meanwhile, I've finished the list of promotional ideas for No-Bagel Emporium, and gotten some business done for Talbot. The top of the list is the obvious place to start.

That only requires a phone call to Bill Nash at NJN TV's *New Jersey Works.*

"Hi, Liz. Nice to hear from you."

"You, too, Bill. Shemar's arm is good as new. No-Bagel Emporium's ready to reschedule that spot about bakeries fighting the no-carb craze."

"Oh. Gee, Liz. When I didn't hear from you we moved on."

"As in on to another topic?"

"Actually, we found another bakery."

He doesn't have to say who. I can guess. "I thought we had a deal. You didn't tell me I had to reschedule before a certain date."

"It wasn't my idea. I like No-Bagel Emporium. Think it has something special. But my boss is an impatient man. The concept was in place. When you guys had to bail, he decided to fill it with another bakery. They're doing a lot of advertising. It's called the West Orange Bakery. Ever hear of it?"

Constantly, in my nightmares. I can't tell him how crushed I am. "So, when does it air?"

"We haven't actually shot the footage yet."

I roll my eyes skyward. *Thank you!* "So then, you could cancel with them and come back to us."

"I can't really do that. My boss, you see. Besides, they had some business possibilities in Miami they wanted to explore before we did the piece. I think they are planning a big announcement of some sort during the taping."

I debate the ethics only a second. "How did the Miami business go?"

"Now that you mention it, I haven't heard from them."

Okay, asking about a rival's business ventures might not be strictly kosher. But Marcus said his investors backed off the West Orange Bakery over "issues."

"I hear they have issues." I wince.

I can practically hear Bill's reporter antennae start to hum. "What kind of issues?"

"I have no idea." Why did I start this? "Lousy bread, maybe?"

"You're not trying to queer your competition?"

Sure I am. "I just heard a rumor. But check them out."

There's a long pause. "If there is a problem, can you be ready to tape this Friday?"

"Absolutely." *Yippee!*

I hang up and put a line through item number one before a massive attack of guilt makes me want to reach for the phone and call Bill back and tell him to forget what I said.

Ordinarily it would never occur to me to even hint at rumor with a stranger. It feels as if I've done something sleazy. But playing strictly by the rules hasn't gotten me very far lately. It's not as if I repeated a completely groundless rumor. They probably cheat and use a packaged starter instead of a Ma. And, dammit, that *New Jersey Works* taping was ours first!

Okay. Item number two: build on Shemar's efforts.

It's not yet three, which means Shemar's probably in bed because it's his night to make bread. Don't think I've had to call him at home more than twice in all the time he has worked for me. He's that reliable. I hate to wake him but this is an emergency.

"It's your party," says a low sultry voice. It sounds like the party is going on at Shemar's end of the line.

"It's Liz Talbot, Shemar. Can we chat a minute?"

"Sure, Miz. T. Hold a sec." Even though I'm sure he put his hand over the receiver I hear enough of his fabulously creative swearing to realize that his observance of our ban at No-Bagel Emporium is truly a sign of respect.

He comes back saying, "Miz T, I need to give you another number. Take five and hit me on the hip."

I do just that. When he answers his cell it's quiet but for the distant sounds of passing cars.

"Shemar, I've been thinking. Perhaps we can turn our training of replacement bakers into a more formal and permanent arrangement with the city high school. Make it a regular work/study program."

"I'm feeling that, Miz T."

"I couldn't do this alone. It would mean a commitment of more of your time."

"True that." There's a long pause. "Six months ago I might have blown you off, Miz T. But I'm going through a priorities adjustment. Having the shorties in the place every day, watching them put it together and take it apart, it's a trip! Whatever you're about to do, include me."

We talk for a few more minutes and my impression is reinforced about what a sharp mind Shemar has for business. If I don't watch it, I'll be working for him!

Number three. Sam.

"Hi, Sam. Liz Talbot here. I have the prelims on your campaign ready."

"Bring 'em by. I'm in the restaurant all evening. I'll make us dinner."

"Actually you should call the office and make an appointment with me for tomorrow. Nancy will work you in." Got to maintain the parameters.

He grumbles low but says, "You want to give me a hint?"

"Certainly. My research indicates that the top-tier restaurants are now all about good service. Food quality's a given. My idea for you will attract a top clientele because it will improve the front of your house. It's a bit unorthodox so it should generate a lot of goodwill for Arnaud's while creating jobs for high school students."

"I don't know. I'm paying you guys a bundle to make me famous."

"How about I make you a philanthropist?"

He swears quite colorfully. "Might as well pave the streets with my income."

"What if you got something very valuable in return?"

His chuckle is the unmistakable humor of a man on the make. "Does it involve spending time with you?"

Jeez. "In a way. Now, just hear me out."

Ten minutes later I get off the line and take a deep breath. I must remind myself to wear a turtleneck to our planning meeting. And a loose jacket.

And then I burst out laughing.

Marcus is right. I've been hunkered down since my divorce. He didn't say that, exactly, but what he did say made me think. And what's come to mind in the past days is that I've been so worried about failure that I've practically guaranteed it. Who said with age comes wisdom? Sometimes longevity just entrenches us in our mistakes.

Six months ago I thought all my troubles were about lack of capital and popular dieting habits of the past few years. But the hard-to-face reality is that my comfort zone had shrunk to the square footage of the No-Bagel Emporium. For four years I've been lost in a black hole of disappointment. Why did I stop looking for creative, innovative ways out of my predicament?

Talent will only get a person so far. Tenacity can bury you unless it's coupled with perspicacity. What I needed was a swift kick in the pants, so to speak. Marcus provided that in his own inimitable way. The one-night stand that wasn't gave me a chance to see myself in a whole other way. Who knew I could be as seductive, mysterious and unapologetic about what I wanted as Sally? Or as fearless?

I went back to my bank this week to arrange a loan against my portion of Ted's estate. It was surprisingly easy.

One look at the will and one hundred thousand turned out to be "a very modest sum for a loan from an estate of this size." So said my new personal banker! From practically bankrupt to persona grata in one easy step.

Almost asked for twice as much, but I don't want to be greedy. Got to keep my priorities straight, and focus.

No-Bagel Emporium is going into renovation mode. New flooring, new paint, new plaster, new tables and chairs, new dishes, the works! I drew up original plans over a year ago when I had plenty to time to daydream. Now I can dust them off, re-calibrate according to my most recent thoughts about the place and hire a contractor. We will have to move slowly. Nothing must interfere with the new business Shemar is bringing in. Then there's my own life which could use a little renovation, too.

I take the cashier's check for fifty thousand dollars out of my bra that I've been carrying around all week. It smells of Narciso Rodriguez For Her. I bought a bottle yesterday at Short Hills Mall. I think I've found my new fragrance and I'm not sharing it with anyone, except perhaps Marcus.

Of course, there is a liability factor with this perfume. My eyes keep glazing over from the sensory stimulus associated with saturating sensual sex.

The check I'm going to return to Marcus. Receiving it from him gave me the confidence boost I needed.

After calling a courier service, I pen a quick note to Marcus. It says: *Thanks but no thanks. This relationship is sexual or it's nothing.* I spray it lightly with perfume and stick it in an envelope.

By 5:00 p.m. I've crossed off all my major deeds for this day. I'm one tired but very happy businesswoman.

Right now the clock is ticking on how much I can accomplish before the weekend, in case No-Bagel Emporium actually gets the gig with *New Jersey Works*.

By Wednesday morning, I'm as grumpy as anybody might be who has lost two nights' sleep. NJN TV hasn't called and time is running out. I dress and drink three or four cups of coffee before heading out the door. I need to get out of the house and choose Talbot as my refuge.

After trading unheard insults with a couple of rush-hour drivers, I discover that someone's in my parking space so I have to park a block away in the rain.

By the time I reach the lobby I'm spoiling for a fight.

"Is Brandi in?" I inquire. Might as well take it out on a deserving person.

"No, Brandi won't be in for a few days." Nancy smiles and waves me closer so we won't be overheard by clients waiting for appointments. "She had a personal emergency."

"Again?" I turn and head for my office.

Nancy pops up from her chair and follows me down the hall. "I think you should hear this. Brandi's had another *tanning* emergency." Nancy sounds as if she's inhaled helium.

"Didn't we do this routine before?" I say without breaking stride.

"This time's different. Brandi is supposed to film Mr. Harrison Buckley's new TV spot today but she couldn't get an appointment with her personal tanner. So she borrowed one of those portable units to touch up her tan herself." Nancy pinches her lips together for a moment. "But there was a hose malfunction and she got inconsistent coverage."

I stop at my office doorway. "How inconsistent?"

"She said she's all polka-dotty, like she's got the measles. It will take up to a week to wear off. Until then, she says she's housebound."

My grump factor drops to zero. Some situations are just their own reward!

By noon I can't stand it anymore. I call No-Bagel Emporium. Celia answers. "Any news?"

"No news." She sounds as if we should be readying the burial shroud for our hopes.

"I'm coming over."

There's not anything I can do by driving a half hour out of my way for lunch but I need to stay in motion. Dreams die hard.

Celia isn't in when I get there.

Shemar, who is behind the register, gives me a quick wave. His lunch line is long and that's good.

"Where's Celia?"

"Miz Celia had an emergency. One of her kids has a fever. She's gone to the pediatrician."

"Then you'll need some help in the back. Let me grab an apron."

I push open the door to the kitchen. A young man I don't recognize with dreads wrapped up in a kitchen towel is busy making sandwiches. Must be one of Shemar's new hires. He grins. "What's cracking, Miz T?"

"Not much." I reach for a smock to cover my business suit. "I'm waiting for a phone call from NJN TV."

"Oh, that." He nods. "We gots the 411 just before you came in. I took the call back here."

My heart stops. "And?"

He grins, showing a gold-capped front tooth. "You got the spot."

For a moment my eyes glaze. I was prepared for no. I could accept no. I—

"We got it? We got it! We got it!"

I don't realize I'm shrieking until Shemar bursts through the door.

"What up, Miz T?"

I rush over and give Shemar a big hug, jumping up and down at the same time. "We're going to be on TV!"

"Huh! Ain't that something?" The usually too-cool-to-groove Shemar gives me a tight squeeze. "Only you better watch yourself, Miz T. You're giving me a happy."

I back off, a little embarrassed. "This is just beginning, Shemar."

He gives me slow, smoldering smile. "No doubt."

"We gonna be famous!" The new guy grins. "You the shit, Miz T! Now you can tell that bitch-ass husband stealer to go play with herself!"

"True that." Shemar crosses his arms high on his chest as his gaze shifts to the new guy. "But you owe the pot fifty cents, Bling."

Chapter 30

"What's this?" Shemar give me a lazy-lidded look as I hand him a bag.

"New duds."

He looks in the bag, then cranks his head back like there's a bad smell. "Aw nawgh, Miz T. I'm happening here in my own gear. Platinum FUBU." He's right. The camera would love his black-and-red Harlem Globetrotters gear.

"You look great, Shemar. But the health department might not agree."

He nods and shrugs.

"This here is messed up," DeVon declares freely when he's pulled his gift out of the bag. "We're gonna look like chump doctors."

"Scrubs are green, dog," Shemar answers. "Hospital green. This is baker's white."

Desharee eyes the drawstring pants with head cocked to one side. "This color's gonna make my ass look big on TV."

"Your ass is big," DeVon answers. "Don't need TV to see that."

Desharee takes a mock swipe at him.

This is my big moment, and I'm a little nervous. We know how to make bread. But we have agreed to let in two strangers, and a camera. Anything could happen, and it will be recorded. I hope nothing falls on the floor. And that my crew remembers to wash hands every time they come out of the restroom, or scratch. We don't use hairnets. I reach up to smooth my hair, scraped back into a ruthlessly tight knot. Maybe we should use hairnets.

In the morning when we open, what if no customers show up? We do have slow Saturday mornings. We put the word out with our regular customers, the new mothers group, and students that they might be on TV if they came by 7:00 a.m. But something could happen. What's the weather prediction?

I hurry over and turn on the Weather Channel. What if we're expecting rain with flooding of Biblical proportions? Even one roll of thunder is enough to keep some people from getting out. We don't have a drive-thru. You have to get out and walk to us. We could have—

"Clear and sunny, all in all a lovely crisp November day is on tap for tomorrow."

I blow out a lungful of relief.

The TV crew of two arrives a little after 10:30 p.m. Bill

wears a glaring red sport coat, which worries me because he could look like a confectioner's sugar-dusted cherry doughnut by midnight. Cameraman Ross has on jeans and a plaid shirt with quilted lining over a gray T-shirt, the sort of rumpled look that won't show dirt, stains or ever look completely clean.

"Thank you so much for this opportunity, Bill." I shake his hand for all it's worth.

"You earned it." He glances at Ross, who's pulling equipment out of his camera bags and then says under his breath, "And thanks for that hot tip."

I give him a questioning look.

He nods and there's a gleam in his eye. "West Orange has issues."

I'm too much of a coward to ask what issues. Just maybe it's better not to know.

After a quick introduction of the crew, we are ready.

Shemar usually begins the evening's work alone in a long narrow mixing room that is stacked floor to ceiling with bins and tubs and boxes of ingredients. The collection of flour and salt and water is not exactly riveting viewing but Shemar's a natural before the camera, all smiles and sly comments, as if he's talking to a female instead of a camera. The scales and charts of baker's percentages sound as complicated as rocket science to the uninitiated, and Shemar makes the most of his moment.

To keep the sleepless-night factor to a minimum I offer mocha lattes and pastries all around.

Bill takes the coffee but shakes his head at the offer of a pastry. "Sorry. I'm on the South Beach diet."

Ross looks embarrassed. "Me, too. Atkins."

Grrr! Who gives a bread segment to a no-carb crew? Oh, but this girl's just getting started.

We make a big production of opening the Ma.

Bill leans over and smells it, then mugs for the camera. "Smells sort of like a brewery."

"You're right." With a gloved hand I lift a glob of Ma up for the camera. "Ma is alive and must be fed daily."

"No kidding?" This comes from behind the camera and earns Ross an off-camera glare from Bill, who clearly doesn't want to be upstaged.

"I never thought of bread dough as alive," Bill says in his best commentator voice. "It's enough to make a person more respectful of his morning toast."

The large mixer starts a slow grind on cue, but I hold my breath as Shemar starts up Shorty. It whines and grinds, then shudders, causing the TV crew to back step.

"It's okay. It's just that the equipment is old. But it's perfectly safe." This speech might go over better if the noise and shimmying didn't all but drown me out.

Just as I'm thinking maybe we need to clear the room, Desharee appears, carrying a bright red scarf loaded with dangling coins from her belly dancing class. "Excuse me, Miz T."

She glides past me and Bill, real slow and smooth, then ties the scarf about the rounded head of the machine. "Shorty is just practicing a little dance I've been teaching her just for your show. She's all about shaking the booty!"

As the mixer operates, the scarf shimmies and shakes, making a lively jingle that draws laughter.

I draw them toward one corner away from the noise with the promise of a look into our ingredient bins. "All the nuts and fruits used in our breads are organic. For instance, we order almonds direct from Italy."

"Why go to all that trouble and expense?" Bill asks.

"One bite of our white chocolate apricot almond bread will answer that question." I lean in, put my hand over his on the mike and say in a low seductive voice, "Too bad low-carb viewers shouldn't taste even one sinfully good bite."

Reaching up, I pop the top on another bin. "This gold-foil-lined box contains my favorite thing in the world, extra-bittersweet dark chocolate from France."

After extracting a small stick I offer it to Bill. "Imagine all that bittersweet cocoa lusciousness wrapped in light flaky layers of warm buttered crust."

When he refuses, I stick the piece in my mouth and do a Marilyn Monroe moue. "Yum! Oh, but I promised not to tempt you anymore."

Bill laughs. "That's good. Give us more humor, Liz."

After that the night goes quickly. They watch fascinated as DeVon mixes up batches of pecan currant sourdough and pinenut polenta asiago. When he dumps those doughs in tubs to rise, I lead the men out to the front, where a different kind of dietary assault awaits.

"We don't live by bread alone. Our cheese specialist, Celia, prepared a sampling of our cheeses. This should be right up your dieter's alley." I roll my eyes, vamping like Betty Boop. "Too bad our audience can't taste what this succulent soft Bleu d'Auvergne does to the bite of good sourdough."

"Well, maybe I could sample just one small slice," Bill says, grinning as if he's just suggested we sneak out back for a bong hit.

"What bread would go with that?" From behind his camera Ross points at a pink rind cheese.

"Perhaps the pagnotta or white sourdough with a touch of quince paste."

"You don't wanna be doing that, dog," DeVon chimes in as Bill tries to finger-lift a bit of soft creamy cheese to his mouth. "The chocolate cherry bread's the bomb with mascarpone." He slips a nice thick slice under Bill's fingerful of cheese.

Bill gives a shrug and sticks it all into his mouth. "Ah!" he exclaims in full-mouth ecstasy. "That's like, wow!"

I wink at DeVon and piece up another cheese sample on ciabatta. "Oh, and you must try this, Bill. It's a small village cheese with the aroma of nuts and herbs, touched off with the flavor of mushrooms. When the cheese reaches room temperature, it gets all soft and sticky." After I hand it to him I lick my fingers ever so slowly.

The things I do to make a living!

Ross is filming as Bill begins to nibble the crust like a man tasting forbidden flesh.

"Good, huh?" I nod. "You *bad* boy!"

After that, it's pretty much a dietary slaughter. And they say women are the weaker sex. Give me a man and a loaf of my bread, and I'll have him eating out of my hand in no time.

We turn on CDs while working the dough.

Shemar rocks out to Kanye West while performing virtuoso, making plain, chocolate and savory croissants.

Desharee shows off her new technique with pastry to Missy Elliott tunes.

At one point I look up to see Ross showing Desharee how to use the camera so she can film them trying their hands at working and shaping dough.

They are amazed by the intensive labor required in an artisan bakery.

"I'll never grouse about the cost of a loaf of bakery bread again," Ross says wearily near dawn.

By the time we open a fair-size crowd is at the door. Rallied once more by espresso, Bill and Ross gamely tackle the customer angle, interviewing a dozen or so. He hears about our stroller mommy breakfasts. Even Rodrigo drops by. And, does the totally unexpected. He buys and eats an entire gooey cinnamon roll.

When they finally wave farewell, I go home and fall facedown in my bed. An honest day's work complete before dawn. Take that, West Orange Bakery!

Chapter 31

"You returned my check." Marcus sounds concerned.

"Let's see. I seduce you and you send a check? Has a certain kind of symmetry."

"Damn. That never occurred to me." And now I like him even better. "Tell me what I have to do to fix this."

"Oh, you give up easily."

He grunts. "You're tough."

"So I'm told."

"No, I like that about you."

"Heard that recently, too."

There's a pause. "Is there something you're trying to tell me?"

"No. Yes." Good sex can wake up a lot of feminine urges like the need to probe for relationship parameters. "Maybe." I take a deep breath. "The last time we were together was the first time I thought seriously about how much I'd really like you to be a regular in my life."

Silence. Maybe I shouldn't be testing the commitment of a man who lives a thousand miles away. He might come across another Brandi-type option before I see him again.

"So, thank you, sincerely, for the check."

"It was in no way a payoff, Liz. I was trying to be support-ive, as an investor."

"I know. But when I said I have part ownership in Talbot Ad-vertising I probably should have been more specific. I inherited half share in a thirteen-million-dollar ad agency. So my days of worrying about money are mostly over."

"Mostly?" I can understand his skepticism.

"I have a lawsuit to settle. With Brandi. But at the very least I'm going to be a very wealthy woman. So thanks but no thanks. The most important thing you could ever offer me was what I got from you the other night at the No-Bagel Emporium."

"I'm getting a visual I think I like."

"Well, shelve it for later reference. You were right about my lack of vision as an entrepreneur. I've been in a slump. And I haven't earned the kind of backing that your business is prepared to offer those who are. But things are about to change."

"You're going to pursue the bread-in-a-box idea?"

"No, some things haven't changed. In order for it to work for me, inspiration has to come to me on its own. It is a great idea but it is not my idea. Understand?"

"Independent." He says the word slowly, as if he's writing it down.

"You get credit for shoving me off square one. You also said business shouldn't come between us. So, the check belongs in your pocket."

"Now that that's settled, want to tell me why the check smells like…you?"

I chuckle. "After you left I went out and bought the perfume you were wearing. When the check came, I didn't want to lose it so I it tucked it into my bra."

I hear him breathe out slowly. "What if I stick it in my shorts for a while and send it back?"

"That would start some really kinky correspondence."

From the corner of my eye I see Edward pause in midstride past my open door and give me a jaw-drop look. I give him the heave-ho signal with my thumb. He winks and moves on.

"So, you don't want my money. You don't need my business support. What do you want from me?"

"Dad!" I hear a voice other than Marcus's through the line. "Game's started!"

"Your daughter?"

"My son, Sean. I have two kids and share joint custody. The compromise of the divorce."

"How joint is the custody?" Many fathers claim the rights of joint custody yet only invoke them when it's to their advantage.

"The divorce gave Deirdre custody Monday through Thursday. Unless I was out of town, I had them Friday through Sunday. Sean's in college now. Hayley's a high school senior." He chuckles. "Girls are hard. The losers she dates!" Thinking of my girls' dating lives, I can sympathize. "I have them both this time for Thanksgiving week. Next question."

I've been meaning to ask about the account from which the check was drawn. Why not now? "And JTM Inc.?"

"One of my businesses. I have a couple. A consulting job for General Mills brought us out to St. Paul five years ago, just before the marriage imploded. Deirdre didn't want to come back east, so we worked it out. My main offices are still in Parsippany, New Jersey."

"That's a heck of a commute."

"I love my kids." There's a pause. "How am I doing on your questionnaire?"

"I think I'm going to enjoy getting to know you better."

"Likewise. So then, next week I'll be in the area. Can we have dinner, see a show, or maybe just meet in the library to talk?"

"What? Are you afraid to be alone with me?"

"Absolutely."

I'm in a much better mood after we hang up. Of course that could be because I'm alone in the office today.

Wonder how the streaky business is going for her? No, let that streaky dog lie.

Our *New Jersey Works* segment is scheduled to air Wednesday, the day before Thanksgiving. I started to tell Marcus about it, but why bother? He'll be in St. Paul and unable to view it. Besides it's local New Jersey news.

Maybe I should put in a call to Bill, just to make certain our segment will air. It's been a while since any good news that came my way wasn't attached to a sledgehammer of complications.

Bill takes my call right away. "Liz, been meaning to call you. My producer was knocked out by the segment's rough cut. Asked to see all our footage. Thinks you're a natural in front of the camera."

"Does he have an opening? We're available."

Bill laughs like he just can't get enough. Guess his job is safe.

I had visions of a big celebratory party for No-Bagel Emporium's TV debut. It didn't pan out.

Sarah has plans with friends tonight because she'll be here with me for Thanksgiving dinner tomorrow. Riley has a performance tonight but she, too, will make dinner tomorrow. Same is true for Sally, who says that spending two days in a row in New Jersey is just too dreary to contemplate.

Celia invited me to her house for dinner and to watch. Bless her. But it's her birthday and I know her husband has a surprise planned for this evening. I said there were the others to think of, and the bakery was a better place for a crowd.

Desharee and DeVon announced that they had respective events to attend. She has choir practice. He said something about taking his mother by bus to his grandmother's in West Virginia for the holidays. Even Shemar has a prior engagement. So I end up at home alone.

As I wait for show time, I'm singing and dancing to Sam Cooke crooning on the oldies radio station, and putting together a spinach salad to go with a piece of leftover schiacciata I brought home. There's barely enough room to cha-cha forward and back in my tiny kitchen but I'm giving it my best shot. Dancing was once my favorite exercise. When I was too young to appreciate the simple joys of shared conversation with the right person, I would happily spend hours on the dance floor with guys in whom I had no interest but as a partner. Tonight, I really could use someone to talk with. One is the loneliest number, and all that.

At the appropriate time, I sit in the dark and watch. Bill comes on screen first. He must have come back on another day to do the intro. He's outside the shop in the bright sunshine.

"Tired of eating the same prepackaged, mass-produced, microwavable bread, rolls and pastry? Tired of eating the corner-shop pastries that look a lot better than they taste? There's a place in Upper Montclair where bread-making is lifted to an art form. Jazz Great Carmen McRae put it this way, 'Blues is to jazz what yeast is to bread.' No-Bagel Emporium is a bread lover's Jazz Hall. And Liz Talbot is queen of this Mardi Gras."

Hmm. Must have impressed ole Bill. For the next ten minutes, I watch my life's work and my colleagues on view. There's no doubt we're having fun, and no doubt I need to lose fifteen, twenty pounds. Shemar comes across as *smoo-vee*. Desharee has a lot of snap. DeVon's a born salesman. As soon as the show is over my phone rings.

"Darling, you're wonderful on camera."

"Thanks, Sally."

"Did you hire the crew for looks? That Shemar is quite something."

Sally's call is interrupted by Riley's. "You were so good, Mom. You should think about doing a regular show."

And then Sarah. "I told a couple of people at work and they watched. Now they want me to bring bread back from No-Bagel Emporium after the Thanksgiving holidays. I think I'll host a wine and cheese at my apartment featuring your breads."

And then Celia. "My family is so impressed. They finally get why I love where I work. Even I forget how hard it all is. That's because you make it look like fun. You're going to get calls. You watch. Someone is going to want you to do your own show."

My own show? I'm elated by the thought that had never entered my head. Really, despite the Food Channel and the "Iron Chef" cook-off shows that are spreading like wildfire I never thought of me as camera worthy. Maybe I really could...? Oh, but it's only family and friends encouraging me.

About 1:00 a.m. the phone rings. "What up, Miz T?"

"Hi, Shemar."

"I peeped the show on my TiVo just now." I can feel his grin coming through the line. "Damn, Miz T!"

"We were good, weren't we?"

"You're kinda happening before the camera. And I got a few moves. We should have our own show."

Well, why not? My karma has got to be clearing, rising and improving. Right?

Chapter 32

"Wow! Mom! You made everything!" Riley and Sarah stare as bright-eyed as the children they once were at the decked-out No-Bagel Emporium Thanksgiving feast.

"It just took a little of this and that." Actually, a whole lot of this and a great big lot of that. But what's a holiday for if not to be festive?

The girls and I still get together for all the holidays. And I don't take that lightly. One day there will be serious partners and then husbands and children of their own to take priority over a mother's prerogative to wear herself out with festive meal preparation. However, this year my temporary domicile wouldn't even hold the three of us and a turkey.

It occurred to me to ask to borrow Sally's kitchen. Without Tony, she is at loose ends this year. No Punjab excursions. No

Bali hideaways. However, there is the all together real doubt that she would have allowed the odors of full-scale Thanksgiving dinner preparations to penetrate her silk-draperied world. Her dinner parties are catered and brought in. No mess, no splatter, no leftover smells.

So the family is dining at the No-Bagel Emporium this year. We're closed for the four-day holiday so that new flooring and painting can be done. Of course, we're catering like crazy for customers who have a weekend full of out-of-town visitors who need bread for turkey sandwiches, croissant and cinnamon bun breakfasts, and cheese trays for impromptu gatherings.

But today it's just me and mine.

Besides, I've been working on a list of family priorities, and Thanksgiving seems like a good time to share.

Shemar helped me push together a couple of tables and cover them with a good cloth from home. Dug out my silver candlesticks, china and silver from storage and laid a table I'd be proud to serve anybody. And these are my most favorite bodies.

"That's gorgeous. The centerpiece is edible." Riley turns to me. "How did you have time?"

Sarah sniffs the air and her eyes brighten. "Did you make a turkey?"

"Complete with the carcass." The thing about the holiday is, no matter whether you're having two or twenty, the menu stays the same, at least in my family. The dishes are sacred and time honored, and fattening enough to fell an ox.

"There's also dressing, sweet potatoes and fresh cranberry sauce."

"What about the dressing?"

"Made with focaccia bread crumbs, cremini, oyster and shiitake mushrooms, steamed chestnuts and sweet and smoky Cubana chicken sausage with plantains and garlic."

"Ahhh!" Riley's in a half swoon of ecstasy. "You're killing me. I've got to have a bite. But if you tell anyone!" Life is rough for a vegetarian at holiday time.

"For you I made butternut squash soup. There's pumpkin silk pie with a pecan crust and apple pie." It's a lot for four weight-conscious women but it wouldn't be Thanksgiving if we didn't have enough leftovers to cart home and nosh on for a week.

A few minutes later Sally sweeps in in a fox fur stole with a chauffeur bearing wines from her superior cellar. What could be better?

Well, maybe if Riley and Sally were speaking things could be better. They aren't openly hostile, but Riley refuses to meet her grandmother's eye as the rest of us chat. I suppose Sakdu is still the sore subject between them. So then, every family reunion is bolstered by food, lots and lots of it.

Two hours after that, waist buttons are discreetly loosened, shoes have been kicked aside, and the smiles of family conviviality oiled by a continuous pouring of wine ring the table. We're ready to tackle my list now.

I tap my wineglass with my knife. "I'd like to call to order the first of what I hope will be an annual conclave of the Blake/Talbot women. We're all adults now so it's time we took stock of our adult lives, sort of a family assessment. And I've taken the liberty of making a list of issues each of us needs to address."

Sally reaches for the list I've picked up. "I'm the eld—sen—I am the richest. I should preside."

"No, thank you. Unless you're agreeing to take on the role of family matriarch permanently, I'm in charge."

Sally shrugs elaborately. "You needn't be rude."

I take a breath and begin pacing. "Call me crazy but I've been giving it some thought and have come to the conclusion that, contrary to appearances, we are a lot more conventional than we would like to believe. We are each, in her own way, stuck in a comfort zone that is ruining our lives."

This get me some lifted brows and murmurs to the contrary, but not right-out verbal dissention.

"Okay. Let's begin with the fact that as adult women we are dealing poorly with the man in each of our lives."

"Some of us have more than one," Sally murmurs.

My girls exchange glances and then turn inquiring gazes to me.

"You're seeing someone?" Sarah asks.

"Who?" Riley demands.

"The dishy Mr. James," Sally supplies. "My question is who the other lucky fellow is."

"Mom's dating two men?" Sarah sounds alarmed

"And sleeping with at least one of them," Sally contributes with a kissy face at me.

"Mother!" My girls cry in unison.

This is going well. Sally is already on the attack.

"Forget my love life. This is about the rest of you."

I give them my best imitation of a sergeant with insubordination in the ranks. "This family is going to hell in a handbasket. We need to shape up."

"Speak for yourself, darling." Sally crosses one elegant leg over the other.

I turn on her. "I've heard all about your condo crisis. I know you're being sued for violating the 'common decency' clause."

"Way to go, Sally!" Riley exclaims.

"No, no way to go." I shake my head. "You destroyed an elevator with a lamp?"

"It was an heirloom Stiffel. Solid brass. The momentum of the weight did it. How was I to know Tony would duck?"

I shake my head and turn to my girls. "I have an assignment for each of you."

"This should be good," Sally murmurs.

My one-eyed squint only gets a shrug from her.

Out of my leather tote I pull a thick oversize packet. "This is for you, Sarah. It's the study guide for the New York bar. The next exam is in the spring. I've signed you up for a refresher course at Columbia. Also inside are applications for four law firms. Fill them out and get them in the mail before Christmas."

"But, Mom—"

"No buts. You're an adult. You're entitled to make mistakes. But when you start taking sick leave to sleep with a man whose idea of self-expression is punching a lot of holes in his body parts then it's time for me, as your mother, to speak up."

She blushes furiously but is silent.

"You're stuck. Because you failed the bar once you think that you don't have what it takes to be an attorney. Fine. That shouldn't stop you from finding out."

"So true. I remember a time when—"

"Not your turn, Sally." I glance at her in case she's about to object. "You are like me, Sarah. We are conventional people."

"You mean boring."

"No. But when we stray too far from conventionality we make fools of ourselves. Jon wasn't a risk, he was an aberration. Put your courage into something worthwhile. You have an excellent mind. Use it. And ask the guy down the hall at work out for lunch. The right man won't find you unless you are looking, too."

"Bravo!" says Sally.

Riley makes *whoo whoo whoo* sounds while waving her fist in circles.

I turn to her. "Now for you. I want you to start auditioning again, Riley. You are a good actress with a lot of talent. But the play you are in is, in a word, awful. It's tactless, graceless, and without any of the redeeming qualities of original storyline, writing or genuine social comment to lift it above peep-show sleaze. You're very good in it, but *it* is awful."

"Bravo," Sally murmurs with a little nod.

"I object!" Riley comes to her feet. "You are just projecting your own conventional female body issues on me. I'm perfectly comfortable in my skin."

"No, you're not. You're acting out. Now, sit down, sweetie."

When she subsides, I continue. "You've been furious with your father since he walked out on us. Imagine how your father would react to your new play?"

Her expression reflects the thought but she's quick to say, "It's art!"

"It's a peep show with good choreography. Now, like most things, show business is mostly about who you know. Why not ask Sally for connections? It's time you two patch up your little differences over Sakdu. Last time I checked he was perfectly free to make his own decisions. If he made a bad one, he should be the one to suffer. Your grandmother—" I see Sally flinch but plow on "—is an exemplary human being who would never knowingly hurt you. You should accept her apology. And because she sincerely didn't mean you any harm she will help pave your way. After all, she knows everyone who's anyone in the Manhattan theater district."

I glance at Sally, daring her to contradict me. "Your grandmother has just been waiting for you to ask for her help. Isn't that right?"

Sally nods. "Anytime, darling. I know just the impresario you should meet."

I look back at Riley. "And when your present performance comes back to haunt you, I hope you have the courage to say, 'I made a mistake' and move on."

Riley hunkers down and wraps her arms about her knees. "You sound like Sakdu."

"Good. Him, you can keep awhile."

I take a steadying breath and turn to Sally.

Sally crosses her arms and recrosses her legs. It's a performance in itself. "I suppose you now think you have something to say to me."

"Especially you! You're the head of this family. You need to accept that, and make it work for you."

"Couldn't I just! But tell me, darling, why this sudden temper?"

Okay, it's my moment for confession. "Because we are wasting precious time. Sarah and Riley have more of it left than you and I."

"But we've always had each other."

"Have we?" I subside in my chair, the heat gone out of me. "Haven't you wondered why I never come to you for more than attitude? It's because you scare me. Yes, that's the word."

"Frighten you, indeed." Sally tosses back the last of her Corton-Charlemagne. "You've obviously had too much wine."

"Maybe. But if you didn't make it so hard not to be intimidated I would probably have borrowed money from you years ago and gotten on with my life."

"Whatever are you going on about?"

To buy a little emotional time before my final confession, I reach with unsteady hands to fill my own glass with the exquisite white burgundy. I pick up my glass, bring it to my mouth for a swallow, and think *here goes!*

"It just occurred to me this week how hard I've been trying to prove to you — and me—that I could succeed on my own, like you have done. Well, I'm done with that."

I look across the table at the fabulous woman who is my mother and feel the thrill of that fact, as I always have, in the pit of my stomach. "I'm not like you. I'm not certain of my world and my place in it. I need encouragement and backing and even then I'm going to occasionally fail. And that's got to be okay from now on."

I lift my glass in a toast. "So, Sally, after forty-seven years of hoping for a change in me, you're just going to have to live with me being average."

"You're not average!"

"Yes, I am. Deal with it." Untoasted but undaunted this once, I take a big swallow of wine. "And, another thing. You need to get Tony back."

The look she gives me makes my stomach queasy. "Careful, darling."

"We all really like Tony," Sarah says timidly.

"We love Tony!" Riley prefers bold statements.

"And you're impossible without him," I say.

Sally tosses her head at this. "I don't need a man in my life."

"Yes, you do. We all do." I glance at Sarah. "We just don't need to settle for anything less than a truly great man."

Sally makes a survey of the room with her eyes. When her gaze comes back to me I swear I catch the tiniest whiff of sulfur in the air. "I suppose I could entertain the idea of Tony crawling back. But there will have to be changes. For one, I'll expect a bigger ring."

"You have bigger rings!" I throw up my arms in exasperation. "The role of demanding diva is aging badly, Sally. Stretch your repertoire. Try groveling."

My daughters gasp.

But Sally has a surprised expression. Little by little her eyes narrow, as if she's actually thinking about what I said.

Finally she picks up and eyes her empty wineglass a second, then puts it down. "Are you done with your lecture?"

"Yes, I believe I am." I certainly have exhausted my own courage on that subject.

"Then, darling, what courageous thing are *you* planning to do?"

I grin. "I'm getting out of the advertising business, because though I'm good at it, I don't like it. And then I'm going to get to know the man with whom I've been having a wild anony-mous affair."

"Affair? You, Mom?" My daughters speak their identical thoughts simultaneously.

Okay, perhaps that was a little too much honesty to share with one's children. I'm finding bravery a tough balancing act.

Sally snatches up her fur stole and wraps it about herself, a signal that for her the evening is at an end. "I think I like you better since you met the next great man. I can't wait to see what you do next."

Chapter 33

The thing about bragging about being courageous is that sooner or later you have to show up as brave or pretty much shut up ever after.

I said I was quitting Talbot Advertising. I didn't say exactly how or when. To do so, I need to settle the estate. To do that, *she* needs to sign the arbitrated settlement. But she's still out of the office that I'm still stuck in.

Sally gives me three days before calling to check on things. "You're still there?" It's an accusation because I picked up my office phone.

"You've heard of two weeks' notice?" Notice how smoothly I evade the question.

"How did the slut take the news?"

"She hasn't been in this week."

"So you haven't really quit." Sally can smell prevarication across the Hudson.

"And you called me to say what?"

"Actually there was another reason. I've got Riley into a casting call with an agent for Broadway National Tour Company. They are taking her on as an understudy."

"That's wonderful! She was grateful?"

"For Riley, yes. It's a Disney production, which she disparages as not legitimate theater. I reminded her it's not much of a leap from her present fairy-tale production."

"And yet a giant step in comfort level for her mother. There will be costumes suitable for viewing by kiddies."

"So then back to your dilemma, darling. You are leaving the slut to her own devices exactly when?"

"When *she* returns to the office, I suppose. I don't want to call just *her* with the news. And I wonder if I should talk with *her* outside the office. Yet, I don't—"

"You're wobbling, Liz. Well, here I am. The backup you always wanted. I've my driver at the ready. We will confront the slut together."

"Thanks, but I have it covered." I search for the two agency contracts that have been lying unsigned on my desk since Monday. Though Sally's powers do not allow her to "see"' me through the phone, these are the props I need. "I was just thinking that I have the perfect excuse to drive out to her home. There are a couple of agency contracts we both must sign."

"Does the slut still sign her name with a heart over the *i?* You can't trust a person that insecure about her place in the world."

Sally's right. She can't be trusted. However, I can't call myself brave if I bring my mother along for backup.

"I'll be fine."

Sally says something about bearding the lioness in her den before hanging up.

Before I lose my nerve, I call her house. The housekeeper answers and says Mrs. Talbot is not available. I say to tell *Mrs. Talbot* that I'm dropping by for her signature on important papers for the agency that can't wait even another day.

The housekeeper puts her hand over the receiver for what is, I'm sure, a conversation with *her*. When she comes on again, the maid says okay I can come if I must.

Such a warm, fuzzy invitation.

Curiosity is a terrible thing. Much as I'd like to ignore the fact that she and Ted had a married life with a house and perhaps a cat in the yard, here I am driving with eager interest toward a house whose threshold I'm sure has been voodoo'd against me.

No surprise they live in one of those ubiquitous neighborhoods that a decade ago was a corn field. There are swings and jungle gyms and bikes and out-of-ground pools, all without the benefit of a single mature tree. It's as if the neighborhoods come in burlap bags and each spring a new batch of two-story McMansions is dumped on open grass areas to take root.

Finally I pull up to her house. A two-story modern colonial with columns and—— Now, that's odd.

Shiny new tract homes can be unnervingly repetitive. Perhaps they had the builder make custom changes to the exterior. The strange thing is that the new Talbot home, with its white siding, deep green shutters and Palladian window above the semicircu-lar entry, looks a lot like our old house. Surely it's just coinci-dence.

The fact that her newer model of my car is sitting on the drive does add a *déjà-what?* aspect to the view.

But I'm not easily spooked.

At the door a young woman answers. "You will follow me, please."

Even without the accent I would know she was a foreigner. There's deference in her tone no American would think of using.

"You can wait in here. I tell Mrs. Talbot you are come." The maid points toward the living room.

But I'm stuck to the spot, struck by a funny feeling as I stare across the hallway. It's a funny strange not funny ha-ha feeling.

That's my carpet pattern on the staircase that loops out of the entry toward the second floor. And—*ah jeez!* The living room has a white sofa and two side chairs covered in celadon silk. They aren't the same design as mine but the colors are identical. And the windows! I remember clearly the argument I had with Ted before selecting traditional shutters over draperies.

But even that thought is stunted by the sight that greets me as I cross the foyer.

Her dining room furniture is the identical Henredon pattern as our old bedroom suite. Once more I feel as if something or someone has been shadowing my life.

Why on earth would Ted seek to copy his former home? And why didn't Sarah or Riley at least hint that this was going on?

Maybe Dad doesn't want you anymore, Mom, but you'll never guess how much he loved your decorating style!

I guess revelations like that just don't trip off a daughter's tongue.

As I wander slack-jawed through the two rooms other similarities keep leaping out at me. Even the wall colors are a match for the home I once loved. Everything in this house that reminds me of "us" was chosen by me.

Could this be some sort of weird visual vindication of my lingering effect on Ted's life?

No, that's probably giving me too much credit. But it might be a karma thing at work.

It's all I can do to keep from phoning Sally. It would take Sally to explain this. I'm pretty sure she would chalk it up to Ted's unconscious desire to make up for his wronging me by arranging things in his new life so that he had daily visual cues to prove he had not cut me totally out of his life.

Or maybe he just liked the floor plan.

I'm so totally glad I sold the house.

This is just too—*icky* weird!

Casually as possibility I pick up an Asian vase that Ted's parents gave us as a wedding present and he insisted belonged to him. Never really liked it. No great loss.

"Mrs. Talbot will see you now."

The housekeeper's voice makes me jump as if I'd been caught leafing through her employer's checkbook. The vase slips out of my hand and hits the carpet.

With a pile so deep I've left a trail of footprints that prove I haven't just been sitting and waiting, the rug cushions the fall.

But, not enough. The Ming reproduction cracks in half like an eggshell and its two halves roll apart to reveal its white porcelain center. Coming here was probably not such a hot idea after all.

"I'll pay for that." Pretty sure I sound defensive but, hey, she startled me.

The housekeeper shrugs. One less thing to dust, I suppose.

I follow her down a long marble hallway, which I would never personally have spent the money on, into what must be a library. It has bookshelves and books on those shelves. It also has a pair of leather wing chairs before a white stone fireplace. And there, before a bay window, she sits behind a desk, dressed in a black long-sleeved turtleneck for a change. The only skin on display is on her face and— Whoa! *She* looks like boiled chicken without the skin.

God, this is weird, seeing her outside the office, in her own home. And she's reading. I mean, she's holding up a book whose title is something about being a shopaholic. Figures.

When she notices me she looks up in alarm. "Oh, I didn't think you'd be here so soon."

"Why? Do you lose many guests in the hall?" The eighteenth-century red Chinese lacquer secretary to her left looks suspiciously like the one I'm holding in storage.

But, one item at a time.

At the moment, her fish-belly complexion is a more interesting topic. "What happened to your tan?"

She sighs and suddenly looks close to tears. Real tears, not that fake squirt of seltzer she can turn on and off for the fellas. Her heavily lined black-mascara eyes give her the look of those velvet painting puppies. "I went into the city, to Elizabeth

Arden, to have them do something about the streakiness. It wasn't going away and I couldn't hide out forever, could I?"

Why not? I was enjoying the peace.

Still, did they boil her in bleach? Even her hair looks paler and drier. I feel the urge to rush out and buy bronzer. "What did they do to you?"

"They used glycol peels and micro-dermal abrasion to take down two layers of skin. I can't even think about being in the sun or using a tanning bed for weeks!" Her hands flutter about her face as if she'd like to hide behind them. "I can't remember when I wasn't tanned. Not in years and years."

Her distress is genuine, even if the reason seems trite. She looks older, drained. Or maybe strung out. I've heard about persons addicted to tanning. The George Hamilton Syndrome.

I smile, mostly in amusement, it's true, but also an attempt to be pleasant. I want her to sign the papers I've brought along. Not the contracts, the arbitration ones. In a good mood she might not even bother to carp about the unfairness of it all. "Why not think of this as a nice break for your skin. Sort of a dermal detox."

She makes a feeble, helpless gesture. "I feel so naked."

I recall what Riley said about dogs hiding after they've been shaved. Maybe *she* uses tanning as her protective layer.

I glance around for a topic and notice a cheapo poster version of a Marc Chagall painting. My skin is beginning to creep. I once begged Ted to buy a limited-edition print of a Chagall.

"Why don't you redecorate while you wait to retan? You love what Logan does with color." And I'll never be able to touch another thing I own as long as I know that she's living the doppelganger version of my former life at this address.

"You think that's a good idea?"

"Yes, start with some modernist pieces." I point to the leather wing chairs. "You could replace those with seating that has clean lines and a minimalist feel."

Her gaze narrows and her false nail tips start doing runs of the scale on her desktop. "Why are you being nice to me?"

"Change of pace? Pity?"

She bristles. "I don't need your pity."

Sigh. She's so predictable. Regroup and try again. "You have a new skin tone. You're going to need new makeup."

She perks up. "Maybe I should make an appointment at the Bobbi Brown counter. A private consultation."

"Sure. And you need more color in your hair." I say this as if I'm accustomed to giving fashion tips. "Perhaps some darker toffee and caramel streaks."

She reaches up to fluff the topknot ponytail held by, I notice, a big rhinestone butterfly clip. "Maybe you're right. Caramel, here and here." She pulls strands free and pulls them forward to examine them. "Or maybe peach and apricot. I hear pink is the newest shade for blondes."

Fascinated that she can become so completely absorbed in the minutiae of her appearance, I sit on the edge of the chair near her desk. "What exactly did you do before you stole my husband?"

She gives me that snotty look I've come to expect. "Why do you want to know?"

"Curious. Did you work? Were you married before Ted?"

"Yes." She tries to fluff her lackluster hair. "I married my high school boyfriend. It lasted six months. And then when I was twenty-three I married a car salesman. He wasn't nice to me." She shrugs. "I used to have confidence issues. My therapist says I didn't value myself enough. She said I should go back to my childhood dreams."

This ought to be good. "What did you want to be when you grew up?"

She smiles. "Rich and famous."

"That's a lifestyle, not a career."

"Yes, well…" She looks past me and focuses on the doorway with a sudden bright smile. The housekeeper has appeared with an express mail package. She lays it on her boss's desk and walks out without a word.

She pulls the package toward her and smiles. "You have something for me to sign?"

"Yes, contracts with two new clients." I pull them out and lay them on the table before her.

She opens a drawer and pulls out two large very expensive pens, only one of which I recognize as a Mont Blanc. It takes longer than one would imagine for her to decide between the pens. Or maybe it's just my own nerves working me.

Finally she picks up the ivory pen with gold filigree. "It's a Krone," she announces as if I care. "It's called the Marilyn Monroe model because the cap of the pen contains traces of Marilyn Monroe's personal lipstick. Would you like to hold it?"

I wince. "No thanks." Who thinks of these things?

She looks insulted. "It's a piece of history."

Sure it is. "You need to initial the first two pages of each copy, and write your name on the last page."

She glances at the top page. "This is new business."

"Yes. Edward and I each landed a new client this week. We were able to make good use of last-minute holiday needs because we weren't overbooked. The fourth quarter should show a profit."

"I suppose I should get a bit of credit for that." She gives her shoulder a little provocative twitch, though it's truly not the same without the sepia-tone skin. "Since Harrison's ads began airing, I can't go out my door without being recognized. Which is why I need to be tanned again as soon as possible. So I'll look like me."

Whatever. "Sign here."

When she has finished touching up the heart over the *i* to her satisfaction in her second signature, she looks up and smiles.

"Good." I pull out the arbitration agreement and lay it on the desk. "Now, as long as you're in a signing mood, and you've got your favorite pen warmed up, let's sign the arbitration agreement." I smile at her. "You'll be happy to know that I'm leaving Talbot right after the New Year."

"You're leaving?" She frowns. "You can't do that."

"Oh, but I can. I've spoken with Lionel. We are going to start interviewing possible buyers for Talbot Advertising after the first of the year. The business is back on its feet. The sooner we sell the better."

"In that case, you'd better see this." She reaches for the package the housekeeper brought in and pulls out an all-too-familiar attorney's pouch. "I didn't want to be the one to tell you but some very serious allegations have been made against you."

I'm not even surprised that she's up to her old tricks of filing a new lawsuit. I'm resigned. I cross my arms. "For instance?"

She looks past me, as though even she can't bring off this one while looking me in the eye. "I've received complaints regarding your activities while employed by Talbot Advertising. Those complaints include accusations of conflict of interest, collusion and conspiracy to defraud Talbot Advertising."

"Oh, really?" I turn to check back over my shoulder. I wouldn't put it past her to want witnesses, but the maid is nowhere in sight. "Just who did I supposedly collude and conspire with?"

She hikes up her chin. "JTM Inc. and Arnaud's Restaurant. You did it to serve the interests of No-Bagel Emporium."

"*Jeez!* You're dragging Marcus and Sam into this?"

She smiles. "I saw that check for fifty thousand dollars."

"Oh, that. I can explain that."

"Save it for the courtroom." She plops down the papers she's taken out before me. "Or, you could just sign your part of Teddy's estate over to me now and I'll drop the allegations."

I snatch the papers from her, rip them once up and down and then across the middle before tossing them in the air. "That's what I think of your threat!"

She makes a sound between a sob and a groan and flings herself around the corner of the desk. "How dare you! Get out!"

I stand up, every nerve in my body vibrating. "Oh, no. I'm not going anywhere until we settle this issue once and for all." I pick up the arbitration agreement. "You're going to sign this. And you're not going to drag Marcus into a mean-spirited, knee-jerk, file-a-suit-a-week spite fest!"

"You called him Marcus. Just how well do you two know each other?"

I smile. "Well enough."

Something changes in her expression, a look of pure rage. "You can't stop me. I will tie the two of you up in court until he's sorry he ever heard of you!"

She grabs for the papers I'm holding as I snatch them back. She lurches forward and catches a sheet, which rips out of my hand.

If asked to swear in court, I will never be able to say who started it.

One minute we are like two more or less sophisticated if furious fashion hounds in a face-off over the last Cole Haan handbag at Century 21. The next we are a pair of snarling bitches in a swinging, slapping, hair-pulling brawl.

I'm past my middle forties and haven't been in a fight since sixth grade. *She* must have taken tae kwon do or some other martial arts classes because before I know it her leg sweeps my knees from behind, and I go down pretty much like a ton of bricks.

I may be older. However, I still have a couple of swift moves. I grab her shirtfront as I fall, and my weight outweighs her weight, so we hit the carpet pretty much in a dead heat. Finally an advantage to being twenty pounds heavier!

I don't know how long we struggle on the carpet, entangled arms and legs, and spitting and cursing at each other. Finally, winded and throbbing in half a dozen places, we reach physical deadlock. We each have a handful of hair. My palm is levered under her chin while she has a death grip on the hair at my nape. I think my lip is bleeding. Her left eye looks fatter than it did moments ago.

My one consolation is the hope that no one else is here to witness exactly what happened.

"Mrs. Talbot!" The housekeeper's voice draws both our gazes in her direction. She's standing in the entry looking as shocked as is appropriate under the conditions.

"Call the police!" Brandi shrieks.

"I wouldn't do that if you don't have a green card," I respond. That's a new low for me, but I'm desperate.

The housekeeper crosses herself and hurries away, leaving us to our fates.

"I hate you!" she says through gritted teeth.

"So what?"

She blinks.

"Don't you get it? I'm going to get half of the estate. What the hell do you care? You're already rich." And that's called reaching a person where she lives.

She stares at me, winded, stunned and wary, then lets me go.

I shove handfuls of sweaty hair from my eyes and stagger to my feet. I've lost a shoe and my stockings are laddered but I don't really feel any pain. I've been in a fight and I didn't lose. That's something.

"I'm not famous."

It takes me a second to realize she's still thinking about what I said last. Jeez, Louise! The woman is relentless in her self-absorption.

There's a brief flurry of voices in the hallway and then Sam appears in the doorway. He looks around the room, spies Brandi and then notices me. Maybe it's my expression, or the way I'm holding my briefcase protectively to my chest but within a second, his affable expression changes. His head drops, his jaw bulges and his hands become fists.

"What the fuck is going on!"

"Liz has been stealing business from Talbot Advertising." She says this in a voice one might use to say "It's my birthday!" And to think I offered the woman cosmetic and decorating advice. The *bitch!*

I look at Sam. "We were discussing the merit of that accusation."

He comes over and takes my face in his hands and eyes me carefully. "You took her on in a catfight?" His face splits in a grin. "Jesus Christ, Liz!"

"Oh, Sam! It's just too awful." Brandi pushes past me to take his arm and wraps herself to his side. "The way Liz took you in. The way she took us all in. All this time, she was lining her own pockets."

Sam glances sideways at Brandi. "What's with your complexion? You been putting stuff up your nose again?"

She gasps and releases him.

The laughter that bursts out of me startles them both. But I can't stop. Inside, I think I'm a little hysterical. "You're seeing each other!"

Sam turns pink. "Sort of. It's nothing serious."

"What do you mean it's not serious?" Brandi jerks away from him. "You said it was serious."

He shrugs. "I said it was for laughs. You got expensive tastes."

"You're seeing Brandi after dating me?" My voice is thin with the helium of surprise.

His head drops. "You won't see me no more, right?"

I smile and nod and glance at Brandi. What was it Sam said about some women use their heads, some their asses? Some men prefer one to the other. Natural selection. Ted. Harrison. Sam. Marcus—no, Marcus didn't play. Some men prefer the other.

Brandi isn't an original. She isn't even especially good. She's just the ordinary variety of cow.

I pick up my purse and head for the door. As I pass Sam I say, "If things do get serious, be sure and get a prenup this time."

And just like that, I'm free. Free of the past. Free of wondering what might have been if— Brandi is yesterday's news.

Oh, m'god! I thought her name and it didn't give me a rush of adrenaline.

Chapter 34

It's the week before Christmas. Northern New Jersey can be a regular chameleon in December. One week it flaunts its mid-Atlantic state status with mornings that are cool and middays warm enough to precipitate the shedding of coats that will be required an hour after dark. The weather can dictate that you diligently water the Christmas tree, if you buck tradition and put it up early, to keep the needles from falling off before Christmas Day. Or it can do a fair imitation of a Norman Rockwell New England winter. We're in transition. My bedroom windows are frosted with lacy patterns, but where the lazy morning sun cuts a sliver through the room, the lace is wet and runny. Mornings spent in bed are the best.

I roll over flat on my back and smile. "Ah."

Marcus opens an eye. "Just ah?"

"Ooh! Ah! Ooh! Ah! Ooh! Ah! Oooh! Aaaahhhhhh!"

"That's better. Sounds like I can safely hit the shower."

I half turn toward him and prop up on an elbow. "Where have you been all my life?"

"Freezing my ass off on the Great Plains, but that's about to change."

I hold my breath as he draws a finger down the length of my nose. When he reaches the tip I can't resist lunging and grabbing his fingertip between my teeth. I give it a lick before releasing it. It's fun to watch his eyes darken with passion. I'm sure I've never had this much fun before in bed. Ever.

He arrived at my door last night, bag in hand, and said every hotel in the tri-state area was full. Would I put him up? I did not call him a liar. I said, absolutely. *Mi casa su casa.*

We both know his reason for being here is much more serious and, best result, will cost him a wad for legal counsel he wouldn't need if he wasn't involved with me. It was a pipe dream to think Brandi would change her mind about the lawsuit. The only surprise is I haven't been sued for assault and battery—yet. But since Marcus walked through my door, we've been playing make-believe and we both needed it.

"Do you want to hear my plans or not?"

I kiss the bulge of his shoulder. "Does it involve more of this?"

He grins. "Better. I've decided that as soon as Hayley goes off to college next fall, I'm going to move my main operations back to New Jersey."

I feel as if I've been splashed with fairy dust. But I know better than to make too many plans too soon.

"You may want to think about that. You've been away from New Jersey for a while. It's brick-busting hot here in the summer. The sky can turn nasty unnatural colors by July. We have road rage and potholes that can swallow a Kia. We believe in public transportation but often abuse it. And we have recycling laws from the third ring of hell."

He reaches up and balances three fingers on the summit of my right cheekbone. "I'll take my chances. It has you."

And when a great man says something like that a smart woman just shuts up.

It's not until he has slid out of bed and padded into the bathroom, his full-noodle frontery on rousing display that I glance over at the clock.

It's seven-forty-eight. In less than three hours we have a court day with a judge and lots of attorneys and several sides with a vested interest in the outcome of the hearing.

I take a deep breath and then again.

I finally made time for a physical after I was tossed out of Talbot Advertising. Okay, the black eye and swollen lip from the scuffle was my excuse. My doctor listened to me explain how I "accidentally" got in a brawl then said, "Basically your health is sound. Lose fifteen pounds. Exercise. And decide what else you would like to be doing with your life, Liz. Because what you are doing is making you crazy inside."

Not perhaps a professional diagnosis, but right on the money.

The truth is I already know what I want. Simple as one, two, three.

One: I want to go back full-tilt boogie into the artisan bakery business. Business is up, thanks to our TV exposure and

Shemar's continuing efforts. We went right from spooky breads to Italian harvest schiacciata. Now our Kris Kringle holiday bread orders are so large we've hired two extra hands.

Two: I want to become northern New Jersey's bread guru. I want to share my joy of baking and eating fine quality bread by teaching young men and women a skill they can use, take with them, and find work nearly anywhere people eat out, which pretty much covers the entire united fifty.

Three: I want to see more of the man currently using up all the hot water in my shower. The first two are life-affirming changes. Marcus is the icing on the cake!

To do the above, I need to come out of this lawsuit pretty much unscathed.

What are the odds?

The phone rings. It's Lionel.

"Good news, my dear. The suit has been dropped."

"What do you mean, dropped?"

"Mrs. Brandi Talbot has withdrawn her suit. It happened late yesterday so we had to wait until the courts open today to verify it with the judge."

I feel as if I can't draw a full breath, rejecting any possibility of relief. "This is just more shenanigans by her. She's withdrawing this one to file another!"

"Now, Liz. I assure you all is well. Mrs. Brandi Talbot even initialed the arbitration settlement."

"Why?"

"As proof of goodwill for not having a contempt charge filed against her for issuing a series of frivolous lawsuits. The judge was not at all pleased she waited until the last minute to withdraw. Her explanation about not being able to show her face in public until today because of a tanning issue didn't sit well with him. In return, she also agreed to pay all court costs, yours included."

Now, maybe I'm a bit slow but... "She signed the arbitration settlement?"

"It's over, Liz. Congratulations. You are a very wealthy woman."

A very wealthy woman. As in worth, say, seven, eight or more million dollars! What can I do with it? What can't I do?

A fair amount of time lapses while I calculate.

When I come out the trance of happy speculation Marcus has reappeared in my doorway, wrapped in one of my new thick-as-a-slice-of-sponge-cake bath towels, his jaw smoothly razored. "Your bed takes up this entire room."

I smile. "I like to keep my priorities straight. Bedroom equals bed equals—"

"Major boinking?" His laughter ripples over me in tiny shivers of pleasure.

"You're making fun of me?"

He puts a knee on the bed and that parts his towel to an interesting degree as he grabs my ankle. He kisses it and says, "Why don't we just call this what it is?"

"And that would be?"

"Cop-u-la-tion."

I sit up as he crawls toward me and put out a hand to arrest him at a more or less safe distance. I sniff the air. "You're wearing our perfume."

He grins. "For luck."

On me, I love it. On him, it makes me a hot and gooey pushover. But we have something else to discuss first!

"We don't have to go to court this morning."

I fill him in quickly, and watch his right brow arch in major proportions to my news.

I conclude with "But I still need to shower, do something with my hair and find the stamina to get through this day. I have to go and sign those papers."

He pushes away the hand I have been using to hold him at bay and crawls right up on top of me, forcing me back against the bedding. "It's going to be okay. The papers can wait."

He kisses me lightly. "After today, things are going to get a whole lot better very quickly."

"Yeah, yeah." I take a deep breath.

"And you and I can settle down and really get to know each other."

"Hmm."

"Hmm?"

I look up at him. "Would you chase a taxi to get to me?"

"Do I have to?"

"Hmm."

"Okay, I'll chase a taxi. When and if I get a chance. On a warm, clear day. As it's pulling away from the curb, and if there's not too much traffic."

I smile. "Good."

He kisses me again, longer and more thoroughly. "So then, promise me that after the holidays you'll find a new place to live."

"What's wrong with where I am?"

He draws back with a grimace. "Damn, Liz—everything."

Chapter 35

"Liz, darling. Tony and I just flew in from Paris. I caught your show this morning on the Food Network. You were brilliant!"

"Thank you, Sally. We're doing two shows a month to see how reintroducing homemade bread to America goes. What about you? Do you have any news for me?"

"You are referring to Tony and me? Yes. I took your unsolicited advice and proposed to the man." There's a pause during which I hold my breath. "He refused me."

"Oh, Sally. I'm so sorry. I should have stayed out of it." Damn!

"No, darling, it's the very best news. Tony said marriage would ruin the very thing he loves best about me, my independent spirit." Her throaty laugher is absolutely angst free.

"To tell you the truth, it was such a relief! I am much better as a lover than I ever would be a wife. Therefore, we are most

definitely *not* getting married! What we are going to do is cel-
ebrate that fact by throwing a very merry no-wedding reception for friends and families in mid-May. I'm waiting for the
peonies to bloom."

"Sounds perfect."

"Now, about your show, darling. You really must insist on
being able to hire your own producer, someone who can stage
you to your fullest advantage. Your production values need improvement. I know the absolutely right person for you."

I smile and listen as my mother, who's never been quite
certain of her role in my life, heaps me full of motherly advice.

"This is so exciting," I say when I have scribbled down a
steno-pad page of her suggestions. "I never really thought that
I'd have to learn about all that goes into producing a TV show."

"I did," Sally says confidently. "You are my child. You were
born to be a star. I always *always* knew it! Wasn't I right?"

"Yes, Sally, you were right."

It seems that without my knowing it, I was plotting the
course of my future, in spite of everything.

A week after we settled Ted's estate, a producer from the
Food Network called me. Said he has been viewing some footage
of our spot on NJN TV. He especially liked the part where I went
all Marilyn Monroe over the chocolate croissants. And the *I Love
Lucy* bit I did with Shemar about the care and feeding of Ma. He
wanted us to come in to the New York City office after the
Christmas holidays to talk about doing a guest-chef spot.

Now, three months later, I'm standing under a spotlighted
counter set up for making bread and ready to smile for the
camera…with my own show.

Off in the shadows Marcus watches. We are in business together, after all. Nabisco has agreed to sponsor the show, and Marcus's private company is sharing executive-producer credits with me. Shemar is my co-host and, with his cred with young people, we are drawing in a new demography for the network.

Celia runs No-Bagel Emporium when I'm otherwise occupied. And business is jumping off! I've never been happier. My karma? Bitchin'!

"Today we are making an original Liz loaf recipe I call pomegranate molasses bread." I pick up a perfectly baked and arranged example, and hold it up for the camera.

"We were meant for bread," I whisper over like a desperate lover. I glance to my left. "You feeling that, Shemar?"

He grins his sexy, mellow grin. "True that, Miz T!"

New York Times bestselling author

CATHERINE
COULTER

Afterglow

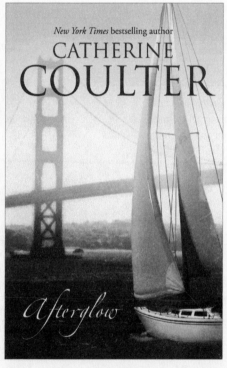

A story of matchmaking mayhem…
and everlasting love.

Available wherever trade paperbacks are sold.

www.MIRABooks.com   MCC367TR

Return to Willow Lake
with Susan Wiggs's novella "Homecoming Season," a heartwarming tribute to cancer survivors and their families.

Miranda Sweeney's life was put on hold after a diagnosis of breast cancer. And now that she has a clean bill of health, she finds her family has drifted apart. Sophie Bellamy, Miranda's best friend, has the perfect solution—a retreat for the whole family on Willow Lake. But can the tranquillity of the lake help the Sweeneys regain what they've lost?

Look for "Homecoming Season" in *More Than Words Volume 3*, an anthology of novellas inspired by the real-life heroines honored each year with the Harlequin More Than Words award.

Visit *www.HarlequinMoreThanWords.com* to find out more, or to nominate a woman who is making a difference in her community.

Proceeds from the sale of the book will be reinvested in Harlequin's charitable initiatives.

Available in October 2006 wherever books are sold.

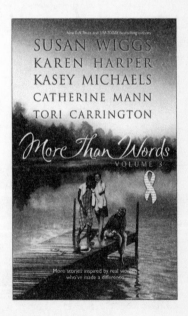

HARLEQUIN

More Than Words

MTW06TR

DIANE CHAMBERLAIN

Her family's cottage on the New Jersey shore was a place of freedom and innocence for Julie Bauer—until tragedy struck when her seventeen-year-old sister, Isabel, was murdered. It's been more than forty years since that August night, but Julie's memories of her sister's death still color her world, causing turmoil in all of her relationships.

Now an unexpected phone call from someone in her past raises questions about what really happened that night. Questions about Julie's own complicity. Questions about the man who went to prison for Isabel's murder—and about the man who *didn't*. Julie must harness the courage to revisit her past and untangle the shattering emotions that led to one unspeakable act of violence on the bay at midnight.

THE BAY AT *Midnight*

On sale in September.

MIRA®

www.MIRABooks.com

MDC341TR